Praise for Lauren Gallagher

"A perfect escape for those who question their sexuality, or for those who are already quite happy with love outside conventional boundaries."
—Library Journal Reviews on *Who's Your Daddy?*

"*Who's Your Daddy* is a story that makes you believe that love conquers all. […] I've read many books by Lauren Gallagher over the years, but in my opinion this is a defining moment in her career."
—Guilty Pleasures Book Reviews

"This is an incredibly emotional story about two people who despite the odds and some pretty big differences manage to find common ground and a love that neither one expected or has ever experienced before. Lauren Gallagher gives us hope that no matter how insurmountable your problems may seem; faith, love, and distance can make a world of difference in emotional healing and finding the love of your life."
—Guilty Pleasures Book Reviews on *All the King's Horses*

Look for these titles by Lauren Gallagher

Now Available:

Who's Your Daddy?
All The King's Horses
The Princess and the Porn Star
I'll Show You Mine
The Saint's Wife

Writing as L.A. Witt
Nine-tenths of the Law
Out of Focus
Conduct Unbecoming
General Misconduct
The Walls of Troy

The Distance Between Us/Wilde's Series
The Distance Between Us
A.J.'s Angel
The Closer You Get
Meet Me in the Middle
No Distance Left to Run (with
    Aleksandr Voinov)
No Place That Far (with Aleksandr
    Voinov)

Tooth & Claw Series
The Given & the Taken
The Healing & the Dying
The United & the Divided

The Only One (with Cat Grant)
The Only One Who Knows
The Only One Who Matters

Kneel, Mr. President

Lauren Gallagher

SAMHAIN
PUBLISHING

Samhain Publishing, Ltd.
11821 Mason Montgomery Road, 4B
Cincinnati, OH 45249
www.samhainpublishing.com

Editing by Linda Ingmanson
Cover by Angela Waters

First Samhain Publishing, Ltd. electronic publication: June 2015
First Samhain Publishing, Ltd. print publication: June 2015

Chapter One

Kent Sinclair hated Camp David.

Well, that wasn't entirely true. The lodge was nice, and it was secluded and secure. The place wasn't crawling with cabinet members, never mind heads of state and their security. Out here, it was just the First Family—James, his wife and their three kids—and their various staff members.

They all rarely came out here, since a trip to Camp David meant James was actually taking a break between his endless presidential duties. Which was great—God knew the man needed as much downtime as he could get—but it made Kent restless. This wasn't like back in the day when they were SEALs and downtime meant licking wounds, cleaning weapons and testing the limits of the human liver.

He couldn't do any of that now. His weapons were as clean as they could get before he'd start stripping off the bluing. He didn't have any wounds to heal, aside from that mostly gone blister on his ankle from a pair of shoes he hadn't broken in properly. And he couldn't drink, because even though the president was on vacation, the Secret Service was not.

As always when they came to this place in the remote woods of Maryland, Kent was fucking *bored*.

It wasn't so bad right now, at least. He was lounging in the rec room, watching James and the kids playing Super Mario Kart on the big screen. James looked more relaxed now than he had in quite a while. He reclined on the floor between the twin toddlers, dressed down in a T-shirt and an old pair of sweats with NAVY emblazoned on the thigh.

He was still obviously President Broderick, though. He was practically in pajamas, laughing with his kids while they chased each other around an animated race-car track, but he could never completely shake the look of the leader of the free world. He'd had a press conference this morning, and his graying dark hair was still arranged the way it always was when he had to appear in public. He'd tousled a few strands when he changed out of his suit and into his faded T-shirt, but otherwise, it was neat and severe. Professional. Presidential.

Knowing James, his appearance reflected his mind—even while he was playing with his kids, part of his brain was on his job. Steering Luigi's green cart around the track, collecting coins and trying to knock Princess Toadstool out of the running, James's mind was almost surely churning through budget issues that he and Congress had been locking horns over for three months, not to mention the simmering conflict in South America. While Congress hashed out some details and tried to reach a consensus about how to address that conflict, James's wife and advisers had all but dragged him kicking and screaming out of the White House for a desperately needed week off. Now that he'd been here for a few hours, he didn't seem to be fighting it, but this was probably as relaxed as he was going to get.

Until he went to bed, anyway. There were other distractions there that would take his mind off peace negotiations and military mobilizations. He'd have something else to think about, and Kent would be going insane. It wouldn't be long either—the kids were already starting to flag, and once they were tucked in, they'd zonk out in no time. Then James and his wife would go to their room, Kent would retire to his, and the house would be dead silent.

Almost dead silent.

Maybe it was the acoustics. Maybe it was the vents. Maybe it was that California-king-size bed in the master bedroom. Whatever the case, Kent could hear everything from his own room across the hall. Every creak. Every moan. Every muffled, playful laugh. *Everything*.

It wasn't even standard procedure for the head of security to stay across the hall from the president like that—there were round-the-clock agents keeping a close watch on the place—but James had insisted. He wanted Kent close by, even when his shifts were over. Even when Carlene was apparently doing everything in her power to pull James's mind off his never-ending duties.

Kent shook himself and pushed those thoughts away. James was married now. He'd moved on. Kent was fortunate to have a skill that could benefit—and protect—his longtime friend, and he was happy to use that skill to stay close to him. Being able to hear James and his wife at night was merely collateral damage. Just like seeing James in tailored suits all the time, watching him play the leader he was born to be, but not being able to touch him. Ever.

Note to self—when we get back to Washington, go out and get laid. Stat.

"What do you guys think?" James sat up and stretched gingerly. "Bedtime?"

Nobody protested. Justin, one of the three-year-old twins, was already out cold, half on his dad's lap and half on the floor. Even Joey, the oldest, was starting to nod off. He was five and insisted he was much more grown up than his younger siblings, so he deserved to stay up later, but on rare nights like this when everybody was up late, he never outlasted the other two. Especially Natalie, the other twin—she was the spitfire of the bunch. James joked that her blood must be half Red Bull or something. Like father, like daughter, as far as Kent was concerned.

But even Natalie, like her brothers, was winding down. While her dad and older brother played, she'd been yawning, stretching, and rubbing her eyes.

James looked at each of his children in turn, then up at Kent. "Guess I'd better put them to bed before they pass out."

"Good idea." Kent pushed himself up out of his chair. "You need a hand?"

"Sure. Thanks." Their eyes met, and James's tired smile made Kent's stomach flutter.

Kent quickly broke eye contact, though. He knelt and let Joey climb on his back for a piggyback ride while James scooped up the sleeping twin. Natalie stretched a bit but followed her dad out of the room on her own power.

Outside the boys' bedroom, Kent carefully let Joey down and turned to James. "We playing golf tomorrow?"

James exhaled, running a hand through his hair. "I don't know. I need to sleep off some of this jetlag first."

Kent pressed his lips together. They'd all flown back last night from a short trip to the West Coast, sleeping for a few hours before this morning's press conference and this afternoon's drive to Camp David, and James was dragging ass. He had always been the first to bounce back after their team had gone on a mission that involved days on end of sleep deprivation. The first few months after his inauguration, he'd been the same way. But the last year and a half, all it took was a meeting with another head of state to knock him on his ass for a few hours—Kent couldn't help thinking that two years as president had already taken more out of James than all the years he'd spent as a SEAL.

"Well, let me know." Kent clapped his shoulder gently. "You need to wind down, and we've both got our clubs."

"Sounds great." James offered another exhausted smile. "We'll figure it out in the morning. It also depends on if Carlene's got anything planned with the kids."

"Of course." Kent returned the smile. He didn't like James's wife, but he'd never hold it against either of them for wanting to spend time as a family or a couple.

"We'll see how it goes." James gestured toward the bathroom, where the kids were starting to squabble over who got to squeeze the toothpaste. "I should go supervise that before it gets out of control."

Kent laughed. "Yeah, good luck with that."

"I'll call you if I need backup."

He replied with a mock salute and then watched James disappear down the hall to take care of the kids. The demands of being president kept James away from his family more than he liked, so whenever he was able to be there for the bedtime routine, he insisted on handling everything. The occasional duty of making sure the kids brushed their teeth, put their pajamas on and were ready for a story was probably one of the few things keeping him sane these days.

While James took care of the kids, Kent went into the kitchen to hunt down something to eat. Much as he craved a beer, he never drank anymore unless he was actually on leave. It was hard to imagine there'd ever been a time when he and James had routinely gotten blackout drunk, put on their uniforms and reported for duty before they could've passed a field sobriety test. God help James if any photos or videos ever surfaced from *that* era, especially during an election.

In the kitchen, Kent rifled through the refrigerator. Fine, no beer, but there had to be something he could—

The hair on his neck stood up.

A second later, quiet footsteps came into the kitchen.

He mouthed a silent curse, then put on a poker face and turned around, knowing damn well whose soft steps those were.

Carlene Meyer-Broderick. His other favorite part of spending time at Camp David. There was nothing wrong with her, per se, but she wasn't terribly fond of Kent, and when she wasn't occupied with her duties as First Lady, she rarely missed an opportunity to subtly remind him of that. Kent would've gladly returned the favor if his best friend weren't madly in love with her for some reason.

Tonight, he fully expected her to grab a bottle of Perrier out of the fridge and leave without saying a word, but she stopped and faced him over the kitchen island.

Looking him right in the eye, she said, "I need to talk to you."

Kent hesitated. Her tone had betrayed nothing—including none of her usual hostile annoyance—so he couldn't begin to guess where this was going. "What about?"

She glanced at the doorway she'd just come through, then turned back to him. "James."

Kent gnawed the inside of his cheek. "Uh, okay."

"He's..." She broke eye contact for a moment, and something in her expression softened. "The thing is, the presidency is killing him."

Kent rubbed his neck. "I can't really argue with you there."

She glanced at the doorway again and then met Kent's gaze. "I don't know who else can help him but you."

"Help him? How?"

"I'm not... I'm not sure." Before he could respond, she gestured at the sliding glass door. "Let's go outside. I'd just as soon the kids didn't overhear any of this."

Kent doubted the kids or their father were awake by this point. They'd likely fallen asleep during a bedtime story, as they often did when James let them stay up to play video games. Still, he didn't protest.

He followed Carlene onto the back deck. Out here, security wasn't a concern—no one was getting near this lodge without breaching several checkpoints, and there were motion sensors and cameras out in the yard. If anyone did get close enough, there was always the Sig .357 tucked under Kent's left arm.

Carlene rested her hands on the railing and stared out at the dark woods behind the lodge. Kent watched her. The soft light from inside and the harsher glow of the floodlights picked out the shadows and contours of her face. In this light, it was clear the presidency had taken its toll on her too. Usually, it was nearly impossible to tell. She had the skill of a Hollywood makeup artist, so she was able to hide it all from the public. In fact, she was like a modern-day Jackie Kennedy—every inch poise and perfection.

But like this, dressed down and without makeup, it showed. The heavy circles under her eyes. The gauntness in her cheeks. Kent suspected that if she stopped dyeing her hair, she'd have as much gray around the edges as her husband. They were both still young—she was just forty-one, and he was forty-six—but no one held the highest office in the land without aging prematurely.

Kent hadn't even realized how long the silence had dragged on until Carlene spoke. "Did you know he talks in his sleep?"

"I…beg your pardon?"

"James." She faced him, the exhaustion palpable in her eyes. "He talks in his sleep."

Kent held her gaze, not sure what to say. Not sure how far to tip his hand.

She sighed, looking out at the woods again. "I'm not trying to bait you, Kent. I know about your past with him."

"Oh." Kent swallowed. "I, um…" He couldn't remember James ever talking in his sleep. Then again, Kent usually fell asleep first, and half the time, they were both drunk.

"I've lost count of how many times he's said your name." She laughed bitterly. "He's done it so many times, I…" Her jaw tightened, and she added through her teeth, "He does it all the time."

Kent's lips parted. "He does?"

She nodded slowly, staring out into the night. "During the day, he's withdrawn and depressed. He's moody. His temper is…" Clicking her tongue, she shook her head. "He's a mess."

"I know he is." Tonight, James had been in a good mood—turning off Mr. President and turning on Dad mode usually had that effect on him. Kent shifted uncomfortably. "He's going to be a wreck until this bullshit with the cartels is settled."

"And then another crisis will come along."

He couldn't argue with that. James's presidency had been one thing after another from the start. Kent supposed it was like that for every president— things always looked worse when you were closer to the action.

Carlene fell silent again. Kent wasn't sure if he was supposed to say something more, or if she was lost in thought. Either way, he didn't speak. This conversation was one hell of a minefield, and he wasn't taking a step until he had a better idea why he was out here.

After a while, the First Lady took a deep breath. "The thing is, the more stressed-out he is, the more he says your name." She folded her arms loosely across her chest and turned to him. "I can't help thinking that whatever he needs to help him cope while he's in office, you're the key."

Kent shifted his weight. "What is it exactly that you want me to do?"

"I don't know." She swallowed. "But...I need you to help him. Whatever it takes." She held his gaze, and though there was no hostility in her dark eyes, there was no shortage of intensity either. "*Whatever* it takes, Kent."

"Um..." He regarded her uncertainly. "I don't follow."

"You two have a history." She broke eye contact and glared out at the forest. "Go back to that history if you have to."

"Our hist—" Kent blinked a few times. "Are you...are you asking me to..."

"Sleep with my husband?"

He gulped and then nodded slowly.

Carlene squared her shoulders and lifted her chin slightly, still staring down the trees. "If that's what it takes, then, yes. Honestly, I don't know what he needs. The only thing I'm sure of is that my husband is a mess, and in some way, he's reaching out to you." She shook her head. "I've done everything else I can think of."

"But your marriage—"

"My marriage is a moot point if a heart attack drops him." She set her jaw. "I need my husband to be okay. If that means that he needs you, then…" She waved a hand. "So be it."

"Carlene. You're asking me—"

"*Please.*" She stepped toward him, her eyes echoing the desperation in her voice. "James needs you. I don't know why, or exactly *what* he needs from you, or what will help him, but I know he needs *you.*"

"I… I don't…"

Carlene came a little closer, eyes locked on his. "Kent, I've seen the way you look at him." There was no accusation in her voice. No anger. Maybe some resignation, but nothing more. "And I've…" She sighed. "I've seen the way he looks at you."

Kent's throat tightened. Yeah, he'd seen those looks too, but he'd forced himself not to read into them. "But…what will it solve? If he does need something from me, I can't imagine it would change anything."

"I wish I knew. Maybe he just needs to talk to you. Maybe he needs…" She stiffened a bit. "Maybe he needs more. But at this point, I'm out of options besides just sitting back and watching my husband wither away under all this pressure."

Kent studied her. "I don't even know where to start with him. I mean, I want him to be okay too. But what am I supposed to say? 'Your wife just gave me carte blanche to—'"

"I get it," she snapped. Then her tone and expression both softened. "Look, I'm going to go get some sleep. It's been a long day for all of us." She met his eyes. "The kids and I will be gone tomorrow morning. I've arranged for a short trip with them. You and James will be…"

"Alone."

She nodded. "I assume it goes without saying that anything that happens needs to be discreet."

"Of course."

"Thank you."

They held eye contact for a moment longer, and then she turned to go, leaving him standing there with his heart in his throat and no fucking idea what to do now.

As she reached for the door, Kent said, "I would never take him away from you, you know."

Carlene stopped with her hand on the door and looked over her shoulder. "The last couple of years are proof enough of that. If you had wanted to during that time, I'm sure you could have."

Kent blinked. "James would never leave you."

"Maybe, maybe not." She pushed her shoulders back, though her posture lacked its usual effortless confidence. "But I don't think he's ever stopped loving you."

That hit him right in the chest. James had never uttered the words to him, not even to reciprocate.

Carlene went on, "And...he trusts you with his life. If he does, then so do I."

Kent had no idea what to say.

She took her hand off the door and faced him fully. "Kent, I can't lose my husband. My kids can't lose their father. I need..." She exhaled. "I need you to bring him back to us."

Kent swallowed hard. "I'll do what I can."

"Thank you." Carlene stepped closer and, to his surprise, hugged him. When he returned the embrace, he was stunned by how thin and frail she felt. They weren't even halfway through James's term—at this rate, the presidency wasn't just going to kill *him*.

"Do me a favor, Carlene," he said softly.

She drew back and met his eyes, suspicion darkening her gaze. "Hmm?"

"Take care of yourself too."

Carlene nodded. "I will."

"When will you be back? With the kids?"

"I'll meet James at the White House in a week."

"All right. I'll...see how it goes."

"Good. Thank you."

With that, she turned to go again, and he didn't stop her this time.

Alone on the deck, he rested his hands on the railing and looked out at the dark forest as the conversation replayed in his mind.

This was dangerous. He and James had already tested their friendship a few too many times—sharing women, sleeping together, one disastrous attempt at a relationship. It was a miracle they'd remained this close, and after the last time had nearly pushed them apart for good, they'd vowed never to cross those lines again. The sex was amazing, but it wasn't worth losing his best friend.

But this presidency *was* killing James. It must've been even worse than Kent had thought if it had driven Carlene to this.

What was he supposed to do, though?

In the past, he and James had helped each other cope with the stress of their job with booze and sex. Sometimes they teamed up to give a woman the night of her life. Sometimes it was just the two of them. But there was always liquor and there was always sex. Kent didn't even know how to cope otherwise, so how the fuck was he supposed to help his best friend—and ex-lover, and the goddamned president of the United States—cope? Playing the role of commander in chief was, by its very nature, a stressful job. Every president came away looking decades older. There was nothing Kent could do to minimize that stress, and he was fairly certain that his job description with the Secret Service didn't include "if needed, get the president drunk and shove a dick in his mouth".

Still, there had to be something he could do. There had to be some reason James kept calling his name, and Kent refused to let him down. He wouldn't hesitate to walk through fire for James. Hell, he hadn't hesitated for a second when James had handpicked him for his Secret Service detail—if there was anyone on this planet for whom Kent would take a bullet, it was James. Kent would do whatever it took to keep him from going off the rails.

But what *would* it take?

Chapter Two

On her way to the bedroom, Carlene stopped to check in on the children. All three were tucked into their beds. Joey was curled up beneath his covers, but the twins were sprawled out like someone had thrown them there. She couldn't help smiling as she picked up the stuffed Angry Bird that Justin had dropped—the twins had always slept like starfish, starting as soon as they were born. Probably enjoying the fact that they finally had some room after sharing so little space before birth.

She double-checked that their suitcases were packed. They'd all be on the road early tomorrow, and she wanted everything in order before the car came. The quicker and quieter they could slip away, the better.

The suitcases were ready and the kids were sleeping peacefully, so Carlene left them for the night and went back up the hall to the master bedroom.

James was in the shower. He'd left the bathroom door open, as they both tended to when they were showering—a leftover habit from their kids' infancy, when they'd wanted to be able to hear any cry of distress. A side effect of that was they'd both long ago gotten used to the other walking in and out, so she didn't bother saying anything as she stepped into the room. No doubt he was aware of her presence—his SEAL training ran deep—but he didn't acknowledge her. Which was also normal. They could usually move in the same space in comfortable silence, not necessarily saying anything but aware of each other and completely at ease.

Except tonight. As she brushed her teeth and took out her contacts, Carlene's stomach roiled. She'd been nauseated as she debated approaching

Kent, and now that she'd done it, she felt even worse. The wheels were in motion, but she wanted to hit the brakes. Alone with James in the bathroom while they went through their nightly routines, everything was normal. It had to be. She was wrong about James. About Kent. About everything. This was a huge mistake, and she'd regret it forever if she didn't stop it *now*. She needed to drop her toothbrush, hurry across the hall, bang on Kent's door and tell him she'd changed her mind.

And if she did, she'd be relieved right up until James murmured his ex-lover's name in his sleep. Again.

Carlene's gut turned to lead. She glanced at James's blurry silhouette, and her heart sank. Maybe she wasn't doing the right thing. Maybe this would be a disaster.

But what was the alternative? There was none. She'd tried to find one, failed and accepted that this was how it needed to happen.

She finished brushing her teeth and left the bathroom to change into her pajamas.

Her thoughts drifted to Kent. The man wasn't the ripped, tanned SEAL he used to be. Some of his old injuries had slowed him down, and he wasn't quite as religious about working out as he had been during their military years. Neither was James. Instead of six-packs, they each had smooth, flat abs these days. James had lost some muscle-tone, so she imagined Kent had too, but they were hardly flabby. They were battle-scarred, graying, and both bastards could grace the cover of a men's fitness magazine if they wanted to.

Especially since neither had carried and given birth to three kids. Two at the same time.

As she stripped down to a T-shirt and panties, Carlene didn't dare look at herself in the mirror. No sense comparing herself to the guys. Specifically, the guy whose body hadn't been ravaged by time and pregnancy, and whose name her husband kept saying in his sleep. The guy her husband had insisted on having as his head of security, keeping him around far more than standard protocol dictated. To the point that it raised eyebrows. Hers, anyway.

But were those eyebrows going up for a reason?

Something had happened between them during their SEAL days. It could've been anything from a drunken fuck they'd regretted in the morning to…more. James had never gone into detail. She'd never asked and he'd never told. Something had definitely happened, though, and there was still something between them. She trusted James fully when he insisted he'd never cheat on her with Kent or anyone else. She believed him right up until he said there was nothing between them now. Maybe there wasn't anything that either of them openly acknowledged, and maybe they never acted on it or touched or spoke of it, but it existed.

And whatever it was, she'd just given them the green light to let it out of its cage.

Shit. This wasn't going to end well, was it? After all, she'd heard the old saying that if you love something, let it go, but she was fairly certain that didn't include "even if that means letting your husband sleep with the man he's been in love with since before he met you."

In the other room, the shower stopped.

Carlene's heart jumped. She glanced at the bathroom door and gulped. There was time to turn this thing around.

But then, minutes later, James stepped out of the bathroom, wearing only a pair of faded blue boxers, and the second she met his eyes, she knew there was no going back. He was exhausted. His cheeks were flushed from his shower, but he still managed to look pale, especially when his complexion contrasted so sharply with the circles beneath his eyes.

He smiled at her but didn't say anything. She returned it, though it was a struggle, and then turned around to brush her hair before bed.

James came up behind her, and the brush stopped midstroke when he wrapped his arms around her waist. He kissed her cheek. "You've been quiet tonight."

"It's been a long week."

"Yeah, it has." He sighed and leaned down to kiss the side of her neck. "I'm sorry to keep dragging you and the kids everywhere."

"We knew what this was when you signed up for it."

"Still." Another soft kiss.

"It's… We can manage." Her stomach coiled tighter. After a moment, she took a deep breath, turned around in his embrace and met his eyes. "Listen, the kids and I are going to my mom's house. Tomorrow morning."

James blinked. His arms tensed around her waist. "Tomorrow?"

She nodded. "We'll, um, meet you back in Washington. In a week."

"A week?" He tilted his head. "What brought this on? I thought we were going to—"

"I know. I know." Carlene sighed and ran a hand through her hair. "I just…"

"Carlene." He gently cupped her face and looked in her eyes. "Is everything okay?"

I want it to be. I hope it will be. But right now…

She swallowed, then forced a smile. "It's fine. I just think the kids are tired of Camp David. I want to take them someplace they'll enjoy." She put her hand over his against her cheek. "You need some downtime too."

"That doesn't mean I want to be away from you and the kids."

Her chest tightened. "It's just for a few days." *I hope.*

He chewed his lip but then offered a tense shrug. "Okay. It'll probably be better for them than being stuck here." He kissed her cheek, and as he released her, added, "It'll probably be good for you too."

"Hopefully." *Hopefully even better for you.* She stood up on her toes and kissed him lightly. "It's only a week. I'll be back before you know it."

He again smiled as he tucked a strand of hair behind her ear. "I'm already looking forward to it."

She smiled back, and after one more kiss, they let each other go.

They climbed into bed, and he turned out the light. For a long time, they were quiet, but he wasn't asleep yet. His breathing was too fast for that.

Carlene was acutely aware of his body heat beneath the covers, the warmth radiating off him as if trying to draw her closer to him. And she wanted to be closer to him. Especially tonight.

She was exhausted. He *had* to be.

But still…

There was no telling how things would go after tomorrow. Her marriage might not exist anymore after she turned Kent loose on James. She believed James when he said he loved her, but she had to accept the possibility that Kent held a piece of her husband's heart that she could never touch. Which meant that tonight might be all there was left.

Heart pounding, Carlene snuggled toward him. He welcomed her closeness, wrapping his arm around her shoulders. She ran her fingers down the center of his chest, and when she reached his abs, the muscles contracted beneath her fingertips.

"Didn't realize you were feeling…" He trailed off into a groan.

She ran her hand over the front of his boxers, and his whispered "*Fuck…*" gave her goose bumps. He was so suave and professional as president, but behind closed doors, he could be as crude as the scruffy SEAL she'd fallen in love with. She traced the outline of his hardening erection through the thin fabric. A shudder ran through him, and he lifted his hips, pressing into her palm.

She grinned into his kiss. "Like that?"

"I fucking love it." He turned his head and found her lips in the darkness. Light kisses. Deeper ones. Breathless ones as she slid her hand beneath his waistband and stroked him, hot skin on hot skin, until he was damn near thrusting into her tight grip.

They tangled up beneath the covers, holding and touching each other in between stripping away the few layers of clothing they'd each worn. When there was nothing left, Carlene rolled onto her back, and as James got on top, narrow hips settling between her thighs, her pulse quickened. Again when his cock slid inside her.

Their bodies moved together the way they always did—smoothly, fluidly, every muscle well-practiced in the art of arousing the other person—and Carlene tried her damnedest to be into it the way she'd been in the early years. Back when sex happened in the heat of the moment and the only desperate telepathic message she'd tried to send him was that she wanted to come so badly she'd forgotten how to speak. Especially back when he'd just retired and there was nothing threatening to send him into an early grave except his penchant for motorcycles and fast cars. Back when whatever he'd had with his on-and-off Navy SEAL lover was a distant memory.

She rocked her hips just the way she knew he liked it, and he buried his face against her neck. Every hot huff of breath was shorter and sharper than the last, and then there were the whispered curses, and she rolled her hips a little bit more, and his whole body tensed. James groaned and shuddered, his hips jerking as if he might get a little deeper inside her as he came.

Then he relaxed.

He collapsed beside her and held her close as they kissed for a long moment. But then his lips left hers, and he whispered, "You didn't come." He slipped his hand between her legs. "Can't have that."

Carlene gasped as his fingertips brushed over her clit. She parted her legs for him, and he kissed her in the darkness as he teased her right to the edge. His fingers were wonderfully talented—nimble, gentle, never too rough or too light, and God, but the man knew his way around a woman.

But her orgasm stayed just out of reach, and slowly, the truth settled in: it wasn't going to happen tonight. Her mind was just too far away and in too many other places to let her body surrender completely.

So she gasped, she shuddered, and she dug her nails into his arm, and she didn't give him a single reason to think it wasn't genuine. She lifted her hips off the bed, pressing against his hand, and she moaned like she meant it. She *did* mean it—he turned her on, and he knew how to please her like no other man ever had—but this was all she had tonight, and she prayed to God he believed her.

As she relaxed, James kissed her softly and withdrew his fingers. Fresh guilt gnawed at her. She'd never been one to fake orgasms, but lately, it was either that or stop and talk about why she couldn't come. And she'd rather fake it than spoil one of these increasingly rare moments of intimacy.

James wrapped his arms around her, and they each slowly caught their breath. As the dust settled, they didn't separate physically, but she felt him drifting away from her as he often did. When they had sex, he was right there, fully present in every kiss and every touch, but the minute it was over, he started sliding back into that place she couldn't get to. It hadn't always been like that. Only in recent months, around the same time the stress had started wearing him down and he'd started talking in his sleep.

She gave herself the space of a heartbeat to wonder if he'd pull away from Kent like that, and then she banished the thought and held him tighter. James held on too, strong arms around her making it *almost* seem like he was still in the moment with her. She couldn't even put her finger on what it was that made her feel like he was slipping through her fingers. Her imagination, maybe? Fearful thinking?

Eventually, she turned on her side to go to sleep, and he molded himself to her back.

"I love you," he murmured against her neck, sounding far away even while he held her.

"Love you too."

In no time, he was sound asleep, his breath drifting softly across her skin. His hand rested against her stomach, and she laced her fingers between his in the darkness.

Hopefully, he wouldn't dream much tonight. Or at least, not enough to wake them both up at all hours, sometimes by twitching and murmuring, sometimes by thrashing and crying out. The first night or two of a vacation, he usually slept soundly for a good twelve hours, likely catching up on at least some of the sleep he'd been missing. After that, all bets were off.

She actually felt guilty about leaving right now. She hated sleeping away from him. Those nightmares jarred him, sometimes leaving him sweating and pacing for a while before he could finally go back to sleep. He never talked about them, though. What was going on in his mind—what he did and what he saw—was his and his alone. Flashbacks, maybe? Lifting the veil on some of the PTSD he swore he didn't have? There was no way to know. All she could do was help him come back to reality and calm down. When she was with him, she could wake him up as soon as he started freaking out. When he was alone, as he would be for the next week, he would be stuck in the dreams until he could rattle himself awake.

But he wouldn't *be* alone. She doubted he'd spend even one night by himself while she was gone. What happened after that… Well…

If James really was in love with Kent, then it was what it was. At this point, her primary concern was his mental health. If Kent was the answer to maintaining James's sanity, and a byproduct of that was the two of them realizing they wanted and needed to be together, then so be it.

The mere thought of losing James broke her heart, but deep down, she was afraid she'd lose him no matter what. Either to his presidency or to his bodyguard. At least if it was the latter, he'd be safe, maybe even happy. Kent was better than a heart attack.

But she hoped and prayed it didn't come to that. The heart attack or the man James had never gotten over.

I know you love him, James, she thought as she stroked his hand with the pad of her thumb, *but please, please don't stop loving me.*

Chapter Three

Carlene was gone.

Heart in his throat, James sat up in bed. Her glasses and cell phone were gone. There was a conspicuous void next to his suitcases where hers had been stacked last night.

Though she'd told him she was taking the kids to her mother's, she hadn't even woken him up for a kiss good-bye. Or had she? He couldn't remember anything after they'd fallen asleep together last night, and waking up alone after that felt weird. Her absence felt weird.

He looked at her side of the bed. It was hard to believe they'd made love here last night, right there in the middle, and then slept so close together, and now…she was gone.

She's just taking the kids on vacation. Relax.

But somehow, it felt different. More decisive and final than just a little trip so the kids could have a breather. She'd been uneasy when she'd told him last night, and then she'd been hungry, almost demanding in bed, more than she'd been in a long time. And now she was gone.

What the hell?

In the bathroom, where her contact lens case and toothbrush usually sat beside the sink, was a small envelope with *James* written across it in her distinctive handwriting.

His heart dropped. *No, Carlene. Please, no…*

The last ten years flashed through his mind. It couldn't be over.

Please…

A queasy feeling rose in his throat. With unsteady hands, he opened the envelope and slid the letter free.

He unfolded the paper. Instantly, the words *leaving you* caught his eye and sent his stomach all the way into his feet. But then he read it more closely.

James,

This will all sound strange, but bear with me.

First, let me be clear: I'm not leaving you. I want things to be okay between us, but first, they have to be okay with you. And I don't think they are.

But… I don't know where to start. I want you to do whatever you have to in order to be okay. If that means being with someone else—

James flinched and shoved the letter aside. Someone else? He didn't want to be with any other woman. He loved *her*, damn it. How could she even think he'd want to cheat on her? And, Jesus, even if he did, it wouldn't be while he was a sitting president. It was all he could do to be a husband and father while he was in office. Carrying on an affair? Not a chance. It mystified him that those before him had managed to do so.

James steeled himself, picked up the letter and continued reading.

If that means being with someone else, even if it's just to get something out of your system, then you have my blessing. I love you, I want you to be all right and I won't leave unless you want me to.

Love,

C.

That wasn't going to happen. He wasn't laying a hand on anyone. No way in hell. And wanting her to leave? He couldn't begin to get his head around that. Especially over the last few years, from the time his political campaign had begun picking up speed, he had no idea how he could have made it through without her by his side. Even while she'd been struggling with that hellish second pregnancy and the twins arriving early, and then recovering from surgery while the babies were in the NICU, she'd been stronger than anyone had any business being. She'd encouraged him to campaign like hell, cheering him on from the hospital and then at home. She'd kept him sane over the phone without ever hinting that she was running on sleep that had to be counted in minutes instead of hours, struggling to keep up with two newborns and a toddler in between all the post-op complications that had plagued her for months.

Ask her to leave? Not in this lifetime.

Beg her to come back? As soon as he could reach her.

If a few of their previous rough patches were anything to go by, she'd turned off her phone and would avoid any other form of communication until she was good and ready to be contacted. There were Secret Service agents with her, but he'd only use them to reach her if there was an emergency involving blood or fire.

For now, he'd have to wait until she wanted to be reached, and hope to God she didn't change her mind about the "not leaving him" part.

Equal parts shaken and numb, James got dressed and went into the kitchen. The Secret Service guys were around, but the kitchen was empty, thank God. He wasn't ready to face anyone, including the stoic professionals tasked with keeping him alive.

He poured himself a cup of coffee and went through the motions of adding cream and sugar. Not that it mattered—he didn't taste any of it. The caffeine probably wouldn't even help now. He'd developed an immunity to that during his campaign. But it was something to do, and something to occupy his hands and—

"James?"

Kent Sinclair's voice almost sent James's coffee mug to the floor.

James slowly turned around to face his longtime friend and bodyguard, and when their eyes met, his blood pressure skyrocketed.

Oh shit.

Yes, Carlene was the only *woman* James loved.

But Kent…

Oh shit was right.

Kent studied him. "You okay?"

"I…" James set the cup down before he dropped it. "Carlene's gone."

Kent swallowed. "I know."

"No, I mean, she's…*gone.*"

"She left? Like, left you?"

"No. Well, yes. Sort of." James scrubbed a hand over his unshaven face. "Christ, I don't know. She left a note, and she said she's not *leaving* leaving, but…" He lowered his hand and met Kent's gaze. "Something's wrong. With us. I don't—"

"I know."

"What?"

"I know. Carlene and I talked last night."

James stared at him. "What did she say?"

"To put it bluntly?" Kent took a breath and glanced around, as if to double-check they were alone. "She told me to do whatever you needed me to do."

James blinked. "I don't—"

A shadow passed the window, turning both their heads. Just another Secret Service agent making the rounds.

Once the man was gone, Kent faced James over the kitchen island. "Let's go someplace a bit more private. We should, um, talk."

James's heart thundered. He wasn't sure he wanted to have this conversation. In fact, he was damn sure he didn't want to have it. But if Kent knew what was going on, then maybe he knew how James could bring Carlene back.

So, wordlessly, he followed Kent down the hall to the office a few doors past their bedrooms. James balked at the threshold. Behind closed doors with Kent had always been a dangerous place to be. In their past life, they'd gone into rooms—bedrooms, motel rooms, offices—to talk, and not a lot of talking ever happened.

But James was married now. Even if he hadn't been, the fact remained that the past was just that, the past, and they'd both agreed to move on and let it go.

Cautiously, he walked into the office and shut the door behind him, sealing them inside the room. Kent drew the curtains over the window.

James's heart sped up. "What's going on?"

"What's going on," Kent said quietly, "is that your wife is worried sick about you. You're—"

"So she left me?"

"It's…a bit more complicated than that."

James folded his arms. "How so?"

"Basically…" Kent lowered his gaze, chewing his lip like he'd always done when he was trying to figure out what to say. "She thinks the stress of your job is eating you alive. Quite honestly, I think she's right."

James leaned hard against the door. "No one ever said this was going to be easy."

"Of course not." Kent held his gaze, one eyebrow up a little. "But I think it's driving you into the ground harder than you're letting on."

"It's not that bad." Except his voice didn't sound convincing at all. James's shoulders sagged. He couldn't even present an argument to back up those four words. He was too distracted by Carlene's absence and too fucking exhausted by, well, everything. "Okay, it is. But what the hell am I supposed to do about it?" He dropped his arms to his sides and thanked God for the door keeping him upright. "I can't just take thirty days' leave and go drink myself stupid like we used to. Especially not with all the shit blowing up in South America." He rubbed a hand over his face and groaned. "I shouldn't even be *here* until all of that's settled."

"You need to rest," Kent said. "You'll be useless to everyone if you try to tackle those negotiations again without a little downtime."

"There isn't *time* for downtime." The words barely came out as a whisper.

"The congressional committee needs to consider their options. You wouldn't be doing anything right now anyway."

"Still." James rubbed his temples. "I should be doing something."

"You are." Kent came closer, though he stayed beyond an arm's length away. "You're resting and recharging so you can address all of this effectively once Congress throws the ball back in your court."

James shuddered. He felt useless out here at Camp David while Congress squabbled over some crucial budgeting issues, but he'd feel even worse once it was his turn to make a decision. Making a decision to lead a dozen men into a heavily fortified building in pursuit of a single objective had been enough pressure, especially since the outcome hadn't always been favorable. Not all of those dozen men made it out every time, and James had spent weeks, months, years wondering if he could've done something differently and gotten them all out alive.

Making a decision to send thousands upon thousands of troops into a war zone? James doubted he'd ever sleep again if he fucked this one up.

Kent was right—James needed to rest and recharge before he faced down that massive responsibility. He needed to spend a couple of afternoons on the golf course and then huddle up on the couch with the kids, play Mario Kart until two in the morning before he took his wife to bed and…

James swore under his breath. The kids weren't here. His wife wasn't here. There was no one here but Kent, and after that cryptic note from Carlene and the conversation she'd apparently had with Kent last night, James didn't see himself relaxing and recharging over the next few days. Instead of stressing over his presidential responsibilities, he could worry himself sick over his marriage.

Why now, Carlene?

He wanted to be angry with her for doing this, for throwing this at him while he was hanging by a thread, but Carlene wasn't one to incite drama for its own sake. If she was doing this, then she'd reached the end of her own tether.

He opened his eyes. "What do I do?"

"What do you need to do?"

James let his head fall back against the door. "I have no idea. She's right, though. This job is killing me."

Kent's eyebrows pinched together, but he didn't say anything.

James closed his eyes again and raked a hand through his hair. "You know, they always say being president means being the most powerful man in the world. That wasn't what I was after, though."

"I know," Kent said softly. "That's never been you."

"No, it hasn't." James pressed his fingers into his temples. "I wanted to make changes, you know? Fix some of the bullshit." He lifted his head. "But the power… It's there. It's real. It's…" He exhaled hard, letting his head hit the door again. "I've had the power to make decisions that got people killed before. I didn't realize how much it bothered me until I had that kind of power again. Just having that is… It's draining."

"Of course it is. I don't think anyone ever believed it was easy."

"Yeah, but it's… Now…" James pushed out another breath as he slid down the door to sit on the thick carpet. Elbows on his knees, he pressed his fingers into his temples. "It used to be I'd make a decision that affected the guys working under me. They trusted me to lead them, and I led them. If someone got killed, it fucked me up. Always did. And now, I make decisions that can affect thousands of people. *Millions* of people. If I make the wrong one…" All the air rushed out of his lungs, and he shook his head. Meeting Kent's gaze, he whispered, "Do you know what that does to someone?"

"I know what it does to you." Kent came closer and crouched beside James. "I know what kind of man you are. You don't see human beings as collateral damage. Not even the enemy. It's what made you an effective and conscientious leader. You're the perfect kind of man to have that kind of power because you're the last one in the world who'll abuse it."

"What about when it starts abusing me?" James met his longtime friend's eyes. "There's no outlet in this job. When we were SEALs, I could come home, drink myself stupid and get laid until I forgot why I was so fucking exhausted. But this, it's not something I can take leave from. Even out here"—he gestured at their surroundings again—"it's still there. The responsibility, I mean. It's just this…" James rubbed the bridge of his nose. "Look, I don't regret running for president. And if the GOP tries to put that jackass Dalton into office again, I'll gladly run for reelection. I just… Sometimes I wish I could have that weight off my shoulders for a little while, you know?"

"You need it off your shoulders for a while," Kent said. "It's killing you."

"Evidently it's killing my marriage too."

Kent put his hand and James's arm, probably oblivious to what that did to James's already sky-high pulse. "It's not killing your marriage, James. It's killing *you*, and that scares Carlene."

James stared at Kent's hand. Abruptly, the contact lightened, and Kent withdrew his arm.

"Sorry," he muttered.

"It's okay." James swallowed. "Why is she coming to you? I… Shit, I didn't even think you two could stand each other."

Kent shifted uncomfortably, avoiding James's eyes. "She, um… She thinks I can help."

"Help? How?"

"Any way I can."

James studied him. "Meaning?"

Kent fell silent. A good long time passed before he finally turned to James. "Answer me something." He locked eyes with him. "If we had your wife's blessing to—"

"*What?*" James's jaw fell open. "What the hell are you talking about? Did you ask her if we—"

"No! No, of course not." Kent shifted around and sat against the wall beside him. "She came to me." He chewed his lip. "How much does your wife know about us?"

James hesitated. "I told her you and I had… That we've slept together." He swallowed hard. "That it's in the past."

Kent flinched. Subtly but unmistakably. "Maybe she isn't so sure about that." His eyebrows rose a little, and James caught himself wondering if Kent wasn't so sure about it either. It *was* in the past, though. Right?

"What did she say to you?" James asked.

"That she thinks you need something she can't give you."

James's stomach flipped. "Such as…?"

Kent didn't speak, and the truth gradually clawed its way to the surface.

"Why would she think this"—James gestured at both of them—"is what I need?" He shook his head. "I don't get it. I don't… What she's doing…She says she's not leaving, but she's gone, and—"

"*James.*"

His teeth snapped shut. He held Kent's gaze.

"Carlene loves you. There's no way in hell she would've come to me like that if she didn't."

James swallowed. So many questions, so few words to convey them.

Kent went on, "She can see just like I can that you're buckling under all this stress, and she thinks somehow…" He paused, studying him, then softly added, "She thinks I can help you."

"By what? Fucking me?"

"If that's what you need." Kent's blunt matter-of-factness didn't usually catch him off guard. Then again, he wasn't usually being bluntly matter-of-fact about the two of them having sex for the first time in years, with or without Carlene in the picture.

"Jesus." James rubbed his eyes. "Why wouldn't she talk to me about this?"

"I can't imagine it was easy for her."

"Still. She's my wife." He looked up. "I can't lose her, Kent."

"She doesn't want to lose you either."

"Then what the hell is she doing?"

"Everything she can think of to save you."

James didn't know what to say. Kent didn't speak either. Eventually, they both stood. James wanted to lean on Kent for balance and…more than balance, but he drew away and started pacing, his bare feet nearly silent on the plush carpet. "This is insane. I can't… I mean…"

"I know it is. But under the circumstances, I think you can be forgiven for doing whatever it takes to keep your head together for the next couple of years."

"Including you?"

Kent's lips pulled tight.

Silence fell between them. James kept pacing. Outside the window, a radio crackled, and one of the Secret Service agents muttered a few words into it, his voice fading as he wandered past.

James stopped, facing the curtain-covered window, his skin prickling as if every hair on the back of his neck were searching for Kent's exact position behind him. "I don't know what to do."

"Do you want me to kiss you right now?"

The question weakened James's knees. His stomach turned and his mind screamed *No!*, but his body tingled at the thought of kissing Kent after all this time. "I…"

Well, do you?

Oh, wasn't that a loaded question? He'd never stopped wanting Kent. Never. He'd suppressed it, tamped it down and kept it hidden away from everyone, especially himself, and he'd long ago vowed never to act on it. He was a married man now, for God's sake. He loved his wife. Cheating on her? Out of the question.

But whether or not he was willing to cheat wasn't the same as whether or not he still wanted the only man who'd ever gotten this far under his skin.

James squared his shoulders and faced him. "Ever since we were SEALs, a day hasn't gone by that I haven't wanted you to kiss me."

Kent swallowed. "Is that an invitation?"

Yes. Holy shit, yes.

"I don't know what it is," James whispered as Kent stepped closer. "I don't…" *My God, I could touch you right now.* "I don't know what the fuck is going on."

Kent reached for James's face. They held their breath as his hand hovered there, and then his fingertips trailed tentatively across James's cheek, sending a shiver through both of them. Then the other hand came to rest on James's shoulder. Kent's thumb moved back and forth along the collar, just grazing his skin and raising goose bumps beneath James's shirt.

Kent chewed his lip. "Carlene wants you to be okay, James. So do I."

"But how is this"—James gestured at both of them again—"going to do anything but complicate things?"

Kent's hand slid into James's hair, bringing back memories he'd tried like hell to forget. "I don't think anyone's pretending it'll make things simpler."

"Then what are…"

The way Kent shivered almost dropped James's legs out from under him.

Their eyes locked. Kent's hand didn't move. James didn't pull away. There was nothing logical or rational about this, no analysis pointing to this strategy as the lowest risk/highest gain scenario, but logic and strategy didn't exist in Kent's gaze. It never had. He'd always been the hothead, the wild one, and yet somehow, he'd always been James's anchor. The one who could bring James down to earth or wind him up and send him into the stratosphere, and somehow, he'd always known which way James needed to go.

Heart thumping against his ribs, James took a small step forward, narrowing the distance between them to a sliver Kent would have to cross.

And he waited.

Barely breathing, barely standing, he waited.

Kent didn't move in—he drew James to him.

Their lips met. Softly at first, touching so tentatively that it almost tickled, and then Kent tilted his head and kissed him full-on.

In a heartbeat, everything else in the world just melted away. Disappeared. If anything still existed, it no longer had a name. It didn't matter.

James opened to Kent's kiss, inviting him to deepen it. As he always did,

Kent took the invitation. He pulled James closer and held him tight as he explored his mouth, his breath hot on James's cheek and his fingers twitching on James's scalp. It was everything James remembered and more—the kind of kiss Kent had always used to promise him more. The kind of kiss that had always turned James on more than the most passionate foreplay with other men.

Kent broke the kiss. Panting against James's lips, he whispered, "What do you feel?"

Hot. Holy fuck.

"I…" He held Kent's gaze, struggling to form thoughts and words and whatever else might help him figure out what to do just then.

"Tell me what you want." Kent licked his lips. "Tell me what you need, James."

I want you. I want everything we had before.

I need…

James's heart sank. Guilt twisted beneath his ribs, and his throat constricted around his breath.

I need my friend and I need my wife.

Where the hell did sleeping with Kent fit into that picture?

It didn't. It couldn't. No matter how much James wished, it wouldn't.

James sighed. "I'm sorry. I can't do this." He brushed past Kent. "I need to go for a run."

He fully expected a hand on his arm or a sharp *wait*, but none came.

Chapter Four

Kent stared at the open doorway for a long moment. How James could go running right now, he had no idea—Kent could barely stand after that kiss. He sank into one of the chairs in front of the massive mahogany desk and cradled his head in his hands.

Of course, he could barely stand, but he also couldn't sit still. For once, his restlessness wasn't that ever-present worry that something might happen to James while he was out of sight. There'd been threats, after all. Not everyone was happy that he'd won the election against the conservative favorite, and many speculated he'd be just another fuck-up in the never-ending presidential clusterfuck. Some were more than happy to resort to violence to end the Bush-Clinton-Bush-Obama-Broderick series of disasters.

Out here at Camp David, though, Kent knew James was safe. They were within a secure compound, and even a team of highly trained SEALs would be hard-pressed to make it this far—prior to joining the Secret Service, Kent had been on the team of eight ex-SEALs and Green Berets tasked with trying. Only three of them had come within a hundred yards of the lodge, and they'd worked with the Secret Service to close those security gaps.

And whether James liked it or not, a contingent of Secret Service agents were always hot on his heels when he left the lodge.

So he was definitely safe.

But Kent couldn't relax. Not with that conversation ringing in his ears and that kiss tingling on his lips.

He sat back in the chair and stared out the window, chewing on his thumbnail and trying—and failing—to get comfortable. That probably wasn't an option for a while. His mind was going in too many directions for his body to settle.

What the fuck were they supposed to do now? They'd kissed for the first time in too long, and he didn't know if he regretted it or not. He'd never found anyone who made him feel the way James did, but James had found someone else, and with or without Carlene's blessing, that kiss wasn't a line they should've crossed. Was it?

"Whatever it takes, Kent."

He closed his eyes and rubbed his temples. Did she have any idea what she was asking him to do? He'd gladly fall into bed with James without a second thought, but not if it meant destroying his best friend's marriage or losing that best friend to the awkward aftermath. He'd worked too damned hard to fix things with James after they'd both screwed up one time too many. No matter how good the sex was—and it always was—it wouldn't be worth it. Even if Carlene weren't in the picture, this was dangerous territory, and with her in the picture? Jesus.

But…what am I supposed to do?

"Whatever it takes, Kent."

He swore into the stillness and scrubbed a hand over his freshly shaved jaw. If there really was something Kent could do for James, and if that really meant stripping down and getting into bed together, then he'd happily do it. He'd walk through fire for that man.

But it wasn't that simple. Just the thought of sleeping together was definitely not helping James's stress level. Quite the opposite. So it was counterproductive well before any clothes came off.

Kent stood, opened the curtains and stared out the window at the forest surrounding the lodge. If Carlene thought sex with Kent was the solution, she couldn't possibly have thought it through. That, or she really didn't know much about their past. James was notoriously tight-lipped about things, even with those closest to him. As far as he was concerned, everything existed on a need-to-know basis, and it was quite possible that extended to his wife knowing about his sexual history.

She knew they'd had sex, but it was way more complicated than that. James and Kent had thrived as friends with benefits—no strings, no bullshit, just the most amazing sex whenever they felt like it. Their one and only attempt at a relationship had been a disaster, culminating in a drunken argument in a bar in Estonia that had damn near gotten them both court-martialed. Thank fuck nobody on high had known it was a lovers' spat—they'd just assumed it was two hothead SEALs who'd had too much to drink, because God knew *that* never happened. Kent and James had been forcibly separated until they'd cooled off and sobered up, and warned that one more word out of either of them would result in disciplinary action.

It wasn't just one of those fights that evaporated in the wake of a hangover, though. The bitterness had lingered on, and they could barely look at each other. A few nights later, they'd tried to fuck, but it was clear that something had changed between them. They'd given up before either had gotten off, and one of them—Kent couldn't remember who now—had left.

It was the last time they'd ever touched like that. Eventually, they'd resolved things, and they'd agreed to give it a rest—the sex, everything—for a while. Spend some time apart, get their shit together, and maybe they could go back to being casual fuck buddies again.

Then James had been injured in a training exercise, and he'd been stuck stateside while the team deployed. During that deployment, after a mission was over and the guys were celebrating with shitty beer in a shitty bar in some shitty country, James's absence hit Kent hard, and he realized he couldn't do this anymore. He was in love with him and couldn't pretend otherwise, so he'd vowed that as soon as he was back in the States, he'd take James somewhere private. He'd fuck him the way he loved to be fucked, and he'd tell him, and they'd find a way to make it work this time.

In the present, in that silent office in the backwoods of Maryland, a lump rose in Kent's throat. He would never in a million years forget that homecoming.

When he'd stepped off the plane, when he'd seen James for the first time in too long, and when…

Kent blew out a breath.

When he'd realized James was there in front of him, but gone forever.

He shook himself and left the office. There was no point in pacing alone in there—sooner or later, one of the other agents would get curious. He did have a job to do, after all. Protecting the president, not pining after him.

So he walked out to the kitchen and poured himself a cup of coffee. There was activity in the foyer. Voices, footsteps. James.

Kent swallowed a mouthful of coffee, grimacing at the bitter taste. Which may have been the coffee, or it may have just been the taste that had taken up residence in his mouth while he'd wandered through those ages-old memories.

Another agent—Agent Roberts—strolled through the kitchen. He offered Kent a slight nod and, thank God, didn't try to make conversation. Agents Hall and Perez came in a few minutes later to touch base with Kent about the return trip to Washington, and oh by the way, a couple of the guys needed to make some changes to their upcoming shifts. Family commitments and shit like that. Kent didn't mind—as long as the guys all pulled their weight and didn't abuse the privilege, he was willing to modify schedules as needed. One of the agents assigned to the motorcade upon their return needed to switch with one of the guys currently scheduled to stand watch here at Camp David, so he was on his way up here now to change places. Fine by Kent as long as James and his family were properly protected.

After the agents had left, Kent went out onto the deck with a fresh cup of coffee. His mind kept wandering back to James, and not in the way the president's head of security should've been thinking about the man.

He wanted to believe there was something he could do for James. Maybe he could if what James needed was really as simple as some rough sex. After all, in combat and in the bedroom, they were perfect together. They just couldn't make a relationship work, which hurt like hell. Kent would have James's back forever. No question. But *Christ*, he wished he could have done more. He wished he could've had more, but that ship had sailed.

And really, thank God for Carlene. Even if Kent didn't think too highly of her, James loved her, and Kent was grateful that there was someone who could make James happy. For that matter, someone who was willing to do whatever it took to *make* him happy, even if it meant letting another man into their bed.

Kent sighed. She probably thought she was breaking eye contact in a decade-long staring contest and giving Kent what he wanted, but sex with James was only the tip of a very large iceberg. There was probably a *Titanic* metaphor in there somewhere, but Kent was too fucking tired and distracted to put the pieces together.

He closed his eyes and took in a long breath. This would be an interesting conversation with Carlene. Fuck. Maybe it was time to update his résumé. An ex-SEAL who'd worked as the president's head of security could get a gig anywhere, right? Maybe with less travel. Less bullshit. Less wishing he could render a sitting president unable to sit comfortably for a little while.

He shivered. That ship had sailed, sunk and didn't need to be salvaged. A man could certainly dream, though, especially—

The sliding glass door opened. The hair on the back of his neck prickled. It wasn't Agents Hall or Perez. Somehow, he just knew.

He rested a hand on the railing for balance. "How was your run?"

Quiet footsteps. Halt. A breath. "Would've been better without an army following me around."

"Occupational hazard."

"No shit." James stepped into his peripheral vision, and then he was there. Right there. Right beside Kent at the railing, gazing out at the forest just like his wife had last night.

Kent's stomach twisted around the god-awful coffee. "I'm sorry. About earlier."

"Which part?"

Kent…didn't know the answer.

James exhaled. "I'm sorry. That was uncalled for. You were apparently doing what my wife asked you to."

"Something like that, yeah." Kent turned his head, and his fingertips tingled at the memory of that unshaved jaw. "I just want you to be okay, James."

"I know." James rubbed his eyes with his thumb and forefinger. "And I'm sorry Carlene asked you… That she put you in this…" He made a sharp gesture and dropped his hand but didn't look at Kent. "I don't even know what the fuck is going on."

"That makes two of us." Kent shrugged and didn't remember that subtle motion ever taking quite that much work. "Carlene thinks you still want me, I guess."

James tensed, and his head snapped toward Kent. "I do."

Kent blinked. "But in the office—"

"That doesn't mean I don't want…" James swallowed hard. "Look, I've wanted you since the day I met you, and that's never changed. I doubt it ever will."

Those words ignited a million feelings in Kent, but he tamped them down. No point. Not here. Not now. Not with James.

Especially when James went on: "I can't do this, though." He shook his head. "I can't lose my wife."

"I would never want you to. She doesn't want you to either."

James studied him, twin crevices forming between his eyebrows. "But she thinks I should sleep with you?"

"If that's what it takes to cope with all the stress in your life."

James looked out at the forest. "That doesn't make any sense."

They were both quiet for a moment before Kent finally asked, "*Exactly* how much does she know about us?"

James pursed his lips. "I've told her a few things. She knows we've slept together."

"Is that—"

"Yes, that's all," James snapped.

Kent swallowed.

James sighed. "Sorry. I… Look, what was I supposed to tell her?" His voice was soft and pleading now. "After I put you in as my head of security, and as much as she knows I want you around, how am I supposed to tell her you and I have done more than have sex?"

Kent drummed his fingers on the railing. "Even if it blew up in our faces."

"Yeah." James folded his arms. Not defensively, more like he was trying to ward off a chill even though the day was warm. "It's complicated, you know? I don't like hearing about what she had with exes, and I'm pretty sure she doesn't want to hear it from me either."

More silence. Long, prickly silence.

James lowered his hands. He rested one on the railing, dangerously close to Kent's, though it was impossible to say if that was deliberate. Either way, Kent didn't move to narrow that tiny space.

"So what do we do?" James asked.

"We don't have to do anything. Carlene came to me because she doesn't know what to do either."

"But why?" James shook his head. "Why did she come to you specifically? I mean, what makes her think you and I sleeping together is going to solve anything?"

Kent hesitated. "Apparently you talk in your sleep."

James paled. "What?"

"That's what she said. She…" Kent cleared his throat. "She says you say my name. A lot."

James's eyes widened. "Oh."

Kent was sorely tempted to ask what James was dreaming about when he called out his name, but he wasn't sure he wanted to know. "It's worse when you're really stressed. Like…lately. The only thing she could make of that was that you need me."

James flinched. "Even if I do, what would it change?"

"You tell me."

Silence. More long, tense, uncomfortable silence.

"For what it's worth," James said after a while, "I've never stopped wanting you. Never."

"You said that. And I believe you."

"Still. I don't want you to think this is because of you." He set his jaw. "It isn't. I want…"

"You know I would never try to get between you and your wife, right?"

"Absolutely. I wouldn't have you on my security detail if I didn't trust you. In every way." James swallowed hard. "I'm sorry."

"Don't be." Kent resisted the urge to reach for his arm—even the most platonic physical contact wouldn't be reassuring in this context. "We both know damn well we're better off as friends."

A subtle wince worked its way into James's features and then vanished. "I know."

They held each other's gazes.

After a while, James turned to go, and Kent was alone on the deck again, just like he had been last night after he and Carlene had talked.

He exhaled. Time and again, he'd told himself—and James—that they were better off as friends, but every time he'd watched James walk away, it hurt a bit more. Today was no exception. Though he'd never do a thing to break up James's family or take him from his wife, it hurt.

Kent thumbed a loose piece of wood on the railing. He could usually force back the bitter regret and remind himself that things had worked out for the best. The sting of seeing James's gold wedding ring had faded years ago, and he'd talked himself into accepting the sight of Carlene by her husband's side. Once in a while, he even believed this was how things were meant to be. Sometimes, though, that regret surfaced, and that was what it did now, bubbling up in the back of his mind and making him wish he could change the past.

Yeah, they'd given a relationship a shot in their younger days, and it had blown up in their faces. And yeah, he'd rather have James as a friend than an estranged ex-boyfriend.

But after they'd been separated, and Kent was on his way home from that mission full of close calls, he'd vowed to persuade James to give it one more try. They were older then. More mature. More aware of their own mortality and things that were more important than when and where they'd get drunk. This time, when he saw James again, he'd tell him he loved him and hope like hell that James felt the same.

He'd stepped off the plane, exhausted and jetlagged, and James had been there, and Kent had almost forgotten about DADT and military bearing and all that. What little restraint he'd had left went into keeping that first embrace from turning into a long overdue kiss.

"God, it's good to see you."

"It's good to see you too. Kent, this is Carlene…"

Two months later, Kent had stood beside James in dress whites and watched James and his future First Lady tie the knot.

In the present, Kent cursed under his breath.

And he caught himself wishing that Carlene was right—that sex with him was the answer to James's problems.

But he was starting to think his presence was only going to make things worse.

Chapter Five

A week after Carlene left Camp David, the limousine came to a gentle stop in the White House's North Portico, between the iconic pillars and the front steps.

Not a moment too soon, either. The kids had been wonderful for the entire trip, but after traveling all day long with the requisite crises of ears popping, drinks spilling, turbulence, a lost toy and a lot of tears, everyone was exhausted. Why did she resist hiring a nanny again? She really needed to do something about that.

Thank God for Blake and Steve, two of the Secret Service guys who were absolute saints with children. Blake had pretty much dealt with Justin all day while Steve had been on Natalie detail, leaving Carlene free to take care of Joey's ears and tears. Those two would be getting expensive bottles of something for Christmas, policies be damned.

In the shadow of the huge pillars, staff members busied themselves unloading luggage from the back of the limo. The Secret Service saints helped Carlene herd the groggy kids up the marble stairs and into the massive foyer, and she couldn't remember ever being so thankful to be back in this place. The poor kids needed to rest, and now they finally could.

She thanked Blake and Steve profusely, then turned to the kids. "All right, everyone up to—"

"Daddy!" the three of them squealed in unison, and suddenly the lethargic trio found a second wind. They bolted across the room to the stairs.

And there was James.

He jogged down the steps and knelt, arms out, and let the kids bowl him over.

Carlene's chest tightened at the sight of him—what had gone on this past week?—but she had to smile as he greeted the kids. The presidency had taken its toll on James and on their marriage, but God bless the man, he'd done everything in his power to be a good father.

While he hugged the kids and listened to them chatter over the top of each other, she just watched him. He must've been dealing with some official business just before they'd arrived. She could always tell when he hadn't had any downtime yet because his tie was still tight. He hated ties, hated the "hangman tightness" as he called it, and always jumped at the first opportunity to slide the knot down a little for some breathing room.

"You guys all had fun, right?"

The kids nodded vigorously.

"Good." James tousled Justin's hair. "Okay, everybody go upstairs and unpack, and if Mom says it's okay, maybe we can squeeze in some Mario Kart before bed."

Three sets of eyes were suddenly fixed on Carlene. Four, including James.

"Can we play, Mom?" Joey asked.

James raised his eyebrows, and a playful smile formed.

In spite of all the questions and worries weighing on her, she couldn't help feeling that familiar tingle when he smiled. Or laughing when his eyes added to the little row of "Please, Mom, can we?" in front of him.

"I want suitcases unpacked first," she said. "After that, it's up to your dad."

Immediately, the kids came down and grabbed the tiny suitcases that they could carry, and then rushed past James, nearly knocking him flat as they thundered up the stairs.

Laughing, James rose, and as he did, he finally tugged at that knot at his throat. He slid it down, and when it unraveled, he let it hang without pulling it completely off.

Then their eyes met. His laughter faded. Carlene struggled to hold her smile as she held his gaze, and that effort hurt like hell.

When did things change between us?

He let go of his tie and came closer, and when his hand met her waist, her whole body seemed to twinge and tingle at the same time, as if her senses didn't know what to make of him anymore.

"It's good to see you," he whispered.

Carlene swallowed. "You too."

He hesitated, and for a moment, she thought he might let her go and disappear upstairs with the kids, but instead he drew her in and kissed her. A hundred different feelings rushed through her. Relief that he was here. Nerves over what would happen now that they were in the same place again. That little thrill she always got when she touched him. That certainty that things were about to go south.

When he drew back, her heart jumped into her throat. There was so much they needed to talk about. She needed to know—and didn't want to know—what had happened in her absence, and if James was any closer to sane than before she'd left.

But not out here. Not with staff members and Secret Service milling around.

Evidently, James either didn't want to talk about it or didn't want to do it out in the open, because he didn't bring it up. Instead, he slipped his hand into hers, and in silence, they went up the stairs and followed the noise of the kids settling back into their rooms.

"Think they'll have enough energy to play games tonight?" he asked.

"I doubt it."

He chuckled. "Me too. But maybe for a little while."

"Okay. I need to go unpack anyway." She smiled and nodded toward the kids' rooms. "Even if they're tired, they'll want to spend time with their dad." She struggled to hold the smile. "They missed you."

"I missed them." James stopped, and without thinking about it, she did too. He faced her and touched her cheek. "I missed you."

"I missed you too," she whispered.

Nothing in James's expression betrayed anything. He was never easy to read by any means—probably as much a result of his personality as his SEAL training—but she'd learned his subtle tics and cues.

This time, though, he offered nothing. No anger. No guilt. No hint about what had or hadn't happened in her absence. Nothing.

After a moment, he cleared his throat and took a step back. "I'd better check on the kids. Make sure they're doing what they're told."

She forced a smile. "Okay."

They held each other's gazes and then continued in separate directions. Carlene reminded herself that there was time. They didn't have to hash everything out this instant—she needed to decompress from the trip, and he needed to see his kids.

They would talk. After the kids had spent some time with their dad, after he'd taken them through their bedtime routine, there'd be time for him and Carlene to talk. Behind closed doors, preferably. She and James weren't opposed to the kids seeing them argue or even fight—it was good for them to understand that Mom and Dad didn't always see eye to eye, and that everything would be okay once the disagreement was over. She wasn't so sure about this, though. She and James weren't fighting. They weren't really disagreeing on anything. This was something she didn't know how to process, never mind explain to a kindergartener.

So for now, she'd get herself unpacked and showered, and she'd leave James to the role he filled best of all—Dad.

Chapter Six

Washington was one of those cities that never slept, and it was never completely quiet. More often than not, the distant sounds of overnight road construction, traffic and occasional gunfire peppered the night.

None of it ever really bothered James. He'd slept in worse places.

Tonight, though, it was the silence that unnerved him. The city's usual noise existed in the background, but here on the second floor of the White House, in the master bedroom, where James sat alone and stared out the window, he could've heard a beetle blink.

After just one round of Mario Kart, the kids were done for the night, so he'd put them to bed. When he'd returned to the bedroom he shared with Carlene, she wasn't here. Her phone was on the nightstand, so there was no point in texting or calling. Chances were she didn't want to be reached anyway.

So James had numbly fucked around on his phone and tried to pass the time, but he couldn't even concentrate on simple, silly games, and he didn't dare read the news. Now he sat here, waiting and wondering. Maybe she just needed some time to herself after a day of traveling with the kids. He knew all too well how draining that could be—they were good kids, but being herded around by Secret Service agents and dodging cameras at every turn was exhausting for anybody, especially little ones. By the end of a trip, the poor things could barely move most of the time, and their mother was usually dragging too.

Guilt gnawed at him as it had been doing for the last several days. He wished like hell he could be more useful during those trips, but more often than not, even when they traveled together, he was being hauled in a completely different direction while Carlene wrangled the kids. When he was out of office, he owed that woman diamonds, cruises, a cabin in the woods—anything she wanted was hers, because God knew she'd given up more for him than he had any right to ask.

Including, he realized as the guilt chewed deeper, giving up her place in their bed even though it must have been killing her. Especially when she was offering that place to Kent. Anyone else in the world, she might've been able to take it. But not *him*. And yet…

James sighed.

Right then, the handle on the door turned, and the soft creak of the hinges straightened his spine. He stood, and as she came in, the sight of her made his mouth water and his stomach twist. He'd missed her, and he'd been terrified she wouldn't be here when he came back, but now here she was, and he had no idea what was going to happen next.

Carlene closed the door behind her.

James cleared his throat. "It, um, sounds like the kids had a good week."

"They did."

Did you?

"They're already asleep," he said. "At least, they were when I left their rooms."

A small smile struggled to form on her lips. "They are. I checked on them just before I came in here."

"Good. Good."

Carlene came a little closer. "I'm surprised they had any energy left."

"You know how they are." He offered a tight half shrug. "When they haven't seen one of us in a few days."

That faint smile vanished, and she dropped her gaze. He didn't know how to fill the silence, and apparently neither did she, aside from a murmur of, "I need to take out my contacts."

She disappeared into the bathroom. James sighed. In silence, they went through the motions of getting ready for bed. When they met again in the massive bedroom, the air between them was even more uncomfortable. He was down to boxers, and she wore an oversize football jersey and panties. Christ—nothing quite like being dressed down the way they usually were before they were intimate, and not being able to look each other in the eye.

"We should get some sleep," she said after a moment. "We need—"

"I think we should talk first." His heart sped up. This wasn't a conversation he was looking forward to having.

"It's late."

"I know. But I haven't been able to sleep since you left."

Carlene dropped her gaze. "I'm sorry."

"You don't need to be." He brushed some of her dark hair out of her face and then gently cupped her cheek. "Just talk to me."

She drew back slightly, out of his grasp, and his heart dropped. "This isn't an easy thing to talk about."

"No, it's not. But you've definitely got my attention."

Carlene sighed and sat on the edge of the bed where James had been a moment ago. He joined her. For the longest time, neither of them said a thing, and aside from James's pounding heart and the noise of Washington coming in from outside, the room was silent.

Finally, he whispered, "Why didn't you say anything before you left?"

Carlene avoided his eyes. "What was I supposed to say?"

"I don't know." He reached across the space between them and took her hand. "But you can talk to me. I know… I know this whole thing has been hard on everyone."

She kept her gaze down, instead watching her thumb run back and forth across his, and still didn't speak.

After a while, James broke the silence again. "For the record, nothing happened between us. Between me and Kent, I mean."

Her eyes flicked up, but only for a second. "Oh."

"I mean, it did, but it…" He hesitated, gnawing his lip. "We didn't sleep together."

This time, she met his gaze and held it. "Do I want to know?" Her voice was as difficult to read as her expression—not angry, not hurt, but definitely not happy.

"We..." James sighed. "We talked. We kissed. Once."

Carlene's lips tightened.

He squeezed her hand. "But it just felt wrong. I couldn't do that to you."

"You're not doing anything to me," she whispered. "If it's what you need, then—"

"I need you, Carlene."

The skepticism in her eyes cut to the bone.

James gently freed his hand and got up. He shoved his fingers through his hair as he started pacing. "This whole thing blindsided me. Why didn't you say something?"

"What was I supposed to say? Was I supposed to just tell you that I think you're stressed out, so hey, why don't you go blow off some steam with him?"

James flinched. "I don't know. But leaving, and letting him tell me? I mean, I..." He shook his head. "I don't know."

"I don't either." Carlene stood slowly, rubbing her neck with both hands. "I didn't know what else to do. Maybe I went about it all wrong. I just thought you needed him."

"But..." With some effort, he held her gaze. "Why would you ever think I need anyone but you?"

"Because my name isn't the one you call out in your sleep."

His heart dropped to the floor. He'd known about that, but hearing it straight from her hit him hard. James reached for her waist. "I have dreams about all kinds of things, but you're the one I'm looking for when I'm awake."

"But am I enough?"

His lips parted. "Of... Carlene, of course you are."

"You have no idea how much I want to believe that." She touched his face, her fingertips soft and unsteady on his cheek. "I don't want to lose you, James."

"You're not going to lose me." He clasped his hand around hers and squeezed gently. "I thought you were pushing me away."

"No. Never." She moved in closer, wrapping her other arm around his waist and gazing up into his eyes. "I just want you to be happy."

"I am," he whispered, and pressed his lips to hers.

She didn't protest, and held him tighter as she opened to his kiss. Well, they hadn't resolved much, hadn't gotten down to the root of why he said Kent's name in his sleep or why she thought sex with him would settle something, but they were touching. She was in his arms. For now, that was enough.

"I don't want to talk anymore," he whispered between kisses.

"Neither do I."

So they didn't talk. They climbed into bed, and her jersey, his boxers and her panties all eventually made their way onto the floor. James held her close, the warmth of her body turning him on and reassuring him that, yes, she really had come home, though every movement was slow and subdued, almost lethargic. Even as he moved inside her, it was like there was a layer of something between them. Like back in the days when they'd used condoms, only…more. Separating every place they tried to touch with something just thick enough to dull the senses and temper all the feverish heat.

He tried moving faster, thrusting harder, kissing her more passionately, but…nothing. He was turned on enough to stay hard, but at this rate, even that wasn't going to last much longer.

What the hell?

Beneath him, Carlene relaxed a little. Her arms loosened around him.

He slowed down. There had to be something he could do. Some way to turn her—

"I'm exhausted." She caressed his face. "It's been a long day. Maybe…"

Message received.

"Yeah." He fought to keep the resignation out of his voice, and he withdrew slowly. "Same here."

"Tomorrow night?"

"Definitely." He kissed her once more, then eased himself down beside her.

Neither of them spoke—what could they really say right then? James lay on his back. She lay on hers. His heart pounded in his ears. The city made all its nighttime noise in the distance. Between the two of them, though… Nothing.

After a while, Carlene rolled onto her side, facing away from him. She slept like that sometimes, so he tried not to read too much into it.

The light from outside illuminated her silhouette. James desperately wanted to touch her and draw her in again, but that had already failed once. All he'd do was frustrate them both. If she could sleep, then he wouldn't disturb her.

So he just watched her breathing while he tried to make sense of everything. Because right then, none of it made a damn bit of sense.

Things had been awkward with Kent ever since that first day alone at Camp David. Now they were weird with Carlene too. This tension between them was like a ticking time bomb. Something that couldn't last forever, something that would eventually break somehow, and it scared the hell out of him to think about how that break might happen. Especially since it was far too close to that feeling that had set up shop in his chest during those periods when he and Carlene had skirted divorce. Those periods were just rough patches now, speed bumps like the ones every marriage faced now and again, but at the time, he hadn't been so sure they'd make it past.

Those had happened without the pressures of being president and First Lady. Before life in the spotlight. Before the constant presence of the man she had seemingly resented just for existing.

And long, long before she'd resigned herself to the idea—ridiculous or not—that the only way James could deal with his responsibilities to the public was to have sex with the man who made her bitter just by breathing.

And before James had let himself entertain the thought of seeing if she was right.

Jesus, man. Sex with Kent is not worth losing Carlene. Nothing is.

What the hell am I supposed to do?

James scrubbed a hand over his face. He'd been hanging by a thread for the last few months as it was. Things were going from bad to worse in South

America. Powerful drug cartels had managed to seize control of the governments in Venezuela and Colombia, and both countries were in chaos. Now Congress was chomping at the bit to go to war. The American people were polarized on this and dozens of other issues, but in agreement that James needed to get off his ass and do *something*.

He could cope with being negatively compared to George W. Bush and Barack Obama. It was the part where he had to make divisive decisions about things that would affect the lives of innocent people—and quite possibly send some American service members to their deaths—that was more than he could handle.

Now, lying here in the relative darkness of the master bedroom, he couldn't escape the feeling that his wife, the woman he loved and the mother of his children, was slipping through his fingers. Or the realization that his best friend, now drawn into the crossfire, might be gone too, reduced to unavoidable collateral damage.

James resisted the urge to put a hand on her slender shoulder. His need for reassurance didn't trump her right to sleep. So instead, he just gazed at her silhouette in the soft glow from the outside lights.

I'm barely holding on to my sanity and my country, Carlene.
I can't lose you.

Chapter Seven

On his way down a dark street in Alexandria, Kent pulled back his sleeve and looked at his watch. It was after eleven.

Carlene had no doubt arrived earlier this evening. By now, she and James were most likely in bed. Hopefully they'd fucked each other senseless, collapsed together in that massive bed, and were sleeping soundly side by side, where they belonged.

Kent, meanwhile, wanted to be as far from 1600 Pennsylvania Avenue as he could get. Thank God he had a few options. He kept an apartment just outside of Washington, though he spent most nights at the White House. James helped him with the rent—he knew Kent wanted a place of his own, and respected his need for space sometimes when he was off duty, so he was happy to help offset the cost in exchange for Kent spending most nights just down the hall. It was a lifesaver for Kent those times when sleeping under the same roof as James threatened to drive him insane.

Tonight, even that sparsely furnished and rarely visited bachelor pad wasn't far enough from James. After pacing and fidgeting for hours, he'd finally given up, put on some decent jeans with a button-down black shirt and headed out. He needed to be somewhere else. With any luck, he'd be sleeping somewhere else too. Preferably next to someone hot. Or maybe two. He wasn't sure he had the energy for a threesome tonight, but if he found a pair of willing, attractive men, he'd damn sure make a go of it.

The Hancock, a semi-sleazy gay night club near the old part of town, seemed like the safest bet tonight. Lots of horny, single men, and he'd rarely encountered someone he knew. Parking in this area wasn't necessarily the best idea, but he wasn't fond of cabs. It was just as well his car was a piece of shit since he didn't drive enough to justify having a nicer one, and he didn't leave much in it. If someone broke into it, they wouldn't score more than a few pens and a map of Washington. If they stole the whole damned thing, well then, he'd take a cab home.

After parking, he walked the few short blocks to the Hancock. The club had a short line out front, and he didn't figure he'd have to wait long to get in. The few times he'd been to this place, he'd marveled that they hadn't yet installed a revolving door. Guys went in alone. Guys left with their hands in other guys' back pockets. Kent fully intended to be—and have—one of them tonight, and the sooner the better, so he stepped into line.

Earlier, he'd entertained the idea of going to a BDSM club, but he'd have had to drive a few hours to one. Not that there was any shortage in and around Washington, of course. He'd been to plenty of them. But he was safer driving out to Richmond, Philly or even Virginia Beach or New York. At least that minimized the odds of running into someone he knew, which was a real possibility within the District. That was a lesson he'd learned the hard way.

He'd gone to the Raven's Cage in Baltimore for a few months, and that had been great right up until the night he'd found himself making eye contact with the Speaker of the House while the old man was crawling around on the floor at the end of a leash, his back covered in welts from a flogger and his dick encased in a painful-looking metal cage. That had been a bit awkward. Though he had to admit, it was amusing as hell two days later when he'd struggled to keep a straight face while the man stammered and tugged at his tie during a meeting with James. The usually eloquent Speaker could barely form a sentence the entire time, and whenever he'd glanced at Kent, he'd lost a little more color, to the point that James and the other attendees started asking if he needed some water or a doctor.

There'd been other incidents like that, and they'd been awkward at worst, amusing at best. Eventually, he'd just decided to stay away from Washington. The last thing he needed was something like this coming up during James's bid for reelection.

That was a very real concern too. During the primaries, one of James's political opponents had not only recognized Kent in a dungeon, but approached him and tried to get information out of him. Damning information—something from James's past as a SEAL, or something from his personal life. Anything that could be used against him.

Any other night, Kent would've told him to kick rocks, but that night, things had been a little more complicated. The man must've been biding his time for weeks, waiting for the right moment to make his move, and his patience had apparently paid off when Kent had decided one night to experiment with submission. Kent was, by and large, a Dom, but curiosity and a couple of trusted Dom friends had put him into a haze of subspace one night, and that was when the asshole had made his move. Kent had been flying high, borderline delirious, and thank God one of his Doms had chased the fucker away. To this day, Kent couldn't remember the guy's face, and his friends hadn't gotten a good look at him either.

That had spooked Kent away from local BDSM clubs, and it had also ruined submission for him. If he did have any submissive tendencies, if he was an occasional switch, that side of him was now shut down forever and hidden behind a mental wall. He would never let his guard down like that again.

Playing a Dom, however, was a different story. How it had taken him into his midthirties to figure out he was a Dom, he'd never know, but now that he knew, he craved it. Tonight, he was itching for some of that, for the chance to shut out the world and focus on making some desperate submissive scream, but he didn't have it in him to drive clear up to Philly or down to Richmond tonight.

So here he was, standing outside the Hancock with his hands in his pockets, checking out the guys in line and wondering if any of them were within twenty years of his age. Shit. When did this place turn into a club for college kids? He could've sworn this was the place where he'd hooked up with that silver-fox banker from New York and his bear boyfriend last year. Maybe the older crowd had gotten here early, and it was the young stragglers waiting outside.

A man could dream, anyway.

The line moved quickly, and it wasn't just because guys were leaving almost as fast as they were arriving. The crowd was fairly thin—the line was apparently a result of the bouncers taking their sweet time checking IDs, not to mention a few jackasses who were trying to flirt their way out of paying the cover.

Kids. Kent rolled his eyes. *Get off my lawn.*

His own thought made him snort, which turned a couple of heads, and oh Lord, weren't they cute? Both were young—midtwenties at the most. One looked Filipino, and the other was a redhead. They eyed him, then looked him up and down and exchanged "are you serious?" glances before they went back to fucking around with their phones.

Give me the hairy eyeball all you want, kids. You don't know what you're missing.

Pity too. Now that they weren't looking at him, he took his sweet time looking at them from head to toe. They were both pretty cute, especially wrapped up in designer jeans and expensive haircuts that desperately needed to be messed up. He knew the type—they weren't interested in him now, but one look at the tattoo on his right forearm and they'd be putty in his hands. For whatever reason, guys like that always were.

Let me take off my jacket, and then we'll see what you think of me.

Cradle robber.

Eh, they were obviously legal.

Kent's thoughts at least entertained him long enough to get to the front of the line. The bouncer didn't bother carding him, which was no surprise, and after Kent had paid the fifteen-dollar cover—highway fucking robbery!—he was waved inside.

Kent checked his coat, made doubly sure he still had his wallet and keys on him, and then rolled his sleeves up to his forearms. The partially faded Trident tattoo was the result of being absolutely shit-faced in some backwater shithole town in a former Soviet state, but it hadn't turned out to be a complete mistake. A lot of guys had a thing for SEALs, and the ink always managed to be an effective icebreaker when he was looking to get laid.

Hell, he hadn't even finished fussing with his sleeve before a gorgeous little twink in a tight red shirt walked by and damn near snapped his neck doing a double take. He met Kent's eyes, and his perfectly groomed eyebrow arched. The corner of his mouth lifted too.

Kent grinned back. *Go, go, Gadget Trident…*

Out of nowhere, a much taller guy with bad highlights materialized and grabbed the drooling twink by the elbow. He shot Kent a ball-withering glare, and the two of them slipped into the crowd, but not before the twink threw back one last glance at Kent's arm.

Kent chuckled and slowly made his way to the bar. Okay, so this place might be populated by pretty young—but very, very legal—college kids, but he wasn't looking for someone who could carry on an interesting conversation. He just wanted someone to fuck so he didn't think about James and—

Stop thinking about him, then. Find someone hot and get the hell out of here.

First things first, though. He flagged down the bartender and ordered a beer. Even the bartender was cute—a gorgeous African American man who *might* have been approaching thirty—but Kent didn't spend much time checking him out. Bartenders had shifts to finish, and Kent was in the mood to, well, find someone hot and get the hell out of there.

So he offered a polite smile, tipped the man well and then turned to check out the rest of his options. He downed almost half the bottle in a couple of swallows. It was tempting to shotgun the whole thing, but for one, it was cold enough to make his teeth ache, and for another, he didn't drink much these days. He was here to find a warm body for the night, not set himself up for a one-night stand with the porcelain god.

With a little alcohol steadily working its way into his veins, he surveyed the crowd.

Turned out it wasn't all young guys after all. There were a few thirtysomethings hunched over tables, chatting along the edges of the dance floor and, like Kent, scanning the mob of people like lions searching for just the right zebras. An uncomfortable-looking guy sat alone at a booth, barely touching his beer except to peel the label. He was easily in his late thirties, possibly into his early forties, and fidgeted and pursed his lips like he wanted to be anywhere but here.

That makes two of us, amigo.

Kent took another sip of beer and was just about to head toward the booth when another guy stepped right into his line of sight. From partway across the room, the blue eyes and cocky swagger caught his attention, and bam! They made eye contact from several feet and quite a few people away. He was on the young end—twenty-five, tops—and hot. Smoking hot. He was a little bit shorter than Kent, and every bit of him was lean, sculpted muscle. His hair was cut high and tight. Something about his posture made Kent think Marine, but whatever the case, the guy was almost certainly military.

The vaguely Slavic angles of his face and his vivid eyes made Kent forget all about that guy at the booth who looked...who seemed... Whatever. *This* guy.

A subtle nod acknowledged Kent, and slightly narrowed eyes made his pulse jump. Kent grinned. The guy grinned back.

Kent knew that look well. It was the look of a man who was a little buzzed, a lot horny, and who didn't want to know anything about a guy beyond his oral hygiene and maybe his dick size. Even that last part wasn't a deal-breaker so long as a guy was a nonsmoker with a working relationship with his toothbrush.

Jackpot.

Kent pushed himself away from the bar and started toward him.

They met somewhere in the middle, where other guys were dancing, and that devilish grin was even hotter close-up, but it was impossible to interact out here. It was like trying to stand and talk in a damned blender, so they made their way off the floor and toward the edge of the room, and before they'd even introduced themselves, Kent decided he liked standing close to him. The guy had a hot body that had been lightly doused in an intriguing cologne, and his eyes were hypnotic, especially whenever they caught the light as they flicked toward Kent's lips.

It was too loud to hear the guy's name, and Kent didn't really give a shit what his name was anyway. The guy was drinking what looked like a Samuel Adams, so Kent dubbed him Sam and called it good.

Small talk was as impossible as hearing each other's names, but it gave them a reason to stand close together. Each time one tried to hear what the other was saying, it was another excuse to get even closer, until Kent's lips brushed beneath Sam's ear while he tried to ask if he could buy him another beer.

Sam shivered, arching into that touch until the light brush was a kiss on his hot flesh. The beer was forgotten. Kent snaked an arm across Sam's midsection, his dick hardening as Sam's abs contracted beneath his touch.

Kent lifted his head. Holy fuck, those eyes. Now they were gleaming, and he knew he hadn't misread Sam—this guy wanted to get laid, and he wanted to get laid now.

Please tell me you'll kiss one-night stands on the mouth. Please tell me—

Right then, Sam grabbed him and kissed him. Hard. On the mouth.

Oh fuck yes. Jackpot, jackpot, jackpot.

"You live around here?" Sam asked.

Kent grinned. That wasn't small talk in this club. It was code for "let's figure out who lives closest and go there."

"My apartment's not very close by."

Sam deflated slightly, a hint of a pout on his thin lips. Then he shrugged. "We'll get there." He nodded toward the back of the club, where the men's rooms were, and said something that sounded like, "You want to?"

Quickies in dirty restrooms really weren't Kent's cup of tea, but he had a hard-on and a lot of bullshit on his brain, so the sooner he had a dick to focus on or someone focused on *his* dick, the better. Men's room it was.

They made their way down the hall and into the restroom, where it was definitely quieter, though Kent's ears were ringing from the dance floor. There were other guys in here, but none of them gave him a second look and he didn't give them one. He did give the men's room itself a cursory glance—it was surprisingly clean, thank fuck—and then let himself be dragged into the stall farthest from the door. As soon as the stall was latched, Sam grabbed the front of his shirt and tried to push him back a step, but Kent just chuckled.

"I'm sorry," he growled. "Did you think you were calling the shots?"

He didn't give him a chance to answer before he shoved the guy up against the stall divider, and felt more than heard the little moan of pleasure just as he pulled Sam into a deep, horny kiss. Kent pressed against him, and Sam wriggled back, making sure Kent felt every hard inch of him.

Sam slid a hand in Kent's back pocket. Kent grabbed his wrist and pinned his arm to the wall, and the guy groaned—obviously he'd taken it as a show of dominance rather than an instinctive reaction to an invasive hand, and he *liked* that show of dominance, and Kent decided that was good enough.

"Tough guy," Sam murmured. "Guess that tat's not fake?"

"Not fake. You like Special Force—"

The kiss answered him well enough. Sam had been turned on before, and now he was squirming and panting between kisses. Kent's head spun. If he told Sam to drop his pants and bend over, the guy probably would. Definitely should've brought some condoms in with him instead of leaving them in his jacket pocket.

But this would do for now, especially when Sam wrestled his hand free and shoved it between them. Long fingers groped him through his jeans, and he pressed hard against him, grinding Sam's hand between both of their hard cocks.

Kent groaned. "Get the feeling you...like it rough."

"If it doesn't hurt, what's the point?"

Oh. Fuck. *Yes.*

Sam tugged at the button on Kent's pants. The button came free, and Kent cursed as Sam drew the zipper down, and again when Sam's hand slid beneath the waistband of his boxers. Sam's slim fingers were slightly cool and strong as hell, and Kent gasped when they wrapped around his cock.

"I had a feeling you were hung," Sam growled into a kiss. "You walk like a guy who's packing."

"G-glad I didn't disappoint."

"Not at all."

Kent couldn't even continue the banter. Eyes squeezed shut, he fucked into Sam's fist and tried like hell to keep kissing him, but damn...

"Good thing I brought condoms," Sam murmured, dipping his head to kiss Kent's neck. "Gonna need 'em tonight."

"Did you bring enough?"

"Define *enough.*"

Kent swallowed, struggling to speak as the delicious friction on his dick screwed with his brain. "Costco pack should do it."

Sam groaned softly. "I love the way you think." He kissed Kent's throat, pressing so hard Kent was surprised he didn't feel teeth. He stumbled back, then hit the wall on the other side of the stall and tilted his head to the side, inviting more lips and, please, please, teeth.

"J-just don't leave marks," he murmured.

A hot huff of laughter made his breath catch. "None at all?" He flicked his tongue across Kent's skin. "Or just none above the collar?"

Lauren Gallagher

"Above the collar."

"Noted." Sam tugged Kent's shirt down slightly and pressed his teeth into the newly exposed collarbone.

Kent moaned, gripping Sam's short hair tighter.

"I'd say we should get out of here," Sam said, working his way back up Kent's neck. "But before we go…" He squeezed Kent's dick and added the slightest twist to his strokes.

"Oh, fuck."

"Yeah. We're gonna do that. Soon."

"Good."

Jesus, this was exactly what he needed tonight—a hot, eager guy stroking him while they made out against a wall, both of their bodies feverish and trembling. He needed to get this man alone in a place where they could strip down and fuck. Where they could make all the noise they wanted, and maybe test the limits of some furniture, and go through a few condoms before the end of the night. Oh yes, this was exactly what he needed.

"We should… We should go somewhere else."

Sam kissed him again. "We will." He stroked Kent faster, and the message was crystal clear—they weren't leaving until one or both of them had gotten off. Kent loved the way this guy thought. Get the first quick one out of their systems, and then take their time fucking each other into the ground later. Was Sam a top? A bottom? Did he go both ways? Kent didn't even care. As long as he fucked as well as he kissed, and his whole body moved with the same skill as his hand, and—

Suddenly the hand was gone, and so were the lips against his, and then his cock was surrounded by a talented, eager mouth.

Kent braced against the wall. "Oh my God…"

This was no tease. This was a one-way ticket to a fast, powerful orgasm, and Kent was damn sure going to return the favor as soon as it was over, assuming he didn't go out of his mind before they even reached that point. "Holy shit…"

Get up, he wanted to say. *Get on your feet and turn around so I can fuck you.*

But for some reason, the words didn't come.

Get up. I want to fuck you until you cry. Get up, James

64

He opened his eyes and—

Froze.

Rationally, he'd known all along that he was in a dingy restroom stall at the Hancock with a stranger whose name wasn't really Sam. Yet somehow, he was truly surprised to find himself here instead of tangling up with James.

He was here, with his dick in a stranger's mouth, and his mind was somewhere else. 1600 Pennsylvania Avenue, to be exact.

And the stranger in front of him, sucking his cock and occasionally gazing up at him with those gorgeous blue eyes with the pupils blown, was suddenly way too familiar.

Oh, goddammit.

"Shit." Kent pushed himself back as far as the wall would allow. "Stop, stop."

"What?" Sam sat back on his heels, showing his palms as if he'd been confronted by police. "What's wrong?"

"N-nothing." Kent shook his head. "I mean, I...can't. I'm sorry."

Sam's eyebrows shot up, and he lowered his hands a little. "You're hard. I'm hard. What's the problem?"

"It's..." Kent swallowed as he tucked his cock back into his pants. "Complicated."

Sam laughed and rolled his eyes. "Whatever." With a shrug, he stood, zipped up his own pants and stalked out of the stall, leaving the door swinging behind him. A second later, the restroom door opened, letting in more noise from the club, and shut again. Sam was probably well on his way out to the dance floor in search of someone who'd see things through.

Good luck. Not that he'd need it.

Kent stepped out of the stall and went up to the sink. There were still others in the bathroom, but they still didn't pay him any attention, and he still didn't look at any of them. They were preoccupied, and he was... He was a fucking wreck.

He leaned over the sink and splashed some cold water on his face.

Get it together. Come on.

A whole club full of hot guys, and he had to gravitate toward *him*. One look, and Kent had wanted him, and there they'd been, and he hadn't made the connection until the worst possible moment, and now…

Fuck.

Maybe finding a man tonight was a bad idea. He supposed he could go somewhere else. Maybe a straight club—he could always find a woman. Though he was more into men, he certainly found women attractive, and tonight, the ladies had the added bonus of being as far removed from James as possible.

Except for the fact that the majority of nights he'd ever spent with women had also been spent with James.

Fuck. Fuck!

All he'd wanted to do was come here, get laid and forget the married man he couldn't have.

So he'd found Sam. And he'd damn near hooked up with Sam. And he'd been on the verge of coming in Sam's mouth or on his hand or wherever.

And right *then* he'd realized Sam was the spitting image of a young, horny, single James.

Kent met his own eyes in the mirror as a few drops of water slid down his temples and his cheek. He had it bad, didn't he? A hell of a lot worse than he'd had it before. Or at least worse than he'd let himself admit before.

What the fuck do I do now?

Chapter Eight

The next morning, in the White House's immense dining room, Carlene surreptitiously watched James from across the broad table. The kids were already gone for the day—Joey had been ferried to his private kindergarten, and the twins had gone off with a preschool tutor. The cavernous room was almost empty. Even the Secret Service were standing outside the door rather than looming in the background with the pastel wallpaper and elegant paintings. It was just James, Carlene and heavy, uncomfortable silence punctuated by the quiet clink of silverware on plates as they picked at their breakfasts.

Carlene took a sip of coffee. "You okay?"

James nodded and nudged his plate away. "Just thinking about tomorrow."

Carlene's own food suddenly didn't look so appetizing, but she kept picking at it and made herself take a couple of bites. She didn't need to worry James. "The committee's reconvening, isn't it?"

"Yeah." He exhaled hard. "Sounds like they're going to push to go to war."

Carlene resisted the urge to squirm uncomfortably. "Do you think you can talk them out of it?"

"I doubt it." He rested an elbow beside his plate and rubbed his forehead. "I'm not sure how much longer they're going to let me outmaneuver and stall them before they go around me." He lowered his hand and met her gaze, his eyes tired and his face pale—she wondered if this was what had made his sleep so restless last night, or if it had been the weirdness between them. Maybe both. He absently ran his thumb along the edge of his plate. "I think the only thing stopping them is they know damn well that voters defer to me when it comes to military operations."

"As well they should," she muttered. "You've got more combat experience in your little finger than the entire damned House."

"Yeah." He fidgeted, and she thought he might have shuddered just before he added, "They know the only way any of them can send the country to war and still get reelected is if I'm in agreement that it's the only possible solution."

Carlene swallowed. "Is it?"

He lowered his head and rubbed the back of his neck. "I've been asking myself that for weeks. I... Fuck, I don't know."

"What other options are—"

He dropped his hand on the table with a heavy *smack*. "I don't fucking *know*, all right?"

Carlene jumped.

James exhaled. "Jesus. I'm sorry. I'm..." He shook his head. "I'm sorry."

"It's okay," she said, barely whispering. She thumbed the handle on her coffee cup and avoided his eyes. Cautiously, she asked, "What happens next if it is the only option?"

He didn't answer right away. Probably choosing his words carefully. He rarely snapped at her, and when he did, he was hesitant to speak again until his temper was completely contained. God bless the man—he had a hell of a temper, but he'd only ever lost it at her one time. She'd gotten right up in his face and warned him against ever speaking to her that way again, and against even *thinking* of speaking to their future children that way, and he must have taken those words to heart. Though he could be moody, especially when his job pushed him to his limit, he'd never, ever let fly at her like that again. Even when they argued, or when he raised his voice at the kids, it was nothing like that one hellacious fight.

Finally, James sighed and shook his head, and his voice was calm and even as he said, "I've been trying to come up with a solution, but I don't know. The cartels have access to too many military resources now. They're making more threats against US interests." He gnawed his lip for a moment. "If they keep waving missiles at us and everyone else, we may not have a choice but to send in troops to neutralize these assholes before they kill more innocent people."

"But you don't want our troops getting killed in the process."

James closed his eyes and nodded. That meeting tomorrow was going to be the death of him—he nearly always spent the first thirty minutes or so after something like that getting sick, and he was already starting to look green just talking about it.

He swallowed hard, as if it took a lot of effort. "I know as well as anyone that's what they signed up for. You volunteer to serve, you volunteer to go in and possibly die when shit like this blows up. But I…" He grimaced. "It was different when I was a SEAL, you know? If I gave the order, I was going in with them. I don't like the idea of giving the order for troops to go into combat while I sit back here with my dick in my hand." He pressed his elbow into the table and rubbed over his face again. "If I'm going to send them in, I should be going in with them."

"You were elected to lead from here," Carlene said softly. "Not out there."

"I know." He lowered his hand and met her gaze. "But I know what's out there. I've seen it. How—" He took a deep breath, and softly asked, "How can I send someone else's kids into that?"

Carlene's stomach clenched. The hurt and worry in his eyes were palpable. She was beginning to understand why only the sleaziest and most coldhearted members of humanity slithered their way into politics. People like James cared too much about people to make decisions that could impact, disrupt or end their lives.

She reached across the table, and he met her halfway, clasping their hands together between the candleholders and centerpieces. She squeezed gently and locked eyes with him. "Whatever decision you have to make, I know it won't be easy. If it was, then I'd question what kind of person you were." She rubbed her thumb alongside his hand. "But I have complete faith that the decision you make will be the right one."

He studied her, and eventually a faint smile came to life. With his middle fingertip, he drew tiny circles on the inside of her wrist. "I'm glad someone will."

She returned the smile, hoping it was more convincing than his. "I doubt I'll be the only one. The fact that you're making Congress budget for taking care of soldiers and their families speaks volumes. The American people know you genuinely care about them, and you're not going to just send our guys into combat and hope for the best."

He nodded. "Let's hope so. And…" He cursed softly, watching their hands instead of looking in her eyes. "Let's hope they do come up with that budget. Because if shit keeps escalating"—he lifted his gaze—"I may not have a choice but to send in troops, with or without a safety net."

Jesus. No wonder he couldn't sleep these days.

No wonder…

Carlene's chest tightened. No wonder he'd been shaking and calling for Kent last night.

She pushed that thought away and squeezed his hand again. "Let's hope it doesn't come to that."

"Yeah." He gently freed his hand and reached for his coffee. Eyes unfocused, he murmured, "Let's hope."

With the committee reconvening tomorrow, Carlene didn't see much of James. His agenda for the day was packed full of meetings with advisors, diplomats and military leadership. Combat operations were becoming a very real possibility, especially as news trickled in about more and more bloodshed in the cities thanks to rival cartels and civilian uprisings. Worse, there were rumors that the cartels were "reappropriating" some military transport equipment for the purpose of moving narcotics and God knew what else into the United States.

The media was going insane. Americans were demanding action. Congress was pointing fingers at James, blaming him for inaction, which only fueled the media fire, which only infuriated the population.

So there were meetings. Nonstop, one after the other, behind closed doors, with a nonstop stream of people coming and going from the West Wing with their faces contorted into scowls and grimaces.

It was nothing short of a miracle that James was able to join Carlene and the kids for dinner. By the time the family sat down, though, he was a million miles away. He tried his best to keep it under the surface and be completely engaged as Joey told him everything he'd done at kindergarten today, but Carlene could see it in his eyes—he was in another world.

Carlene barely touched her food. When the kids couldn't hold their exhausted, preoccupied father's attention, that wasn't a good sign. What the hell was she supposed to do about it, though?

Her mind kept going back to the same place it had gone when she'd tried to come up with a solution over the last few months—Kent. It was hard not to return to that solution over and over when she heard his name so many times a night, especially last night, when James had not just called out for Kent but had sounded on the verge of breaking down every time.

Just thinking about it almost brought Carlene to tears herself, and she took a deep swallow of wine to keep the lump from rising in her throat. She had to try Kent again. There was nothing else she could do.

After dinner, she set the kids up with a movie they'd seen hundreds of times, even if using an electronic babysitter did make her feel guilty as hell. It was necessary this time, though. For the sake of Mom and Dad. Especially Dad.

And they didn't only have the TV as a babysitter tonight. A couple of the Secret Service guys hung around even though their shifts were over. They never seemed to mind doing that—they were both single, both adored kids, and they always seemed even more engrossed in *Finding Nemo* than the little ones were.

With everyone situated in the White House's family theater, she went looking for Kent.

His shift was over, but he spent most nights here. Hopefully he hadn't gone back to his apartment tonight.

It turned out he hadn't—she found him in the South Portico, sitting on the marble steps and gazing out into the night beyond the white pillars on the other side of the lane, where cars sometimes pulled up during the day. His jacket was unbuttoned, his tie loose, forearms resting on his bent knees with his fingers dangling in between.

She glanced around. The portico and the lawn were as deserted as they ever were. Staff, drivers, guests—there was always someone coming and going. Several Secret Service agents were nearby, of course, including a K-9 wandering past with a German shepherd on a leash, but they were all out of earshot.

"Hey."

He sat up straighter. If his reflexes were anything like her husband's after all those years as a SEAL, he'd known she was there before she'd even seen him. She hadn't startled him, but she was willing to bet he'd been hoping she wouldn't say anything.

She cautiously came a little closer. "Can I talk to you?"

Kent turned and looked up at her, and Carlene was the one who startled. She hadn't expected the pronounced, heavy circles beneath his eyes. His shoulders were down, as if the only thing holding him upright was the thick bulletproof vest beneath his shirt. Though it was hard to tell in this light, his complexion looked a few shades lighter than usual, and his eyes... Had he slept at all last night?

She shifted her weight. "Are you okay?"

"Is that what you came to talk to me about?" Irritation laced his tone.

"I... No, but I—"

"Don't worry about me." He folded his hands between his knees and focused on something beyond the pillars. "What do you need?"

She chewed the inside of her cheek. Maybe this wasn't a good time. Kent obviously had a lot on his mind, and she'd have bet money it pertained to why she'd come looking for him. "It can wait. Never—"

"Is this about James?"

She hesitated. "Yes. It is."

Kent rubbed a hand over his face, his palm rasping across his five o'clock shadow. "I can't help you. I tried. He's..." He shook his head, and bitterness dripped from every word as he added, "Whatever he needs, it isn't me."

"Shit." She wrung her hands just to give them something to do. "He's going to be a mess tomorrow if something doesn't give."

Kent put up his hands. "Don't look at me. I tried."

"He's not—"

"Why are you pushing so goddamned hard for this?" Kent growled. "What makes you think there's no other solution to—"

"Because I'm fucking scared, okay?"

He drew back a little, eyes wide.

Carlene squared her shoulders and forced herself to hold his gaze. "I'm scared that if I'm reading him wrong, and there's nothing you can do to help him, then there's nothing any of us can do. And that's just not something I can accept right now."

Kent's lips parted, and some of the hostility drained from his posture.

Carlene cleared her throat. "Maybe I'm crazy. I don't know. But there has got to be some reason why he keeps asking for you."

"Have you tried asking *him*?"

"Of course I have."

"And?"

Carlene folded her arms. "I get about as much out of him as you do."

Kent lifted a shoulder in a tense half shrug. "Then I don't know what to tell you. I really don't." He stood and faced her, staying one step below her so they were nearly eye to eye. "Whatever's going on in his head..." Another shrug, this one almost as taut as the last. "I'm not sure there's much you or anyone else can do."

"I can't accept that," she whispered. "His job is going to *kill him*, Kent."

He glared at her. "You don't think I know that? Or that it's not ripping me apart as badly as it is you?"

She took a startled step back. Despite his reputation as a hothead SEAL, Kent had always been mellow, sometimes to the point of irritating, and she'd never heard him raise his voice before.

They both looked around, and a couple of nearby agents had turned their way.

"We should take this inside," he said.

Carlene nodded. Without a word, she turned to go into the mansion, and he followed her. The last thing either of them—or James—needed was a paparazzo with a telephoto catching a "tense moment" between the First Lady and the president's head of security.

Neither spoke until they'd stepped into an empty room and closed the door, sealing them off from the rest of the world.

When Kent faced her, his expression had softened. "Look, I'm sorry I snapped at you. But you've..." He pushed out a breath and shook his head. "Carlene, even if your idea is somehow going to help, you've got to realize you're asking more of me than just fucking him so he can blow off steam."

"I know. I'm sorry too."

"I've done everything I can. I can't keep pushing the issue with him for his sake, but also mine."

She rubbed her eyes. "Fuck."

"What exactly do you want me to do?" The anger was back in his voice. "Keep at him until he gives in? Then what? Do you think things will just be perfect and smooth between him and me after that? Or between *you* and him? And Jesus Christ, do you think I *enjoy* being rejected by the one that got away?"

Carlene pulled in a sharp breath.

Kent's eyes widened as if he'd gone further than he'd intended. Then his shoulders dropped. "I'm... Look, I'm sorry, but you've got to understand where I'm coming from on this. I would never do anything to hurt your marriage, but don't think for a second that the only feelings I have for him are physical."

The admission sent her heart into her feet and made her chest tighten.

Kent went on, "I love him, okay? I always will. But he's married to you, and I respect that. I mean it when I say I'll never stand in the way." His lips pulled tight for a second as if his rock-steady composure was wavering a bit. "If he needs something from me, it's his. Always. No matter what. Just don't...don't assume it's easy to put myself in a position to be turned down by him." Kent swallowed. "Or if he says yes, watch him go back to you afterward."

They held each other's gazes. Carlene had no idea what to say, or how to feel, or what to think. She'd long suspected that Kent was still in love with James, and she was almost certain James was still in love with him, but hearing it was a punch to the gut. One she'd brought on herself—what was she *thinking*?—but a punch nonetheless.

Kent took a step back. "If I think of something that'll help him, I'll let you know. But this? I'm not discussing it again."

With that, he turned to go.

"Kent, wait."

He stopped and, after a moment's hesitation, faced her.

She sighed heavily. "I'm sorry. I...didn't really think about how this would affect you. I thought..."

His features hardened. He didn't speak, but his eyes said it all: *You thought I could fuck him without feeling anything.*

"I'm sorry," she said again. "I wasn't trying to hurt you. I promise."

He eyed her warily for a moment, but then relaxed a bit. "I know. You were trying to help James." Kent glanced at the door, a pained expression in his eyes. As he shifted his gaze back to her, he said, "I want to help him too. I just don't know if there's anything I can do that he'll allow, or that won't make things worse."

"Or that won't hurt you in the process."

He winced. Then nodded.

"I'm so sorry, Kent." She ran a hand through her hair and tried not to look at him. Her throat ached and her eyes stung with the threat of tears, but she quickly composed herself. She was not quick to crack, no matter what was pressing on her last nerve, but the further James frayed, the more she struggled to keep herself together. "I don't want to hurt you or anyone else. I'm just worried sick about James."

"I know. So am I."

She wiped at her eyes just to make sure no stray tears got loose. "Do you think there's anything we can do to help him?"

He shook his head. "I wish I knew." He paused. "Talk to him. I will too. Maybe...maybe we can find some way to help him cope with the stress."

"And if what we talked about before *is* what he needs?" As much as she didn't want to believe it, every time Carlene heard James whisper Kent's name in his sleep, she had to accept that it was a very, very real possibility.

Kent avoided her eyes. "I promised him a long, long time ago that there was nothing I wouldn't do for him." He finally lifted his gaze and met hers. "I fully intend to keep that promise."

Carlene bit her tongue to keep from asking how far that promise actually went.

So all she whispered was, "Thank you."

Chapter Nine

There wasn't enough coffee in the known universe to counter the last few sleepless nights, but that didn't stop James from trying. He paced in the Oval Office, coffee cup in hand, and tried to strategize the impending meeting through the haze of fatigue. This shit would be a lot easier if meeting with lawmakers were like one of the combat ops they were pushing him so hard to authorize. Sure, things could and did go wrong during those ops, and the best-laid plans went to hell as soon as bullets started flying, but he couldn't count the number of times he'd calmed and centered himself in the back of a cargo jet or a Humvee by replaying the plan in his mind. Once he was in the thick of things, he'd improvise, but at least he had a plan going in, and that plan was what kept him sane until he hit the ground.

For shit like this? It was all verbal. He could think of things to say, come up with questions to ask, but he couldn't predict the responses. He couldn't play out a conversation in his mind, at least not past the first three or four comments. Somehow, going into a building that was quite possibly wired with C4 and in the path of a missile was less unsettling than going into a room full of overpaid corporate puppets who'd say and do whatever it took to convince him to send legions of eighteen-year-olds into a combat zone.

James shuddered and took another swallow of coffee. At least that would keep the nausea at bay until after the meeting. He hadn't gotten sick during a meeting yet, and he wasn't about to start today.

"Mr. President." A staff member leaned in through the door. "They're ready for you."

Well, *now* he was awake.

He straightened his jacket and glanced at his flock of advisors. Admiral

Stein met his gaze and offered a reassuring nod—no matter the outcome of this meeting, wheels were already turning and things were happening. Then James glanced at Kent, whose tired eyes also offered reassurance.

I've got this. James slowly released a breath. *Time to face the assholes who somehow got elected.*

He left the Oval Office and headed for the conference room. It still struck him as weird to be the president on his way to meet with Congress. He was supposed to be one of *them.* Six months after he'd retired from the SEALs, he'd stood up and announced his intention to run for the Senate. As it happened, the GOP was pushing a presidential candidate with a million corporate interests and a throbbing war boner, and the Democrats had grabbed James—a no-name politician, but a decorated soldier who believed combat to be a last resort—and made him their golden boy. They didn't want him in Congress. They wanted him in the White House.

Suddenly everything had been going a million miles an hour. James was in the spotlight as the presidential hopeful. His wife was pregnant. He was the frontrunner. Twins were on the way.

Then the twins had come early, and he'd nearly dropped out of the race to focus on his family, but Carlene had urged him to stay the course.

"You're what this country needs," she'd insisted. *"I'll hold down the fort at home."*

So he'd gone on even though it killed him to be away from his wife and babies—particularly when he found out later that her recovery had been rougher than she'd let on—and after the primaries came and went, James found himself on the ballot against the warmonger Republican, running for president instead of the Senate. With his wife, his toddler son and his thriving year-old twins by his side on election night, he'd won by a landslide.

Thank God too. If that asshole had won, there would've been troops on the ground in Venezuela and Colombia the second the cartels had made an aggressive move, the soldiers' futures and families be damned.

Now if he could just keep Congress from overriding him and going to war anyway...

As he entered the conference room, the senators and representatives stood.

James took his seat, and all around him, chairs creaked and groaned as everyone else did the same.

"When we left off last time," James said, "you gentlemen were going to put together a budget and prove we can afford this operation and the long-term care of soldiers and their families. Have you?"

Several of the congressmen shifted uncomfortably.

Senator Baxstrom cleared his throat. "The funding is just not there."

"Then our troops won't be either. We have to find another option."

Senator Lee thumped the table with his fist. "We need to take decisive action, Mr. President! Or else we're just waiting for an attack on American interests. Sir, they're using *military*-grade transport equipment to move narcotics onto our soil."

"Then I would suggest we get a budget together so we can—"

"It's not that simple. Combat operations are expensive, and it's not always possible to conjure the funding from thin air in time to respond to a threat to our people and our national security."

"Then we need to rethink what we're doing with our money," James said. "If we can't afford to go to war, then we need to double our efforts to negotiate a peaceful solution."

"With all due respect, Mr. President"—Senator Gorton shook his head—"we are running out of options, and we are running out of time to exercise them. Deploy the troops and send a message to—"

"With all due respect, Senator," James said through gritted teeth, "our troops are people, not a message. For that matter, I would say I have significantly more firsthand knowledge of what we'd be deploying our troops *into*. I will *not* send in our young men and women out there to come home in boxes until we have exhausted every possible peaceful solution."

"You're asking us to negotiate with terrorists."

"And *you're* asking our soldiers to die for the purpose of making a point, without even having the decency to make sure their families don't live in poverty for their trouble."

The rest of the committee glanced back and forth across the table, but no one spoke.

James looked around the room. "If we have no choice but to send in troops, then we must take into consideration the inevitable damage this conflict will do to our service members. I am not authorizing troop movement of this magnitude until there is an irrevocable guarantee in place that those troops and their families will be taken care of."

Senator Lee raised his gray eyebrows. "And if that's not possible?"

"Then we have no business going to war."

The senator started to speak, but James shot him a look that shut him down fast.

"Senator, have you ever been the last person a traumatized soldier talked to before he killed himself?"

Senator Gorton sat straighter, his eyes widening. "I... No."

"I have. And as I have said repeatedly, I will not authorize mobilizing our troops until Congress guarantees that soldiers like that have the resources to deal with the trauma *you* are asking them to endure." He narrowed his eyes. "Am I clear this time?"

The man swallowed. "With all due respect, Mr. President," he said, his voice low and cautious, "this situation is quite a bit more significant than any of our personal histories and tragedies."

James ground his teeth. "Meanwhile, those personal histories and tragedies are quite a bit more significant than whether or not you get reelected, so you'll forgive me if I focus on the human aspect of this conflict rather than the political one."

Everyone at the table drew back a bit.

Senator Baxstrom folded his hands and inclined his head. "Then what do you propose the United States do? We can't take this situation lightly. We can't do *nothing*."

James glared at him. "Do not assume for a second that I'm taking this situation lightly, or that I won't act. I'm taking this very, very seriously, but what I refuse to neglect is that we're not sending in a 'show of force' or 'taking decisive action'. We're talking about mobilizing human beings."

"Human beings who volunteered to serve," Baxstrom said.

"They volunteered to serve their country," James said. "Not to die in the name of political reindeer games. Until I can look every last one of them in the eye and tell them their service is necessary, and that they and their families will be taken care of regardless of the outcome, they're not going anywhere." He thumped the table with his index finger. "Give me a budget, or give me another solution."

The various congressmen exchanged uneasy glances.

Finally, Lee spoke. "The only way we're going to come up with the budget you're asking for is to cut funding to other areas. And a tax increase may be necessary."

"We may not have much choice," James said. "But I'm not sending a single soldier into South America until you do."

Baxstrom sighed heavily. "All right. We'll reconvene in one week with a budget. But one way or another, we must take action, Mr. President."

"Agreed," James said coolly. "And that action starts with your budget."

The senator scowled, but he didn't argue. In fact, no one argued, and at long last, the meeting was adjourned. Congress had one week to present him with a budget, and then he'd have to make a decision. Mobilize the troops, or don't mobilize the troops.

As soon as he was out of the conference room, James clenched his jaw and damn near sprinted to the men's room down the hall. No one got in his way or tried to stop him. They'd all gotten used to this routine.

And as he always did, James got into the room just before he started heaving violently.

He'd worked well under pressure when he was a SEAL, but the magnitude of this crisis was more than he could handle. He had yet to make it out of a meeting with this committee without getting sick—he quite literally couldn't stomach these fucking negotiations.

The only reason he could get through the meetings at all was knowing he had an ace up his sleeve. What the committee—indeed, any member of Congress—didn't know was that the budget negotiations were also a stalling tactic. He was buying time because, unbeknownst to anyone without clearance several levels above Top Secret, there were boots on the ground in Venezuela already, and another contingent was on its way into Colombia. As of three nights ago, SEALs were moving in to cripple the drug cartels from the top in a coordinated attack. They'd cut off the two dragons' heads while Congress worried about the bodies. If things went as planned, the cartels would implode, and Colombia and Venezuela would be back under their own leadership, and they could settle the two civil wars before it all erupted into something even bigger.

Godspeed, boys.

That ace up his sleeve was a double-edged sword, though. He had to keep Congress believing that military operations depended upon them forming a budget. He had to hope they'd keep stalling and stalling like they often did. He needed them to stall so he could buy time for the Special Forces, but he also needed to get that budget just in case the covert ops failed and there was no other option but to send in troops.

James coughed a few times and spat, then flushed the toilet and stepped out of the stall to rinse out his mouth. He desperately needed to go collapse in a dark, quiet room somewhere and decompress, but he was lucky everyone gave him this momentary reprieve. After all, duty called.

He gave himself a look in the mirror and made sure he was composed and collected. His eyes were a little red and watery as they often were, but there wasn't much he could do about that. The press wasn't around, so he didn't worry about it.

He tugged at his jacket, adjusted his tie and went back out into the hall.

No one gave him any grief. His advisors and security detail were standing around in clusters, talking quietly amongst themselves or looking at phones or paperwork. As soon as they noticed him, they all straightened and watched him, waiting for him to give some indication that they could proceed with business as usual. He glanced at Kent, who gave him an "are you okay?" look.

James pursed his lips. He really missed the days when his weak stomach— usually triggered by nerves, booze or both—would get him ribbed by the rest of his team. The secretary of state was hardly going to toss him a bottle of Pepto-Bismol and call him a pussy, and he was pretty sure the Speaker of the House wasn't going to suggest he eat a plate of ghost pepper hot wings to settle his stomach (SEALs could be dicks sometimes).

Ah, the good old days.

James cleared his throat. "What's next on the agenda?"

Just like that, everyone descended on him. Papers were shoved into his face. People threw questions and schedule changes at him. So much for that quiet, dark room.

As he was herded from the meeting to a press conference about the South American situation, a familiar shape beside him turned his head.

Kent studied him. "You all right?"

James nodded. "Yeah."

"You sure?"

He half expected a reassuring hand on his shoulder or his arm, and he wasn't sure how to feel when that touch didn't come. He supposed he and Kent had made a bit too much physical contact recently, and it was best not to push it. Even if he desperately needed it right now. He couldn't count the number of times they'd been stealthily moving through enemy territory, where a wrong step or the faintest sound could get all of them killed, and a slight touch to the shoulder meant *I'm here and I've got your back*. Sometimes it was Kent, sometimes it wasn't, but it was enough to give him the courage to take the next dangerous step.

But that wasn't happening now, and James still had to take that step. The press was waiting. The nation was waiting. To a degree, the world was waiting.

No pressure or anything.

James took a deep breath. Squared his shoulders.

And walked out to meet the press.

Usually, James liked arriving at Camp David. Just going through the checkpoint at the front gate was enough to relieve some of the tension in his neck and shoulders. Even though he knew the media would be all over him—how dare he take yet another vacation, just like every president before him did at every possible opportunity?—he couldn't help releasing his breath and smiling at the prospect of some sleep, some golf and, best of all, some time with the kids.

Tonight, though, he spent the entire trip dreading their arrival. Away from the chaos of his job, away from the pressure of an impending war, he would have nothing to focus on but the chaos of his suddenly fucked-up relationship.

Relationships? Whatever. Even losing himself in a night with his wife had become complicated. Tense. Uncertain.

Sitting in the back of the limo, he rubbed his aching forehead and tried to relax. He hadn't had a drink in a long time, but he was thinking he might break that dry spell tonight. Once he had a few moments alone at Camp David, he was planning a brief fling with the hip flask he'd slipped beneath his jacket before he'd left Washington. Booze wasn't an easy thing to come by without raising eyebrows, but he'd topped off the flask with bourbon, and if that wasn't enough, he'd had a bottle of tequila hidden in the bedroom for a long time.

The first night, thank God, Carlene didn't say much to him. She left him and the kids to some video games to unwind, and when she joined him in bed, they made love. He tried to tell himself they were both exhausted, and that was the only reason it felt halfhearted, but he wasn't convinced.

They barely saw each other the second day, right up until after they'd had dinner with the kids. He'd gone into the bedroom to put his phone on the charger, and when he turned around, there she was.

Carlene gently closed the door. "Can we talk for a few minutes?"

James nodded. "Okay."

"About this…um…the conversation we had about Kent."

He flinched. There were plenty of things they probably needed to hash out, but God, not this again. "What about it?"

She shifted her weight and folded her arms beneath her breasts. "Have you given it any more thought?"

James blinked. "I beg your pardon?"

Her eyebrow rose.

He rubbed the back of his neck and sank onto the edge of the bed. "Is there really a right answer to that?"

Carlene gave a tight half shrug. "I don't know. I'm not sure I know anything anymore except that—"

"Except that you're convinced I want to sleep with Kent."

"Am I wrong?"

No, you're—

He threw up his hands. "For God's sake, why are you suddenly so convinced that I do want to sleep with him?"

"Suddenly?" She snorted, and her tone was laced with barely contained anger as she went on, "There's nothing sudden about it, except that I'm finally not in fucking denial over it. I've been listening to you saying his name in your sleep for the last year. What am I *supposed* to make of that?"

His stomach lurched. "It's... Carlene, it's just dreams, okay? I've never stopped dreaming about the missions he and I went on."

"He wasn't the only member of your team. Don't try to tell me you two just worked closely together, because you've told me enough stories, we both know you'd be calling out—"

"He's the only one I ever slept with, if that's what you're getting at," James growled. "But that's in the past. These are just dreams, for God's sake."

"Just dreams?" Her arms tightened across her chest. "Then tell me why this didn't start until *after* you were elected."

He studied her for a moment. "After I was elected? Or after Kent became my head of security?"

"Both, now that you mention it."

He barely kept himself from rolling his eyes. "I don't know. I honestly don't." He showed his palms. "I mean, Jesus Christ, I can't help what I say in my sleep, all right?"

"No, but you can at least tell me the truth about him."

"I've told you the truth." James stood and dropped his hands to his sides. "We ran missions together. We drank together. We—"

"Fucked," she said through her teeth.

"Yes, and I was honest with you about that from the get-go."

"You were, but I understood that it was in the past." She inclined her head. "This last year or so, I haven't been so sure."

"Because I have fucked-up dreams? Because I say shit while I'm asleep? What do you want me to say?"

"I want you to tell me the truth."

"What difference will it make either way? What will it change?"

"If it won't make a difference or change anything, then why not tell me?" She narrowed her eyes. "Why can't you just answer the question? Yes or no,

James. Do you want him or not?"

He gritted his teeth. "Carlene, I—"

"I've seen the way you look at him." Anger kept her voice taut and low, but the slightest waver cut him deep. "I've seen that, I've heard you call his name in our bed, and all I want to know is—"

"Yes. Yes, okay?" He made a sharp, frustrated gesture. "I still want him. I never stopped wanting him."

No surprise appeared in her expression, but the tightness of her lips told him the confession had hit a very tender target.

He sighed. "I'm sorry, Carlene. I don't know what there is to say. Yes, I want Kent, and I probably always will, but that doesn't change this." He pointed at her, then himself. "I love you. That's why I married you. That's why I have a family with you. You're my wife, the mother of my children, the—"

"Your First Lady." Her eyes narrowed again.

James held her gaze. Every time he replayed those three words in his mind, the venom came through clearer and clearer. His stomach dropped. "Are you... are you suggesting..."

"Am I wrong?"

"Yes!" He stared at her, his throat constricting as the accusation set in. "I married you because I love you. That had nothing to do with my political career."

She arched an eyebrow.

James studied her. "I feel like you're not going to be happy until I tell you that our marriage is a sham and I'm really in love with him."

"Are you?"

Yes. "It's in the past."

"That wasn't my question."

"But it is the answer. I was in love with him back then, yes. And I'm attracted to him. I've never lied to you about either of those things."

"No." She clenched her jaw and raised her chin a little. "But I don't think I quite understood just how much you loved him then or how attracted to him you are now. Not until I started waking up to the sound of his name in the middle of the night." Before he could respond, she asked, "Do you ever dream about me?"

James blinked.

She rolled her eyes and sighed, her shoulders dropping. "Just yes or no. Please?"

He chewed his lip.

"Forget it." Carlene put up her hands. "I'm done. I need some air."

"Carlene."

She halted with her hand on the doorknob and turned her head, making her face visible in profile, but she didn't speak.

He had to force the words out: "You wouldn't want to be in the dreams I have."

Carlene was still for a moment. Then she pulled open the door and disappeared out into the hallway.

James closed his eyes and rubbed the bridge of his nose.

She was convinced the presidency was going to kill him, but he was starting to wonder if it would kill his marriage first. They'd fought—and walked out and slammed doors—more in the last two years than they had in the eight years before that.

How the hell do I stop this?

Carlene must've gone for a walk or something, because James didn't see her again until after he'd put the kids to bed. When he came into the bedroom to call it a night himself, she was there, but neither of them said anything.

Without speaking, they got ready for bed. Little things that made almost no significant sounds at all—the faucet, brushing teeth, Carlene's glasses case snapping shut—were like gunshots tonight, hammering home the silence between husband and wife.

He climbed into bed beside her and killed the light, but the tense quiet lingered. This wasn't something they could just sleep off and face it down over coffee in the morning. James was wide awake. Judging by her breathing, so was she, but he didn't know what to say.

Eventually, she beat him to the punch. "I'm sorry," she whispered. "For what I said about why you married me. About it being political."

"I'm sorry I ever made you think that was true."

"You didn't. I…" She sighed. "It was out of line."

James turned on the bedside light. They weren't going to hash this out in the dark. Then he moved closer to her, hoping and praying she wouldn't push him away. She didn't—when he wrapped his arms around her, she melted against him.

He kissed her forehead. "I think we've both said things we don't mean. This life is a bit more than either of us expected."

She exhaled hard, her breath hot against his chest. "Isn't that the truth."

"I'm sorry." God, that sounded so useless. He stroked her hair. "I should've gone for the Senate."

"No, you shouldn't have." She draped her arm over his waist. "You're the best man for this job. It just… It takes its toll."

"Yeah, it does." He closed his eyes and held her for a little while, not sure what to say and even less sure what to do. They were in this for the long haul. There was already mounting pressure to run again, but he wasn't entirely certain he'd make it through this term, never mind another four years. Or several months of campaigning while being in office. Thank God Carlene didn't seem to mind his rapidly growing population of gray hairs.

"Can I ask you something?" She shifted a bit, and he released her so she could draw back a bit and look him in the eye. "And will you be completely honest?"

Oh shit. "Yeah. Of course."

Carlene swallowed. She searched his face. "If we had never met, what do you think would have happened to you and Kent?"

James released a long breath as he brushed a few strands of hair behind her ear. "Honestly, I don't know. We tried to make it work once, but—"

"You did?" Carlene raised an eyebrow. "I thought you guys just hooked up."

"Most of the time, yeah. But we gave it a shot once."

She inclined her head a little bit. "And?"

"And…" A million memories flooded his brain. James shook his head. "If I'd known then how it was going to turn out, I never would have let it happen."

"Why?"

"Because I almost lost my best friend over it." He shrugged. "Kent and I, we've got something not a lot of people have. I won't lie about that. But… Well, to be honest, if we'd given it another shot, we probably would have killed each other. It's just not in the cards." He touched her cheek. "I won't pretend not to have feelings for him, but I chose to make a life with you."

She chewed her lip. "Why didn't you ever tell me? That you two had a relationship?"

"I didn't think you wanted that much detail about my past. Kent and I have a long, sordid history, but it's just that—history." He lifted his eyebrows slightly. "I…never really thought we'd be having some of these conversations, you know?"

"About you sleeping with him in the present?"

"Yeah. That."

"I didn't either. But those dreams…"

"I can't explain them."

"You can't?" she asked, her voice soft. "Or you won't?"

James winced. A little of both, actually, but he didn't know how to explain that either. "They're just dreams. I'm sorry it hurts you to hear it, though. I wish there was something I could do."

She sighed but didn't speak.

He molded himself to her and stroked her hair. "I love you, Carlene. Don't ever doubt that."

"I don't," she whispered. "But I know you have feelings for him. If you need—"

"Don't."

"Just hear me out." She freed herself from his embrace and rolled onto her back. James pushed himself up on his elbow beside her, and Carlene touched his face. "Your job is killing you. I can see it and so can he."

He flinched. "I'm fine."

"No, you're not." She caressed his cheek. "We can argue all night about whether you can cope with it or not, but the thing is, if he can do something for you that I can't—"

"Carlene, please—"

"Hear me out," she said again.

He pressed his lips together and held her gaze.

Carlene ran the pad of her thumb along his cheekbone. "If there's something between you two that you need, then I don't want to stop you. I'd rather share you with him than lose you to this job."

"You're not going to lose me. Even if I wanted to be with him, I told you, it didn't work. It would never work."

She lifted one shoulder in a tired shrug. "I'm not going to argue about it. But...look, I trust you. As long as you're honest with me, I want you to do whatever you need to do to take care of yourself."

It took him a moment to make sense of what she was saying. To read between all the lines and comprehend everything. "You're serious."

"Completely. Whatever you need to do."

"Even if that means sleeping with him."

Carlene nodded.

"I would never cheat on you."

"No, you wouldn't." She combed her fingers through his hair. "I'm giving you my blessing. As long as you're honest with me about it, then it's not cheating."

"It's still adultery."

"But no one's lying."

He trailed the back of his hand along her arm. "I want *you*, Carlene."

"Maybe you need more than me." She kissed him lightly. "I'd rather go down that road than watch you keep withering away under all this pressure."

James sighed. Then he rolled onto his back again, and she cuddled up against him, resting her head on his shoulder. He wrapped his arm around her, and she draped hers across his stomach. "Yes, the stress is killing me, but I don't see how having sex with Kent would help."

"I don't either. I just know what I hear in the middle of the night." She slid a little closer to him. "And it happens more when the stress is really bad."

James cringed. He'd had no idea. God knew how long this had been going on. How many times he'd murmured the name of his former lover while lying right beside his wife in their marital bed. That must've been on those nights when he had that recurring dream.

She continued, "So all I can think is that when you're that stressed, you need him. Somehow."

He rubbed his eyes. There was no way to explain to her what he dreamed about on those nights. Especially since that would only make things worse. Meeting her gaze again, he said, "If, hypothetically, you're right…" James paused, his heart pounding. "How long would something like this go on?"

"That's between you two."

"It is, but…" He swallowed. "There's a big difference between you giving your blessing for us to spend a night together, and giving us carte blanche to do this indefinitely."

"As long as it needs to, then."

They were both silent for a while. Minutes, at least. He never once thought she'd drifted off—he knew her breathing patterns way too well, and she was far too tense—but neither of them spoke.

Finally, with a lump in his throat, he whispered, "What about us?"

"What do you mean?"

"If something does happen with Kent…" He held her a little tighter and buried his face in her hair. "What…what does that mean for us?"

Carlene cuddled closer to him, sliding her leg over the top of his. "I'm not going anywhere. Not unless you want—"

"No." He ran his hand up and down her arm. "I don't want you to leave."

"I don't want you to leave either."

"But if I'm sleeping with Kent…" James flinched. Was he really considering this? Was Carlene on to something?

"We'll make it work," she whispered. "I trust you. If you trust him, then so do I."

Of course he trusted Kent. He'd trusted the man with his life more times than he could count. This wasn't about trust. It was about… Fuck, what *was* it about? And what the hell was he supposed to say to his wife?

She covered his hand with is. "Do you need him?"

James swallowed. "Honestly?"

Her body tensed ever so slightly against his. "Yes."

He closed his eyes and took a deep breath. "To tell you the truth, I don't know what I need. I just don't know."

She was silent for a little while. "Promise me something."

"Okay?"

"If you figure it out, you'll tell me." She lifted her chin and met his gaze in the low light. "And if it is him, you'll be honest with me about it."

James's chest tightened. She seemed to have accepted that he was being drawn toward Kent, to the point she was shoving them together so they could be done with it already, and it hurt like hell to hear his wife so resigned to the idea of him being with someone else. "Carlene…"

"Please." She touched his cheek. "If this were just ordinary stress, it'd be one thing. But you're the president. You've got responsibilities and demands on you that I can't even imagine." She ran her thumb along his cheekbone. "I will happily share you with him if that'll help you get through this term without driving yourself into an early grave. All I'm asking is for you to be honest about it."

James smoothed her hair. "You remember all those times you told me you were worried you weren't cut out to be First Lady?"

She scowled, probably annoyed by the subject change. "Of course."

James lifted his head off the pillow and kissed her gently. "I don't see how any man ever made it through being president without a woman like you at his side. You're amazing." He kissed her again, drawing it out for a moment, and then whispered, "Yes, I promise, I'll be honest about whatever happens."

"Thank you." She tucked her head beneath his chin. "I love you."

He wrapped his arms around her. "I love you too."

And he hoped to God that was enough.

Chapter Ten

The walls of Camp David were closing in on Kent as they often did, but it was worse this time. The weird tension between James and Carlene—between all of them—was palpable. James could barely look at Kent. As near as Kent could tell, the kids hadn't caught on, and he hoped like hell that didn't change.

He didn't see much of Carlene. She was around, but their paths rarely crossed. Probably for the best.

James too, but now, as the sun went down and the forest around Camp David turned dark, he was out on the deck, leaning on the railing with a glass cradled between his fingers.

Kent hesitated, not sure if James was in one of his "everyone leave me the fuck alone" moods, or if he'd be okay with some company. Worth a try, and after pouring himself some iced tea, Kent stepped out onto the deck.

James turned. When their eyes met, he relaxed a bit. "Hey."

"Hey." Kent stopped beside him and set the iced tea on the railing. "Everything okay?"

James jumped as if the question had startled him, but then shrugged. "Yeah, it's fine."

"Is it?"

James chuckled dryly and gazed out at the woods. "As fine as it ever is in this fucking job." He shook his head. "I swear, I didn't think it was possible for this much bullshit to exist."

"You did twenty years in the Navy, James. You know damn well bullshit is infinite."

"Yeah, but since when does it roll *uphill*?"

"This is why I got out and became a glorified security guard, my friend." Kent laughed and clapped his friend's arm. "No way in hell I'm dealing with that crap."

"Smart man." James's humor faded, and his gaze grew distant. He sighed. "I don't know how all this shit is going to play out. All I know is I pissed off a lot of people the other day."

"No shit."

Congress and the media were having a field day with James's speech from the press conference. He'd publicly announced that before he would entertain the idea of mobilizing the military to settle the brewing conflict, he'd ordered Congress to formulate a budget that would cover the projected cost of the entire war. More than that, he demanded a budget written under the assumption that this conflict would be as costly or more so than the Iraq or Afghanistan wars. *Further* infuriating lawmakers, he'd forced them to include substantial funding for postwar care of wounded and traumatized veterans, as well as families of service members who were killed.

It was a risky maneuver. Some thought it was a sign that he was backing out on his promise to stay out of the escalating conflict, and that once Congress presented a budget, he'd be gung ho for an invasion. Others saw it as evidence that he was too much of a coward to make a decisive move and stop the bloodshed, not to mention halting the increased—and militarized—transport of drugs into the United States. That he was stalling, hoping that other nations would step in and settle it, or that the conflict would fizzle out before he was forced to make a decision. Some taxpayers were freaking out over the possibility of higher taxes. Others were convinced that this apparent sign of weakness would invite an onslaught of narcotics—maybe even a full-scale invasion, according to the most alarmist of the bunch—on US soil. There was a ton of speculation that Congress would call James's bluff.

Kent, meanwhile, was still rattled by the comment James had made during the committee meeting about being the last person a soldier spoke to before taking his own life. Joker's death had shaken everyone on the team, and Kent doubted he was the only one haunted by it to this day. They'd all known Joker was losing it, and everyone—his family, the team, their command—had tried to help him. The night he'd called James, crying and wasted, saying he was done, just done, James had sounded the alarm to every member of their team, but Joker put his gun in his mouth before anyone got there.

The only silver lining from that tragedy was that it was ultimately what had sealed James's decision to run for office. He'd seen far too many people dying for nothing—or for oil—and he'd lost one friend too many to stand by and let it continue.

And now here he was, digging his heels in while Congress tried to force his hand and go to war again. Kent couldn't begin to imagine that pressure.

He drained his glass—God, why couldn't it have been whiskey?—and set it on the railing. "You think they'll come up with a budget?"

James shook his head. "They can't. Not without jacking up taxes and pissing off voters."

"Sounds like you're playing chicken with them."

"I am." James reached into his back pocket. "God help me if I lose." Before Kent could respond, James brought his hand up and unscrewed the top on a stainless steel hip flask.

Kent's eyebrows jumped. "I thought you stopped drinking."

"I did." James took a swallow and grimaced as it went down. Then he tilted the flask toward Kent. "You want in on this?"

"I'm on the clock."

"And I'm the president." He poured a splash in Kent's empty glass. "I won't tell if you don't."

Kent shrugged and picked up the glass. He clinked it against the flask, and they each took a drink. After Kent had forced down the bitter booze, he made a gagging noise. "Jesus. I forgot how bad your taste in bourbon is."

James laughed. It actually sounded genuine, if quiet and tense. "Well, it was either this or drain cleaner."

"Which would probably be better than this shit." Kent grimaced. "What is *wrong* with you?"

"Ask Fox News. I'm sure they have an opinion on the subject."

Their eyes met, and James and Kent both laughed.

Then they fell silent. They looked out at the dark forest but didn't speak. James took another swig from the flask. Kent swirled his glass a bit, the ice tinkling softly, but couldn't quite bring himself to finish the last of the… whatever the hell that swill was called, since it sure as fuck wasn't good bourbon.

This wasn't that comfortable silence they'd sometimes shared over the years. Kent recognized this feeling, like the air between them was loaded with a conversation they needed to have, but neither knew how to start it. They'd been there before. Standing together, staring out at nothing, not saying a word while Kent wondered if he should say something, or if there was something on the tip of James's tongue, or if breaking this silence would somehow do more damage than just letting the unspoken thoughts go.

Eventually, James spoke. "It's been a long couple of weeks. I should get some sleep." He paused. "So should you."

Disappointment and relief mingled in Kent's gut. "Yeah. I'll probably turn in in a bit."

"All right. I'm calling it a night, though."

"Okay. I'll see you tomorrow."

"See you tomorrow." James squeezed his arm gently, oblivious to the shiver that contact sent through him. "Good night."

"Good night, James."

After James had gone, Kent took another sip from his mostly empty cup, searching the melting ice for even the faintest trace of that god-awful booze.

This job was supposed to be a stressful one, and he'd known that when he'd signed up. After so many years as a SEAL, he didn't know what to do with himself if he wasn't stressed.

But this was pushing his limits. Hard. For the first time, he was starting to wonder how much more he could handle.

After James was out of office, he'd have Secret Service protection for the rest of his life. That didn't necessarily mean Kent, though, and if he was honest with himself, Kent wasn't even sure he'd make it through James's term. If James was reelected, Kent would have some decisions to make. Part of his job meant standing in the background during meetings like the one today. Though he'd managed to avoid the degree of PTSD a lot of his team members struggled with now, he had his share of ghosts following him around. Listening to rich, powerful men talk about sending young people—barely more than children— into combat zones in the name of political gains and messages to foreign powers was enough to wake up some of those ghosts. Enough to send him back to that edgy feeling that had driven him into many, many bottles during his active duty days.

He wasn't so sure he could listen to that shit for another two years. Another six? Doubtful.

Whether or not he stuck around for the rest of James's presidency, Kent was pretty damned sure he wasn't in for the long haul. When James was out of office, maybe Kent could go buy a piece of property in the backwoods of someplace no one had ever heard of, and golf and fish until his number was called. They could stay in touch via email and whatever technology came into existence in the future.

Kent's shoulders sank. He was kidding himself if he thought he could stay that far away from James. And if he thought he could be that close to James without touching him. And if he thought there was any outcome that would end with him keeping both his sanity and the man he'd tried like hell not to fall in love with. And…

Kent rubbed his eyes.

And damn James for not leaving the flask out here.

Kent couldn't sleep, which didn't surprise him. Too keyed up. Too worried about James and every other goddamned thing.

He wondered if James could sleep. Or if he and Carlene were okay. For a long time, he'd listened to the stillness, hoping and praying to hear those creaks and moans and muffled laughter from the room across the hall. As much as it drove him insane to listen to the two of them having sex, at least that would mean that James was okay enough to shut everything out and focus on his wife.

But tonight…nothing.

Until around one in the morning, anyway.

Kent was still lying in bed, staring at the ceiling, when a door opened across the hall. He stiffened. It was definitely the master bedroom door—he'd memorized the creak of every hinge in this house. He could tell if one of his agents stepped out onto the deck for a smoke, or if one of the kids sneaked out to the kitchen and opened the cabinet where the cookies were kept.

A gentle knock on his bedroom door brought him to his feet. What the hell?

He hurried to the door and opened it. "Carlene? What's going on?"

She shifted her weight, her oversize T-shirt threatening to slide off her shoulder, messy strings of hair falling into her face. She had her glasses on, and in her eyes, there was no hostility or anger. Just resignation, desperation and the unmistakable shine of tears she was trying to hold back.

"It's James." Carlene swiped at her eyes, nearly dislodging her glasses. She glanced back at their bedroom door before she squared her thin shoulders and met his gaze again. "He's dreaming again. Nightmares." She folded her arms beneath her breasts and shifted her weight. "He hasn't said your name yet, but it's only a matter of time."

Kent's heart seemed to plummet and speed up at the same time. He glanced past her at the bedroom door, which was open a crack. "What…what should we do?"

"I don't think there's anything 'we' can do." Bitterness laced her wavering voice. She sniffed sharply and wiped her eyes again. "I know I'm asking a lot, Kent. I know things aren't easy between you two." She gestured at the door, and as she did, a tear slid down her face. "But he needs you. Like, *now*."

"Carlene, I—"

"Please," she whispered. "I don't care what you do. Talk to him. Comfort him. Fuck him. Get him drunk. I don't… I don't care." She moistened her lips. "There's nothing the two of you could do together that's worse than listening to him in pain that I can't do anything about."

Kent's gut clenched and his chest ached, both for James and for her. Nothing about this felt right, but standing by and letting James unravel didn't either. With the memory of Joker's downward spiral so close to the surface right now, Kent couldn't justify going back to bed and leaving James and Carlene to their own devices.

He took a breath. "Do you want to sleep in here?"

Carlene hesitated. "I…"

"It'll be more comfortable than the sofa, and the kids won't ask questions."

Her jaw clenched. "The sofa will be okay. They're used to me sleeping there once in a while." She must've seen the question in his eyes, because she added, "James snores sometimes."

You should hear him when he's been drinking. But Kent bit down on that comment and just nodded. "Okay."

Carlene turned on her heel and disappeared down the hall, her bare feet almost soundless on the thick carpet.

Once she was gone, Kent went into the master bedroom and carefully shut the door behind him. There'd been a time when that quiet click would have been enough to jolt James out of a sound sleep, but maybe time had tempered some of those paranoid reflexes, because James didn't stir.

The room wasn't completely dark. James and Carlene kept a small night-light in here in case one of the kids came in after a bad dream or something. With that subtle glow, Kent could see his way to the bed, and he could make out James's features—the ones not buried in the pillow.

His heart thumped hard against his ribs. James was still for the moment, no sign of the nightmares that had apparently woken his wife, but he wasn't completely relaxed either. His brow was furrowed, his lips taut—there was no way in hell this was restful sleep.

Kent wasn't quite ready to climb into this bed and take Carlene's place, so he eased himself onto the edge. James didn't move, though he didn't relax either.

Kent gazed over his shoulder at the empty space beside James. It should have been inviting. Sharing a bed with James? God, he'd dreamed of that countless times in the years since he'd last done it for real.

This was a mistake. With or without Carlene's blessing, there was no way in hell he'd be able to sleep in this bed. This was the bed James shared with his *wife*.

James twitched beside him. Then he jerked. "Sinclair."

Kent's stomach flipped.

"*Sinclair*." James shuddered. He murmured something incomprehensible, then said it again.

Shit, what was he dreaming about? They'd been through all kinds of hell together. It could have been anything. How many times had James relived it in his sleep like this?

James's breathing sped up. A bead of sweat slid down his temple, and though Kent couldn't understand what he was murmuring now, the tension in his forehead was painfully visible.

With one arm at the ready in case James startled—old reflexes died hard—Kent touched James's shoulder. Abruptly, James stilled, but he didn't take a swing at Kent.

"Hey. Broderick." Kent stroked James's arm. "Broderick, I'm right here."

James tensed.

"It's me. I'm right here."

James's eyes fluttered open. "Sinclair?" He sat up slowly. "Kent? What are..." He glanced at the other side of the bed, then around the room. "Where's Carlene?"

"She's sleeping downstairs." Kent took James's hand. "She sent me in here."

"In the middle of the night?"

"You needed me."

"But...how..."

"Carlene wants you to be okay. So do I."

James stared at him.

Kent's heart pounded—what now? "You were dream—"

James grabbed him.

And kissed him.

And they both froze.

Neither moved at first. Maybe it was disbelief, maybe they just needed to hit Pause for a second to get used to the idea, but after a little while, Kent tilted his head slightly and nudged James's lips apart. Though James had made the first move, he resisted now, his lips firm as if he wasn't sure about going further. But then—cautiously, it seemed—he relaxed and let Kent take over and deepen the kiss. His fingers twitched on Kent's neck. Kent slid an arm around him, hot skin brushing hot skin and sending Kent's body temperature soaring.

They pulled apart, though not completely—still holding on to each other, just not kissing.

James blinked a few times and drew his tongue across his lips. His expression was a mess of confusion. *Why are you here? Why am I here? What the fuck is going on?*

Kent touched James's face. "You needed me," he whispered again. "So I'm here." He initiated the kiss this time, and James didn't even try to resist. He melted against Kent, sliding a hand around the side of Kent's neck and pulling him closer.

Without breaking the kiss, Kent shifted around, and once he was facing James fully, he guided him back down onto the mattress. His thigh brushed James's thickening erection, and Kent pressed against him, making sure James could feel him getting hard too.

This was wrong, and messed up, and there was guilt and confusion swirling in Kent's mind, but he'd been craving this—James's lips and body pressed against his—for too long to talk himself out of it now. This was better than leaving James to his nightmares, right?

This is what she wanted us to do, he told himself as he slipped his fingers beneath James's waistband. *This is why I'm here.*

And God, if this was what James needed, then…

"Tell me what you want," Kent breathed. "What do you need?"

James dug his fingers into Kent's shoulders. "You."

The confession rattled Kent, and it seemed to have the same effect on James. They both froze again, and when Kent lifted his head to meet James's eyes, his own fear and confusion reflected back at him.

Kent swallowed. "I don't know what we're doing."

"I don't either." James ran trembling fingers through Kent's hair. "I just know I don't want to stop."

Stopping wasn't an option. From that first kiss, it had been out of the question.

Kent moved in for another kiss. "I don't want to stop either."

"Will you do something for me?" James asked, his voice soft and shaky.

"Anything," Kent murmured.

"Don't stop until you can't move."

Kent's lips brushed James's throat as he said, "I always wear you out long before that point."

"I know." James dragged his fingers up Kent's back. "That's what I'm counting on."

Kent lifted his head and met James's gaze, and understanding slowly dawned.

Fuck me until I break, James's eyes begged, *and then keep going until you do.*

Deep down, Kent wanted to take his time, to savor every moment and make every kiss last. God knew when or if they'd ever be in bed like this again.

But that wasn't what James needed tonight. Even before James had spoken, there'd been a hunger in his kiss and his embrace that Kent knew very, very well—the quiet, simmering desperation of a man who wanted the kind of sex he'd still feel next week. No foreplay. No blowjobs. Just get on top, get inside, and fuck me as hard as you can.

Kent was already out of breath as he said, "We need lube."

James gestured at one of the bedside tables. "Top drawer."

Kent didn't ask why James and Carlene kept lube handy—maybe they were into anal, maybe she just needed it sometimes—but he was damned glad they did. "Condoms?"

James hesitated. "I haven't been with anyone but Carlene in ten years." He raised his eyebrows.

"It's been a while for me too." *In spite of my best efforts.* "I'm clean."

"I trust you."

Kent swallowed. "Me too." He withdrew the lube from the nightstand and set it beside the lamp.

They both stripped out of what few clothes they'd been wearing, and when Kent picked up the lube again, he thought James whispered, "Oh God…"

He paused. "You okay?"

James nodded, gaze fixed on the lube in Kent's hand, his eyebrows pulling together.

Kent poured some of the clear, cool liquid in his hand. "I'll go slow."

"No." James shook his head slowly and met Kent's eyes. "Not tonight."

Kent gulped. Momentarily distracted, he almost poured too much lube in his hand, but stopped before it ran onto the sheets. "You want it hard, then."

"*Oh* yeah."

"Get on your knees."

James didn't hesitate for a second. Kent lubed himself up, and then put a little on James as well, only because it had been so long. James liked friction, even if it was painful, but not if he hadn't been fucked in a long time.

Kent glanced at the bottle on Carlene's nightstand. Then again, maybe James *had* been fucked recently? He shook that thought away and focused on James.

He guided himself to James and eased himself in, carefully pushing past the ring of muscle. Christ, James was tight—he felt fucking amazing, especially as Kent worked himself deeper and picked up speed.

"Oh God," James groaned and rocked against Kent, driving him in even harder.

Kent grabbed his hips and pulled him back, until his dick was buried all the way inside James, and he held him there. "Did I say you were calling the shots tonight?"

"N-no..."

"Then don't move." Kent withdrew just a little, then slammed into him hard enough to make James whimper. "You get exactly as much as I give you. No more. Got it?"

James didn't speak. He just shivered.

Kent grabbed James's hair and jerked his head back. "*Got it?*"

"*Yes.*" Another tremor went through James, and he was suddenly so tight that Kent sucked in a sharp hiss of breath.

"God, you feel amazing," Kent murmured. He let go of James's hair and started moving again. Started thrusting. Fucking him deep, hard, fast, exactly the way James had always begged him to.

James shifted onto one arm, and with the other, reached under him. Kent didn't have to ask what he was doing—if the rapid motion of his shoulder and elbow hadn't given him away, the low groan and the way he tightened around Kent's dick did.

Kent dug his fingers into James's hips and fucked him even harder. His own orgasm kept threatening to creep in, but Kent wasn't done. As long as James could form a coherent sentence, Kent wasn't stopping.

James shuddered, gripping the edge of the mattress. "C-can I come?" The words were little more than a moan.

"Yes. Come for—oh, fuck..." Kent's vision went white for a second as James gasped and clenched around him again. Kent fucked him good and hard, all the way through his orgasm, until James sounded like he was damn near crying. Kent was about to stop, but then James rocked back against him again, encouraging him to keep moving. Kent considered reminding him who was in charge tonight, but hell, he was too turned on to care at this point. He wasn't about to say no to anything that involved fucking James.

And being pounded like this after he'd already come had to hurt, but James kept slurring, "God, don't stop…" He wasn't rocking back or meeting Kent's thrusts anymore—he probably couldn't move by now—but, "Please, please, don't stop."

James's arms trembled, and Kent thought they might collapse under him. There was an easy solution to that, fortunately.

"Turn over," he growled, and pulled out.

James started to turn over, but Kent couldn't wait. He grabbed him and forced him onto his back, and he pinned him to the bed, kissing him hard while he held him down. James shuddered beneath him, moaning into his kiss and rubbing his dick against Kent's. Fuck, Kent hadn't been with any man in way too long, but James? God, he was overwhelming. No one ever surrendered as completely as he did, held on to Kent as tight as he did—it was no fucking wonder Kent had never been able to resist him.

He pushed himself up and shoved James's legs farther apart. James arched and squirmed, reaching back to grab the pillow as if that could somehow steady him as Kent guided himself back in. As Kent slid into him, James groaned, and when Kent started fucking him, James's mouth moved in soundless curses.

Kent lowered himself enough to almost meet James's lips, and James met him halfway—he lifted himself up on his elbow, slid the other hand into Kent's hair and kissed him breathlessly.

Kissing him, fucking him, feeling the heat of his body against and below and around him, Kent completely lost himself in James. In the kind of sex he'd been aching for with the man he'd never stopped pining for.

Whether or not this was what James needed, he couldn't be sure, but he was pretty fucking certain this was what *he'd* needed for a long, long time.

Kent groaned and fucked James even harder, and James fell back to the bed. Kent's body trembled and tingled, and the sight of James lying beneath him sent him over the top, and as Kent's vision blurred, he forced himself as deep as James would take him. He shuddered and took a few more hard thrusts before he couldn't take any more. He held James tight, forbidding him from moving because even one more stroke would've been too much.

James's limbs seemed weak and boneless, but he held on anyway, his whole body trembling between Kent and the covers. After a moment, though, James's arm slid off Kent's back. Then the other. Kent's grip loosened, and his legs started feeling like rubber. He pulled out slowly, gasping as his hypersensitive cock slid free.

James whimpered softly.

"You okay?" Kent murmured against his neck.

"Uh-huh." James shivered. "Feel…amazing."

"Good." Kent nearly sank onto the bed beside James, but somehow, they both managed to clean themselves up before they collapsed into bed.

They'd had sex like this before, and James usually crashed hard afterward, sleeping like the dead for hours. This time, though, he was awake. He was lethargic, his eyes heavy-lidded, but he was definitely awake. For how long? Anyone's guess.

Kent absently trailed his hand up and down James's arm. "Can I ask you about something?"

James shifted a bit. "Sure."

"What were you dreaming about?"

James tensed a little but didn't pull away. He shook his head. "Nothing."

"Nothing?" Kent's hand stopped. "The same recurring dream of nothing?"

"It's…" James sighed. "All right, it's not nothing, but it's kind of stupid."

"Try me."

James didn't respond immediately. After a lengthy silence, he said, "You remember that mission to Kazakhstan? The one that went to shit?"

Kent shuddered. If there ever came a day when dementia took away his ability to remember his own name, he would still remember that mission with crystal clarity. "Yeah."

"Remember when you came to my barracks room before the hearing?"

How could he not? James had been under investigation for fucking up the mission. It was bullshit, of course—things had gone to shit, but it hadn't been his fault. Nevertheless, there'd been an inquiry, and there'd been whispers that James was going to take the fall for letting three fellow SEALs get killed.

Before James was called in for one of his hearings, Kent had gone to see him in his barracks room. In spite of the hellish mission they'd just completed, and the grief and the chaos and the certainty that their careers—especially James's—were over, or perhaps because of all that, they'd done the only thing they could think of. They'd fucked. Violently. Desperately. Until James was in tears and Kent nearly was.

In the present, goose bumps prickled his arms. "I don't think I'll ever forget that."

James lifted his chin and kissed beneath Kent's jaw. "Neither will I."

"So it's nightmares about the mission?"

"No." James settled against him again. "It's about the day in the barracks." Kent furrowed his brow.

James went on, "Whenever I have that fucking dream, I'm just sitting there in the barracks. Alone. Getting more and more freaked out over the hearing, and wishing like hell you'd show up." He swallowed hard. "But you never do."

Kent's heart sank. What was he supposed to say to that?

James sighed. "When it really happened, I'd been hoping you would, but I'd… I was so fucked up, I didn't even know how to find you, you know?"

Kent knew how that went—there'd been times when a mission left him so shaken that it took all the concentration he had to work a coffeepot or a cell phone. After that particular mission, it had taken him three days to even try the remote control for the TV in his barracks room.

He pulled James closer. "I'd never desert you." *Not even when it hurts to be close to you.* "You know that, right?"

"I know." James draped his arm over Kent's chest and pressed a soft kiss onto his skin. "But goddamn, that dream fucks me up every time."

"I can imagine."

Kent didn't push the issue, though, and he shifted the subject to a more benign conversation like kids and last night's game. They talked until James's voice started to slur a little, as it often did when he was tired. Sure enough, within a few minutes, he was sound asleep on Kent's shoulder. Carlene been right—the man did snore sometimes, and apparently not just when he was drunk.

Kent wasn't annoyed. It had been too many years since he'd held James, and the snoring only meant he was here and he was real.

But Kent still wasn't completely sure why *he* was here.

Why me and not Carlene?

Because of that fucking dream about the day in the barracks in Germany a lifetime ago. But of all the things James had been through as a SEAL, and all the things they'd been through together, why did that night in particular keep coming back to him? Why now?

Kent closed his eyes and let his mind go back to that distant time and place.

Men died on missions. It was a brutal but real truth of being a SEAL. But that mission should have been easy. It was a simple extraction in some backwater town in a former Soviet state. Twelve guys would go in, twelve guys would come out with two hostages in tow, and after the hostages had been handed off at the base in Germany, twelve guys with shiny new medals would drink themselves stupid in their favorite bar outside of Munich.

But they'd landed in Germany, shell-shocked and disbelieving, with two of their guys and one of the hostages in caskets, plus a third team member who wouldn't survive the night.

Everything in Kazakhstan had gone just fine right up until they'd been driving out of the town in a pair of nondescript vehicles. Suddenly there'd been a checkpoint that hadn't been there three days before. Suspicious-looking soldiers who didn't buy their alibis or expertly forged credentials.

Then the soldiers had abruptly stopped questioning them and started backing away from the vehicles, changing their collective tunes and waving them through, but taking their sweet time moving the roadblock. The guys had all known something was wrong, had all gone for the doors and made it out of the vehicles, but the mortar had come out of nowhere.

Shrapnel hadn't even landed before the bullets started flying. Deaf and bleeding, the SEALs had fought back, but the momentary shock from the explosion had slowed their collective response for a few precious seconds. Long enough for three bullets to drop Smitty.

They'd fought off the soldiers, stolen their vehicles and weapons, and gotten the hell out of there to the pickup point on the other side of the river. Smitty was already dead. A hostage had died in the blast. Pentz had bled out in the helicopter. Holloway was touch and go all the way back to the base, but went into cardiac arrest in surgery. It was the stuff of nightmares, and like Joker's death, Kent doubted he and James were the only ones who *still* had nightmares about that mission years later.

In Germany, they'd all been treated for their wounds, and the higher-ups immediately launched an investigation. Kent had long suspected it was the death of the hostage—not the three SEALs—that had prompted the fury and the inquiry, but nevertheless, they were all being questioned even before being released from the hospital.

At first, all the surviving team members had been separated so they could issue statements without influencing each other. After the initial round of hearings, though, they didn't need to be sequestered anymore. Kent suspected that letting them interact was a serious breach of protocol, but those in charge didn't want to be tasked with trying to contain a team of angry, grieving SEALs from each other. Whatever the case, the restrictions had been lifted, and they'd all stayed close.

Everyone except James.

Though the mission's failure and their teammates' deaths had not been his fault, he carried the weight on his shoulders. He'd been the team leader. He should have gotten his men out safely. The whole time in Munich, he'd holed up in his barracks room, not eating and not sleeping, and—if Kent knew him—no doubt spending every waking and sleeping hour reliving the mission over and over again.

"You've gotta go talk to him, man," one of their teammates had said to

Kent. "If anybody can shake him out of that, it's you."

Kent never knew for sure if any of the guys knew that he and James had slept together, but it was well known that they were close friends. And yeah, Kent was about the only one who could shake him by the shoulders and bring him back to reality. He wasn't so sure that would work this time, though.

Still, he'd gone to the barracks. All the way there, he'd wondered how James would take his presence. Tell him to fuck off? Indifference? The man could be moody as all hell when he was stressed, and sometimes he just wanted to be alone.

What Kent hadn't expected was for those tired, bloodshot eyes to meet his, and for James's stoic exterior to crack just enough to reveal the "thank God you're here". And now, years later, knowing what he did about that dream James had when he was stressed, Kent realized James had been hoping he would show up. Had he been too proud to ask? Too fucked-up in the head? Kent would probably never know. But James had hoped he'd be there, and Kent had been, and they'd stood in that tiny room, the low hum of the vents the only sound for the longest time.

Finally, James had said, "They're going to crucify me."

"No, they won't."

"They want to blame someone."

"They can't blame you. They can try, but everyone knows you had no way of knowing—"

"I know." James kneaded the back of his neck with both hands. "I know. But I... I keep seeing it all over again, and there was nothing else I could... I just can't..." He exhaled hard and let his head fall forward. "Fuck. I can't think anymore." Leaning back, he swore under his breath. "I am so fucked at this hearing."

"No, you're not. You're in the right. I guarantee everyone on the team backed you up."

"I know. I know. I just... I need to just..." James scrubbed a hand over his unshaven face. "Shut down. Forget. I can't drink. I can't get stoned. All I can do is…" He'd tensed, then lowered his gaze.

Kent put a hand on the side of James's neck. "What? Tell me."

James swallowed and, after a moment, met Kent's eyes. "Will you do something for me?"

"Anything."

If James had been any farther away, Kent wouldn't have heard him as he whispered, "Fuck me until I don't care anymore."

Kent's fingers twitched on James's neck. He didn't want James to see he'd been caught off guard, though, so he said, "Yes, I will. But only under one condition."

James nodded.

"Before I fuck you," Kent said, struggling to keep his voice even, "you're going to get on your knees and suck my dick."

James was already on his knees before Kent finished the sentence. He fumbled with Kent's zipper, and then did exactly what he was told.

And Kent, true to his word, had fucked James into oblivion.

In the silent master bedroom in Camp David, Kent opened his eyes. His stomach twisted and knotted, his heart speeding up as if he was on the verge of an uncomfortable epiphany.

The sex he'd had with James over the years always happened one of three ways.

One, they were drunk, bored and horny.

Two, they were sober, bored and horny.

Three…

Kent's heart didn't know if it wanted to sink or speed up. Maybe a little of both.

On those nights, when it wasn't the booze or the boredom, it always seemed like James was at his breaking point. Like he was about to unravel completely, and though he never said the words out loud, his body language and his moans and his sheer hunger might as well have been a plea for Kent to push him to and beyond that breaking point. One command from Kent, and James was on his knees, thanking him and begging for more at the same time.

Those were the nights when Kent left marks. Teeth marks. Scratches. Bruises from holding him down or shoving him against walls and furniture. The nights when he tortured James by forbidding him to come, and then rewarded him with an orgasm that nearly made him pass out.

The afternoon in the barracks had been like that. Kent had barely been able to move afterward. His hips had been sore, his knees weak, his back aching, and he'd been fucking exhausted.

James had slept right up until he'd needed to shave, put on his uniform and report to the hearing. In fact, he'd slept harder than Kent had seen in all the nights they'd spent together. When he woke up, his eyes were clear, his shoulders were squared, and he faced down that hearing like a drill instructor facing down a formation of recruits.

Kent gazed at the shadowy outline of James's body beside him. He stroked James's hair as he mentally compared that day in the barracks to tonight, and the pieces fell into place.

He kissed the top of James's head.

I think I know what you need.

Chapter Eleven

Carlene tossed and turned all night on the couch. She didn't hear anything from the master bedroom, but the lodge's construction was good for muting sounds between rooms and floors. The kids were well out of earshot too, thank God. Hopefully asleep.

Rubbing a hand over her face, she swore into the silence of the rec room. Maybe it was time to send the kids on a vacation to her parents' house. Both grandkids and grandparents would be thrilled at the idea. More to the point, she wouldn't have to worry about the remote but terrifying possibility of some very awkward explanations about why Uncle Kent slept in Mommy and Daddy's bedroom while Mommy slept downstairs.

She made a mental note to call her mother this afternoon. First, it was time to face the day now that her husband and his former lover had spent the night together. Hopefully, Kent had done whatever James needed to decompress, even for a few hours. And hopefully, Carlene could look them both in the eye.

Lying here in the light of day, she was less and less optimistic. She'd been so certain that James needed Kent, that somewhere between the two of them lay the answer to James coping with the demands of his job, but she hadn't let herself think about the aftermath until now.

Shit. What have I done? What did I encourage them *to do?*

She refused to go back into the master bedroom until she was sure the two of them were out of bed. Or at least Kent. Seeing James in their bed would be awkward, but she wasn't sure she could handle seeing Kent there, even if she'd sent him in herself.

So for now, she got up off the couch, found her glasses on the coffee table, and wandered into the kitchen for some coffee. The first of many, she guessed, given how tired she was after that sleepless night.

While she sipped it, she listened. Eventually, doors opened and closed at the other end of the hall. The master bedroom's shower came on.

They must've been awake, then. Kent back in his bedroom, thank God. James taking a shower. It occurred to her that things could have gotten incredibly awkward if she'd taken Kent up on his offer to sleep in his bed. Carlene brought her coffee up to her lips, ignoring the sudden prickle of goose bumps. He would've been polite and considerate, no doubt, but she could only imagine how that would've played out.

"Um, thanks for letting me sleep in your bed. It's all yours."

"Yeah, ditto. Your husband too."

"Right. Good. Thanks."

"Right. Um…"

Well, at least that had been avoided, and now she didn't have to avoid her own bedroom, so she finished her coffee before heading down the hall.

James was in the shower, bathroom door open as per habit.

Carlene stepped into the bathroom. She didn't look at the blurred shape of James through the frosted glass doors, and instead took off her glasses and busied herself with her contact lenses.

The first lens was on her finger when the shower stopped. Carlene froze. Her stomach lurched into her throat. Was she ready to face him? She didn't have many alternatives, though. Hurrying out of the room would only make things worse.

Carlene concentrated on putting in her lenses while James dried off. Though she could see his reflection in her peripheral vision, she didn't let herself focus on him. One thing at a time. Start with being in the same room. Move up to eye contact. Talk. Pretend it wasn't weird to have to take baby steps toward a conversation with her own husband.

The sound of bare feet on tile had never made her hair stand on end like it did just then. In the mirror, she could see him moving closer to her, but she couldn't convince herself to turn her head and meet his gaze. She stood, she waited, she held her breath.

He stopped.

Right behind her, close enough for her to feel the warmth of his body, he stood still for a moment. She glanced in the mirror—he'd wrapped a towel around his waist, but his torso was bare, the dark hair on his arms wet and plastered against his skin. The thin fan of hair in the middle of his chest and the narrow trail leading down from his navel were probably that way too, but she couldn't see them, and she suppressed a shiver at the memory of all those times she'd run her fingers through it, or let a fingertip drift down that slim line when she wanted to turn him on.

Did Kent know how that little touch could make James gasp?

Carlene forced that thought away.

Then James moved again. He came a little closer, paused and wrapped his arms around her from behind. He kissed the side of her neck but didn't meet her reflection's eyes.

So many emotions and sensations shot through her. Fury that he'd have the nerve to touch her so close on the heels of a night with Kent. Relief that he still wanted to. Guilt that this was all her doing. An ache in her throat over how awkward their effortless marriage had suddenly become. An entirely different ache that, even after all this time, he so easily ignited inside her.

She turned around within his embrace and held him too. She rested her cheek against his shoulder, and James kissed the top of her head. She didn't look up at him. He didn't say anything.

But at least he was here, and so was she. They were touching. Tenderly and affectionately, if silently, they were touching.

After a while, he loosened his embrace, and they drew apart. Finally, their eyes met.

Whenever she saw him like this—scruffy from not shaving, hair wet and unruly—her heart sped up, and even with all the guilt and uncertainty roiling in her veins, this time was no exception. Time and duty had grayed his hair and lined his face, and he was as sexy now, if not more so, than when they'd fallen into her bed the night they met.

James brushed a few strands of hair out of her face and tucked them behind her ear as he'd always loved to do. His hand lingered, barely touching her skin, but raising goose bumps all over her nonetheless.

Then he drew her back in, tipped her chin up and pressed his lips to hers. It was a soft kiss, a short one, but it sent electricity through her body. As if the mere confirmation that he still wanted to kiss her meant he still wanted to do even more with her, and that was enough to both turn her on and put her mind somewhat at ease. If they weren't leaving for Washington in a couple of hours, she'd have dragged him into the bedroom and made damn sure he still wanted her, but he'd promised to take the kids out hiking in the woods around the lodge first. Tonight, when they were back at the White House, he'd be all hers.

She hoped.

James broke the kiss and met her eyes. A smile played at his lips, and she managed a slight one too.

Without either of them saying a single word, he released her, offered one last lingering look and left the bathroom.

She watched him go, and as she did, she tried not to notice the slight hitch in his gait. Sometimes his back bothered him, not to mention the knee he'd had operated on a few times, and that must've been all it was.

Except that just before he disappeared around the corner, she caught a glimpse of a shadow on his back, just above where the towel was wrapped. No, not a shadow. A bruise. Though she had only a fleeting second to look at it, the shape burned itself into her mind. Something told her that if she asked him to, Kent would be able to fit some part of his hand over that mark.

She slumped over the counter. They had, hadn't they? With her blessing, at her insistence, they had. Now she didn't know how to feel about it.

Had she done the right thing? If she hadn't, could they come back from this? Was the damage reparable?

He'd touched her, though. And kissed her. That was promising, right? Or was he just trying to compensate? To cover up a guilty conscience and a wandering eye?

And what about Kent? In her mind, she saw the palpable concern on Kent's face when they'd talked in the hallway last night, and her stomach lurched again. How would this affect the guys' friendship?

Way to go, Carlene.

By the time she stepped out of the bathroom, James was gone. Probably making sure the kids were up and ready to go.

She got dressed and headed out of the bedroom. There were voices down the hall—the kids, and occasionally James—so she left them to their morning routine while she went into the kitchen.

There, she found Kent. He was leaning against the counter, quietly drinking coffee. She guessed, anyway. He usually had a coffee cup in hand when he was in here, but she couldn't look at him to confirm one way or the other.

Carlene couldn't look at him, but she couldn't avoid him either. As the morning went on, and James and the kids got ready for their hike, Kent's presence loomed around every turn. That was one of the drawbacks of being married to the president—the constant Secret Service presence. There was no taking a vacation anywhere, not even to Camp David, without a swarm of armed men following them around. Carlene had gotten used to that in fairly short order, but she'd never been quite comfortable with Kent. Not when she knew he and James had a history.

Now, there was no escaping Kent. Worse, there was no escaping their history, because that history had become the present. Being around Kent and James at the same time had always been uncomfortable, but knowing they'd been intimate recently made her skin crawl. She wasn't opposed to men being lovers, but…her husband. The man who was slipping away from her a little at a time. Going back to the man who'd been there long before she'd entered the picture. With her blessing, no less. With her all but shoving Kent into their marital bed.

What have I done?

Saved him. That's what I did.

Right?

She forced back the lump in her throat and tried not to hear the ghosts of the sounds she'd imagined hearing all through last night. It was just the house settling. Nothing more.

Sounds or not, though, she didn't have to ask—not Kent, not James—if they'd had sex. There was far too much evidence to deny. The slightest hitch in James's gait. Kent gingerly rubbing his lower back when he thought no one was looking. The mark on James's hip. The impenetrable silence between all three of them.

But she couldn't deny that James was a hell of a lot more relaxed this morning. He tended to carry his stress in his forehead, his brow pinching with deep thought until the crevices between his eyebrows had left permanent grooves. Last night, he'd been so wound up, she wouldn't have been surprised if he'd had a wicked headache by the time he'd gone to bed. Today, that tension was gone. His eyelids were a little heavy, his gait a little slow, but she supposed that was par for the course. He probably hadn't slept much last night.

Despite the obvious fatigue, he looked better than he had in a while.

Whatever you did, Kent… Thank you.

While James and the kids headed out for the afternoon, Carlene poured herself another cup of coffee. Thank God—a little time to breathe. Maybe they could talk tonight. Or maybe, if he could move and if he had any inclination, they could make love. Remind him with a few kisses and touches that she was here, because she was suddenly terrified that one night with Kent might've erased her from his mind.

As she stirred in the creamer, her skin prickled with the visceral awareness of the man standing beside her.

She turned around. Over the kitchen island, their eyes met.

Carlene swallowed. So did Kent. He was back to the picture of professionalism—the black suit, the crisp white shirt, the little blue lapel pin that all the Secret Service guys wore—but something had changed in him. There was an odd softness in his eyes this time that even the uneasy quirk of his eyebrows couldn't mask, and his posture was less Navy SEAL fight-or-flight and more civilian calm. As if something in him had relaxed for the first time since she'd met him. Or he was just too tired to maintain the usual posture. Too tired from…

God. I can't.

She cringed inwardly and quickly gathered her coffee and tried to make a graceful escape. "Kitchen's all yours."

"Carlene, wait."

Shit.

She turned around. "Hmm?"

"Can we talk?" Kent's tone was guarded, his expression offering nothing.

Carlene's pulse sped up. She set the cup on the counter to avoid dropping it. "Is this about last night?"

He nodded and started to speak, but she put up a hand.

"Don't. If it's good for him, great, but whatever happened, I…" She shook her head. "I don't want to know."

You win, Kent. Please don't rub it in.

"I think you need to know," he said. "It's important."

Carlene flinched. "I don't—"

"Please," he whispered. "I wouldn't do this if I didn't think it would be good for James. And for you."

She swallowed hard but let him talk.

Kent was quiet for a moment, gaze unfocused and brow furrowed. Then he took a deep breath and looked her in the eye. "I think I've figured out what he needs."

Carlene ground her teeth. "So I've noticed." Immediately, she regretted the venom in her tone. She wasn't being fair—she'd all but shoved them into bed together. The fact that the aftermath wasn't what she'd expected—hell, what *had* she expected?—wasn't their fault. "I'm sorry."

"It's okay." He studied her, but then shook his head. "But, what he needs, it's…it's not me."

"It's…what?"

Kent chewed his lip. His eyes lost focus for a moment, and he drummed his fingers on the kitchen counter. Finally, he said, "When James says my name in his sleep, it's because he's dreaming about a particular incident in Germany."

Carlene steeled herself. "Do I want to know?"

"It'll be hard to hear, but I think a few things will make sense if you do."

"Okay."

"I can't go into any more detail than James can, but we had a mission go bad." Kent shifted slightly, almost masking the shudder. "He was our team leader at the time, and the military always has to blame someone when something goes to shit. The assumption was that he'd fucked up. Gotten three of our guys killed."

Carlene's breath stuck in her throat and refused to move.

Kent went on, "The day of the hearing, he was holed up in a room in the barracks, and I went to check on him. Things, uh…went a little differently than I thought they would, let's put it that way."

Well, those were some pieces she could put together well enough—when James was stressed out, he craved sex. She wanted to believe that if she'd been in his life at the time, and she'd walked into that barracks room, he'd have wanted her just like he'd wanted Kent. That was getting harder and harder to believe, though.

She folded her arms beneath her breasts. "So you went to check on him and ended up sleeping with him."

"Sort of."

"Sort of?" Carlene laughed humorlessly. "Did you or didn't you?"

"I did." His voice was so quiet she could barely hear him. "But it wasn't that simple. It wasn't the sex he wanted. It was…" Kent's eyes lost focus. Whether he was remembering—fondly, no doubt—or just trying to figure out what to say, she couldn't tell.

Without meeting her gaze, he said, "How much do you know about

BDSM?"

The bottom fell out of Carlene's stomach. "What?"

He hesitated, then looked at her. "How much do you know about it?"

Carlene fidgeted, folding her arms tighter. "Probably more than I'd like to, given where this conversation seems to be going."

Kent took in a long breath. "James and I were into that sort of thing. Sometimes. Kind of."

She winced. "Oh God." Then, "What do you mean, 'sort of'?"

"I mean, it's just something we did. We didn't talk about it, and for all I know, he never thought anything of it. I sure didn't until years later, but I've put some pieces together since then. And that day in his barracks, it..." He swallowed. "I won't say it got out of hand, but it was pretty intense."

Carlene glared at him. "What's the point, Kent? Or do you just want to rub it in that—"

"I'm not rubbing anything in." He put up his hands. "Just bear with me."

"Fine," she said through her teeth.

Kent glanced at the hallway, as if James and the kids might suddenly materialize. "After that, um, afternoon, James handled the hearing flawlessly. Barely even broke a sweat while they grilled us all up one side and down the other. He told me later he didn't think he would've made it through without me, and I never quite knew what he meant by that until now."

Carlene clenched her jaw so hard it ached, but she didn't say anything.

"He told me he dreams about that day a lot," he continued. "But it's not the hearing or the sex. He dreams about being in the barracks room and waiting for me, but I—" Kent's voice caught slightly. "But I never show up. He's just... sitting there alone in the room."

She still didn't speak but silently begged him to get to the goddamned point. There was only so much she could stand hearing about her husband longing for someone else like that.

"He calls out my name because he's freaking out that I won't be there. But the thing is, it's not me he's looking for." Kent paused, watching her for a few seconds as if he thought she might lash out. "It's not me. It's what we did. To make a long story short, when we were in that room in Germany that afternoon, he was completely submissive to me. More than he'd ever been before. After it was over, he faced the most stressful hearing of his career as if it were nothing."

Carlene glanced down the hall, then met his eyes again. "What are you saying?"

"I'm saying your husband is a submissive. Most of the time, he can live without it, but when he's under serious amounts of pressure, he *needs* the domination to center him. Anchor him." Kent held her gaze with what seemed like a lot of effort. "He doesn't need me, Carlene. He just needs to be dominated."

She stared at him, unsure what to say or what to make of any of this. Fooling around with a little bit of kink was one thing. *Needing* it? And James, needing to be dominated? She shook her head. "That doesn't make any sense. James is a born leader."

"He is, and that's exactly the kind of person who sometimes needs this sort of thing."

She raised an eyebrow.

Kent's cheeks colored a little. "I've, uh, done some reading about it."

"I see." She unfolded her arms and rested her hands on the counter's edge. "But why? I mean, he's never struck me as the type who wants to...*submit*." She couldn't help wrinkling her nose at the thought. It wasn't the dominance and submission, though, just the idea of James wanting to play that role. Or needing it. Especially in the bedroom. He could be aggressive to the point of violent, which she loved, and it was hard to imagine him wanting to switch those roles. "James just... He doesn't seem..."

"He's a born leader, and he's in a position of power," Kent said. "Which means sometimes he needs to hand over that power for a little while. Just give the reins to someone else so he can take a break for a bit."

"That's..." Carlene pinched the bridge of her nose as she struggled to comprehend all this. Dropping her hand, she said, "That means letting someone take over in the bedroom?"

Kent shrugged. "That kind of situation can be about as vulnerable and powerless as a person can get. And really, he's the president. Where else *can* he hand over that much power and control?"

"Fair point, I guess." Carlene chewed her lip. "So this is what the two of you used to do. Back then."

Kent shook his head. "Not…not consciously. I didn't know anything about any of this until years later. But we'd…" He paused, meeting Carlene's gaze. "Look, we both know you don't want the details, so let's just leave it at that. Bottom line, I didn't make the connection until last night. I thought he just liked…" Another pause. Kent swallowed. "It's what he needs now. That's about all I can tell you."

Carlene folded her arms, struggling not to get defensive as Kent let on about more than she'd ever wanted to know about their past. "What does this all mean, then? In practice? I mean, what am I supposed to do? I don't have the first clue how to do that. I'm not… I'm not into that stuff."

"I could teach you."

She blinked. "I beg your pardon?"

"It's probably not what you're imagining. You don't have to dress in head-to-toe leather, or whip him or chain him or anything."

Carlene squirmed. "What *would* I have to do?"

"Take charge."

"Take charge?"

"Tell him what you want him to do. Phrase it as an order. He does what you want, and he doesn't come until you say so."

Heat rushed into her cheeks and she looked around, suddenly mortified at the prospect of someone overhearing him talking like this. "That's…that's it?"

"It's a good start. For now, just let him know that you're in control. Get a feel for that, and maybe I can show you how to put him into that headspace."

Carlene's lips parted. There were so many surreal parts of that sentence, she couldn't even fit them all into her head. Space? Control? Kent showing her how to do anything in that context? What the hell?

"I know this is weird," Kent said. "But as far as I can tell, that's what James needs."

"Why hasn't he said anything?"

"I'm not sure he even gets it, to be honest."

"Then how do you know?"

Kent's eyebrow rose slowly.

Carlene showed her palms. "Never mind. Forget I asked." She cleared her throat. "So, what now?"

"Just try it," he said. "I don't know if you're wired for it, or—"

"Wired for it?"

"Yeah. Some people are naturally Doms, some people are naturally subs, and some...aren't."

"And if I'm not?"

"Then..." He shook his head. "I don't know. At this point, all you can do is see how it goes. If it doesn't work, we can always figure something else out."

Carlene swallowed. She wasn't sure she wanted to know what the alternative would be.

Chapter Twelve

The visit to Camp David was much too short for James's liking. He always had to be dragged kicking and screaming away from his job, but once he had some downtime, it was hard to come back. Especially when he'd barely had a chance to catch his breath.

But such was his job, and he'd rest when he was out of office. So the family returned to the White House that afternoon.

James put the kids to bed that night and took his time heading back to the master bedroom. He and Carlene had managed to avoid each other for most of the day, aside from the quiet drive back from Maryland. The thought of facing Carlene tonight made him uneasy to say the least. After all, they hadn't yet spoken about what happened last night with Kent. For that matter, he hadn't spoken to Kent about it, but he'd promised his wife he'd be honest about it, and the silence was grating on him.

She knew. That brief, wordless exchange they'd had this morning had conveyed that clearly enough. Besides, she'd been the one to send Kent into their bedroom.

With every step he'd taken since he'd gotten up this morning, he'd been reminded that, no, what he and Kent had done hadn't been a dream. It had been real, and every ache and bruise their interlude had left wouldn't let him forget it. Not that he necessarily wanted to. Evidently Carlene was right—he *had* been needing Kent. He'd needed to be thrown down, held down and fucked into the ground until he couldn't see straight. In that respect, he felt spectacular now.

But… Carlene.

James paused outside the bedroom with his hand on the doorknob. He glanced at Kent's door. They needed to talk too. Clear the air. Define what this was and, most importantly, what it wasn't.

But first…

He took a deep breath, turned the knob and stepped inside.

"Carlene?"

No answer.

He leaned back out into the hallway. "Carlene?"

From another room, she replied, "I'll be there in a minute."

Fair enough. He could at least grab a shower and get ready for bed. They had most of their heart-to-hearts in bed anyway.

He'd just started brushing his teeth when the bedroom door clicked shut. His scalp prickled and heart fluttered. She was here. Almost showtime. Why the hell was his stomach knotted worse than it had been before those fucking congressional committee meetings?

Not that it mattered. She was here. He was here. All he had to do was get in the same room with her and get this conversation over with.

In a minute. No time for that shower, but just one more—

"Honey," she called from the bedroom. "Could you bring me my glasses case?"

He looked around and found it on the counter. "Yeah, just a second." He quickly finished brushing his teeth, took one last glance in the mirror, and then picked up the case and started out of the bathroom.

And halted.

And stared.

Carlene stood beside the bed. At least, he was pretty sure it was her. James blinked a few times, taking in the sight of this woman who was so familiar, and yet…not.

Jaw slack, he looked her up and down. Her hair was down, tumbling over her shoulders, and he was pretty sure she hadn't worn that shade of red lipstick in a long, long time. He was absolutely certain he hadn't seen that dress before.

Black, snug, and modest in the most erotic ways—the skirt ended just above her knees, leaving her slender thighs to his imagination, and the top only dipped low enough to offer the faintest hint of cleavage. As much as she'd been afraid that three kids and an emergency C-section had ravaged her body, she had no idea how incredibly sexy she was. If she'd been hot at thirty-one, the first time she'd lured him in with that grin and a tight red dress, she was fucking stunning now.

"Wow." His gaze stopped at her eyes. "Carlene, you look—"

"My glasses case?"

He looked down at the plastic case he'd all but forgotten about. "Right. Sorry." He came closer and handed it to her.

Carlene set it on the dresser and faced him again. "Kneel."

The terse command didn't quite register. "Sorry, what?"

Carlene lifted her chin slightly, her expression hardening, and pointed a blood-red nail at the floor in front of her. "I said, *kneel*, James."

His lips parted. Though his mind couldn't comprehend what was happening, his knees sure figured it out. Everything below his belt did too—by the time he was kneeling at her feet, his dick was well on its way to fully hard. "What's…what brought this on?"

Carlene didn't answer. She combed her fingers through his hair. Tenderly, slowly. Enough to nearly lull him into a trance. He'd been on his knees in front of her before—he loved kneeling beside the bed so he could drive her mad with his tongue—but not like this. Never at her command.

His eyelids started to slide closed.

She grabbed his hair and jerked his head back.

His eyes flew open. He stared up at her, skin prickling with goose bumps, and God, he was hard. So, so hard.

"Everything I say, you're going to do. Understood?" The steely edge of her voice turned his brain to liquid.

Anything you say. Anything at all. Holy shit, baby…

Her grip tightened, and his scalp burned, which did nothing to bring his thoughts into any semblance of order. "Answer me, James. Do you understand?"

"Y-yes." He blinked his eyes into focus. This was all so bizarre and out of the blue, and yet he couldn't fathom giving her any other answer. "Any… anything. Everything." What the hell?

A gentle smile softened her expression and warmed his entire body. She relaxed her grasp on his hair, then stroked it again. Her light touch, coupled with the lingering sting in his scalp, drove him wild, and without thinking about it, he pressed against her palm, seeking more.

He had no idea what had gotten into her. Why they were doing this instead of having an awkward conversation about why his entire body ached.

He didn't ask, though.

Because he didn't want this to stop.

"Look at me."

His eyes flew open—he hadn't even realized he'd let them slide closed again.

Her fingertips brushed his cheek, sending a shiver through him as she gazed down at him. "You're going to…" She chewed her lip. The firmness in her expression faltered. Uncertainty creased her forehead, and she swallowed nervously.

He touched her leg. "Tell me. Whatever you want."

She put her hand over his on her thigh, and after a few heartbeats, the confidence came back. "You're going to do whatever I tell you."

James nodded slowly. He'd never seen this side of her before, but holy Christ, it was hot. Five minutes ago, he'd been prepared for an uncomfortable conversation. Now he was prepared to move a mountain if she told him to, just as long as she kept on talking to him like that.

"You don't do anything without my permission." Her eyebrow arched. "Understood?"

Another nod, faster this time. "Understood."

She smiled. "Good."

He smiled back, his skin tingling beneath his clothes.

She took her hand off his. "You're going to start by taking this dress off me."

Oh. Yes.

He started to stand, but she snapped her fingers, startling him right back down onto his knees.

"I didn't tell you to stand."

He blinked. "I... But you..."

"Did I?"

"N-no, but how can—"

"Did I tell you to stand?"

The command in her tone went straight to his balls. Fuck, if she kept that going, she'd probably talk him right into an orgasm without so much as laying a hand on him.

"James? Answer—"

"No." He swept his tongue across his lips. "No, you didn't." He paused. "M-may I? So I can take off your dress?"

That smile. Holy fuck. Subtle, gentle, every bit the woman he'd made love to thousands of times, and yet her eyes remained firm and commanding. Two radically different and equally intoxicating sides to the same gorgeous woman.

"Yes," she whispered. "You may stand."

For the second time, he started to stand, pausing to let his knee adjust to the idea of straightening out and bearing weight. As he rose, his whole body ached and protested, which he'd certainly expected, but the light-headedness caught him off guard. He grabbed the bedpost for balance.

Carlene touched his arm. "You all right?"

"Yeah, just..." He took a deep breath and let it out. "A little dizzy. I'm okay." *Dizzy* didn't even describe it. His head just felt...weird. Spacy. Like his equilibrium had gone out the window and even gravity was questionable at this point. He'd felt that before, but not often. Only when he was already well on his way to one of those mind-blowing orgasms that would make him black out for a few seconds. Not while he was still standing, still dressed and still figuring out what the fuck was going on. By the time he'd reached this point in the past, Kent already had him—

His own thought startled him. He shook himself—tonight was about Carlene, not the man who'd left him bruised and aching last night.

"Are you sure you're okay?" Carlene asked.

James met her gaze. Her expression had changed to pure concern, but she still had a commanding aura about her. He grinned and took his hand off the bedpost. "Yeah. I'm good. Let me… Let me get that dress off you."

She studied him for a second, then withdrew her hand and stood a bit straighter. Her features hardened. Though she didn't say a word, the "Yes, get to it" in her expression was unmistakable.

Yes, ma'am…

He'd helped her take off her dresses more times than he could count, and it usually played out the same way—he'd make a "turn around" gesture, and she'd face away from him, holding up her hair so it wouldn't get tangled in the zipper. Then she'd giggle and tell him to stop screwing around when he ignored the zipper altogether and focused on kissing her neck and her shoulders. Then her hair would fall, and her hands would be over his as he wrapped his arms around her, and more often than not, it would end with the skirt hitched up to her hips, Carlene bent over the bed, and James fucking her while she clawed at the comforter and begged for more.

This time, James was aroused beyond belief, and he wouldn't have hesitated to bend her over and fuck her. It wouldn't have lasted long—he was so turned on, he was sure he'd lose it after one or two thrusts, and he *never* went off that quickly—but God, it would be hot.

But she didn't tell him to fuck her, and he didn't tell her to turn around like he always did. This time, though he wasn't entirely sure why, he went around behind her. He carefully gathered her hair and laid it over her shoulder, well out of the way of the zipper. The exposed curve of her neck made his mouth water, and he bit his lip as he fought the temptation to steal just one soft kiss on that beautiful skin.

Something told him, though, that a stolen little kiss wouldn't work in his favor this time.

He held the top of the dress's back in one hand and carefully drew the zipper down. As it cleared her bra strap, he mouthed a silent curse—she really was pulling out all the stops, wasn't she? She hadn't worn that red lingerie in a long, long time, and he hoped like hell she'd worn the matching garter tonight too.

Guilt knifed its way past the fog of arousal. His hand stopped, holding the zipper pull just above the small of her back. Was she doing this because of last night?

"Carlene." He cleared his throat. "What we're doing… Is this because of—"

"Do you want to stop?"

"Not if you're enjoying it."

She turned her head so her face was visible in profile, and her grin turned his knees to water. "Then why are we stopping?"

"Uh…" *Yeah, James. Why* are *we stopping?* "Sorry. Sorry. Um…" He shifted his gaze to his hands. And the zipper. Which wasn't all the way down yet. "Sorry," he murmured again and continued opening the back of her dress.

At the very bottom of the zipper's open *V,* a line of bright red lace peeked out. James's pulse quickened again. Oh fuck. She was wearing the garter.

Heart pounding, James pushed one of the dress straps off her shoulder. Then the other. The whole thing slid down, and as it pooled at Carlene's feet, James mouthed *Jesus.* The red lingerie emphasized every smooth, perfect curve, just like it always had. No panties, either—her gorgeous ass was completely bare, framed by the straps on the garter. Across the top, the garter belt sat just below that faded blue rose tattoo that only he and a discreet Myrtle Beach artist knew about.

Every instinct screamed at him to slide his hands over her hips and pull her closer, but he didn't move. She hadn't given him permission. She'd worn the most sensual pieces of clothing she owned, and any other night, he'd have been buried to the hilt in her by now, but her earlier commands, backed up by that look in her eyes, kept him still.

And marveling at how unspeakably hot this was.

Slowly, Carlene faced him. A few dark strands had fallen down beside her eyes, and his fingers curled at his sides as he resisted the urge to brush her hair behind her ear.

Her grin almost drove him back to his knees. "You like this, don't you?" She took a step toward him, her red satin bra brushing his shirt. "Doing what I tell you?"

"I…" He struggled to untie his tongue. "Yeah. I do. How did you know?"

The grin broadened, and her eyes narrowed as she reached forward and tugged his shirt free from his waistband. "A little bird told me."

"A little—" James blinked. "Did—"

"No more talking."

The sharpness in her voice made his teeth snap together.

Her expression turned serious. She put her finger over his lips. "You don't need to worry about anything tonight except doing what I tell you to. Got it?"

"Mmhmm."

She lowered her hand. "You *are* enjoying this, right?"

"Absolutely."

The grin returned. "Then do what I tell you to, because I'm enjoying it too."

"Y-yes, ma'am." He was definitely curious about that little bird—a little Secret Service bird, no doubt—but then she was pushing his shirt up and off, and then her nails were dragging down his chest, and…the conversation faded into the back of his mind.

She leaned in close enough to almost touch her lips to his. "The first thing you're going to do is make me come."

Oh… Jesus…

"Yes, please," he whispered, his own breath ricocheting off her lips as he fought the urge to move in for a kiss. Her commanding presence was magnetic, as if she'd not only assumed authority but created her own gravitational pull. Only the fact that he was forbidden to do a thing without her permission kept him almost literally digging his heels in to resist that pull. He swept his tongue across his lips, very nearly brushing hers in the process. "How?"

"Good," she whispered. "Not assuming anything."

Her approval almost knocked his knees out from under him.

"What do I do?" he breathed.

She closed her fingers around his wrist and guided his hand between them. "Fingers only."

James nodded. That was easy enough.

"But you can't touch me with your other hand." She let their lips brush this time, scrambling all his thoughts completely, and he almost didn't understand when she said, "Other hand behind your back."

Confusion kept him frozen for a couple of seconds, but when her fingers twitched on his wrist and her posture straightened, panic shot through him—*do what you're told, idiot!*

He put his free hand behind his back.

Carlene's grip and posture relaxed. "Good." She drew his hand in closer, and he sucked in a sharp hiss as his fingertips grazed her skin. He was taller, so he had to drop his shoulder slightly as she guided him to her pussy, but he didn't protest.

He forgot to breathe altogether when his fingers slipped between her legs and along her wet pussy lips. His head was spinning, and he realized her command would be harder to obey than he'd thought. Leaning forward slightly fucked with his balance. Touching her but not touching her was sheer torture. Clenching his fist against his back to remind himself not to bring his hand around and hold on to her made his other fingers tense, which made it impossible to do those slow, soft circles that she loved so much. So he had to relax that hand and simultaneously concentrate on the left hand staying put while the right hand drove her wild.

All the while, as her breathing sped up and she whispered her approval now and then, her lips were *right there.*

"Is this... Is this good?" he asked.

"Mmhmm." She wrapped her arms around his neck, probably for balance, and rubbed against his hand like she always did when she was getting close. "Very good. You're…so good at this."

James bit his lip. He didn't know what turned him on the most—Carlene on the edge, her soft, slurred praise or her body rocking slightly against his. He imagined himself throwing her down and fucking her, and he prayed that'd be her next order, and the anticipation was driving him almost as crazy as her impending orgasm seemed to be driving her.

She gasped. Her balance faltered a little, and he almost grabbed on to her with his free arm just to steady her, but she held on tighter and leaned on him harder, and her hip rubbed up against his clothed cock, and suddenly it wasn't just Carlene's balance on the line. Tempted as he was to reach for her, he was afraid she'd slam on the brakes, so he just moved one foot a few inches to widen his stance and give him a more solid base.

"Oh God," she murmured. "Keep…"

James circled her clit faster, keeping his touch soft enough not to hurt her, and Carlene gasped again. A shudder jolted her from head to toe. Her arms tightened around his neck.

And right when she came, she lifted her chin and kissed him hard. Deep, aggressive, breathless, until she collapsed against him and panted, "S-stop."

He stopped.

At first, neither of them moved. She held on to him and caught her breath, and he held on to her so he could—

Oh fuck!

He'd thrown his other arm around her without even realizing it. His heart flipped. "Shit. Sorry. I—"

"S'okay." She loosened her grasp and eased herself onto her own feet. "Under the…under the circumstances, I'll let it go."

"Thanks."

Their eyes met, and her smile relaxed him as much as it turned him on. Her eyes were gleaming now, wild and yet somehow still in total control.

He swallowed. "What do you want me to do now?"

Carlene thought for a moment, glancing around the elegantly appointed bedroom. Finally, "I'm going to lie across the bed." Her voice was hard but somehow unsteady at the same time. "And you're going to fuck me. Understood?"

Words. What the hell were words?

So he just nodded.

"Good." She hoisted herself onto the bed. "*Now.*"

She didn't have to tell him twice.

Though his hands were shaking and his mind was a mess, he undid his belt and zipper without any trouble. He didn't even bother taking them off completely. Once his pants and boxers were past his hips and out of the way, that was good enough for him, and Carlene didn't protest, especially not when he shoved her legs apart, guided himself to her pussy and thrust all the way inside her.

They were both still. Regardless of how many times they'd had sex before tonight, that first stroke took his breath away this time.

"Fuck me," she repeated. "*Now.*"

"Yes, ma'am," he breathed. He withdrew slowly, then slammed into her, and her little gasp damn near made him come apart, so he did it again. And again. "Is this... Is this how you want—"

"Perfect," she panted. "D-don't you dare stop."

"I won't. No fucking way."

Carlene whimpered softly. Then she rolled her hips, changing the angle of his thrusts enough to make his breath catch, and before he could recover from that, she dug her nails into his back and raked them across his shoulders.

"*Fuck*, Carlene," he moaned. "I don't know what's gotten into you tonight, but..." He held her tighter and thrust harder. He fucked her harder than he ever remembered fucking her, thrusting into her tight, hot pussy until his muscles burned and his wife—his beautiful, sweaty, disheveled, *demanding* wife—was nearly in tears. And, Jesus, so was he. His eyes stung and his body ached, and he couldn't get enough and he couldn't take any more, and he hoped and prayed this wasn't a one-time thing.

I will fuck you like this every night if you ask me to, baby.

If you tell me to.

If you order *me to.*

The thought made him shudder.

She hooked her leg over his hip, and the angle changed again, and he could barely keep his eyes from rolling back. Much more of this, and—

"Holy…*shit*…" He gasped for breath. "C-can I come?"

"No." She dragged her nails up his back, grinning when he sucked in a breath. "Not yet." Her pussy, her body, her nails, her voice—they all conspired to drive him insane, especially as she whispered over the creaking bed, "You won't come until… Oh my God…" She pulled in a breath. "Not until I say so."

Fuck. *Fuck!* He gritted his teeth and squeezed his eyes shut and didn't dare let his rhythm falter, didn't dare let his orgasm take over.

"Oh God," he murmured. "Please, Carlene."

She said nothing, and James didn't dare push. He was well past the point where he would've—could've—held back under normal circumstances, but he kept fucking her despite his aching muscles, kept giving her all he had, kept himself from coming just…a little…longer…

"James." She grabbed his hair, holding it tight enough to sting and letting her nails bite into his scalp. She lifted her head off the pillow and gently pressed his face into her throat, and her lips nearly touched his ear as she whispered, "Come."

And the world exploded.

All the tension broke at once, and he was distantly aware of her holding him against her neck as if to muffle a cry. Of his body moving of its own volition, of shaking violently and forcing himself as deep inside her as he could. Of her nails between his shoulders and her thighs squeezing his hips.

As his vision cleared, he collapsed over her, and for the longest time, they both just panted.

"That was…" He touched his forehead to her shoulder. "That was *insanely* hot."

She moaned an affirmative and ran shaking fingers through his hair.

Eventually, he lifted his head and met her eyes. "We should do this again."

Carlene grinned up at him. "Oh, we will."

He didn't have the energy left for a full-blown shudder, but the subtle shiver that went through him was enough to make his breath catch.

"We should get ready for bed." She stroked his hair again. "Unless you want to fall asleep like this." She might as well have just uttered a powerful incantation—as soon as she said "fall asleep", his eyes and body were heavy, and he was close to doing exactly that.

Somehow, he found the energy and willpower to lift himself off her. They stripped out of what clothing still hung from their limbs and collapsed into bed together.

He couldn't begin to explain what had brought this on, or what had awakened this side of her, or why this side of her had turned him on so fucking much. All he knew was that it had aroused him and exhausted him, leaving him lethargic and beyond satisfied. But…why? What did that little Secret Service bird say to her? And was this because of last night? What the hell did all of this mean?

But he couldn't string any words together. He wasn't even sure he could've understood any answer she gave him.

So he'd ask her in the morning. For now, he held her against him, closed his eyes and slept like the dead.

Chapter Thirteen

Something had changed.

James looked…shell-shocked? Kent couldn't quite put his finger on it, but there was definitely something different about him this morning

Hopefully it wasn't the phone call that had roused him at six in the morning. As near as Kent could tell, James had long ago gotten used to being dragged out of bed at all hours of the night, even when he was at Camp David, but whatever news had come down the line could have rattled him.

But Kent couldn't ask because a carload of advisors had arrived at a hair past seven, and now James was surrounded by officials in suits and uniforms. So much for downtime. That was an occupational hazard, of course, just like when they'd been SEALs.

The meeting dragged on and on, a whole conference table full of people grilling and advising James, practically interrogating him about what he was going to do about *the Situation*. James responded calmly and coolly as he always did, giving answers and orders and demanding more answers and updates from the men sitting around him. Kent didn't pay much attention to the specifics of what was going on—he was too busy watching James and trying to figure out what was different.

At almost noon, the meeting broke for coffee, and while a few of the men stepped outside for cigarettes, James released a breath and sagged in his chair.

Kent seized the opportunity and casually stepped closer. "Are you okay?" he asked, keeping his voice as hushed as possible. "You seem a little—"

James met his gaze and sent a jolt of electricity right down Kent's spine.

"Yeah. I'm, uh… I'm good."

Kent almost had to take a step back. Holy shit. Apparently what he'd taken as being shell-shocked or distracted was quite the opposite. Up close, eye to eye, James didn't look out of it and ragged. If anything, his focus was razor-sharp, his eyes a hell of a lot clearer than they'd been last night. Or any time recently, for that matter.

James pushed himself up out of his chair, wincing a little as he did. Probably that gimp knee pestering him again. Rubbing his lower back gingerly, he said, "I'd better get some coffee while I can."

Kent gave a slight nod. He and Agent Roberts stayed on James's heels on the way out to Laurel Lodge, where meetings took place. Some of James's advisors and staff members were here at the house, waiting to accompany him. They were standing around in the living room, coffee cups and smartphones in hand.

It was here that Kent and James crossed paths with Carlene, who was herding the kids outside. The advisors and staff members who knew her and the kids greeted her politely, and those who didn't were introduced, but Kent didn't hear any of it. He was too busy staring at James and that look he was giving his wife.

Suddenly, James's state of clarity made perfect sense.

Well done, *Carlene…*

After all the introductions and greetings, she turned and continued outside with the kids. James's gaze lingered on his wife for a few seconds, and then he shook himself and shifted his attention back to leading the group into the living room.

Kent glanced after Carlene. Then he grinned to himself and followed James.

By the time James's meeting adjourned, a flurry of activity had taken over Camp David. Fur was flying back in Washington because of the South America situation, and James needed to cut his trip short and go deal with it face-to-face.

They wouldn't leave right away, though. By the time they made the hour drive back to Washington, the freeways would be stacked up with commuters. James preferred to travel in the off-peak hours unless it was a dire emergency—traffic in that town was hellish enough without the presidential motorcade making it worse.

In the meantime, James's phone was glued to his ear while Carlene made sure the kids got their things packed up.

Kent checked on the other Secret Service agents, and once he'd made his rounds, he took a few minutes to relax out on the deck. In this job, he'd learned early on to seize any opportunity that came along to catch his breath. He never knew when it would come along again.

The sliding glass door opened.

Kent glanced over his shoulder and stood straighter. "No rest for the weary, eh?"

James groaned as he shut the door behind him. "It's to be expected. Especially when I've got congressmen who are more concerned about elections than resolutions." He rolled his eyes.

"Think you can unfuck this situation?"

James slid his hands into the pockets of his trousers and shrugged. "I can unfuck the situation if they'll work with me." He strolled a little closer and stopped beside Kent at the railing. "The media shitstorm? That might be out of my hands."

Kent grimaced. He'd stopped reading the news years ago since most of it was bullshit spun into golden bullshit for the sake of ratings. "How bad is it?"

"Apparently, I'm indifferent to the fact that the cartels have access to military equipment now, and I'm putting money ahead of them using that equipment to bring drugs into the States." He scowled. "Not to mention innocent people being slaughtered or the possibility of a double civil war in South America." Bitterness dripped from the words as he added, "Since money is more important than people who aren't white."

Kent's jaw fell open. "They played that card?"

James nodded, cheek rippling as he clenched his teeth. "Days like this, I wish I could tell them the shit that's going on behind the scenes."

"No kidding." Kent didn't have the clearance to know the specifics of this situation, but he had the experience to read between the lines. After all, how many times had he and James gone in on covert missions to defuse situations before wars broke out? If he knew James, then there were—

"So, I take it you and Carlene talked."

Kent's head snapped toward him. "I… What? I mean, we… About what?"

James lifted an eyebrow. "Don't play stupid."

"I'm not." Kent showed his palms. "Look, Carlene and I have talked a lot lately. Which part are you asking about?"

James's eyes widened. "How many parts *are* there?"

"Um." Kent debated how many cards to show. "Look, she came to me because she was worried about you."

"Which is how you and I ended up in bed."

"Right." He gnawed the inside of his cheek. "And after that night, I put a few pieces together. About what I thought you need to help you cope with the stress."

James tilted his head.

Kent shifted, trying and failing to get comfortable under his friend's scrutiny. "It all made sense after you told me about your dream about Germany. The part where I don't show up."

James broke eye contact, and it was his turn to shift and fidget.

Kent continued, "It's not me you're looking for."

"What?" James looked at him again. "What do you mean?"

"I mean, that day in Munich, we—" He glanced around, double-checking they were alone, and lowered his voice anyway. "That wasn't how we usually fooled around, you know?"

James rolled his shoulders as if to mask a shiver. "Right. It wasn't."

"I didn't realize it at the time, but if I'm reading that day right, and the night we spent together recently, it's not sex that you need, and it's not me."

"So what is it?"

Kent chewed his lip again. James was as sexually adventurous as any man he'd ever been with, but even the wildest cum slut with a duffel bag full of toys didn't necessarily embrace kink very gracefully. Not everyone wanted to be analyzed or labeled, especially not by people discussing them out of earshot. They just wanted to be whipped, tied, gagged and fucked, not told this was some kind of *thing* with its own acronym and web forums.

James folded his arms loosely across his chest. "Just tell me. Obviously you've already told my wife."

Kent winced. "I wasn't trying to go behind your back. I was only trying to help. So was Carlene."

"I get that. But I need you to spell it out for me so I can wrap my head around it."

"You want the short version or the long version?"

James lifted one shoulder slightly. "Start with the short version, and we'll go from there."

"Okay. The short version is that you're a submissive."

"A…" James blinked. "Come again?"

"A submissive." Kent licked his lips. "You get off on being obedient and compliant. More to the point, you get off on someone *making* you obey and comply." He paused. "You get off on being dominated."

James's eyes lost focus. "Dominated? Submissive?" He shook his head. "I don't even—wait, is that why Carlene was, um…" His eyes flicked up and met Kent's. "That's why she was being so, uh, aggressive last night, wasn't it?"

Kent nodded. "I gave her some pointers and told her what I thought you needed." He hesitated. "How did she do?"

The way James's eyes slid closed for a second answered him well enough. "She sure seemed to enjoy it."

"Did you?"

James met his gaze. Wordlessly, he nodded.

Kent rested his hands on the railing and held on, resisting the urge to adjust himself and draw attention to the effect James's silent confession had on him. "Afterward, um… How did you sleep?"

"Better than I have in ages."

"Then it must have helped."

James's lips quirked and his eyes lost focus, as if he was mulling over the suggestion. Then he nodded. "Yeah, I guess it did." He furrowed his brow as he looked at Kent again. "But…how did you know?"

"I know you," Kent said quietly.

"Yeah, you do. But…" James studied him.

Kent fidgeted under his friend's scrutiny. "You said yourself that one of the worst parts about your job is having that much power because it's such an enormous responsibility. Submission gives you a chance to turn that off for a little while. You submit to your Dom and let them take all that power and control. You can just check out and enjoy the ride."

James stared out at the trees, eyebrows pulled together and lips tight, the very picture of concentration. No doubt trying to make sense of what Kent was telling him.

"Think about it," Kent went on. "We didn't fuck like we did in Germany very often, but every single time I can remember, it was when you were buckling under pressure. The investigation after the mission went south. After Kazakhstan. Those were the nights you came to me and practically begged me to fuck you until you forgot your own name. Neither of us knew what we were doing or if there was a name for it, but you needed to be submissive, and I guess we stumbled into me dominating you." He shrugged. "And it worked."

James nodded slowly, apparently processing everything. "What about you?"

"What do you mean?"

James turned to him. "Are you, what, a dominant? Or did we just—"

"Yes. I'm a dominant."

James arched his eyebrow. Then he laughed softly and shrugged. "Guess that explains why we were so good together in bed." He paused, and his expression turned serious. "But if you're a dominant and I'm a submissive, why were we such fuck-ups when we tried to date?"

"Just because we're compatible in bed doesn't mean we could make a relationship work. It sounds like you lucked out—if you slept as well as you did last night, then Carlene must've gotten the hang of it right off the bat."

"Yeah, she did," James breathed.

"You said she enjoyed it."

"I think so? I haven't really had a chance to even talk to her about it today. But she…" He lost focus again for a second. "She seemed to, yeah. So, what I need is this…domination, submission, whatever? Not—" He gestured at Kent, then himself.

"If it's helping you, then yeah. I'd say it's what you need."

"Oh." James didn't tip his hand far enough for Kent to figure out how he felt about that. That wasn't a surprise. Kent just hoped he hid his own disappointment well enough—as much as he wanted James and Carlene to be able to resolve this on their own, it stung to have a taste after so long, and then be shown to the door.

"Well. Um." James cleared his throat. "We'll be heading back to Washington this afternoon. I should…" He waved his hand at the lodge behind them.

"Yeah. Good idea." Kent shifted his weight. "Talk to Carlene when you get a chance. About all this. Make sure you two really are on the same page."

James's brow creased. "Okay. I will."

"It sounds like you are," Kent said. "If she went there, and it worked for both of you, then you're probably good."

"True." James shook some of the tension out of his shoulders. Then he smiled and met Kent's gaze. "Thanks, by the way. You might have saved my sanity."

Kent returned the smile. "Anytime."

They held eye contact a moment longer, as if one of them might say something, but Kent didn't know what to say, and James offered nothing.

Without another word, James went back into the house.

Kent sagged against the railing. Part of him wanted to call James back out here and ask what this meant for them. Now that they'd figured out what James needed, and it was rapidly becoming clear that Carlene could provide it for him after all, then did Kent have any further role in this?

Carlene had come to him as a last resort. Now she had another solution, and Kent wasn't needed.

He took a deep breath and pushed his shoulders back. Yeah, it hurt, but this was the right thing. Carlene could give James the stress relief he needed. James had the power exchange that would allow him to balance the burden that came with his job. Carlene no longer needed to be afraid that her marriage was at risk because her husband was having sex with his former lover. All was as it needed to be.

And sooner or later, Kent would get over it.

Chapter Fourteen

The family had barely arrived at the White House before James vanished into the West Wing. Carlene's stomach had been in knots as she watched him go, flanked by security and staff members. He hadn't said two words all the way from Camp David, and he'd been a million miles away even while he'd absently clasped their fingers together. Earlier, he'd seemed like he was focusing better, and he hadn't said a word in his sleep last night, but as soon as the family had piled into the limo, he'd gone quiet and stayed that way.

Now he was on his way to save the world, and she whispered a prayer just like she always did that he had his head together and knew what he was doing.

She didn't see him again until that evening, well after she'd had dinner with the kids and put them to bed. She'd gone to check on them one last time—they were sprawled out and sound asleep, of course—and come back to the master bedroom, and he was there.

He'd shed his jacket and tie and was sitting on the edge of the bed, taking off his shoes.

"Hey." She shut the door quietly behind her. "How did everything go?"

"Same shit, different day." He slid off his remaining shoe and set it on the floor by the other one. "I gave a statement to the press that will hopefully convince the public that I'm really not stalling or putting money ahead of people." He rolled his eyes, cursing under his breath.

"I can't believe anyone would think that about you." She folded her arms loosely and came a little closer. "But then, I know you."

He lifted his gaze. "Yeah. You definitely do." A faint smile played the corners of his mouth. As he stood, he added, "I especially can't argue with that after last night." He put his hands on her waist. "Everything you did last night, it was… Well, your timing couldn't have been better."

Relief cooled her veins. "Glad it helped."

"It did. A lot. To be honest, those meetings were a clusterfuck." He whistled and shook his head. "I don't know how I would have gotten through today without what you did."

"Really?"

"Yeah. It was… It was weird. Kind of like everything just rebooted. I don't think I've slept like that in a long time."

"No, I don't think you have." She smiled. "I didn't think it would have that much of an effect that quickly, but if it does, great."

He tucked a strand of hair behind her ear. "You won't hear me bitching about it."

"Good. And, um, I'm sorry I went behind your back," she said, barely whispering. "To Kent, I mean. I should have—"

James silenced her with a soft kiss. "Don't apologize. It's okay. I promise."

She wrapped her arms around him. "I'm just glad we found you an outlet."

"Me too." He embraced her and kissed the top of her head. Then, in a playful voice, he said, "Any chance I could talk you into it tomorrow night? Before I meet with the committee again?"

Nerves and arousal both fluttered in the pit of her stomach. She drew back a bit to meet his gaze. He was grinning, as she expected, but there was a glimmer of something in his eyes that gave her pause. Though he was being playful, an unspoken "*Please…*" was carved into the creases in his forehead, and it was uncannily similar to the way he'd looked at her from down on his knees last night. It was a plea hidden inside a little joke, and she could almost feel his heart pounding as he waited for her to answer. She even thought he might've been holding his breath.

Carlene raised her chin and narrowed her eyes. "Talk me into it? Or beg me for it?"

His eyebrows shot up. His hands twitched on her side, and he gulped.

And wow, that was surprisingly hot.

She let her hip brush his and drew one fingernail along the side of his neck. "Well, Mr. President. What's it going to be?"

His Adam's apple jumped again. "D-do I need to get on my knees?"

Carlene let her grin form slowly, and she loved the way that seemed to fuck with his balance and his breathing. "I think in your mind, you're already there."

"Yeah. You could say that."

"Mmhmm. We'll save your knees for tomorrow night."

He released a ragged breath. "I'm looking forward to it."

"I'll bet you are." *So am I.* "Tomorrow night, after all your meetings are over, you're going to meet me in the master bedroom." She ran her thumb along his lower lip. "You're going to do anything I tell you to. Understood?"

James nodded.

She arched an eyebrow. "Understood, James?"

"Y-yes." He cleared his throat. "*Yes.* Understood." He was standing a little straighter now, shoulders back as if he were in his younger military days being barked at by a superior officer.

That could be hot...

She tucked the thought into the back of her mind. "Good. Tomorrow night."

"Thank you," he breathed.

"For tonight, I think we could both stand to sleep."

"You're telling me. Mind if I grab a shower before bed?" The slight uptick of his eyebrow made her wonder if he was just politely bringing the conversation to a close, or if he really was asking permission. Or both.

"Go ahead."

One last kiss, and they both went into the bathroom—James for a shower, Carlene to take out her contacts. While he showered, she put on her glasses and went back into the bedroom.

Her mind drifted to tomorrow. James would be under an absurd amount of pressure, and if this dominance and submission really did help as much as it seemed to, he'd definitely need it tomorrow. And after that. With this crisis getting worse by the day, and the constant avalanche of responsibilities that were part and parcel of being in office, James would be frequently burning the midnight oil. Even if they now knew what he needed to stay sane, would they even have the opportunity?

Well, one night at a time.

Carlene exhaled slowly. The pressure was on tomorrow. She'd caught him off guard at first, but he knew the game now. Would it play out the same way without the element of surprise? What if he needed more? If he needed her to get him deeper into... What had Kent called it? Subspace?

Carlene's blood turned cold.

What if she did it wrong? Or it wasn't enough?

James had a possible war on his hands.

Suddenly, she understood fully why he needed to let go of his role sometimes—power came with pressure, and her palms were sweating from the pressure of having power over one person. James had to do right by *millions*. At least he had advisors to help him through the tough spots, offering guidance and advice and—

Wait. She had someone too.

Without a second thought, she grabbed her phone and sent a text to the one person who could walk her through this.

Need some advice—find me after breakfast?

James had another meeting first thing in the morning, so, as they often were, Carlene and the kids were on their own for breakfast. Wrangling a five-year-old and a couple of toddlers was never a simple task, and Carlene was so completely focused on them that when she stepped out of the family dining room, she nearly crashed into Kent.

Kent, who was waiting to speak to her.

Because she'd asked him to.

Oh shit. That's right. We need to talk. About…what?

He tilted his head. "You rang?"

"Uh. Yeah. I…" The fog lifted off her mind, and she remembered why she'd texted him and asked him to come find her. She glanced at the kids. "Let me take care of them first. I'd rather not have them overhearing us."

"Understood. I'll meet you in the South Portico."

"Good. Perfect. Give me, I don't know, half an hour or so."

Kent pulled up his jacket sleeve to check his watch. "Half an hour. I'll be there."

Carlene took the kids to their rooms to get them ready for their day. She made sure Joey had his backpack and that his uniform was on right and his shoes were tied, and then sent him off to his private kindergarten. Once he was gone, she took the kids to one of the rooms near the master bedroom that had been converted into a playroom. She'd finally given in recently and hired a couple of nannies to keep an eye on them throughout the day—though she preferred not to let strangers raise her kids, this whole First Lady gig had come with a pile of responsibilities too, and the nannies had turned out to be a lifesaver.

With Joey off to school and the little ones playing happily under their nannies' watchful eyes, she went outside to the portico to meet Kent behind the tall white pillars.

When she found him, he was leaning against a pillar and looking at something on his phone. As she approached, though, he spoke without looking at her.

"Copy that."

Carlene cocked her head. Then she realized he was talking into his radio.

He acknowledged her with a slight nod as he continued his conversation. "The demonstrators haven't been violent or made any threats, but add some extra agents to the South Lawn as a precaution. Four on foot, and two K-9s in case someone throws anything over the fence."

Carlene scowled. Protesters and demonstrators weren't unusual, especially in light of things like the South American crisis, but they unsettled her. The

White House wasn't just some government building in Washington—it was where she and her family *lived*.

"I'll walk by again myself in"—Kent glanced at his watch—"thirty minutes. If anything changes out there, I want to know." After another moment of back and forth with whoever was on the other end, Kent hung up. He shoved his phone into his jacket pocket, adjusted something on the earpiece he always wore when he was on duty, and then turned to her. "Sorry about that."

"Don't be." She smiled. "You're doing your job and keeping my husband safe."

"Definitely doing my best there." He glanced at his watch again. "Sorry I might not be able to stick around long. I need—"

"Totally understand. What you're doing is more important."

"Well, I have some time now." He lifted his eyebrows. "You wanted to talk?"

"Yeah, I…" Carlene paused, glancing around as if anyone might be close by, before looking him in the eye. "So I think I know what you mean about…" One more sweeping glance around the portico. "About what James needs. Especially after, um…"

"Last night?"

"Last night." Her cheeks burned. She folded her arms loosely, as if that might keep her from fidgeting. "The thing is, I still don't know exactly what I'm supposed to *do*. It's all well and good to say 'dominate him', but…how?"

"What do you mean?"

"Well, I'm supposed to tell him what to do, turn everything into a command." She shrugged. "But I'm… I'm kind of at a loss for what to tell him to *do*."

"Yeah, that's understandable. But really, it can be anything. The important thing for him is the domination and the commands. That's what'll put him into subspace."

"Subspace. That's what made him zone out a little, right?"

Kent nodded. "It's…it's kind of a trance state that happens to a submissive, but it's usually while they're doing pain play. I don't think James is into that, but he does go into space. It's… I've been told it's not the same thing." He shrugged. "I really don't know. All I know is, when he's in that submissive mindset, he goes into *some* kind of space, and I'm thinking that's what he needs more than anything. It gives him a chance to check out and not think about anything except what he and his Dom are doing."

Carlene eyed him.

Kent continued, "I guess you could call it sensory overload. It's not like with a masochist who's getting flooded with endorphins because of pain, but there's still adrenaline, there are still some endorphins involved, and God knows what other brain and body chemistry."

"Oh." She chewed the inside of her cheek as she tried to process everything. "So, if he does this, how did you not figure it out years ago? Back when you guys…um…"

"I didn't know what *any* of this was until long after you two got married. Ever since that night I spent with him at Camp David—"

Carlene flinched.

"—I've been thinking back and trying to fit all the pieces together, and I've seen the pattern."

"I see." She tapped her fingers on her upper arm. "So is this how James and I are going to have to do things forever? I thought he enjoyed what we did before."

"I'm sure he does. And no, I don't think it'll be all the time. Hell, sometimes he might even want to turn around and dominate you."

"Did he ever, um, dominate you?" As soon as she asked, Carlene regretted it. She really didn't want to know what they'd done together. Not recently, and not in the distant past.

"*No one* dominates me," Kent said quietly. "Not even James." His tone was guarded, as if he was holding some cards *very* tightly against his vest.

But she didn't push.

"So you tried it?" he asked.

She nodded.

"Did you enjoy it?"

Carlene's hackles went up. "I *beg* your pardon?"

"I'm sorry." Kent shook his head, his cheeks coloring. "That…sounded a little better in my head. Some people can't be dominant in the bedroom, some people can. I just meant… How did it feel to be the dominant one? Like something you could do again? Or would want to?"

As her hackles came down, Carlene mulled it over for a moment. "I think I could, yeah."

Especially if James keeps responding the way he did.

She blew out a breath. "But, like I said, I'm just not sure how. When we were in the middle of it, I went to tell him what to do, and I kind of drew a blank."

"It's not something you learn overnight."

She laughed humorlessly. "I doubt anyone offers lessons."

"It's…" Kent went quiet again, this time for the better part of a minute. Finally, he lifted his gaze to meet hers. "There is one possibility, but I'm not sure how well you'll like it."

Carlene exhaled hard. "Try me."

"Well, I…" Kent hesitated. "I could show you."

"Show me?" She blinked. "How?"

"I'll top him. Dominate him." He swallowed. "While you watch."

Carlene's lips parted. "You… You want me to watch you fuck my husband."

Kent laughed. "Well, when you put it like that, it suddenly sounds ridiculous."

She tried to glare at him, but apparently she couldn't help laughing. "I guess it's no weirder than anything else that's happened so far."

"No, probably not." He turned serious. "To be absolutely clear, I'm not suggesting this to rub anything in your face or force you to see something you're not comfortable with. But I have experience with being a Dom. And it's sometimes easier once you've seen someone else do it."

She tried and failed not to stay still. "I suppose we don't have many alternatives."

"Well, there's one, but I don't think it's really feasible under the circumstances."

She arched her eyebrow.

Kent shifted a little. "I... Regardless of how discreet people can be, I don't think it would be a good idea for the president or First Lady to be seen in a BDSM club."

Carlene snorted and clapped a hand over her mouth. "God. I'm sorry."

"It's okay." Kent chuckled.

"Can you imagine the headlines?"

Kent burst out laughing. "Oh, I could think of a few."

She managed a genuine laugh, which, she had to admit, unwound some of the knots in her gut. "Yeah, maybe that wouldn't be a good idea."

"No, probably not. I don't know what else we can do. Besides, you know..."

"You dominating him while I watch."

Kent nodded.

Carlene mulled over the idea. It was unnerving, the thought of being in the room while her husband and his ex-lover were intimate. Just imagining two men together was enough to make her uncomfortable. Those two? Oh, this would be weird. But if anyone could help her be what James needed...

"Okay." She exhaled. "He's asked me to do it again tomorrow night. Before he has to meet with the committee."

Kent's eyebrows jumped. "He's really on board with this, isn't he?"

"Apparently."

"All right, then. Why don't you send me a text tomorrow, and I'll join you when you're ready for me?"

How surreal, discussing an invitation to their bedroom as if it were casual dinner plans.

"Sure. Okay." She lowered her arms. "I guess I'll see you tomorrow?"

Kent nodded. "Yeah. I'll see you tomorrow."

They both started to leave, but she paused. "One more thing."

He turned to her, eyebrows up.

Carlene smiled. "Thank you."

Kent returned the smile but didn't say anything, and then left the room.

And for the millionth time, Carlene wondered what the hell she'd gotten herself into.

In the White House master bedroom, chewing on her thumbnail, Carlene hadn't been this nervous since the night of the election.

James was in the shower. The second he'd gone into the bathroom, she had texted Kent, and he'd immediately responded: *On my way.*

She could text him and rescind the invitation. Maybe she'd be a little clumsy and have to fumble her way through it, but she could dominate James on her own. She'd find her footing eventually.

Except with tomorrow's meetings looming over his head, James needed it done right. He needed someone who knew what they were doing, and that someone was on his way here.

A sharp tap at the door made her heart skip. She took a deep breath and crossed the room to let him in.

Here goes nothing...

She opened the door. "Hey."

"Hey." He glanced around. "Where's James?"

"Showering." She stood aside. "Come on in."

He stepped into the room, and Carlene shut the door behind them. As he looked around the bedroom, she looked right at him. He was in a suit, but his hair was damp, and his jacket sat on his torso a little differently than it usually did. She suspected he wasn't wearing the bulletproof vest underneath it.

Wore it just for the occasion, did you?

Well, James had told her a few times he liked a man in a well-cut suit...

She couldn't deny that she did too. Especially without the vest underneath, which usually added the slightest hint of unflattering thickness around his chest,

Kent looked amazing. In fact, this must've been a different suit altogether—the way it fit him, there probably wasn't room for a vest underneath.

She couldn't help letting her eyes follow the smooth lines.

Under his left arm, the line wasn't so smooth.

Did he...

Did he wear his gun?

And why was that thought turning her on?

Kent turned to her, and she jumped, her cheeks burning.

He cocked his head. "You okay?"

"Yeah, I'm..." She forgot what she was trying to say right then, because something about the way he'd turned emphasized that line beneath his arm. Yes, he had worn the gun. And yes, that was turning her on. "I'm good."

He didn't seem convinced. "Are you sure about all this?"

It's growing on me, now that you mention it. She nodded. "Unless you've come up with any alternatives."

"Not really, no. Nothing that doesn't involve other people potentially finding—"

"This will be fine, then."

He studied her, his brow creased with uncertainty, but then shrugged and let the subject drop. They sat in silence and waited, Kent alone with his thoughts and Carlene alone with her nerves. Though she couldn't come up with a single alternative, it was surreal to be here and doing this. Two men together was a weird thing to imagine. If they were into each other, fine—that was between them. But she wasn't so sure she wanted to *watch* it.

Maybe she should've downloaded some gay porn first. Gotten used to the visual. To the idea of two men doing...whatever it was that two men did together.

Oh, wouldn't the NSA have a field day with that? Finding out someone had downloaded gay porn in the White House? Tracing it right to the First Lady's personal laptop? Maybe that wouldn't be such a good idea after all.

It was too late anyway, because Kent was here and the water in the other room had just shut off.

She mouthed, *What do I do?*

He nodded toward the door and mouthed back, *Tell him.*

Right. Because it was certainly that simple.

But Kent knew what he was doing, so Carlene took a deep breath. On the way to the bathroom, she stopped and glanced back at Kent once more. He gave her a slight nod, and she continued. She walked into the bathroom as James stepped out of the shower.

He glanced at her, then did a double take and froze. "What?"

So much for not wearing her nerves on her sleeve.

Carlene took a deep breath. "Listen, um… About what we did…the other…"

"Yeah?"

"I, um…" She swallowed hard. "If that's what you need, then it's what I want to do for you. But I'm not completely sure I know how to do it."

"You did just fine the other night." He wrapped a towel around his waist and then reached for another to dry himself off. "I had no complaints. That's why I was hoping you'd do it again tonight."

"Still, I think I can do better. With…" She bit her lip. "With some help."

James looked up from drying his arms and chest. "Help?"

"Yes."

His eyes widened a bit. "Kent?"

Carlene nodded.

James's Adam's apple jumped. "Oh."

"Is that…okay?"

"You tell me. I didn't think you two got along."

She resisted the urge to fold her arms just for something to do—she didn't want to look defensive. "We both want to give you what you need, so he's going to show me how." She paused. "Tonight."

"To—" James looked past her, and she didn't have to turn around to know Kent had appeared behind her. The second the guys made eye contact, something shifted in James. His shoulders tensed slightly at first, but then slowly relaxed. His eyes were wide, and he started breathing *just* a bit faster. It was as if the very promise of being topped by Kent was enough to send him halfway into that headspace. "Holy fuck."

"Dry off." The sharpness in Kent's voice raised the hairs on the back of Carlene's neck. "When you're done, keep that towel on and meet us in the bedroom."

James blinked. "Um…"

"Did I stutter?"

James's eyebrows flicked up. Then he resumed drying off.

A gentle hand tugged at her shoulder. Carlene followed Kent back into the bedroom.

There, he faced her. "You can call this off at any time for any reason. I'll give him a safe word, and you can use it too, or you can just tell me to stop. No questions asked. Okay?"

Carlene nodded. "Okay. What do… I mean, while you two are…" She closed her eyes and exhaled sharply, frustrated with her own inability to speak. Looking up at him again, she asked, "What should I do?"

Kent smiled, a mix of warmth and mischievous playfulness in his eyes. "Pull up a chair and enjoy the show."

Enjoy the show. Right.

Soft footsteps turned both their heads. James appeared in the bathroom doorway, his damp hair finger-combed into some semblance of order and the towel around his waist as instructed. His gaze darted back and forth between his wife and his head of security.

Kent beckoned to him, and James immediately approached as if Kent's gestures were hard-wired straight to whatever part of his brain controlled his limbs.

Carlene's heart sped up. Time to pull up a chair and enjoy the show, apparently.

The room had no shortage of antique furniture. Between the two bureaus, there was an elegant and comfortable armchair, so Carlene took a seat. It occurred to her how ridiculous this was. Someone had put in the effort to find and acquire this lovely and undoubtedly expensive chair for the president's bedroom. She wondered what that someone would've thought if they'd known it would eventually be used by a First Lady to watch her husband be dominated by a Secret Service agent.

Oh hell. Maybe this wasn't the first time. A Bush or two could have had a kinky streak that no one knew about.

She snorted and immediately clapped a hand over her mouth.

The guys eyed her.

"What?" Kent asked.

"Nothing." She tried and failed to smother a giggle. "I'm sorry. Nothing."

Kent shrugged and faced James again. "Look at me."

James's head snapped toward Kent.

Kent touched his face, and James closed his eyes for a second, but then opened them and looked up at Kent, as if he'd forgotten himself briefly. Neither of them spoke for a long moment. They just stood, facing each other, gazing at each other, with that single point of contact between Kent's palm and James's cheek.

They were nearly the same height, though Kent's shoes gave him a slight advantage, and yet Kent seemed to tower over James. When he raised his chin, James lowered his, and the optical illusion was even more pronounced.

Kent withdrew his hand. "Lose the towel."

James obeyed so quickly, Carlene wondered if the towel had simply fallen off. Given the commanding tone of Kent's voice, it wouldn't have surprised her.

Kent stood in front of James. One fully dressed—shirt, jacket, tie, gun. The other completely naked. Both men were erect too. They stood so close together, the head of James's rock-hard cock could almost brush the obvious swell beneath Kent's fly.

Carlene's pulse sped up. Nerves, of course. Right?

Kent nodded downward. Immediately, James dropped to his knees at Kent's feet, bare legs on the cream-colored carpet in front of those highly polished black shoes.

Kent hooked a finger beneath James's chin and lifted it so they were looking each other in the eye. Now that height difference was real, and the effect was incredible. James gazed up at Kent, eyes wide and pupils blown, and Kent grinned down at him. He stroked James's cheek, and Carlene's breath caught. The way they were looking at each other, eyes smoldering with lust and need, didn't make her jealous or angry like it should have.

It was…

It was fucking *hot*.

Oblivious to her, Kent said, "Until I tell you otherwise, you don't give a damn about anything outside of this room."

James managed a nod. "Okay…"

"The only thing that matters is what I tell you to do. Understood?"

James's eyes flicked toward Carlene, and his brow furrowed slightly.

"James," Kent said sharply, making him jump. "Look at *me*." James obeyed, and Kent continued, "Whatever I say goes. Understood?"

James tried to nod, but the finger beneath his chin limited his movement, so he whispered, "Understood."

Kent gestured at Carlene. "Anything she says goes too."

James's eyes darted toward her again. Confusion lingered in his expression, but he was definitely sliding into that headspace Kent had talked about. Sliding into it *fast*. His whole body was far too limber and relaxed for a man with the weight of the world on his shoulders, his breathing too deep and steady.

"James."

He shifted his gaze back up to Kent.

Kent stroked James's jaw with the back of his fingers, and James pressed against him slightly, as if seeking out more contact.

"What matters tonight?" Kent asked.

"Nothing." James swallowed. "Except this."

"Good. And you're going to do, what?"

"Anything you tell me to." James's speech was vaguely slurred, and he spoke slower than he usually did, like he had to carefully form each word.

"Anything?"

"Anything."

Carlene shivered.

"You can stop this any time with a safe word," Kent said. "Tonight's safe word is 'Republican'."

Any other time, Carlene was sure James would have laughed at that, especially with Kent's mischievous grin granting him permission, but he just nodded slowly. His gaze was fixed on Kent, his eyes wide. He looked almost hypnotized. Maybe he was.

Kent beckoned to him. "Stand up."

James rose quickly, pausing only briefly when his knee popped. Back straight and shoulders square, he faced Kent.

"Good." Kent cupped James's neck and drew him in. Their lips were nearly touching, but not. Carlene held her breath, waiting for Kent to bridge that last little gap between them.

Holding him still with the hand on his neck, Kent reached between them and closed his long fingers around James's erection.

James hissed sharply and closed his eyes. "Holy shit."

Carlene's pulse jumped. *Holy shit* was right…

Kent stroked him slowly. "Look right at me. Eyes open. Right on me."

James was struggling to keep his eyes open, but he did as he was told. "Fuck…"

"Not yet." Kent chuckled softly. He leaned in a bit more, their lips just grazing, and added, "I'll fuck you after I'm done fucking *with* you."

James whimpered. His hips started moving in perfect time with Kent's hand.

"You're not going to come until I tell you to." Kent's lips were so, so close to her husband's. "Are you?"

James murmured something Carlene didn't understand.

"Are you?"

"N-no."

"Good." Kent added a subtle twist to his strokes, and grinned at James's frustrated moan. "I don't want you to come yet, because I want you to come while I'm fucking you."

James squeezed his eyes shut. "Jesus..."

"Do you want that, James?" Kent cupped James's cheek with his free hand. "Do you want me to fuck you?"

"Y-yes."

"Wrong answer."

James's eyes flew open. "Huh?"

Kent pulled back, and Carlene lost her breath. They'd been so close, and she'd been so sure the kiss was inevitable, and now...this?

Kent ran his thumb up and down the side of James's neck. "I'm calling the shots. You do whatever I tell you to. If I want to fuck you, you get on your hands and knees and be fucked. Anything you do, it's because I tell you to."

James swallowed again. His hips were rocking slightly, fucking into Kent's fist, and deep crevices appeared on his forehead as he undoubtedly struggled to comprehend what he was being told. "Anything you want. J-just tell me."

"Good," Kent said softly. "Very good."

James released a ragged breath, and his muscles softened.

"So I'm going to ask again," Kent whispered just loud enough for Carlene to hear, "do you want me to fuck you?"

James slowly ran his tongue across his lips. He studied Kent's eyes, seemed to concentrate hard on them, and finally murmured, "Only if you want to."

Kent smiled, and James shivered. Then Kent shrugged off his jacket, and Carlene's clit tingled. Oh yes, he was wearing his holster. Black. Tight. Emphasizing his chest and his shoulders, plus the butt of the gun sticking out from beneath his arm.

She tried not to fidget, afraid a single creak of the chair would tip them off that she was already more turned on than she should've been.

Focused completely on James, Kent drew him in closer, until their lips were once again almost touching. "You learn fast. Always have."

James said something Carlene didn't catch. He tilted his head a little and moved in, but then backed off, mouthing a curse. She couldn't tell if the curse was because he'd almost forgotten himself—again—and kissed Kent, or because Kent's hand kept him from drawing back to a safe distance.

Carlene's head spun as she watched them. As Kent stroked James, as he made James speak when the man had clearly lost his ability to speak, their mouths so close together, and yet not.

Just kiss *him already!*

Carlene's own thought startled her. It also sent a shiver right down her spine and straight to her clit. She'd never wanted two men to make out in front of her. Then again, she'd also never given Kent a second look before tonight, but she sure did now, and wasn't he just a checklist of *holy shit hot*. The tailored suit holding on to his powerful body. The shoes polished to a mirror shine. The naked, trembling man—her husband!—at his command.

Then there was that shoulder holster. It was rarely visible, but now that his jacket was off, it was out in the open. The gun added an irrational but undeniable note of danger, that sharp black pistol elevating him from a man in a suit to a badass motherfucker in a suit. Carlene's mouth watered. There was a reason she'd been attracted to a SEAL in the first place. The gun struck that chord just right, and reminded her this wasn't just a pair of men—this was a pair of men who'd been Special Forces at one time.

And one was naked.

And the other was about to strip off his clothes.

So they could have sex.

With each other.

Suddenly the idea of two men in bed wasn't quite so weird.

And for the love of God, would they just *kiss already*?

"I'm going to fuck you while your wife watches," Kent said in a low growl, still slowly stroking James's dick, "and you're not going to come until I give you permission."

"Fuck…"

"Understood?"

"*Yes.*"

Kent moved closer, until only a fraction of an inch remained between their lips. Carlene held her breath. James held his. Kent held on to James's neck and whispered, "I want to fuck you, and I don't want to wait."

And with that, he kissed James, and all the air rushed out of Carlene's lungs.

Holy.

Fuck.

She couldn't remember ever witnessing—or experiencing—a kiss that passionate. Openmouthed, demanding, each man's brows furrowed as if their kiss required every ounce of concentration. Kent's hand stopped moving, as did James's hips, and for the longest time, they just kissed, James's knees shaking like they were about to go slack as Kent explored his mouth.

Carlene's jaw fell open. If James ever kissed her like that, she was pretty sure she'd spontaneously combust. She was pretty surprised he *hadn't*.

When Kent broke the kiss, they were both breathing hard. Kent swept his tongue across his lips. "Yeah. Definitely don't want to wait." He let James go and took a half step back.

Biting her lip, she uncrossed and crossed her legs. Was watching her only option tonight? Because it was getting incredibly warm in here…

Oblivious to her trying not to come unglued, Kent loosened his tie slightly and unbuttoned the top of his shirt. He took off one cufflink, and as he rolled the sleeve to his elbow, he said, "Get the lube."

James lunged for the bedside table.

Kent turned to Carlene, eyebrows up as if to ask, "So far so good?"

She nodded. He smiled, and she smiled back as James dropped to his knees in front of Kent again, lube in hand. As Kent shifted his attention back to James and continued rolling his sleeves, she couldn't help thinking that so far, what

Kent had done with James wasn't much different from what she'd done with him. To her surprise, that realization made her feel better—maybe she wasn't as clumsy and clueless with this as she thought. Maybe it didn't have to be elaborate as long as James knew who was in charge.

Some more of her nerves settled. Maybe she didn't need this guidance after all. She was glad Kent had offered, though. Seeing was believing, and now she believed she was more competent than she'd thought.

And seeing turned out to be hot. Seriously, *seriously* hot.

Kent jerked his chin toward the foot of the bed. Without a second of hesitation, James moved onto the bed and went to his hands and knees, resting his hands just short of the footboard.

In this position, he was facing her, and their eyes met. A little grin worked its way onto his lips—kind of a silly, loopy expression, like that dopey smile he'd given her last time he'd come out of surgery and was drugged out of his mind.

Still dressed, Kent knelt behind James and slid a hand over his hip, and James's smile faded. James's eyes slid closed. He bit his lip. His fingers curled around the comforter.

Carlene squirmed. She could only imagine everything James felt right then, but the anticipation was palpable.

Kent undid his belt and zipper, dropped his trousers and boxers enough to be out of the way, and positioned himself behind James. He added some more lube and put some on James, just as James had always done for her whenever they'd had anal. Had he learned to do that with Kent? She shook the thought away and watched as Kent pressed against James.

James closed his eyes and let his head fall forward. His shoulders tensed and his arms quivered as he leaned back a little, as if trying to urge Kent deeper. Kent was in no hurry, though—he steadied James's hips and inched inside. Teasing? Being careful? Both? No way to tell, but watching it was… God, it was mind-bending. Especially once Kent was moving smoothly and easily, and his strokes started speeding up. Before long, he was slamming into James, thrusting so hard it must have been painful.

And James? He was quite obviously in heaven. He sank almost onto his forearms, and whenever he raised his head enough for Carlene to see his face, his eyes were screwed shut and his lips were apart as if he were trying to moan but didn't remember how.

Carlene couldn't have looked anywhere else if she'd wanted to. Everything mesmerized her—the fluid motion of Kent's hips, the blissed-out expression on James's face, the way their bodies looked so natural and perfect together. The fact that Kent was dressed—his shirttails falling over his ass, his belt buckle jingling and his tie bouncing with every thrust, the shoulder holster's harness emphasizing his broad chest and shoulders—only added to the masculinity and the raw power of the two of them together. The little groans and gasps were soft, but echoed across her nerve endings and tingled right down to her pussy.

She couldn't stay still any longer, and the antique legs creaked in protest. This was not supposed to be that hot. It was, though. Insanely hot. Two powerful, gorgeous bodies moving together like it was what they were made to do, two men sweating and panting and losing themselves in each other—what wasn't to love?

Kent leaned forward and slid his hand around the front of James's throat and kissed beneath his ear as he fucked him. "Look at your wife, James."

James struggled to open his eyes and then slid his gaze toward Carlene.

And that pure surrender on her husband's face was addictive.

Kent nipped James's ear, then growled, "You're not going to come until she gives you permission."

Carlene's breath caught. So did her husband's. She and James stared at each other, and her whole body broke out in goose bumps.

Kent thrust hard into James and asked, "Understood?"

James moaned softly, his arms shaking beneath him. "Yeah. Under... understood." He held Carlene's gaze, and she couldn't tell if he was silently pleading for her to go easy on him, or if he wanted to be tortured as long as he could stand it.

Not that he had a choice. As hot as it was watching these two have sex, she wasn't about to bring it to a halt anytime soon.

Kent definitely didn't mind—he fucked James hard and deep, testing the limits of that four-poster bed, which squeaked beneath them. James gripped handfuls of the comforter, as if that might hold him in place or keep him in the present or something, and the sounds of ecstasy—low groans and whispered curses—were beyond words.

Carlene was hypnotized. She'd been certain this would be difficult to watch, but now she couldn't have looked anywhere else if she wanted to. This was sexier than it had any right to be—sweat and skin and muscles and *power*.

Kent dug his teeth into James's shoulder, and James was almost sobbing as he pleaded breathlessly, "Please, let me come."

Kent's eyes flicked up and met hers. He must've been close to the edge too—the cords on his neck stood out, as did every muscle in his arm as he gripped James's neck. His lips peeled back across clenched teeth. Oh yeah, he was right there. But he held back, driving into James over and over.

Now Carlene understood why Kent got off on domination. Though Kent was in control of James, he wasn't going to come until James did. Until *she* gave the word. That power—keeping both of them right there on the brink until she was damn good and ready to let them come—was intoxicating.

Kent exhaled, burying his face against James's neck. James squeezed his eyes shut and grimaced. Then he swore.

She grinned. "James."

Both men looked at her.

"Come."

Chapter Fifteen

As soon as the word slipped off his wife's lips, James lost it. The whole world shattered. The air in the room seemed to shatter with the sudden break in tension, and white light exploded behind his eyelids. Then it all went dark.

When the smoke began to clear, he was on his stomach, so his arms must have collapsed beneath him.

Kent collapsed too, dropping onto James's back but holding himself up just enough that James could breathe.

No one moved or made a sound. The room was dead silent except for him and Kent breathing in unison and James's heart pounding against his ribs. He pressed his forehead into the cool sheets, eyes closed and fingers kneading the bed as he slowly came down, slowly returned to terra firma.

Kent panted hard against James's shoulder, his breath cooling the sweaty skin. He pressed a soft kiss to the base of James's bowed neck. "You okay?"

"I'm…" James's mouth was as dry as his brain was scrambled. "Think so."

Another soft kiss, which did nothing to help him collect his thoughts. Then Kent lifted himself up and pulled out, and James wasn't even sure who gasped. Maybe both of them? Hell, he didn't care.

A hand touched his arm. Carlene said something. Then Kent did. Carlene again. James was moving, going from lying down to being partially, then fully upright.

His vision cleared fairly quickly, but his mind took a bit longer. Everything was hazy as he got up and moved. He had no idea how much time actually passed before he glanced to his left, then to his right, and realized he was lying in bed, naked beneath the covers, between Kent and Carlene, who were both dressed and on top of the comforter. Well, sort of dressed. Kent's tie was undone, hanging over his shoulders, and he'd unbuttoned his shirt enough to reveal some of the dark hair on his chest.

James didn't remember getting here. His last clear memory was Carlene and Kent helping him get upright, and someone handing him a towel, and after that, it was all blurry.

He must have drifted off for a little while, because he just now realized they were talking over him.

"…is the same thing we did the other night," Carlene said. "Not exactly the same, but you and I both did a lot of similar things."

"That's perfect. It doesn't have to be much more involved than that." Kent shrugged. "The dominance is the important part. Unless you want to get into bondage, toys, maybe some—"

"Wait, what?" James blinked. "What are you two talking about?"

They both laughed.

Carlene rested her hand on his arm. "He's just giving me some pointers and ideas. So I knew what to do with you."

James arched an eyebrow. "Uh-huh. Seemed like you had a pretty good grasp on it last time."

"Well, after watching him, I think I'll be more *confident* about it."

"Confident is good." James scrubbed a hand over his face. "Okay, how exactly did we get from you two barely being in the same room together, to… *this?*"

Carlene and Kent exchanged mischievous glances.

"Hey, don't look a gift horse in the mouth." Kent trailed a finger down the center of James's chest, and when he reached his abs, the muscles contracted and James shivered. Kent chuckled. "We figured out what you need, and we accidentally stumbled across a way to not want to kill each other."

Carlene laughed. "He's right, you know." She followed the same path Kent had just traced, but with her nail, drawing a sharp, whispered curse from James's lips.

He squirmed between them. "I'm not going to complain. Not if—*Jesus.*" There was no escaping the two of them—Kent's ticklish touch, Carlene's nail—and he couldn't lie still. Couldn't think. The contrast of soft and sharp drove his already fried senses wild. "Yeah. N-not going to complain."

Carlene's touch lightened. "So this really does help? This, um, dominance?"

"Oh God, yes." James clasped her hand in his. "It's like a fucking reset button for…everything."

"Good." Kent rested his hand on James's forearm. "With the way things were going with South America, we were both getting seriously worried. And then all the shit going on with Congress seemed to make it worse."

"Tell me about it," James muttered. Then he glanced back and forth between them. "So, wait. Are you telling me it *literally* took an act of Congress for the two of you to get along?"

Carlene and Kent met each other's eyes and then burst out laughing.

Kent chuckled, trailing a finger up James's arm. "Well, at least those idiots were good for something."

"Miracles never cease, I guess." James turned to Carlene and squeezed her hand. "Are you sure you want to do this? I mean, this—"

"Did I seem like I wasn't enjoying it?"

"Well, no. I mean, what I can remember."

Carlene's eyebrows shot up. "You don't remember?"

"Not…clearly." James waved his free hand in front of his face. "It's all kind of hazy."

"That's normal," Kent said. "Sometimes people get so far into that headspace, and there's so much adrenaline and God knows what else, the memory can be foggy."

Carlene held his gaze for a few seconds and then relaxed a bit, her grasp on James's hand loosening and her shoulder sinking slightly. "Weird."

"Everything about this is kind of weird." Kent smiled. "It'll make more sense as you go."

"I hope so." She turned to James again. "I do like it, though. And if this is what you need, then I'm more than happy to do it."

"You lucky bastard," Kent said. "You married a service top."

"A what?" Carlene and James asked in unison.

Kent grinned. "Someone who's not necessarily a Domme but will be if that's what her partner needs."

"Well…" Carlene laughed cautiously. "Let's, um, see how it goes after I've been the one in the driver's seat without any guidance a few times."

James moistened his parched lips. "There's, you know, no need to rush. If you need more guidance, and you want him around to supervise…"

Carlene and Kent both rolled their eyes.

After a moment, though, Carlene met Kent's gaze, then James's. "Actually, that might not be such a bad idea. Having Kent around."

Kent blinked. "Seriously?"

James's pulse shot up, but he was too stunned to speak.

"Kent knows what he's doing. I'm learning." Carlene lifted her shoulder slightly. "Who's to say we wouldn't be better for James if we did this together?"

If Kent's eyes got any wider…

James pushed himself up onto his elbows. "You're serious."

"Yes." She nodded. "Completely."

James stared at her.

Kent did too, but then he cleared his throat. "Well, I'm not going to say no."

"N-neither am…" James shook his head. "Carlene, are you sure about this?"

She nodded. "I could use the help. Until I find my confidence, I mean."

"That works for me," Kent said. "Next time, I'll sit back and watch her, and offer a little guidance if she needs it. Maybe one or two times after that." He shrugged. "Then I think you'll be in good hands."

A wicked grin materialized on her lips. "I don't know. The guidance is great, but I'm starting to like the idea of a team approach. So many more opportunities to"—she drew her fingertip along James's arm—"make him squirm."

The ticklish touch did, indeed, make him squirm.

Kent raised his eyebrow. "Yeah, I don't think you're going to have any trouble in the driver's seat."

James swallowed. "Gonna have to agree with him, baby."

Carlene switched from her fingertip to her nail, making James gasp and bite his lip. She laughed. "We'll just have to see how it goes, won't we?"

Sitting at the conference room table, surrounded by frustrated, exhausted congressmen, James was rested and clearheaded. Aching in a few places, especially since he'd also fucked Carlene into the ground after Kent had left last night, but he felt great. Centered. Focused.

Bring it on, boys, he thought as he scanned the gathered senators and representatives.

As the meeting got started, Senator Baxstrom absently turned a pen over and over between his thick fingers. "Mr. President, I understand what you want, but it's just not feasible."

"Then we need to find an alternative to invading."

"Sir, we—"

"This is not our war," James said sharply. "I will gladly help our allies in any way possible, but my responsibility—and *your* responsibility—is first and foremost to the American people. I'm not putting American soldiers into body bags or prosthetic limbs unless I can look them in the eye first and tell them that they and their families will be taken care of. Am I clear?"

Senator Lee huffed. "That's a wonderful thought in theory. And none of us"—he gestured at the other congressmen—"want our boys getting killed or wounded. But something has to be done to resolve this conflict."

"Agreed." James gave a single nod. He tapped the reports in front of him. "And you've made it abundantly clear that mobilizing troops is not a viable option without quite possibly destabilizing our economy. Which means we need to consider other possibilities."

Senator Gorton pursed his lips, and James thought the man was stopping just short of rolling his eyes. "What do you suggest, then? The cartels aren't interested in any form of compromise, so diplomatic talks and any attempt at negotiations have fallen apart at every turn."

James narrowed his eyes. "Maybe it's my own experience as a soldier, but I find it hard to swallow that I should send troops into harm's way because elected, appointed and overpaid officials insist on behaving like kindergarteners instead of working toward a peaceful resolution."

"We can't have a peaceful resolution with terrorists, Mr. President," Gorton said.

"But we *can* minimize bloodshed."

"This has been going on for *weeks*," the senator snapped. "We don't have *time* to keep playing these games, sir."

"Then I would suggest that Congress stop playing games and come up with a budget." He folded his hands on top of a stack of reports. "You have one week. No budget, no action."

The senators exchanged glances. Knowing ones, if James read them right— they had cards up their sleeves, didn't they?

"All right," Senator Baxstrom said. "One week. We'll have a budget."

The others nodded, and more glances were exchanged. Several murmured, "One week."

James shifted his gaze toward Admiral Stein, who sat across from him and two seats over. The admiral gave him a subtle nod. He'd briefed James before the meeting, updating him as much as he could about the ongoing covert mission in South America. The men needed more time, but the week James had bought them today would—hopefully—be enough.

James cleared his throat. "Then I guess we're done here."

No one objected, so the meeting adjourned. Everyone stood, buttoning their jackets before shaking hands and slowly filing out of the room.

When there was no one left but Secret Service agents, James sank back in the leather chair and released a long breath. He dared not turn his head and make eye contact with Kent, who was just a few feet to his left, because he was sure everyone would instantly know what they'd done last night. Not that he could turn anyway. For the moment, all he could do was…collapse. Breathe. This battle was over. The ball was back in Congress's court. But the pressure was on, because in one week, depending on the outcome of the twin SEAL missions, he'd have to make a decision. A final, decisive choice. Either the United States went to war or it didn't, and if Congress got its ducks in a row and presented a decent budget, that choice would be his.

For the next few days, though, while he waited for Congress to pull its head out of its collective ass, James could focus on other issues. There wasn't time to slip away to Camp David, catch his breath and relax with his family, but those little interludes with Kent and Carlene were lifesavers.

And if the United States went to war, James was going to need all the help he could get.

Chapter Sixteen

By the time the day wound down, after the press conferences and a gazillion meetings about all the other shit James was responsible for, nobody was in the mood for anything. At eleven thirty, Kent barely managed to drag himself through his bedroom door—no way in hell he was going back to his apartment tonight. He wasn't at all surprised that James had looked like a zombie as he'd shuffled down the hall to his own room—the man had been run ragged since daybreak.

Carlene had looked ready to collapse too. She'd spent the day out with the kids, and that had turned into an unmitigated disaster. The press figured out where she was, and she was hounded by photographers and reporters. Kent was proud of his agents—as per their training, they'd acted as a buffer, keeping the press at as comfortable and safe a distance as they could. Still, by the time Carlene had returned to the White House, the kids were rattled and she was exhausted.

Nights like this, James probably needed the stress relief from Kent and Carlene, but he was far too tired to go through with it, and they were too. He'd need it soon, though, and Kent vowed to keep an eye out for that window of opportunity, when all three of them had both the time and the energy to even think about it. He just hoped like hell that didn't turn into a Catch-22—when James needed to be dominated, he was too busy and exhausted. When he wasn't too busy and exhausted, he didn't need it.

The next day, James spent most of the morning in the Oval Office. He was on and off the phone with countless people. Members of the congressional committee, Kent guessed—no one else seemed to draw that aggravated tone out of James quite so easily. The day after that, same thing.

It wasn't until the third day that James finally managed some downtime while the sun was up. He dismissed his cabinet, and they cleared the room, leaving him with only Kent and three other Secret Service agents. With a subtle nod and a gesture, Kent dismissed them too.

Once they were alone, he double-checked his radio was off—he could hear if someone needed to reach him, but no one would hear his conversation. Then he turned to James, resisting the urge to reach for him. There were cameras in here, after all. "You okay?"

James pressed his elbows onto his desk and leaned forward, rubbing his neck with both hands. "I'm fucking exhausted."

"I know." Kent watched him for a moment. "Is there anything I can do?"

James met his gaze, and that wasn't the expression Kent had anticipated. James's exhaustion was palpable, but there was something else, and it was unmistakable.

Kent took a breath. "If you're that tired…"

"I am. But…" Though James radiated fatigue, that gleam in his eyes said that he'd find a second wind if Kent told him to. That he was this close to begging Kent to tell him to.

Kent pushed his shoulders back and made sure his voice was hard-edged as he spoke. "After you and Carlene put the kids to bed, I want you to wait for me in my bedroom."

A shudder rippled through James. He nodded slowly. "Dressed? Or…?"

"Dressed. Kneeling beside the bed." Kent paused. "I haven't decided what I'm going to do yet."

James released a ragged breath and nodded again. "I'll be there."

Between the end of his shift and when he expected James in his bedroom, Kent had a couple of hours to himself. As soon as he'd downloaded his gun and taken off his radio, he took advantage of that time off.

First things first, he made sure he had a few things at the ready in his bedroom. If James needed this badly enough to play even when he was this tired, then Kent was damn sure going to make it worth his while.

Then he went looking for Carlene.

She was just coming back in from the tennis courts with the kids. Lately she'd been teaching Joey the basics of the game, and the twins usually spent the time chasing stray balls around the court.

She glanced at him and then did a double take. "I thought you were off tonight."

"I am, yes."

Their eyes locked. Understanding drew her eyebrows up, and she turned to one of the nannies she'd *finally* hired. "Make sure they all change and clean up before dinner, please."

"Yes, ma'am," the lady said with a nod, and the pair of nannies herded the kids down the hall.

Carlene waited until they were all well on their way out of earshot before she faced Kent again. "What's up?"

"I, um…" How to broach this subject? He took a breath and kept his voice low. "I think tonight would be a good night to try your hand at everything I showed you. With James."

Her thin eyebrows shot up. "I beg your pardon?"

"He needs it tonight."

At that, she deflated a little. "Shit. I thought it was getting bad." Her forehead creased. "I'm not sure I've got enough of a handle on this. I mean, it's fine to play around, but if he needs it like this…" She paused. "Maybe you'd be better suited. For tonight."

"You'll do fine, but I was thinking we could work together." He cleared his throat. "I mean, I could be there to watch. Like you did that one night."

"I see."

"I, um… Maybe it was presumptuous, but I told him to meet me in my bedroom tonight. I didn't say anything one way or the other about you because

I hadn't spoken to you yet."

Carlene chewed her lip. "So what do I do? I'm just… It went so well the first time, but I'm worried sick I'll screw it up when he really needs me to get it right."

"I'll be there. If you need help, just ask." He grinned cautiously. "As far as what to do, I've got a few tricks up my sleeve tonight that I think he might enjoy."

"Oh really?" Her expression was guarded for a moment, but then a little grin of her own came to life. "Do tell."

When Kent walked into his bedroom at a quarter after nine, James was there. He'd showered recently enough that his graying hair was damp, and he'd changed into some more comfortable clothing. Kent considered chastising him for assuming he was allowed to change out of his suit and tie, but James was still learning how all this worked. And for that matter, there *was* something delicious about the president of the United States kneeling on Kent's bedroom floor in a black Metallica T-shirt with "*please fuck me*" in his eyes.

Kent crossed the room and stood beside James. Neither spoke as Kent stroked James's cheek, but James closed his eyes and pressed against Kent's hand. Kent was actually surprised the man didn't start purring.

"For future reference," he said, keeping his voice low but firm, "if I tell you to show up, that means in the same clothes you're wearing."

James stiffened, and his eyes flew open. He glanced down at the T-shirt. "I'm, uh…sorry. Sorry. I was…you know, with the kids, and—"

"Shh." Kent stroked his cheek. "This is all part of the learning curve. Eventually, there will be consequences if you disobey me or do something I haven't told you to do. But for now"—he ran his fingers through James's hair—"you're learning."

James closed his eyes again. He didn't speak, but the relief was there in the way his shoulders drooped and his breathing slowed.

Kent was about to speak again, but James's head suddenly turned, and a split second later, the bedroom door opened.

James's spine straightened. "Oh God…"

Kent grinned as Carlene stepped into the room and quietly shut the door behind her.

"Right on time," he said.

She smiled nervously. "I wouldn't miss a minute of this."

James's breath caught for a second, and he lifted his chin to look up at Kent, his eyes huge as three creases formed on his forehead.

Kent cupped his face. "Your wife is calling the shots tonight. I'll just be here as a…"

"Technical consultant?" Carlene offered.

Kent chuckled. "Sure, let's go with that."

She laughed, but it was a nervous sound. James stared at each of them in turn, and Kent couldn't tell if he didn't think he had permission to laugh, or if the words hadn't settled deep enough into his brain for the humor to hit.

"Like I said"—Kent stroked James's cheek to draw his attention back— "Carlene's in charge. Anything she says, goes. Understood?"

James gulped and nodded slowly.

Kent inclined his head and arched an eyebrow.

"Understood," James said quickly.

"Good." Kent ran a hand over James's hair one more time and then moved aside to let Carlene step in.

She hesitated, eyes wide and posture rigid.

Kent gave her a subtle nod and gestured toward James, mouthing, *You'll be fine.*

She swallowed. Performance anxiety was a bitch, and his presence was probably a double-edged sword. He was there to help if she made a mistake, but it also meant he was there to *see* if she made a mistake.

"Carlene," Kent said and waited until she looked him in the eye. "You'll do fine. Apparently you did great the last time."

"You did," James whispered, gazing up at his wife.

They both glanced at him, and Kent debated giving James hell—this time for speaking out of turn—but again decided to let it slide. If the slip instilled confidence in the budding Domme, then he could allow it. Stricter rules would come when James and Carlene both had their feet under them.

Carlene pushed her shoulders back. "Do you have everything?"

"Right there." He pointed at a paper bag on the bed. "Whenever you're ready for them."

James eyed the bag, and Kent thought he might've mouthed either *what the fuck?* or *oh shit.*

"Okay. Okay. Good." She nodded and drew in a deep breath. For a moment, she didn't move or speak, but right when Kent was about to offer more reassurance, she stepped forward and took his place in front of James. Her hand hovered in the air between them, James's gaze fixed on it and neither of them breathed, as near as Kent could tell. Finally, she reached for his face, and James exhaled. He pressed against her palm like he had Kent's.

Carlene glanced at Kent, and he nodded once.

Then she looked down at her husband again and inhaled slowly through her nose. When she spoke, her voice had a firm—and confident—edge. "The kids are down the hall, so we'll have to be completely quiet." Her expression hardened, the Domme coming through loud and clear. "Not a sound unless I allow it. Understood?"

James gulped.

Carlene's eyebrow flicked up.

Quickly, James said, "Yes. Understood."

Carlene grinned. "Good."

Kent couldn't help beaming—*that's my girl.*

She withdrew her hand and gestured at the bag on the bed. "Pick that up."

James started to rise, hesitated and settled back on his knees. Then he reached for the bag, straining because it was just beyond his fingertips. Ever the resourceful one, he tugged on the sheet and brought the bag closer so he could grab it. As he lifted it, the paper crinkled loudly, but it wasn't enough to completely muffle the tiny metallic clink.

James paused, eyeing the bag uncertainly, and looked up at Carlene. *What in the world do you have in mind?*

"Safe word?"

"Republican." As soon as the word was out, a tiny smirk tried to appear on James's lips, but he smothered it. He must've finally been seeing the humor in the choice of safe words.

"Good," she said. "Now pull everything out of the bag."

James opened it and looked inside, wisely not sticking his hand in until he knew what was there. Under his breath, he muttered, "What in the..."

"Pull everything out," Carlene reminded him just sharply enough to make him jump.

"Sorry." James reached inside. He pulled out a blindfold and, at his wife's command, set it on the edge of the mattress. Next was a soft cat toy—one of the fuzzy ones that looked like a clump of feathers at the end of a tiny fishing pole.

And finally, the object that had probably puzzled him even more than the cat toy—a Wartenberg wheel. It had a pencil-length stainless steel handle, and at the end was a pinwheel that always brought to mind a spur like someone would use on a horse. More spokes, definitely sharper, but close enough. It was a menacing little thing, one that warranted a side-eye from even the most experienced masochist.

Being neither experienced nor a masochist, James was definitely giving it a wary side-eye. "What is that?"

"Speaking out of turn?" Carlene plucked the implement from him and spun the pinwheel with her finger. "I'll use this thing harder if you don't behave."

"S-sorry." Gaze fixed on the wheel, he shook himself. "Won't happen again."

"Good." She spun it harder, and it made a high-pitched buzzing sound. James shuddered.

"I've never used one of these," she said. "So I'm going to be experimenting on you with it." She held it right in front of his face and pressed her thumb against one of the spokes, letting it visibly indent the fleshy part until it seemed like it would *almost* break the skin. "Sound like fun?"

His eyes darted back and forth from hers to the wheel. He probably wondered if it was a trick question, or if she was legitimately checking to make sure he was into it.

She glanced at Kent, uncertainty etched into her expression as she chewed her lip and raised her eyebrows.

"James," Kent said. "Do you think you can handle the wheel?"

James pulled in a breath. "I can try."

"Do you want to try?"

Without hesitation, James nodded. "Yeah." He looked up at Carlene. "Yeah, I want to try."

Kent met Carlene's gaze. *All yours.*

She turned back to her husband. "Clothes off. Lie back on the bed."

He hesitated. "May I stand? Before I get undressed?"

Carlene smiled, and Kent swore he could feel the rush of warmth through James. There was no aphrodisiac like the master's approval.

"Yes," she said.

James got up, and Kent wasn't sure he'd ever seen the man undress that quickly. In what seemed like mere seconds, the jeans and the Metallica shirt were draped over the footboard, and James was climbing onto Kent's bed to lie back as ordered.

When he was settled into place, Carlene handed him the blindfold. "Put this on."

James hesitated, eyeing it.

She touched his arm, and her voice was soft as she asked, "Are you okay with the blindfold?"

James chewed the inside of his cheek, but then took a deep breath and slipped the blindfold over his head.

Carlene glanced at Kent. He mouthed, *Safe word.*

To James, she said, "Tell me your safe word again."

James licked his lips. "Republican." No humor this time, but repeating the word seemed to ease some of the tension in his face. Some of it. His jaw was still tight, and his fingers curled and uncurled at his sides.

Kent moved closer to the bed and beckoned for Carlene to come toward him. When she did, he whispered, "He might not be ready for the blindfold. It...goes back to some of our training."

Understanding widened her eyes. "Oh."

"Sorry. I should've..." Kent shook his head. "I didn't—"

"What should I do?"

Kent watched James for a moment. "Take the blindfold off, but have him close his eyes unless he needs to use his safe word."

She mulled it over, then nodded and returned to James's side. "I'm going to take this off, but you're going to close your eyes unless you need to use a safe word. Understood?"

"Yes."

She slid the blindfold off, and James released his breath. Guilt hit Kent in the gut—he should've remembered James might be iffy about blindfolds. Especially while lying on his back. Even years later, getting water-boarded in training had that effect on people.

"You okay?" Carlene asked James.

"Yeah." James's eyes were closed, but not super tight. His fingers hands rested at his sides, his fingers moving a little, but not quite so nervously.

Carlene turned to Kent again, eyebrows up as if to ask if it was okay to proceed. He nodded.

She picked up the Wartenberg wheel and played with the pinwheel, pressing it with her fingers, spinning it, rolling it across her own skin. The sound was subtle—little metallic creaks and squeaks—but James's muscles twitched and tensed. With his eyes closed, his other senses would be extra alert, so he probably heard every tiny sound while his imagination thought of a million different things that might happen once those spikes touched him. And a million different *places* where they might touch him.

Kent grinned. Carlene was obviously getting a feel for the implement before she put it on her husband's skin, but she'd noticed his discomfort, and she started capitalizing on it. Spinning the wheel harder so it would squeak louder. Leaning closer to him and rolling it across her own arm.

Kent cleared his throat. She turned, and he gestured like he was running his fingers across his arm, then pointed at James. The wicked grin that spread across her lips went straight to Kent's balls—confident or not, she was definitely getting into this.

Carlene spun the wheel enough to make a high buzzing sound, and before that had even begun to slow, she reached for James with her free hand and let her fingertips brush just beneath his navel.

James damn near came up off the bed, and Kent damn near came unglued. Carlene did it again, trailing her fingertips along James's hipbone, and her husband gripped the sheets, his knuckles whitening and every muscle in his torso contracting beneath her soft touch.

Then she brought the Wartenberg wheel closer to his chest. Just before she touched the spines to his skin, though, she hesitated.

Kent's heart skipped. *Come on, Carlene. Come on, you've got this.*

He opened his mouth to encourage her out loud, but then she flipped the Wartenberg wheel around in her hand, holding it like a pen, and drew its metal end—its undoubtedly *cold* metal end—around James's nipple.

James sucked in a breath, and his back arched. His teeth snapped shut, and Kent chuckled. *Almost let something slip out, did you?* But he was getting the hang of it. Though his senses were probably all kinds of overwhelmed right then, he remembered that he wasn't allowed to speak.

Carlene drew little circles and swirls all over his chest and stomach. The metal was probably starting to get warmer now, and he didn't jump quite like he had on first contact.

Not until she flipped the wheel over again.

And rolled the spikes just above his hipbone.

James gasped so hard, he clapped his hand over his mouth like he'd *just* stopped himself from letting go of more than a stifled, strangled moan. His eyes flew open for a split second, but he quickly squeezed them shut.

Carlene turned to Kent again and gestured at her eyes.

Kent waved his hand and shook his head. *Let it go.* There was that learning curve again, and that momentary lapse had probably reminded James he wasn't blindfolded—that his sight was relinquished voluntarily and was always a blink away—so this time, it could slide.

Carlene nodded. Facing James again, she held the Wartenberg wheel over James's torso, hovering here, then there, as if trying to decide where to put it down this time. On his nipple. On abs that were so tense they were nearly shaking. On his rapidly rising and falling chest.

She settled on drawing a soft fingertip along the lower edge of his rib cage, and as soon as he started squirming from that, she let the wheel drag across the same place, and Kent almost let go of a groan himself. Taunting a submissive's senses, not letting him make a sound—goddamn, he needed to play the role of Dom more often.

"You know," Carlene said, "this might be easier with an extra set of hands." She held up the cat toy and raised her eyebrows at Kent.

Oh hell yes...

He joined them on the bed and took the toy from her.

James shifted a bit, holding on to handfuls of the sheets.

"You get the fun one," Kent said. "But I think I can have fun with this one too." He tickled James's abs with the dangling cat toy, and the way those muscles tightened gave him goose bumps.

"Hmm, yeah, that one looks like fun." Carlene flashed another grin. "But this one is just cool..." She ran the wheel down the center of his abs, and Kent drew the soft cat toy over his nipples. James's jaw clenched, and he squeezed his eyes shut tighter.

Together, they tortured him for what might as well have been hours. Kent countered every spiny touch of the wheel with a soft brush of the cat toy, and Carlene punctuated every featherlight caress with a stroke of cold spikes. By this point, James wasn't hard anymore, but that was to be expected—he was too far into an entirely different state of mind to be aroused in that way. Kent didn't have a single doubt James was enjoying this, erection or not, especially since he was millions of miles away from all his pressure and responsibilities. His mind was almost certainly focused solely on sensations and anticipation. There was no room for wars, budgets, politics. The only decision he had to make was whether or not to obey, and even that one was a no-brainer—especially in this state, Kent doubted James *could* disobey either of them. He was too far gone, too pliable. Good thing he had a Domme and a Dom he could trust implicitly. There were unscrupulous people out there who'd take advantage of a man like this, but not here. Not tonight. James's seemingly effortless surrender left him in the hands of two people who'd make sure he was safe until he came back to earth.

"Think he's had enough?" Carlene's voice was soft, but it was enough to make James jump. She and Kent both stroked James's arms, easing him back into reality.

"Yeah, I think he has," Kent said.

They set the toys aside and pulled the comforter up over James, and then lay on either side of him, both on top of the covers.

After he'd come down a little bit, James rubbed a hand over his sweaty face. "Holy shit."

"Doing okay?" Carlene asked.

James nodded. "Yeah. Just didn't realize how intense that kind of thing would get."

"Yeah, it looked like it was quite a ride." She paused. "What about blindfolds? Is that a no-go, or…?"

James hesitated. "It's…not a no-go, but I might have to work up to it."

"Fair enough." Kent ran his fingers along James's arm. "You don't have to do it at all, though. If you're not—"

"No, I'd like to. Just…a little at a time."

"Good idea."

"Why don't I go get some water?" Carlene smoothed his hair. "You look like you could use some."

James smiled and stroked his wife's cheek. "Thank you."

She smiled back, leaned down to kiss him lightly and then got up. "Kent, what about you?"

"I'm okay. Thanks."

She slipped out of the room, and James was quiet for a little while. Probably settling back to earth after flying like that.

Eventually, he broke the silence. "You just had to give her that demonic thing, didn't you?"

"Demonic thing? What—oh, the Wartenberg wheel."

"The what-enberg wheel?"

"Wartenberg wheel." Kent picked it up off the nightstand where he'd left it after they'd decided to give James a break. He held it up.

James took it. He thumbed the wheel, turned it a bit, then shook his head and handed it back. "That thing is weird."

"Weird good? Or weird bad?"

"Just weird." He handed the wheel back. "But I did like it. In kind of a…"

"A weird way?"

"Yeah."

They both fell silent. Kent glanced at the door Carlene had gone through, and as he ran the backs of his fingers up James's arm, he said, "You really did pick a gorgeous woman."

"Believe me, I know." James laughed quietly. "Except she picked me."

"Did she? I thought you guys met in a bar."

"We did. I was sitting at the bar with some of the guys, and she walked up and said we were going to dance."

"Oh yeah. You told me about that." Kent paused. "And somehow we're both surprised she does this dominant thing so well."

"Hmm, yeah. Good point."

"Good point about what?" Carlene's voice turned their heads as she stepped into the room with two bottles of water.

James chuckled. "We're both just surprised at how surprised we are that you're so good at this."

She arched an eyebrow, and James's breath hitched, but then she laughed. "Yeah, I still can't believe I like it this much." She joined him on the bed, lying beside him, opposite Kent. She reached up and drew a fingertip along the edge of his jaw. "I wish I'd known about this side of you a long time ago." With a grin, she added, "Guess I'll just have to make up for lost time."

James gulped. "Yes, please."

Chapter Seventeen

Long after they'd returned to their bedroom, Carlene and James were wide awake. The bedside light glowed, and they lounged in their bed, talking like they hadn't done since they were dating a lifetime ago. Age-old walls were gone. They hadn't crumbled, they hadn't fallen down, they were just...gone. As if they'd never been there before. And suddenly, Carlene and her husband were wrapped up in each other's arms beneath the sheets, tired and satisfied but not quite ready to let the evening end.

Carlene ran her fingers through his graying hair. "Do you mind if I ask about some things we've never talked about?"

"Depends." He trailed the backs of his fingers down her cheek. "What about?"

"I'm curious about you and Kent. Your, um, history together."

James's hand stopped but didn't lift away. "I thought you didn't want to know about that."

"I didn't before. But now I'm kind of curious."

He swallowed. For a moment, she thought he might close off and change the subject, but instead he said, "What do you want to know?"

"Well, was he your first man?"

"No. That guy was... He was at the Academy." James's eyes turned distant.

Carlene's stomach tightened—had she turned their lovely conversation into something awkward? "You don't have to answer. I'm just curious."

"No, no, it's okay." He shook himself. "Just haven't thought about him in a while." He met her gaze. "Are you sure you want to know about all of this now?"

Carlene lifted herself onto her forearms and met his gaze. "Look, when we first started dating, I wasn't sure about being with a bi guy. I guess I felt kind of,

I don't know, threatened by it." Her cheeks burned. "And maybe a bit...put off."

"Put off?"

"Yeah. I wasn't sure how I felt about two guys together." She flashed him a grin. "Turns out it's pretty hot."

James laughed and rubbed his hand up and down her arm. "You don't say."

"Hey, I was a little slow on that one." She paused. "Not quite sure I missed how hot Kent is, though."

His eyebrows shot up. "Oh *really?*"

Her face was on fire now. "You have good taste in men, I guess."

James laughed again, and a little color rose in his cheeks. "Why do you think I joined the SEALs?"

"Are you serious?"

"Well...sort of." The color deepened. "That's what got me thinking about the SEALs, and the more I looked into actually becoming one, the more I thought, hey, this is me. But yes, it may have started with a few, uh, impure thoughts."

"Guess I can't really judge. I didn't exactly hang around in bars near Little Creek for the atmosphere."

A laugh burst out of James, and he kissed her cheek. "Objectifying our nation's finest, eh?"

She eyed him. "Doesn't sound like I was the only one."

"Guilty."

"Mmhmm. So, the guy at the Academy?"

"Oh, right. Him." James gazed up at the ceiling, eyes unfocused. "God, I can't believe how long it's been."

"Wasn't I in high—"

"Yeah, yeah, yeah." He chuckled, eyelids sliding closed. After a moment, he went on, "I met him my sophomore year."

"What was his name?" she asked, barely whispering.

"Vance." James paused, eyes still closed, and his jaw moved a little as if he were rolling the name around in his mouth. "Cadet Vance. His first name was..." James shook his head. "To be honest, I don't even remember. We all just called him that." He shifted a bit, pushing himself up onto his elbow. "The thing is, I'd known since high school that I was into both guys and girls, but I thought I had to choose between them. I didn't realize… I didn't understand bisexuality. Generally speaking, I was more attracted to girls, so I tried to ignore guys because I didn't want to give up girls." James laughed softly, almost humorlessly. He scrubbed a hand over his face. "It sounds stupid now."

"Not really. I don't think I understood it until I met you." She chewed her lip. "Or really, until very, very recently."

Their eyes met, and some of the tension in his features eased. "You're one of the few women who was willing to accept it. Or overlook it."

That didn't surprise her. Long before she'd met James, she'd known how her female friends felt about men who slept with other men, and so she'd never breathed a word about his bisexuality. And, in truth, she'd been embarrassed to say anything. She hadn't been comfortable with it. She'd turned up her nose at it. But she hadn't told them, and she hadn't told him, because, weird sexuality notwithstanding, she really liked James, so she'd ignored it.

Which all seemed stupid now, but there it was.

James went on. "Anyway, Vance. So I was at the Academy, surrounded by hot, young, fit men. I'd decided in high school that I was only going to date and sleep with women, but damn, being at that place…" He whistled and shook his head. "Then I crossed paths with this senior, and he was… God, he was just…"

"You had a little crush, did you?"

"You could say that. And Vance caught on too. He was my roommate, and we had some classes together, and some mutual friends, so we saw a lot of each other, and I guess he started noticing that I'd get all googly-eyed whenever that other guy was around. Thank God he was the only one who noticed, or at least the only one who said anything. And he was discreet—he waited until we were in our room one night." James paused for a long moment, as if remembering that night, that conversation. Softly, he continued, "When he admitted he had a thing for one of the football players, I was confused because he had a girlfriend back home."

"So he was bi?"

James nodded. "That, or his girlfriend was a beard."

"A what now?"

"A beard. A girl who a gay guy dates so people think he's straight."

"Oh." She quirked her lips. "You learn something new every day, don't you?"

"No kidding." James chuckled but quickly turned serious again. "Anyhow, he was definitely into men, and he swore me to secrecy, since that could get him kicked out of the Navy. I guess he thought I was a safe confidant since I was apparently queer too." James blew out a breath. "Looking back, he was taking a huge risk. I've known a lot of guys who would get defensive as fuck if someone thought they were gay, and anyone else might've gone running to our superiors and ended his career."

"Or beaten the hell out of him," she said quietly.

James grimaced. "Exactly."

"But you didn't rat him out. So what happened?"

"I admitted I was into men and women, and didn't know what that meant, and that was the first time anyone ever told me about bisexuality." His eyes lost focus again, as if he'd gone back to that time and place for a moment. Gaze still distant, he said, "And suddenly Vance wasn't just this good-looking guy who slept a few feet away from me. He was…an option. He was someone who could possibly look at me the way I was looking at that other guy, and that made him so attractive, I could barely hang around him."

"But you were roommates, right?"

"Yeah. So I didn't have much choice. It was a bit awkward for a while. But then he called his girlfriend one night, and she just…dumped him. Out of nowhere. Decided she was tired of the long-distance thing, and she didn't want to be a military wife after all, and that was that."

"Poor guy."

"Seriously. He was devastated. And pissed off. He needed an outlet, but going out drinking wasn't an option, so he turned to the next best thing."

"You?"

James nodded. "One minute he was crying. The next he was ready to put a fist through the wall. The next…" He swallowed hard. "The next he was begging to suck my dick."

Carlene shifted a bit. "So, did he?"

"Oh yeah. And I…reciprocated. After that, we fooled around any chance we had. That went on until we graduated, and then we ended up going to opposite ends of the country and just kind of drifted apart. We stayed in touch for a long time, but just as friends."

"Do you ever…" She hesitated, not sure if she wanted to broach the subject now.

"Hmm?"

She chewed her lip, absently playing with the edge of his pillowcase. "Did you ever worry something like that would come out during the election? That Vance might go to the press or something?"

James's expression darkened, and as he shook his head, he sighed. The words were barely audible, "I can say with a hundred percent certainty that he'll never talk to the press about it."

Carlene didn't push. That was the same tone James used on the rare occasion he talked about Joker or Smitty—she didn't need him to spell out why he was so sure of Vance's silence, so she quickly changed the subject. "What about you and Kent? How did things get started between you two?"

At that, James laughed. "To be honest?" He reached up and smoothed her hair. "We'd known each other for quite a while, but the way we got started was along the same lines of how they got started with you."

She tilted her head. "So, what? You were drunk in a bar full of SEALs, he told you he wanted to dance, and you ended up making out in the backseat of a taxi?"

James shivered, and she wasn't sure if it was at the memory of the night he met her or the night he met Kent. Maybe both. "Well… DADT was in effect, so there was no dancing involved, and it was the men's room instead of the backseat of a taxi, but…"

"You made out in the men's room?" She blinked. "In a bar full of SEALs with DADT in effect?"

He chuckled. "Well, we *were* drunk…"

"I imagine they all were too."

"*Oh* yeah."

"Did anyone find out?"

James shrugged. "Don't know, to be honest. I think some of the guys on our team knew I was into men, and I think some knew he was. And they knew we were damned close. If anyone ever put the pieces together, though, they never said a word." He disappeared into his own thoughts for a moment before he went on. "Our relationship—if you could call it that—was weird. I never thought of him as a boyfriend, aside from that one time we tried actually dating, but we were…"

"Friends with benefits?"

"In a way, yeah. Except it was kind of…more than that."

"How so?"

James studied her. "Are you sure you want to get into this?"

Carlene nodded. "I'm curious. There's obviously a history between you guys, and with what we're doing now…"

"Right. But if it's too much information, I—"

"I'll use the safe word if this gets too deep."

James laughed, then shrugged. "Fair enough." He cleared his throat. "Basically, we kept each other sane. Sometimes it was just fun. We were bored or drunk, and we…well, we did a lot of crazy things, I guess. He was the only guy who knew I liked women and didn't get jealous. Hell, we had the same taste in women."

"Did you guys ever…" She bit her lip.

James cocked his head. "What?" His eyebrow arched. "Did we ever share women?"

"Yeah."

James held her gaze, as if wondering whether he should answer the question. "Yeah. A lot, actually."

"Really?"

"Yeah. It was…" James's cheeks colored again. "It sounds kind of fucked-up to tell my wife this."

"I'm curious. I haven't used the safe word yet."

"True." He took a breath. "One of our favorite things to do together was take a woman to bed and show her the time of her life. Two men completely focused on her."

"That…" Carlene licked her lips. "That sounds kind of hot, actually."

James's eyes widened. "It does?"

"Well, yeah." She grinned. "I imagine you two made those women quite happy."

James stared at her incredulously, but then chuckled. "Well, we thought so." His eyes unfocused, and he absently stroked her hair. "So sometimes it was that, sometimes we were drunk and bored, and sometimes…" James swallowed. "The thing is, when some missions were over, you could just drink them off and move on, but some of them…" That dark expression returned, and he barely whispered, "Sometimes it wasn't that simple."

Carlene's skin prickled. James didn't talk about his combat experience much. Not even the things he was allowed to discuss. Some therapy a few years back had helped him manage the PTSD for the most part, but he preferred not to discuss the things he'd seen and done.

James inhaled slowly. "Sleeping together, it was kind of a way to remind ourselves we were alive. It was a way of telling each other, hey, I've got your back." He idly traced a wrinkle in the sheet with his fingertip. "When you got back from a real bad mission, sex like that sure beat the hell out of sleeping alone or with some stranger who didn't know or care where you'd been."

"So it was therapeutic. Sort of like what we're doing now."

"Kind of, yeah." He met her eyes through his lashes and gently closed his hand around hers. "I didn't realize why I needed it then until I realized what I need now. And thank you. Between the two of you, I might actually stay sane."

She smiled. "Thank God. Because I was worried sick about you."

"I know." He tucked a few strands of hair behind her ear. "But make no mistake—I need you, Carlene. Whatever this is we're all doing together, it's amazing, and I love it. If I had to choose between this and you, though—"

"I'm not asking you to choose. I want you to be happy, and if this is what you need, then it's what I'll happily give you."

He searched her eyes. "But you're afraid of something."

Carlene lowered her gaze.

James tipped her chin up. "I know this wasn't easy for you. Letting Kent into our bedroom. If you're worried about something, talk to me."

She hesitated. But then, hadn't they learned the hard way in the past about letting things fester until they were unbearable? Until a minor conflict turned into World War III?

"You've known Kent a long time," she said. "You guys have been through things, and you've come back from blowups that would've ended any other relationship or friendship. I know there's a bond there, and I guess... I guess sometimes I'm afraid that bond is stronger than what we have."

James's eyebrows shot up. "What? No. No way." He ran a hand up her arm. "Kent and I have a history, but me and you, we're... I mean, we're a *family*. There's a reason I married you and had kids with you, and none of that has anything to do with him."

Carlene gnawed the inside of her cheek. "Whatever you and Kent had, it's withstood a lot more than what we have."

"That's only because I've known him longer."

"I know. And that's part of what I'm afraid of. He's been around longer. You and he have been through things I can't even imagine."

James touched her face. "You and I have been through things *he* can't imagine. Just because we've never been to combat together..." He shook his head. "Carlene, it doesn't matter. I don't *want* to weather anything without you." He stroked her cheek with the pad of his thumb. "The fact that you were willing to bring in Kent in the first place..." His palm warmed the side of her face. "That's going above and beyond."

"It's what you needed."

"And how many women would have been able to accept that?" He pushed himself up a bit and kissed her softly. Settling back on the pillow, he held her gaze. "Can I be completely honest about something?"

"Please do."

He absently combed his fingers through her hair. "I won't lie and tell you that I don't love Kent, or that I never did."

Carlene didn't let herself wince. She knew, and she understood, but it was still hard to hear.

James trailed the backs of his fingers down her cheek. "Do you know what made me realize I was in love with you?"

Wordlessly, she shook her head.

"When I woke up one morning, and the first person I thought of wasn't him." He drew her closer. "It was you. That…hadn't happened to me in a long time. And then it happened the next morning, and the one after that."

She wasn't quite sure how to take that. "So I was the first to distract you from him?"

"No, no. It…" James exhaled. "It's hard to explain. It was like, my feelings for him hadn't changed, but my feelings for you were…" He shook his head. "All I knew was I didn't want to let you go. I knew you were different." He caressed her face again. "And after all the hell you've been through because of me, you're not only still here, but you let him in, even though I know that was hard for you."

"I didn't know what else to do," she whispered.

"I know you didn't." He pressed a soft kiss to her forehead. "And I'm sorry I pushed you to that point. But if anything, this has all driven home one thing that I've known for a long time."

"What's that?"

"That I would be fucking stupid to ever let you go."

Chapter Eighteen

Kent wasn't as young as he used to be. Long gone were the days of fucking someone senseless and still having enough stamina left to do it all over again before sunrise. Something about turning forty and all that shit.

But tonight, as he tried to sleep across the hall from James and Carlene, he was restless. And horny. And so goddamned hard. One mind-blowing orgasm at the hands of the most amazing man alive—and the most beautifully submissive, obeying his wife's order to suck Kent off—and now Kent was turned on as if his body thought he was still twenty.

It had taken him years to figure out this dominance/submission thing, and even longer to make the connection to his dynamic with James. Now that he had, his whole body responded to the mere thought of James on his knees.

The icing on the cake was that James wasn't just his team leader and fellow SEAL anymore. He was the president of the United States. Arguably the most powerful man in the world. While that power was a burden and a source of unimaginable stress for James, Kent couldn't help but be turned on by it.

Because there was nothing in the universe hotter than a man with that much power getting down on his knees. Kneeling at Kent's feet, completely focused on obedience and surrender and beautiful submission—willingly and gratefully offering up the most profound power exchange Kent had ever experienced.

Kent squirmed beneath his sheets. Thinking about it wasn't going to help his hard-on, but he strongly suspected there wasn't much that would, aside from addressing it directly. He did need to sleep tonight, so he slid his hand under the covers, and hissed sharply as his fingers brushed his own dick—it hadn't been that long since the last time he'd come, and every nerve ending was hypersensitive.

Thank God he kept lube beside his bed for just such an occasion. He put some on his palm and gently wrapped his hand around his cock again, startling at the coolness, but the lube warmed quickly. As he started stroking, he couldn't help groaning into the silence. As those already overwhelmed nerve endings came to life all over again, his mind went back to earlier, showing him the most delicious mental porno he'd ever seen.

Kent closed his eyes, and all he saw was everything they'd done tonight. Carlene teasing James with the Wartenberg wheel. James on his knees and flying through space at his wife's feet. James blowing him at his wife's command. He saw that look in James's eyes—longing, begging, grateful, desperate, completely surrendered—and a shudder went through him. And then another. And even still, his orgasm seemed to come out of nowhere, lifting his back off the bed and drawing a strangled moan from his lips as all the tension broke. Semen coated his hand and landed on his stomach, and he kept stroking until it was too fucking intense, and then he sank back down to the mattress to catch his breath. Holy shit.

As his mind slowly cleared, he saw that image again, the one that had driven him over the edge and into a powerful, toe-curling orgasm. Jesus, but that look on James's face was sexy.

Kent opened his eyes. His stomach knotted.

Yeah, that look was sexy, and it wasn't just a fantasy. It was what he'd seen just an hour or two ago, but there was no pretending it had been for him. Not this time. Not even while James had been sucking Kent's dick. In fact, it was entirely possible James had forgotten that anyone besides Carlene even existed, including Kent. For all intents and purposes, Kent had been as material as the Wartenberg wheel—a tool with which James could demonstrate his eager obedience to his wife.

That was how it should've been—a sub so totally focused on his Domme that the rest of the world faded into irrelevance. It meant Carlene had struck the right chord. Dominated him exactly the way he needed.

Which was perfect. With a little more fine-tuning, Carlene would be able to give James the escape that he desperately needed in order to balance his presidential responsibilities with his sanity. James would be back on an even keel. He'd be able to do his job. His marriage would be on the right track again.

And Kent…

Kent would exit stage left and leave them to it. That had been the plan from the beginning. He'd known it, they'd known it and there'd never been any question about it.

Kent just hadn't bargained for how hard it would be. He hadn't thought about how much it would hurt to watch James submit to someone else. Especially knowing that once Carlene found her stride, she wouldn't need Kent's guidance anymore. Once she knew what she was doing and the two-on-one novelty wore off, there'd be no place for him.

He winced. Gazing into the darkness, he tried to tell himself that wasn't a guarantee, even though he'd known from the start that it was. How the hell had he fooled himself into believing, even for a second, that this would end well? Maybe he'd hoped Carlene was right, that James really did need him. But it wasn't Kent that James needed, and that was for the best. A man needed his wife, not an on-again, off-again ex-lover.

Kent sighed and rubbed his eyes. Reality was a bitch, but it was just that—reality. No amount of bargaining with James, Carlene, God or the Devil would change a damned thing.

A smart man would've walked at that point. Carlene had a reasonably solid grasp on dominating James. They were moving in the right direction, and he could bow out gracefully now and save himself a hell of a lot of pain in the future.

But you're not going to do that, are you, Sinclair?

Of course he wasn't. He didn't even try to talk himself into it. This was the chance of a lifetime, one that would never happen again. For the moment, the Brodericks seemed to want and—maybe as a mentor more than a lover—need him, and that was the closest he was ever going to get to James. It would hurt in the end when they decided they could handle things on their own and didn't need him there anymore, but that was a bridge he'd cross when he got there. Maybe this was what it was like to sell your soul. It seemed like a bargain at the time, and the benefits were incredible, but the moment the Devil came to collect, a man learned the meaning of the word *regret*.

Maybe it was, maybe it wasn't. All Kent knew was that for now, he had a place beside James. He could touch him, fuck him, be with him, and he'd savor every opportunity that arose between now and…and the day when those opportunities went away.

But God help him when that day came.

Chapter Nineteen

All things considered, James hadn't felt this good in ages. What Kent and Carlene did to him was nothing short of magic. They wouldn't be able to do it often—traveling, schedules and sheer exhaustion didn't leave much room for breathless quickies with his wife, never mind kinky nights with her and his head of security.

He didn't need much, though. One night would leave his knees raw and his body aching, and without fail, he slept like the dead whenever they were done with him. The next morning, he'd wake up clear and focused, and the effect lingered, especially when Kent or Carlene—or both—were nearby. When his mind started to get scattered, or the stress started to tighten every muscle in his body, when he'd reached that situation point where he couldn't even choose which shirt to put on, one glance from either of them would bring him back down. Center him. Remind him that he'd only have to cope a little longer before they'd give him the escape he craved.

James's duties being what they were, though, finding some time to discreetly slip away with Kent and Carlene was easier said than done. And of course, now that he'd found a way to deal with the stress of his job and the huge responsibilities, the universe decided to fuck with him and make sure he didn't have time for any kind of relaxation. These things always seemed to come in waves, and that wave just had to start *now*.

A few days after the threesome was yet another meeting about the situation in South America. Starting that afternoon, James was thrown into an exhausting week of flying every which direction in between returning for *more* meetings about the crisis. Sometimes with the committee members, sometimes with their respective staffers. Through it all, he barely had time to think about sex, and what little downtime he had was spent sleeping.

Kent and Carlene were run ragged too—Kent had to be wherever James was, and he definitely wasn't as young as he used to be. He was always bright-eyed and diligent when he was on duty, but the second someone relieved him, exhaustion took over. On two separate flights, he was out cold before Air Force One had even taxied to a runway.

And Carlene had mostly stayed stateside, traveling to her own engagements around the country in between taking care of the kids.

Today, he realized just how right Kent and Carlene had been about him. How centered and focused he'd felt the morning after the night with them, and how centered and focused he *didn't* feel now.

But there was no time, there was no privacy, and the pressure was building.

No matter how desperately he needed some time alone with his two lovers, duty called, and when he hit the end of that week that he'd given Congress, there was no escape—the committee had a budget, and now he had to make a decision.

Several South American leaders called a meeting in Mexico City to discuss the next step, which would most likely be joint combat operations. Everyone was still holding out hope for a peaceful resolution of sorts, but with ruthless drug cartels involved, it wasn't likely. James just prayed like hell that the SEALs finished the job, because they were running out of time.

Early in the morning the day before the meeting, accompanied by Carlene and Kent and the usual entourage of staff and security, James headed to the air base where Air Force One was waiting to take them to Mexico. It was the usual routine—getting on base, boarding the plane, the long flight, landing in a place he'd never been before, smiling for cameras, being greeted by heads of state. By the time they were on their way to the luxury—and insanely secure—hotel, he was exhausted and queasy from the pressure, especially with a doomsday clock ticking and Congress tapping its collective foot.

In the limo, he leaned forward and rubbed his neck with both hands.

Carlene squeezed his shoulder. "You all right?"

He didn't have an answer. He was all right, and he wasn't all right, and he wasn't entirely sure which way was up. There was so much riding on this summit, and so few options to resolve the situation peacefully.

Carlene squeezed his shoulder harder, almost enough to make it hurt.

James sat up and met her gaze.

Something in her expression…changed. The shift was subtle, probably nothing anyone but him would have noticed—her eyes were narrow, the corner of her mouth turned up just so.

James swallowed.

She took his hand, her grip firm. Then her eyes flicked toward Kent, who sat across from them beside another agent. The other agent was looking at his phone and seemed oblivious to the silent exchange going on around him.

Kent flashed her that wicked grin of his. Then Carlene faced James again, and she spoke so softly that he doubted anyone else heard her. "How are you feeling?"

"Tired."

"*How* tired?"

Her eyebrow arched, and his heart skipped.

"Um…"

She sat beside him. "I think you need to clear your head before tomorrow."

"Yeah. I think so too." He paused. "Any ideas?"

The look in her eye sent his body temperature soaring. "Yes, as a matter of fact." She put her arm around his waist, kissed his cheek and whispered, "After everyone is settled in and we have the suite to ourselves, you have ten minutes to take a shower and be waiting for us."

He gulped. "Ten—"

"Ten minutes."

James's pulse shot up.

"Understood?"

James glanced at Kent, who still grinned. At the other agent, who still didn't notice. Back at Carlene, who raised her eyebrows.

He nodded. "Y-yeah. Understood."

"Good." She smiled and squeezed his leg, then sat back against the seat as if nothing were going on.

James barely kept himself from adjusting the front of his pants. No sense drawing any attention. He didn't dare look at his wife or head of security either, so he stared out the window at the passing scenery.

This was a country he'd never visited, scenery he'd never seen before, but he couldn't even drink it in or make sense of it. He also couldn't think about why he was here or what would happen tomorrow.

All he could think was, *Drive faster...*

Naturally, James didn't have time.

The minute they arrived at the hotel, their hotel suite was a flurry of activity. Secret Service had already inspected it for surveillance equipment, bugs or anything else that could pose a threat to James. Then staff members flooded in with luggage while advisers hammered James with questions about tomorrow's summit. Finally, though, everyone left so he and Carlene could rest for a while before they had to meet with all the heads of state for a formal presummit dinner.

But before James could even loosen his tie, there was a sharp knock at the door.

He groaned. "What now?"

Carlene scowled on her way to see who it was. "This had better be important."

She opened the door.

Admiral Stein.

Shit. It *was* important.

Carlene didn't stick around—she knew these conversations were above top secret. Kent too stepped out into the hall, leaving James and the admiral alone.

James's heart sped up. "Any news from the team?"

Stein nodded. "The Venezuelan cartel is doing its damnedest to keep word from getting out, but we've confirmed that three of the eight top officials are dead, and four more are in custody."

James slowly released a breath. "And the last one?"

The admiral chuckled. "Ran off into the trees like a goddamned coward." Turning serious, he added, "We've got boys on his tail, though. He can run, but he can't hide."

"What about the Colombian situation?"

The admiral's face fell. "We're awaiting word. There were some…setbacks."

James's chest tightened. "What kind of setbacks?" Because God knew that could mean anything.

"Don't know yet." The admiral shook his head. "We've lost contact with them, but they may have gone dark on purpose."

"Let's hope." James folded his arms tightly. "The summit is in less than twelve hours. I've bought as much time as I can—if I can't confirm that the cartels have been removed, we're looking at a military mobilization." He exhaled hard. "I want the teams on standby to pull out if necessary. Get their transports in position, and have them ready to fall back on a moment's notice. I don't want them in there if bombs start falling."

"Understood," the admiral said. "They're close, though. Assuming nothing has gone catastrophically wrong, there's time for them to neutralize the cartel without the need for war. Not much time, but it's what we've got."

"I know." James swallowed. "The second you hear anything, I want to know about it. Day or night."

"Absolutely, sir."

The admiral left, and Carlene and Kent returned. Finally—*finally*—everyone was gone except for those two.

There was precious little time, but they had some privacy now. So, true to her word, Carlene turned to James and nodded toward the bathroom. "Ten minutes."

James didn't hesitate. His mind was in a million different places, but he was damn sure going to seize the opportunity to let Kent and Carlene send him out of his mind for a little while. With tomorrow looming, with the clock ticking down to a war he was scared couldn't be avoided, he needed all the distraction he could get.

He hurried into the suite's massive bathroom and didn't bother taking in the luxurious surroundings. There'd be time for that later, when his wife and bodyguard weren't tapping their watches in the other room.

He quickly stripped out of his clothes and took one of those superfast showers he'd learned to take in the military. Soap, rinse, shave, done. All the while, he was vaguely aware of the fatigue in his body, and the apprehension over tomorrow, and why he shouldn't have been in the mood for any of this, but Carlene had told him to shower and join them. And at least one body part wasn't too tired for it—he was half-tempted to jerk off just to relieve the insane tension, but there would no doubt be consequences for that.

So he got himself cleaned up and dried off, and then stepped out of the bathroom and into the bedroom. Kent and Carlene weren't there, but he doubted they'd gone far.

According to the clock on Carlene's side, he had two minutes to spare. He quickly turned down the bed, combed his fingers through his wet hair and then knelt beside the bed.

And waited.

Chapter Twenty

Kent watched from the sidelines as James went through preparations for the summit. After weeks of back and forth, with bombs and missiles pointed across borders, it came down to this. Representatives from all over South America were here in Mexico City, along with James and several other leaders and ambassadors. In T-minus thirty-some-odd minutes, they'd gather behind closed doors, and they'd either pull a peaceful strategy out of the ether, or James would be announcing to the American people tonight that the nation was once again at war.

James was getting it from all directions. Advisors, a couple of generals, the secretary of defense and a bunch of people in suits whom Kent had seen but couldn't readily identify. They grilled James, advised him, threw hypotheticals at him, warned him about this or that quirk from this or that ambassador, and at least two of them were loudly skeptical about one of the leaders' interpreters. At best, the guy sucked as a translator. At worst, he deliberately fucked things up. Either way, James was advised to take the man's comments with a grain of salt and demand clarification if anything seemed off.

In the middle of it all, with the knot of his tie pressed snugly against his throat and a lot less color in his face than he'd had earlier, James was holding it together, but barely. Kent knew him too well to believe that poker face. Panic was working its way into his posture and his expression—the creases deepening in his forehead, the straightening spine, the way his whitening knuckles gripped a handful of reports.

Subtly, Kent brushed James's arm with his elbow. James definitely felt it and must have known it was deliberate—otherwise that faint shiver was just a coincidence. Kent held his breath, hoping to God this worked the way he thought it would, rather than dangerously distracting James at the worst possible moment.

I'm here, James. Breathe.

James inhaled deeply, let it out slowly and then pushed his shoulders back.

It wasn't enough, though. This summit was too huge, the outcome too important, and subtle signals weren't cutting it. Not with all these people throwing questions and comments and God knew what else at him. In seconds, the nerves were working their way back into James's taut shoulders and clenched jaw.

While he had absolute faith that James could go into that meeting and knock it out of the park without any intervention, Kent knew better than anyone how to help him focus.

So, with a whispered a prayer that this wasn't a colossal mistake, Kent ignored the crowd of dignitaries and tapped James's shoulder. Their eyes met—*dear God, you are sweating bullets.*

Kent stood close to him and turned so no one would hear him or see his lips move, and quietly said, "Clear the room."

James faced him. "But we have to—"

"You heard me."

James's eyebrows jumped, and then his Adam's apple did too.

Oh yes. You heard me. And you're not going to argue, are you?

James coughed into his fist. He scanned the room, his expression betraying nothing, and for a moment, Kent thought he was going to tell him to get back against the wall with the rest of the agents.

But then, in his podium voice, James said, "I need a few minutes." Nodding toward the door, he added, "Alone."

Kent didn't move, but no one batted an eye. For a sitting president, "alone" was a relative term, and the Secret Service might as well have been James's own shadow.

Agent Perez hung back, but Kent waved him toward the door. The agent raised his eyebrows. Kent gave a slight nod. The agent shrugged and followed the others.

Behind the last straggler, Kent closed the door.

And just like that, the thickly crowded room was empty, and it was just Kent and James in a luxury hotel room. Voices thrummed faintly in the hallway, and there was noise coming in from the street below, but in here, it was quiet.

"What's going on?" James asked.

Kent started toward him. "You looked like you could use a break."

James laughed bitterly. "What I could use and what I can realistically get aren't necessarily—"

"Kneel."

James blinked. "Come again?"

"Kneel."

"I…" James stared at him. "Here? Right…right *now?*"

"I think I was clear."

James's lips parted and his eyes widened. "I'm mediating a goddamned *war* in"—he looked at his watch—"fifteen minutes."

Kent raised an eyebrow. "We shouldn't waste time, then, should we?"

James opened his mouth to protest but snapped his teeth shut. He studied Kent, disbelief etched in every line across his forehead, and Kent was pretty sure he was teetering between telling off his employee and obeying his Dom.

Almost a minute passed. Neither of them spoke. Neither moved.

But then, slowly, holding Kent's gaze the entire way, James went to his knees on the plush carpet.

Kent stood close to him, and he touched James's face. He didn't say a word—just gazed at him and stroked his cheek.

James fought it at first, and Kent didn't have to ask why. He was wound up and nervous, and he wasn't in the mood for this or anything else. Today was about preventing a war and protecting the lives of soldiers and civilians alike. It wasn't about sexual power play. It would be a defining moment in James's presidency, and the outcome would affect millions. This was no time for bedroom games.

But Kent just stood there, caressing James's face and gazing into his eyes the way he did when he was taking over for the night. All he had to do was wait for James to hand over the reins. James only had fifteen—fourteen—minutes. Kent had all the time in the world.

Something in James started to shift. The tension in his forehead melted away. He rested his hands on his thighs, and with each passing second, his shoulders sank a little farther.

And finally, he bowed his head, breaking eye contact and pressing his face against Kent's hand. The breath he released was long and slow, as if he'd been holding most of it this entire time.

"Good," Kent said softly, his voice barely carrying over the distant chatter coming from the hallway. "Just breathe."

For a couple of minutes, that was all James did—he knelt at Kent's feet, head bowed, and just…breathed. His eyes were probably closed, though Kent couldn't see them.

After a while, Kent pulled a chair out from the table covered in reports and folders, and he positioned it right in front of James. He took a seat, bringing himself closer to James's level while deliberately remaining above him. For a solid minute, he just stroked James's hair, and they both just breathed.

Finally, Kent put a hand on James's shoulder. "How do you feel right now?"

"Nervous." James lifted his chin and met Kent's eyes. "I'm freaking—"

"No." Kent pressed down on his shoulder. "How do you feel now? Kneeling in front of me."

James closed his eyes and exhaled. "Like I'm okay."

"Like you've got this?"

"Yeah. Exactly."

"Good. Remember this. Remember *exactly* how you feel right now." Kent let that sink in. He let James take a few slow, deep breaths, eyes still closed, and then whispered, "Look at me, James."

James's eyelids slid open.

"Do you like the way you feel?"

James nodded slowly.

"Commit it to memory. Got it?"

Another nod.

"You won't be able to see me during the meeting." He squeezed James's shoulder. "But I'll be there. I'll be right behind you, right where I always am." He paused. "So you'll be on your own, and I know you'll handle it fine."

James shivered.

Kent caressed his face with his other hand, keeping the first firmly on his shoulder. "When you start getting that panicked feeling, or you're overwhelmed, I want you to remember this. Understood?"

James swallowed. "I…think so?"

"Good." Kent smoothed James's hair. "I want you to remember this feeling, and when you do, I want you to remember that you don't have to be in control forever. That power and responsibility? It's temporary." He rested his hand on the back of James's neck and looked him straight in the eye, their faces inches apart. "It's temporary, and it's finite, and when this meeting is over, your wife and I will be waiting to take it off your shoulders and put you on your knees. Just like this."

James closed his eyes. The muscles beneath Kent's hand loosened slightly.

Kent softly kissed his forehead. "You've got this. And when it's over, we've got you."

James released another long, ragged breath. He lifted his gaze and met Kent's eyes. "Thank you."

Kent smiled. He touched James's chin with two fingers, and then leaned in for a light kiss. He let it linger for a moment—this wasn't the time or place to turn him on, but it was a damned good time and place to let him know he was safe, secure and loved.

Kent broke the kiss and stood, nudging the chair back as he did. He offered a hand to James, who accepted it, and Kent helped him to his feet.

James closed his eyes and took a deep breath. Then he opened them, and Kent's own breath nearly caught. He still had that vaguely glazed look, his pupils a little bigger than they normally would be under this light, but at the same time, he was clear and focused, and getting more so by the second.

Kent lifted his eyebrows. "Ready?"

James squared his shoulders. "Yeah. I'm ready."

Chapter Twenty-One

Carlene would've recognized that look from a mile away.

James eyes were bright and focused, his shoulders relaxed even though his spine was straight. Calm and collected even while he was nervous as hell—definitely better than the shaking wreck he'd been when she'd left him to his advisers earlier.

She didn't have to ask why. Not with Kent walking behind him.

Jealousy flared in her chest, but that wasn't the only thing heating up beneath her skin. They'd only been alone for a short time. What exactly had they done? Her mind's eye showed James sucking Kent off. Or Kent backing James up against a wall and stroking him off, whispering in his ear the whole time.

Neither of them had a hair out of place, though, and there wasn't a drop of sweat on either of their faces. They weren't even a little bit flushed. If they'd done anything, they'd done a damned good job of cleaning up afterward. There was no telling what exactly they'd done, but it had focused James and leveled him out. With everything on the line today, Carlene was more than a little grateful for that. And turned on by it, but acting on that would have to wait.

"Ready?" she asked, forcing a smile.

James nodded. "I think so, yeah."

"Of course you are." She kissed James on the cheek. "Good luck."

He smiled, gently turned her head toward him and pressed a soft kiss on her lips. Then, without another word, he let her go and headed toward the room where the summit would be held.

She met Kent's eyes. He offered nothing. No gloating, no apologies, no confessions, no denials. It was what it was.

Although jealousy lurked there in the center of her chest, she hoped to God that whatever Kent had done would carry James through this summit.

You've got this, James. You were born for this.

James was sweating, and it wasn't from the heat. The pressure was immense and getting worse by the minute. After three hours, the summit was heading very quickly in a direction they'd all tried so hard to avoid—war. With the cartels refusing to budge, the northern part of South America was in utter chaos. Cartels were battling cartels. The Colombian and Venezuelan militaries were in a chokehold—no one wanted to engage in a civil war, but soldiers who refused to obey were shot without hesitation. Something had to change, and if the SEALs couldn't dislodge the drug lords, then there weren't any other options. Even if they'd succeeded in Venezuela, Colombia couldn't be ignored.

The conversation shifted from avoiding the war to cooperative strategies to minimize civilian casualties. Peru and Ecuador weren't thrilled at the prospect of American warships along their coasts but, under the circumstances, were willing to allow it. Panama's leadership was grudgingly willing to allow nuclear warships through the Panama Canal, but with strict strings attached.

The president of Panama said something in rapid-fire Spanish. His interpreter opened her mouth to speak, but right then, the door opened.

Admiral Stein stepped into the room. The group fell silent and stared at him. He cleared his throat. "Pardon the interruption. Mr. President, a word?"

Every head turned toward James. His heart sped up—the admiral's expression offered nothing.

James rose, buttoning his jacket. "Excuse me for just a moment." He didn't wait for acknowledgment and hurried into the next room with the admiral.

Once all the security and Secret Service had cleared out of that room, Stein cut right to the chase. "We've just been contacted by the ops leader in Colombia."

James's heart was going a hundred miles an hour now. "And?"

Stein smiled. "The mission is complete. Every member of the cartel's leadership is dead or in custody, and those in custody are ready to surrender power back to the Colombian government."

James closed his eyes and pushed out a breath. "Thank God."

The admiral gave him a moment, as if to let the news sink in, and then asked, "What's our next move?"

"That depends on the summit," James said. "There's inevitably going to be chaos and the potential for violence until this all calms down, so I want ships en route to both countries. This is now a humanitarian effort, not a combat mobilization, and I want people and supplies on the ground ASAP."

"Yes, sir."

James dismissed him, and the man was already on his phone to Washington before they'd even left the room. While the admiral took care of getting ships to South America, James went back into the conference room and grinned. "Gentlemen, I have excellent news…"

While Carlene waited for the summit to end, her mind kept wandering back to those minutes during which Kent and James had been alone.

Good God. What if Kent hadn't figured out James's penchant for submission before today? James would be a nervous wreck. He'd still have made it through the negotiation—he always did—but she had no doubt he'd have come out looking like he was about to have a heart attack. It had always terrified her when he got sick after a meeting like that, and he always did.

But he'd never gone so calmly into this kind of meeting. Jealousy and insecurity aside, the fact was that Kent had done exactly what she'd asked him to—brought James back to earth, restored his sanity and given him what he needed to face his duties.

Thank you, Lord, for bringing that man into our lives.

She supposed there was something a little off about thanking the Christian God for the man who used gay sex and kinky mind games to center her husband, but, well, there it was.

The jealousy insisted on burning there in the back of her mind, but she pushed it away. They'd planned it this way from the start, hadn't they? Kent helping James with stress relief, behind closed doors and away from her? The fact that Kent had found a solution that included all of them didn't mean there couldn't be interludes like this, where James had a need and Kent had the answer.

It was all part of settling into this strange arrangement. She'd get used to it.

A burst of activity startled her out of her thoughts, and she looked up as the conference room doors flew open. James was one of the first to come out, and her heart raced. Like any other politician, he was good at faking a smile when he needed to, but she could always see the truth in his eyes, and when he turned to her, meeting her gaze from across the room, tears pricked at her own.

He was happy. Genuinely happy and visibly relieved. And he didn't run for the men's room to get sick.

What he did do was hurry across the hall and throw his arms around her. "It's over," he murmured. "We're not going to war."

Carlene's breath caught. "Are you serious?" Of course he was. He'd never joke about that, and he couldn't have faked his elation if he'd wanted to. But what else was she supposed to say?

"They're dragging us down to a press conference." He kissed her cheek and released her. "I have to go. But…it's over."

"Good. Well done." She squeezed his arm, and they exchanged smiles just before the mob of security and dignitaries herded him down the hall to another room. She followed, staying back with the wives of the other leaders and their own security details, and they stood off to the side during the press conference. Her heart was in her throat as the microphones were set up and the reporters waited impatiently for a statement. What had happened? It was over? How?

Finally, the conference began. Flanked by the rest of the summit attendees, James and two others stood at the podiums.

To the thrill—and applause—of everyone gathered, James and several Central and South American heads of state announced that the cartels had surrendered effective immediately.

James's voice was smooth and confident as he said, "Both nations have the full collective support of all of us as they work to reinstall their governments. The United States pledges to do everything in our power to ensure the transition back to peace is smooth, and I have ordered two battle groups of American ships to South American waters to aid in the process. With the help of our friends"—he gestured at the other dignitaries—"I'm completely confident this can be accomplished quickly and without further upheaval for the Colombian and Venezuelan people."

More applause, followed by more pledges for support and cooperation to make sure the damage done by the cartels was repaired.

The press conference was followed by a formal photo of the dignitaries, and there was to be a celebratory dinner that evening. Just like last night, they had a few short hours to get themselves rested and dressed for dinner, and the limo whisked James and his entourage back to the hotel.

As soon as they were in the room, Carlene dismissed everyone. "He needs some time to decompress. We'll be ready to leave at six o'clock."

James sank into a chair as Carlene closed the door behind the last stragglers. "It's over." He let his face fall into his hands, and Carlene thought his whole body was going to liquefy as his back slumped and he whispered again, "It's over."

She touched his shoulder. "You did it. I'm so proud of you."

He laughed dryly and lifted his head. "Other people did. I just stalled Congress and the summit long enough for them to get it done."

"Even still, you avoided a war."

He held her gaze and finally managed to smile before he rubbed his hand over his face again. "My God, I could sleep for a month right now."

"Maybe you should sleep, then. I think you've earned it."

"I need to—"

"James."

He faced her.

"Sleep." She nodded toward the bed. "There is nothing in the world you need to do right now that's more important than getting some sleep."

"Is that an order?"

Carlene eyed him. "Yes. Yes, it is."

He grinned and touched his forehead in a playful salute. "Yes, ma'am." Then he kissed her softly and headed toward the bed. He managed to get his jacket unbuttoned, but otherwise, when he collapsed on the bed, he was still fully dressed. He hadn't even taken off his shoes.

Carlene didn't say anything, though, and he wouldn't have heard her anyway—he'd barely settled onto the mattress before he was snoring softly.

She smiled down at him and gently stroked his hair. It didn't seem possible to wake him at this point, but she didn't want to take the chance, so she tiptoed away from the bed and out of their suite. Out in the hallway, she carefully shut the door behind her.

"How is he doing?" Kent's voice startled her.

She turned around and smiled. "He's wiped out, but he's good. Really good."

Kent nodded. "Good. And thank God he was able to play this game and draw things out long enough for them to get the job done."

"He was born for this, apparently." She sighed. "I'm just amazed this whole process didn't kill him."

"It didn't because he's damn lucky you stepped in and found a way to keep him sane until it was over."

"I'm glad it worked." She hesitated, then met his eyes. "Whatever you did before the summit, it must've helped."

"What we both did, Carlene. Last night?"

She shifted her weight. "But this morning, you—"

"It was both of us. Not just me." Kent exhaled. "I think he would've pulled it together either way and made it through the meeting, but anything either of us can do to help to keep him from losing his mind…"

Carlene nodded. "So, where do we go from here?" She folded her arms loosely. "I mean, it's only a matter of time before there's some other crisis."

"Agreed. Which means the stress will be there for the rest of his term."

"What do you suggest?"

"There's no reason we can't keep doing what we're doing for him." When she arched an eyebrow at him, he added, "We don't have to be rivals."

"But how does something like this play out?"

Kent shrugged. "One night at a time. We give him what he needs and play the whole thing by ear."

Carlene wasn't sure how she felt about playing it by ear when it came to bringing someone else into her marriage indefinitely. Especially when that someone else was *him*. But it had worked so far, and it had turned out far better than she'd anticipated when she'd approached him in the first place, so maybe she was overthinking it.

She met his gaze and nodded. "Okay. One night at a time."

Chapter Twenty-Two

After far too many weeks of far too much bullshit, the crisis in South America was over.

The Colombian and Venezuelan governments had returned to the capital cities and were slowly picking up the pieces. Per James's orders, contingents of American troops had gone into both countries on humanitarian missions to help restore the damaged infrastructure and keep peace while the governments found their footing. Not everyone was thrilled with that part, claiming it was an example of American imperialism and nothing more than a quiet invasion, but so far, everything was progressing in a civil fashion. It didn't hurt that someone leaked a few videos of sailors wheeling food, medical and building supplies down the ramp of an aircraft carrier onto a Venezuelan pier, or of Marines distributing the same to relieved locals.

There was still work to be done, but the worst was over. James could breathe again. And sleep, for that matter. At least until the next crisis, anyway.

Throughout the fiasco with Colombia and Venezuela, he'd allowed himself to be dragged to Camp David whenever the ball had been in someone else's court, and those little breaks had become fewer and farther between as time went on. By the time the crisis was officially over, James was exhausted, so when Carlene suggested taking the family on a real vacation, he didn't protest.

He was especially on board with it when a software billionaire with family in Colombia offered the First Family access to her private Hawaiian island.

"My mother's house had bullet holes in the windows," she'd told Carlene. "Now my nieces and nephews will be able to play outside again. My home is yours as long as you want it."

And so, for the first time since James started campaigning for office, the Broderick family would be miles away from cameras and cell phone reception. Of course the island would be teeming with Secret Service, and there'd be satellite phones in case James suddenly needed to return to the States, but they'd be, for all intents and purposes, alone. The press thought they were in the Caribbean, and some of the island's CCTV cameras had even been shut off to give the lens-weary family a break.

Before leaving, though, James had one more responsibility that he refused to delay. Flanked by uniformed personnel who would've been miles above his pay grade during his SEAL days, James followed a fluorescent-lit hallway into a windowless room in the basement of the Pentagon.

As soon as he stepped into the room, two dozen men with gold tridents on their chests snapped to attention and saluted him sharply.

James straightened too and returned the salute. He didn't waste any time going into the ceremony., Having received a few medals in secret ceremonies like this, it was surreal to be the one presenting them this time. Knowing how tedious these ceremonies could be, he kept his speech brief and to the point. He'd agonized over it longer than he did many of his speeches because he'd been there before, standing at attention while the president thanked his team for their service. He knew all too well how hard it was not to roll his eyes at political lip service coming from people who'd never even put on a uniform, and God help him, he did not want to sound like that to these men. Not when he'd been in their boots and had the scars to prove it.

As he moved from SEAL to SEAL, presenting their medals, he made sure to shake every hand and take the time to exchange a few words with each man. This ceremony was keeping them away from their families, who they were kept away from more than enough already—the least he could do was make them feel like it was worthwhile. They weren't terribly forthcoming with conversation, though. Nervous, maybe. He'd been to countless war zones himself, and he'd still gotten a bit tongue-tied the first time he met a president.

One commander gave him a firm handshake and quietly said, "It's a shame we couldn't do this in public, sir. My husband would have been thrilled to meet you."

Husband? God, times really *had* changed, hadn't they?

James smiled. "Tell you what, Commander. Arrange a White House tour, and I'll do my best to be there to meet you both personally." He looked around at the rest of the men. "That goes for all of you and your families. My SEAL brothers are always welcome in my house."

With that, some of the formality in the room lessened. The men smiled when he approached them, and for a little while, even dressed in a shirt and strangling necktie, he felt like he was one of them again.

By the time he left, he felt pretty fucking good. Even though the men couldn't speak of the ceremony, and they couldn't wear their medals or talk about the mission, he hoped he'd made an impression. He'd always been dubious of politicians who expressed how grateful they were for what he and his men did.

Hopefully, these men believed him. Because he knew, he understood and he couldn't begin to express his gratitude.

After all, this small roomful of men had prevented a war.

After hours on end of traveling—made worse by all the efforts to keep the First Family's whereabouts under wraps—they finally arrived on the billionaire's island.

The second they stepped off the private boat, James was in heaven. White sand beaches. Clear, turquoise waters. Perfect surfing conditions.

Best of all—no cameras. The only people who knew they were here were some top-level members of his cabinet in case they needed to reach him, and the handful of staff and Secret Service who'd arrived with them. Carlene had even opted to give the nannies some time off so she and James could be parents for a little while.

A boardwalk led them from the sheltered, private pier to the house, which was tucked back behind such thick foliage, it might as well have been in the middle of a jungle. It was a spectacular house too—five stories, built in an exquisite Spanish style with a red tiled roof and cream-colored walls. It was covered with decks, balconies and huge picture windows, and at its ground level was a cabana stocked with surfboards, boogie boards, snorkel gear and a pair of kayaks.

"This place is amazing," Carlene said, staring up at it from the boardwalk. "Think the inside matches?"

She grinned. "Only one way to find out."

They hurried inside like a couple of kids discovering a brand-new toy store. They weren't disappointed—top-of-the-line kitchen. Huge, plump couches in front of a giant flat screen. A massive playroom for the kids. The family planned to spend as much time outdoors as they could, but if it rained or they wanted to do something after dark, they sure as hell wouldn't get bored.

The bedrooms were nothing to sneeze at either. There were enough guest quarters—attached and detached—to accommodate everyone they'd brought along and then some. Kent had a beautiful room down the hall from the master bedroom, and there'd be Secret Service scattered all over the place, day or night. James had also given them all strict orders to take some time off too—if they were off duty, he wanted them out on the beach, in the pool or whatever it took for them to relax.

While Carlene took the kids down to have some lunch, James took his and her suitcases up to the master bedroom.

Holy shit. More like master suite. It was bigger than the one in the White House, and he swore it must've been twice the size of the tiny one-bedroom apartment they'd rented when they first moved in together. As a bonus, the enormous bathroom had a hot tub that, he couldn't help noticing, would comfortably accommodate three adults. Oh yeah. This was exactly the kind of vacation he needed.

He set the suitcases on the California-king bed and was about to start unpacking, but the sunshine coming in through the sheer curtains was just too enticing.

The suitcases could wait. He walked out onto the balcony, rested his hands on the railing and let the warm sea breeze ruffle his hair. He closed his eyes and took in a long breath of the salty air.

If there was one piece of advice he'd heard a hundred times over between the election and his inauguration, it was to seize every bit of downtime, rest and relaxation he could get his hands on.

For the next ten days, he planned to do exactly that.

Chapter Twenty-Three

One of the best parts about their little island paradise was a tiny, protected lagoon. The water was calm and quiet, and part of it was shallow enough for the little ones to play. Carlene and James did some snorkeling while Kent watched the kids. She was quickly falling in love with this place—she hadn't experienced this kind of tranquility or privacy in far too long.

A few days into the trip, while James and the kids were busily building a sand castle at the edge of the water, she watched from the shade of a small cluster of trees.

Two figures in black wetsuits were heading up the beach toward them with surfboards tucked under their arms. Kent and Roberts, one of the off-duty Secret Service agents, had gone out to tackle some waves, and it looked like they'd gotten good and soaked. Kent was limping a little, but not enough to alarm her. He'd put his body through the same wringer James had over the years, and she didn't imagine that an afternoon of surfing did much for the joints of an aging ex-SEAL.

She chuckled to herself. *Getting a little old to be playing twenty-year-old, are we?*

As they approached, Kent handed off his board to Roberts, clapped him on the arm and continued toward Carlene while the other agent returned their boards to the cabana.

They'd both presumably put on sunscreen—Carlene wouldn't let any of them out of the house without it, because she'd apparently turned into her mother—but Kent was a little pink across his cheekbones. His forehead too, now that she looked closer. He'd probably have a white outline when he took off his sunglasses.

"You know you're supposed to reapply the sunscreen, right?"

He laughed sheepishly. "Sorry, Mom."

She rolled her eyes but laughed too. She held up the bottle of sunscreen she kept for the kids. "Might be too little too late, but…"

"Thanks." Kent took the bottle from her. "Mind if I join you?"

"Not at all." She moved over on her towel to make room for him.

Kent sat beside her, keeping a comfortable space between them. After he'd slathered on some sunscreen, he handed the bottle back and gestured out at James. "Looks like he's enjoying himself."

"He is." She smiled. "This is the most relaxed I've seen him in a long time."

Kent nodded. "Yeah, me too."

She hugged her knees to her chest as she watched her family. "I can't imagine how bad things would have gotten if you hadn't figured him out."

"I don't get all the credit. I never would have worked it out if you hadn't opened the door."

"Maybe. But still… Thank you."

"Thank *you*," he whispered, "for letting me stay involved."

She turned to him.

His already pink cheeks colored a bit more. "I mean… I didn't…" He shook his head and shifted his attention to James and the kids. "I just meant it's been good for me too. And it means a lot that you trust me enough to…"

"I know what you mean. And you're welcome. I think it's been good for both of you. For all of us."

Silence fell between them, and she had no idea what needed to be said. This wasn't a conversation she'd ever imagined happening with Kent, though with the way things had gone recently, it shouldn't have surprised her.

Either way, she didn't quite know where the conversation needed to go, so they both watched for a long while as her family abandoned their half-finished sand castle to peer at something in the sand. Maybe a crab or a shell or something—it was impossible to tell from here. The kids were obviously fascinated, though, crowded around their father and looking at whatever it was.

James carefully picked it up and lifted it to their eye level, holding his palm flat. Carlene could see a small whitish object, but she couldn't make it out. James pointed at it, as if describing it to them and showing them all the little details.

She smiled. Moments like this were few and far between while James was president, and she reminded herself to send an enormous gift basket to the saint who'd let them use the island.

Suddenly, James jerked his hand back, and whatever was on his palm fell to the sand. He shook his hand out, grimacing, and the kids giggled and clapped as they watched the object—a crab, apparently—skitter away across the sand.

Kent chuckled. "Trust him to get his fingers too close."

Carlene's stomach fluttered. She'd almost forgotten Kent was even there, but there he was, sitting beside her in a sandy wetsuit and smiling as James and the kids searched the sand for something else.

He turned to her, and his smile dropped.

They each cleared their throats and gazed at the water again.

After a moment, Kent stretched his legs out and pressed his toes into the sand. "For the record, this wasn't what I had in mind when I suggested dominating him."

"What do you mean?"

"I mean it…" He paused, watching James in the surf with the kids. Then he turned to her, his dark sunglasses masking his eyes. "It wasn't some ploy to elbow my way into your marriage."

"I know." She gave a slight nod and turned to gaze out at her family. Yeah, this conversation was weird. Especially because of how she *didn't* feel right then. From day one, there'd been a part of her that felt threatened by Kent, but at some point, that had gone away. Recently, she'd come to realize that no matter what feelings Kent had for James, everything was trumped by his desire for James to be happy, and nothing he did—in her presence, anyway—smacked of a desire to take him away. When Kent told her he didn't want to harm her marriage, she believed him. If he truly was determined to make sure James was happy, he'd succeeded. He'd taught her how to do the same, worked together with her, and all her adversarial feelings toward him were just…gone.

Carlene took a deep breath. "For the record, I'm glad you're in his life." She faced him. "Not just to help me figure out how to dominate him, or for the threesomes. Just…in general."

"Really?"

"Yeah."

More silence. Comfortable this time, but still awkward in its own way. Where did the conversation go from here?

Out of the blue, Kent said, "I'm glad you're in his life too."

"You are?" She turned her head. "I didn't think you liked me. Before, um…"

"I didn't." Ah, there was the bluntness James had always laughed about. But Kent went on, "Obviously, I was wrong." He absently played with the edge of his wetsuit's sleeve. "The thing is, James worships the ground you walk on. It just took me a long time to figure out why. But the night you came to me at Camp David and said you wanted me to help him, I think that's when I realized how wrong I was about you." He took off his sunglasses and looked her straight in the eye. "To do what you did took some serious guts. And it made me realize that…" He paused again, pursing his lips as if he couldn't quite find the words. "That you were something I always believed James deserved, but I was afraid he'd never find."

Carlene swallowed. "And that was?"

Kent held her gaze for a moment, then looked out at James again, and the surf almost swallowed his soft response: "Someone who loves him as much as I do."

Any other time over the last ten years, that confession would've made her seethe with jealousy.

But she'd seen them together. The way they touched and looked at each other. If Kent had wanted to pull him away, or James had wanted to leave, it would have happened a long time ago. Yes, the two of them loved each other, and there was no denying it, but that love didn't threaten her. It didn't threaten her marriage, her family.

In fact, when she'd been convinced Kent was what James wanted and needed, he'd instead guided her, taught her what she needed to know to give her husband what he needed, and always seemed ready to fade back into the woodwork as soon as the word was given. The love he had for James was as palpable as it was nonintrusive.

Carlene's throat tightened, and she reached for his arm.

His eyes shot toward her hand, then met hers.

She squeezed gently. There were a million things she could've said right then, but none of them seemed to do the moment justice.

Kent's gaze flicked down to her hand on his arm, and she nearly withdrew it, but then he put his hand on top of hers.

Her chest tightened. He swallowed.

Eventually, they withdrew their hands and broke contact. Then eye contact.

This time, she didn't feel the need to fill the silence.

She simply sat beside him, watched James and the kids with him, and let the moment be.

Chapter Twenty-Four

James was in heaven on this vacation. Not only was the possible war off his shoulders, and not only did he have some much-needed time off with his family, but whenever night fell, Kent and Carlene were *relentless*. They'd been here five days already, and last night was the first time he didn't have sex with either of them because they were all blissfully exhausted. He hadn't slept like this since before his eldest child was born.

Though he didn't need the domination here like he did in Washington, it was the most amazing opportunity for the three of them to try new things, find their stride, and really get the hang of what they were doing. James was beyond grateful that they were willing to do this, and relieved as all hell that it actually helped—when the time came and he was hanging by a thread, he was completely confident that they'd be able to center him and anchor him. Wasn't it just a bonus that the solution to his stress was this enjoyable for all three of them?

Tonight, Carlene was nowhere around when Kent ordered James to the bedroom. Kent's hair was damp, but he was wearing his shirt and tie as if he'd just gotten off shift. What exactly did he have up his sleeve?

"What about Carlene?" James asked, though he was already on his way up the stairs on Kent's heels.

"She knows what we're doing." Kent gave a wicked chuckle over his shoulder. "She's got some plans for you later on."

Jesus. These two are going to kill me before this vacation is over.

Bring it on...

In the master bedroom, after James had closed the door behind them, Kent didn't waste any time: "Strip."

Yes, sir…

James did as he was told and set his clothes on top of the dresser.

Kent flicked his eyes downward.

Instantly, James's knees buckled, and he knelt at Kent's feet. The second he hit the carpet, his entire being seemed to settle—his body relaxed, his mind cleared. He took in a long breath through his nose, and he caught a whiff of the cologne Kent had used since their younger days. He'd wear it on a night out when he was looking to get laid, and James couldn't count the number of times he'd been the one breathing it in while they made out in a men's room or fucked on a hard motel bed. He'd started wearing it again recently, and it made James's palms sweat.

Kent ran his fingers through James's hair. "I want to try some new things tonight."

James straightened a little, equally intrigued and nervous. "Such as?"

"Well…" Kent paused. "I'd like to try a blindfold again."

"Okay. I think we've done this enough that I'd be willing to give it a try."

"Excellent. We should probably hold off on tying your hands, though. One thing at a time."

A prickly feeling itched along James's spine. He'd never been a captive, thank God, but there were moments in his training that had definitely made an impression, and his skin crawled at the thought of being bound. "Yeah, one thing at a time."

Kent nodded. "Lie on your back with your hands behind your head, then. You're physically able to move them if you need to." He narrowed his eyes slightly. "But you won't. Not unless your wife or I tell you to."

As James stood, that prickly feeling changed to a decidedly more pleasant tingle. He lay back on the bed and laced his fingers together on the pillow. Normally, he'd be lying like this to watch TV or relax, but assuming this position while he was naked and his incredibly devious lover was standing there had the opposite effect. He wasn't uncomfortable, and he definitely felt safe, but relaxed?

Not so much.

Beside the bed, Kent held James's gaze as he slid off his necktie. "Are you absolutely sure about trying the blindfold?"

James licked his lips. Being blinded had been another less than pleasant aspect of training, but didn't give him quite the same feeling of revulsion. In fact, watching Kent slowly wind the necktie around his hand, he had quite a different response to the idea. "Safe word still applies, right?"

"Always."

"Then yeah, I'm sure."

Kent unwound his necktie and grinned. He climbed onto the bed beside James. "Lift your head."

James obeyed, and he willed the fight-or-flight response to calm down as Kent put the tie on him like a makeshift blindfold. This was safe. There was no one here who'd hurt him, and Kent wouldn't leave him. Kent was here, so he was absolutely safe. End of story.

Resting his head on his hands again, James breathed slowly and evenly, letting Kent's familiar cologne settle his nerves. His pulse gradually came down, and the fluttering in his stomach eased—Kent was definitely going to fuck with his head, but all feelings of danger settled.

"Is this all right?" Kent asked softly.

James nodded. "Yeah."

"I'm getting up, but I'm not leaving. Okay?"

"Okay."

The mattress shifted, and he followed Kent's movements. Footsteps. Clothes shifting. Shoes coming off.

James swallowed. More deep breaths—excitement this time, not nerves. Or at least, not those initial nerves. He was always a little nervous that he wouldn't do what Kent or Carlene told him to, wouldn't please them, but he could deal with that. Just a little performance anxiety, not actual concern for his well-being.

Inhale. Exhale.

James's skin broke out in goose bumps—Kent had moved away from him, but the cologne lingered. Even after a good minute of being separated, he could smell it fairly strongly. Kent was hardly the type to marinate in the stuff, though. What little he wore fucked with James's head, but that didn't take much.

Still, even as Kent moved around on the other side of the room, James could smell it. Almost as if it were—

Oh God.

The cologne was on the tie. Not a lot, just enough to keep him tuned in to the light scent. With the blindfold on, his remaining senses were on high alert. Every brush of skin on fabric came to him as if it were happening right next to him instead of—he guessed—a few feet away. The sounds painted a picture of Kent stripping out of his suit, carefully folding each garment and setting them aside. He realized now that the window was open, and the distant splash of the gently rolling surf made it all the way up here as if it were right outside. The salty air, the faint artificial coconut of sunscreen, the soft sweetness of the hand lotion Carlene had left on the nightstand.

And above all that, the hint of cologne, which may as well have been someone lying beside him and whispering Kent's name in his ear.

"How are you doing?"

Shit. Kent's voice made all his senses go haywire. The room had been so quiet, and suddenly…sound. Voice. Words. Fuck.

Kent's hand warmed James's arm. "James? You okay?"

"Yeah." James licked his lips again. "Yeah, I'm good. Just, um, getting used to it."

"Safe word?"

"Republican."

"Good." The hand lingered for a moment, then squeezed gently before sliding off, leaving behind a cool spot. "You're going to lie perfectly still." Kent's voice was gentle and commanding at the same time. "Hands behind your head, feet where they are. You can squirm." He chuckled, and added, "In fact, I hope you do."

Oh God…

James opened and closed his hands, his palms sweaty against his fingers. "Okay."

"No sounds. No orgasms. Understood?"

Oh, James understood, but what the hell did Kent have in mind? What was he going to do that meant James had to make a conscious effort to be silent? To not come?

"Understood?" Kent asked, his voice tinged with impatience.

"Understood."

"Good."

The mattress moved, and James's mind's eye painted him a picture of Kent sitting beside him. Naked? He could've sworn he'd heard the man undressing, but without visual confirmation, he couldn't be—

A soft, ticklish touch erased his thoughts.

It took a second for him to pinpoint that a single fingertip was drifting up his thigh. Then that contact vanished. Everything was silent and still for several seconds before a finger appeared and lightly circled James's navel, making every muscle in his torso contract. That touch also disappeared after a few seconds, replaced a moment later by three—four?—fingers running down the side of his rib cage.

Nothing Kent did would've been particularly erotic in its own right, but like this, it was hot. James couldn't see his expression or body language, so he couldn't anticipate what would happen next. His senses were on such high alert, every featherlight touch might as well have been a kiss right on an erogenous zone. A finger along the inside of his elbow, soft trails drawn across his abs, a nail along his collarbone—James's body responded as if Kent were already balls deep in him. He broke out in goose bumps. He struggled to find breath, and struggled even harder not to make a sound.

In the background, something clicked, but there was too much tactile distraction for him to give the sound more than what amounted to a passing glance.

Until the mattress shifted slightly beside him.

On the wrong side.

And not as heavily as if Kent were there. For that matter, Kent was on James's left side, so…

James held his breath.

Kent's fingers trailed over his nipple. His other hand teased James's hip.

And then there were more. The softest, lightest touch imaginable on his balls, and it was enough to force all the air from his lungs.

He barely snapped his teeth together in time to keep from cursing out loud. Kent's command for silence rang clearly enough in his ears to stop him from making a sound. That wasn't easy, though, not with fingers—Kent's *and* Carlene's now—running all over his body. His stomach. His arms. His legs. His cock and balls. Staying silent was far easier said than done with them teasing him like this.

Even when they both lifted their hands away and brought them down in different places, he immediately knew whose touch was whose. Carlene's fingers were softer, slightly cooler. Kent's were calloused, and he'd always had warm hands.

Can't really say the same about his feet, though.

The random thought cut through the fog like one of those moments of profound clarity that happened while he was drunk, and just like he often did when he was drunk, he laughed.

Every finger touching him stopped.

He gulped. "S-sorry."

One by one, each finger lifted away. His nerves tingled, searching for the contact again. Carlene and Kent were still there—he could hear them both breathing, feel them on the mattress on either side of him—but they didn't speak and they didn't touch him.

Though the ticklish touch had been fucking torture, this was even worse. Just like the night they'd used the Wartenberg wheel on him, his whole body was electrified as his nerve endings searched for *something*. The warm sheets beneath him didn't help—their constant, dull contact only amplified the lack of anything but cool air touching him elsewhere.

And…shit, what if they had the wheel again tonight? That possibility made his skin even more sensitive. Especially since they weren't touching him now. At all. Anywhere. *Fuck.*

"James." Kent was whispering, but the single syllable cracked across James's senses like gunfire.

James inhaled slowly. "Y-yeah?"

"I said no sounds. Right?"

"Right. Sorry. Won't…won't happen again."

"Good." Carlene this time. "Think we should give him another chance?"

"Of course." Kent's weight shifted, and then his breath warmed James's nipple a split second before he flicked his tongue across it.

It took every fragment of control James had left, but he didn't make a sound. He refused. Knowing these two, they'd keep him from coming for hours to punish him, and there was no way in hell he'd survive that tonight.

"No coming," Kent reminded him. "No sounds."

"No matter how much you want to." The wicked playfulness in Carlene's voice fucked with his pulse. "No matter how much we tease you."

As if on cue, Kent's callused fingers encircled the base of his cock, and James had about two seconds to think *oh yes—oh shit!* before Kent's tongue ran around the head of James's cock.

No sounds. No sounds. No…oh God…no…sounds…

But Kent's mouth was so, so good. He'd come a long way since his clumsy younger years, and now he knew exactly how to use his lips, his tongue, even his teeth. James had to fight hard against the urge to push his cock deeper—it wasn't allowed, and besides, Kent knew what he was doing.

Jesus Christ, Kent…

James let a soft, barely audible whimper escape, and clenched his teeth and pressed his lips together to silence himself. At least that gave himself something to focus on besides *don't come, don't come, don't come,* and he managed a few calming breaths through his nose.

Which helped.

For a second.

Carlene shifted and lay beside him on the bed. She pressed her lips beneath his jaw, which sent a ripple of electricity straight down to his cock, drawing his attention right back to that amazing blowjob and his impending orgasm.

"You're not going to make a sound, are you?" Carlene whispered in his ear. James shook his head.

Her nail materialized in the middle of his chest, and she drew little sharp-edged circles as she murmured, "You're not going to come, are you?"

Fuck…

He shook his head again.

"That can't be easy," she said. "With everything he's doing?"

Goddammit.

Kent took James's cock all the way into his mouth, inch by inch, and slowly lifted back off. When Kent started to go down again, James thought he could cope with it this time, but suddenly, Carlene's lips were against his, and he was at the mercy of two of the most talented mouths on the planet. Kissing Carlene, being expertly teased by Kent—this was torture of the sweetest kind.

And still, their hands were on him. Fingers drew circles. Nails drew lines. Palms warmed skin, leaving cool spots when they moved away. All while he tried to remember how to make out with Carlene and remember not to come on Kent's tongue. He couldn't even distract himself with unpleasant thoughts just to keep his orgasm at bay—Kent and Carlene consumed his attention, his focus, and demanded that he concentrate solely on the need for a release he couldn't have until they were good and ready to give it to him.

After ages, Carlene broke the kiss. "Think we should let him catch his breath?"

Kent didn't immediately stop, but when he did, James took in a few gulps of air, taking advantage of what might only be a few precious seconds of *not* being overstimulated.

"I think so," Kent said. "I suppose we should let him come eventually."

Yes please!

"Well," Carlene said with a laugh, "let's not get too carried away."

Damn it.

Carlene gently removed the blindfold. James blinked a few times, trying to bring them into focus. When his vision cleared, he looked to his left, then to his right. After being blind for what seemed like hours, and opening his eyes to the two of them, the arousal was unbelievable. Especially since they were both close enough to touch, but he hadn't been given permission, so all he could do was look.

And he could have looked at them all night.

Carlene was beside him, dressed in a tank top and shorts, sitting on her hip with her legs draped over the edge of the bed as if some sculptor had carefully positioned her in the sexiest way imaginable.

Opposite her, Kent was kneeling, though even on his knees, there was nothing remotely submissive about his posture, and not only because he was looming over James. He simply radiated power and control, and that had always drawn James in like a magnet.

James's eyes flicked toward Carlene again. The way she sat was relaxed but hardly lazy. Spine curved but shoulders back, eyes up and cool even as they gleamed with mischief and arousal, and the more James glanced at each of them, the more he realized how flawlessly she complemented that aura of power from Kent. Not in the way James did, by submitting to him and letting himself get drunk off the other man's control, but by radiating a calm control of her own. As if she was absolutely certain she could, if she wanted to, put Kent on his knees as easily as she did James, just as Kent was probably certain he could make her kneel too.

Carlene grinned and trailed her fingertips beside James's erect cock. "Look how turned on you are. We might have to do something about that."

James bit back a whimper.

"I think you're right." Kent shifted a bit and lay beside him. "If you could have anything right now," he whispered, his breath hot on James's ear, "what would it be?"

James bit his lip. Oh, on any other night, there would be so many ways he could answer that. And it was easy to say "just make me come", because his body was aching for the orgasm they'd kept out of his reach for so long, but he didn't. Here, now, lying between these two like this, there was only one thing he wanted. One fantasy he would have sold his soul to see come to life.

He swallowed. "I want… I want to watch you fuck my wife."

Kent's body tensed. So did Carlene's. They exchanged a look James couldn't read.

"You don't want…" Kent met his eyes. "If you want us to get you off, we will. You've certainly earned it."

Tempting. So tempting. "I want to come, but…that would be…"

To Carlene, Kent said, "What do you think?"

"Hmm." She moved away from them, toward the edge of the bed, and as she stood, said, "I think these shorts might be in the way." She paused, hands on her waistband, and when her gaze shifted toward James, her eyebrow flicked up. "You're sure about this?"

"If…" He cleared his throat. "I want to see it. But only if it's what…what you two want." Please, please, please…

Carlene's gaze shifted again, looking past him, and judging by the hitch in Kent's breath, their eyes had met. That eyebrow climbed a little higher, as did the corner of her mouth.

Carlene stood. The shorts came off. She hooked her thumbs under her panties, and neither man breathed while she slid them down her long legs.

Kent touched James's arm. "You're going to sit over there." He pointed at the chair beside the dresser. "And you're going to watch. Got it?"

James nodded and did as he was told.

It was a smaller, more modern chair than the one Carlene had sat in the first time she'd watched Kent top James, but sitting like this to watch them definitely reminded him of that night. As if his cock weren't already painfully hard.

Carlene still had on her tank top as she climbed onto the bed, and she was about to take it off, but Kent moved from lying down to sitting up, and when their eyes met, her hands stopped. God, but that was hot—she was half-naked, he was completely naked and fully hard. They were both on their knees, facing each other, and just like Kent hadn't been when he'd knelt beside James earlier, neither of them looked the least bit submissive.

She came closer. He moved closer. They met in the middle, his prominent cock nearly touching her hip and her erect nipples nearly touching his chest. Kent curved his fingers around the back of Carlene's neck and drew her in. When they were just inches apart, he brought his hand around to the front of her throat. She locked eyes with him and pressed against his palm, her gaze a mix of defiant and daring and *don't put it there unless you mean it.*

James gripped the chair's armrests to stop himself from stroking his dick. Watching the two of them, he was liable to come, and that wasn't allowed yet, and God, he was pretty sure he was about to find out if it was possible to come without touching himself at all. Carlene and Kent hadn't even kissed yet. They were staring each other down, his hand on her throat and her eyes full of challenge, and if this got any hotter—

Carlene grabbed the back of Kent's neck, pulled him in and kissed him.

It wasn't the kiss that made James's head spin. It wasn't the fact that Kent still had her by the throat, or the fact that she was kissing him as aggressively as she'd kissed James the night they met.

It was that momentary shock on Kent's part. When his whole body seemed to freeze, fingers loosening on Carlene's neck for a second, free hand splaying in midair like he didn't know what to do with it.

James *felt* that shock, his own body twitching for a second as if someone had slapped him. The power between them was palpable, shifting back and forth from moment to moment—when he grabbed her, when she kissed him, when he regained control and seized her hair, giving her that same startle she'd given him. Two people who could drop James to his knees with a look, pushing each other's buttons and winding each other up with a subtle volley of control.

James couldn't sit still. He didn't dare touch himself, and the only reason he remembered to breathe was to keep from getting light-headed. He wasn't about to pass out and miss a second of this.

Steadying Carlene with a handful of her hair, Kent drew back, and the horny, almost predatory glances they exchanged turned James on even more. Carlene narrowed her eyes a little. He released her hair, and she released the back of his neck. Then she wrapped her fingers around Kent's wrist, pulled his hand away from her throat, and guided it down to his own cock.

"That should keep you busy for a minute," she said, and Kent's hand started slowly stroking as if it had a mind of its own.

Holy fuck.

Carlene peeled off her tank top. As she started on her bra, she grinned at Kent. He grinned back.

Then he turned to James. "This is what you want? To see me fuck her?"

James nodded, mesmerized as he watched Carlene take off her bra, and somehow managed to whisper, "Yes."

Kent gulped. Why the hell was that so hot? Seeing him turned on and tripped up like this?

Behind him, Carlene dropped her bra off the side of the bed. "Do we need condoms?"

Kent paused. "Um…"

"We're all clean," James said. "Her tubes are tied. It's up to you two."

"Oh. I guess we don't need—"

"Good." Carlene lunged at him and shoved him back onto the mattress. One smooth rolling motion of her hips, and Kent gasped. So did James—the sight of his best friend's dick buried all the way inside Carlene's pussy was beyond hot.

She steadied herself with her hands on his shoulders and went to town on him. Riding him hard, taking every inch of him over and over again. Kent didn't grab on to her. He didn't thrust up or try to take over. He rested his hands on her hips, but he must not have held her very tight, since her rhythm didn't change. He let her control the speed and everything and…*fuck*, that was a hot sight.

James's heart pounded and his head spun and holy hell, he was going to have to do something about this erection before he lost his mind. He knew exactly what it was like to be beneath her, to have her riding his cock fast and hard, and he wanted her. He wanted *him*. He wanted to watch them like this all damned night.

She leaned forward a bit, and Kent ground out a low "Holy shit…" as she changed her angle and her speed. James's pulse sped up—she was getting close, wasn't she?

Oh yes. Her neck and chest were pink, her nipples rock hard, her eyes squeezed shut, and she ground against him, no doubt rubbing her clit against his body while she fucked herself on his cock.

James gripped the armrests. Just thinking about what Kent must be feeling made his balls tighten—Carlene was trying to make herself come, and her pussy was always insanely tight when she did this, and in Kent's position, James would've been struggling not to lose it himself.

Kent lifted his head and closed his lips around one of her nipples. She whimpered and grabbed his hair like she often did to James. Kent kneaded her ass with one hand, and God knew what he was doing to her nipple with his mouth, but judging by her shudders and deliciously unladylike cursing, she loved it.

Carlene threw her head back, and the cry she released went straight to James's balls, driving a low groan from his lips as he watched her fall apart on top of Kent. Her whole body shook—hell, the whole bed shook—and James couldn't help cursing with a mix of frustration and arousal. Watching was hot as fuck, but goddamn, he wanted to be inside her right then, feeling every shudder and jolt of her orgasm.

She'd *just* started to come down from her orgasm when Kent pulled her down, kissed her—

And threw her on her back.

In a heartbeat, he was on top of her, and he was fucking her, pounding her deep and hard while she gasped and moaned. Every time he slammed into her, his lip curled slightly from exertion. She clawed at his back and his ribs, and that just drove him on.

James just sat there, staring. Holy shit. Watching the two people he loved more than life itself fuck each other like their lives depended on it was hotter than it had any right to be. At this rate, the fucking *bed* was going to come.

"James," Kent panted. He nodded sharply toward the floor beside the bed. "Knees."

James scrambled off the chair and dropped to his knees. The carpet bit in, but he didn't care.

Kent groaned as he fucked Carlene harder. Then, abruptly, he pulled out, rolled to his feet in front of James, and forced his dick between James's lips. He thrust into his mouth, just pushing the limits of James's gag reflex, and almost immediately, Kent groaned. The sweetness of Carlene's pussy mingled with the salt of Kent's semen, and James couldn't stop himself—he grabbed his own cock, stroked it just a couple of times, and came *hard*.

When the dust began to settle, dread clenched his stomach. He was going to pay for that, wasn't he?

Kent stroked his cheek with a shaky hand. "You weren't supposed to come."

"I know." James cringed. "I'm sorry."

"Look at me, James."

He hesitated, but then lifted his chin, wondering what they'd do to make sure he didn't disobey again.

To his surprise, though, Kent grinned. "We pushed you pretty far tonight. Did some new things." He cupped James's cheek. "Just this once, I'll let it go."

Relief nearly turned James's spine to liquid. He pressed his face against Kent's palm. "Thank you."

Chapter Twenty-Five

Kent couldn't stop thinking about that night. For the rest of the trip, his mind kept wandering back to the night he had sex with Carlene for the first time.

It wasn't guilt. No shame either. In fact, he had a feeling things would be more balanced now, that this trifecta would work even better this way. Between that night and the conversation he'd had with Carlene on the beach, most of the lingering tension between them had gone away.

But still, that night had shaken something in him. Even when the three of them fooled around again—which they did almost every night for the rest of the vacation—that weird, undefined feeling just kept gnawing at him.

The last night of their vacation, as everyone was staging luggage in the downstairs foyer, it clicked.

While James was up with the kids, helping them organize their things, Carlene was down here directing the show. Things were getting a little chaotic, as they often did when so many people were traveling, but she was cool and collected and kept everything in order.

Kent was on his way through the foyer to get his own luggage when Carlene turned to him.

"Oh good, you're here." She gestured at a small stack of suitcases. "Grab a couple of those and take them down to the boat."

The command wasn't terse or bitchy, not even all that forceful, but didn't invite a lot of protesting either. They had a narrow window of time to get everyone on the boat and get back to Oahu before sundown, after all.

And apparently it was effective because Kent didn't even realize she'd given him an order until he was halfway down the boardwalk with an armload of someone else's suitcases.

What the hell?

He paused and glanced back. Then he shook himself and kept walking.

After he'd returned from dropping off the luggage, he retrieved his own suitcases from the room and took them out to the boat as well. On his way back up the boardwalk, Carlene's voice halted him in his tracks.

"Kent?"

He turned around.

Carlene cocked her head. "You okay? You've seemed a little out of sorts the last few days."

"Yeah, I'm…"

She neared him, stopping an arm's length away. "What's this about?"

Kent cleared his throat. "I've, uh, just since we started this thing with James, I've been thinking. About some things. About myself."

"Such as?"

"Well…" He swallowed. "There's something I need, and I… Lately, I've been thinking I might be able to get it from you. If you're willing."

She studied him for a moment but then shrugged. "Well, I think I owe you one. What do you have in mind?"

He hesitated. "To put it bluntly, I want you to top me."

"You… I beg your pardon?"

Kent gulped, his stomach roiling with nerves. "It's something I've only done once. And that one time was… It went bad. And I've never been able to trust someone enough to do it again. Not until now."

Carlene's lips parted. "But I thought you didn't submit."

"I don't. I mean, I'm a Dom, and I…" He shook his head. "It's not quite that black and white, I guess."

Carlene pursed her lips. "Do you really think I can do that? I'm still learning how to do this."

"You definitely can. You've caught on incredibly fast." He chuckled. "You're a natural Domme, Carlene. And you're just the kind of woman who wouldn't take shit from me."

She laughed. "No, I definitely wouldn't. Well, it could certainly be fun." The sparkle in her eyes killed any second thoughts he had left, especially when she added, "I think you'd be a fun challenge compared to James."

"Oh yeah?"

"Yeah. He submits willingly. You?" She winked. "I might have to put you in your place now and then."

Kent gulped. Oh, this *was* going to be fun.

Voices in the next room turned both their heads, and they looked as James helped the kids and their suitcases into the foyer.

Carlene tensed. "You, um…" She faced Kent again. "You don't mind if I talk to James first, do you?"

"Absolutely not." Kent shook his head. "I want everything on the up-and-up between all three of us. If he's not comfortable, then…" He shrugged.

"I'll talk to him." She offered a faint smile. "I'm sure he'll be fine with it."

Kent smiled back. "I hope so."

"Yeah, me too." She gestured at the foyer. "I should see if they need any help."

"Right. Of course. I need to go chase my guys down and make sure they've got their shit together."

"Okay. When we get back to Washington, we'll…"

"Right." Kent paused. "One thing, though."

Carlene lifted her eyebrows again.

"James isn't into pain," he said. "I am."

Her eyes widened and her forehead creased. "Pain?"

Kent nodded. He cringed inwardly, certain she was going to balk at the idea and tell him to forget everything.

But then she flashed him the same grin that must've lured James in that very first night over a decade ago. "Sounds like fun." She winked. "Guess I should do some reading."

With that, she was gone, leaving Kent standing there with his jaw on the floor and a hardening erection in his shorts.

It was hard to say when they'd eventually find the opportunity for this, but when they did, one thing was damn certain:

It was going to be *intense*.

Almost three busy weeks after the First Family returned to Washington, Kent had just finished checking on some of his agents when he ran into Carlene near the corridor leading to the West Wing.

"When is your shift over?" she asked.

"Depends on when James's cabinet meeting is over."

"Do you have plans this evening?"

"I—" Kent suddenly recalled their conversation on the island, and his pulse jumped. "No. Not...not yet."

"Are you staying here tonight?"

"You tell me."

She grinned, and her eyes narrowed just a bit. Oh yes, they were on the same wavelength, weren't they? "Text me when you're off duty. I assume your room will suffice?"

"Uh, yeah." He moistened his lips. "And James is on board?"

Carlene nodded. "I'm sure he'd enjoy being here too, but he needs to sleep. And I got the impression you wanted this to be just you and me, so..."

"So my room. That works."

"Perfect. Text me, and I'll meet you there after the kids are in bed." She paused, looking him up and down. "Oh, and show up dressed like that."

"With...with or without the holster?"

"With, of course." Her eyes gleamed. "But lose the vest."

Kent's body temperature rose. "Yes, ma'am."

She left him to finish his shift, and he swore the only thing that got him through the day and into the evening was years and years of training. He was always alert and vigilant, never daring to let his guard down around James. After all, a threat could happen anytime and come out of nowhere, regardless of how much the head of security was dying to clock out and fuck the First Lady.

Eventually, though, his shift ended. By the time Carlene came into his room, he'd showered and put a shirt and tie back on with the holster over the top but no bulletproof vest on underneath. Carlene had gone casual—comfortable jeans and one of those low-cut blouses she couldn't wear to official engagements without causing a scandal—and she looked hot as always. Especially with that spark in her eye that said she fully intended to give Kent what he'd asked for tonight.

Kent gulped. "I, um, I don't know if you'll need them, but..." He pulled two sets of handcuffs out of his pocket and tossed them on the bed, metal clinking loudly against metal. "I slipped an extra pair past security."

"Abusing your security clearance, are you?"

"Hey, I get checked like everybody else." He winked. "But I also know how to get things through without raising any eyebrows." He gestured at his briefcase, which was propped up against the nightstand.

"Oh?" Her eyes darted toward the cuffs, then to the briefcase, and then back to him. "So what else did you bring in?"

"A few things. Getting stuff past the security checkpoint *is* a bit of a challenge, but I've managed to get things through."

"This should be interesting."

"Hopefully, yes."

"What's in the case?"

He picked up the briefcase and set it on the foot of the bed. The latches snapped, making him jump for some reason, and he pulled a bundle of folders from inside. They were held together by a thin piece of cord, and on each end of the cord was a metal clamp being used as a makeshift paperclip.

Carlene watched him, arms folded beneath her breasts. "Am I supposed to make you file papers while I talk dirty to you?"

He paused. "Well, that wasn't what I'd had in mind, but that could be kind of hot."

She laughed and rolled her eyes.

Kent chuckled. He slipped the cord and clamps off the papers and held them up, letting them dangle like a miniature set of jumper cables. "Nipple clamps."

Her laughter stopped abruptly, and she stared. "I beg your pardon?"

"You heard me."

"And their purpose is…"

"Does what it says on the tin."

Her lips formed a silent *O*. She hesitated for a moment, then unfolded her arms and held out her hand. "So they just…clip on?"

"Yeah." He draped the cord over her fingers. "You can pull on them, twist them, attach them to something else." Goose bumps prickled his back at the thought. "Anything to make them hurt."

She raised an eyebrow. "Kent, I've had three kids. My pain tolerance in that region is probably a hell of a lot different from yours."

Kent laughed. "Probably. That's what safe words are for."

"Good point." She held the nipple clamps for a moment, running her fingers along the cord between them. Her brow furrowed, and he thought she might've been wondering what on earth she was supposed to do with them.

But then she started playing with the retractor that adjusted the cord's length. And pinched one of the clamps a bit to open it. Opened it all the way. Then a little bit. She tested it against the side of her finger, and then let it bite the fleshy part of her fingertip.

Kent gulped. Oh God. She was testing it. Just like he'd test a flogger by swinging it a few times, hitting it on his own palm, forearm and thigh, she was figuring out what they could do, what they felt like.

She stretched it out to its full length and ran a sweeping gaze along the taut cord. Then she looked at him. Her eyes narrowed slightly, darting from one side of his chest to the other, then up to his face, and a smirk formed on her lips. Kent's dick was quickly getting hard—holy shit, what was she plotting?

Still holding the cord between her fingers, she gave him a slow down-up, and his knees turned to water. Maybe she had some lingering doubts about whether the domination shoe fit, but more and more, he could see the natural Domme coming out of her. It was a travesty that she'd made it into her forties without knowing that side of herself existed, because damn, she was good.

Carlene met his gaze. "Strip."

Without missing a beat, he started undressing. Jacket first. Then his shoulder holster. Out of habit, he took the pistol from the holster, dropped the magazine and cleared the chamber before he set it all on top of the dresser. He'd done that a million times—he'd been able to do it in his sleep since his first year in the Navy—but the motions weren't as smooth and practiced now as they usually were. Muscle memory kept him from fucking it up, but nerves and an incredibly distracting erection slowed him considerably.

He started on his shirt. At least that part was easy.

Carlene drummed her fingers on the footboard, her nails tapping out her impatience, and suddenly the buttons of his shirt weren't so simple anymore.

"Come on, Kent," she said sharply. "Unless you don't want to do this?"

"I do. I do." He forced a button to cooperate and figured he'd unbuttoned his shirt enough to just pull the damn thing over his head. Once it was off, he peeled off his undershirt and stripped out of his trousers and boxers too. Naked and on autopilot, he started to go to his knees, but her eyebrow flicked up, and he froze.

She eyed him. "I don't recall telling you to kneel."

The hard edge of her voice made his mouth water. "S-sorry."

She nodded sharply toward the bed. "On your back. Hands up against the headboard."

He obeyed, stretching out and resting his hands against the vertical slats. There was no doubt in his mind he was about to be cuffed to it, but Carlene didn't just slap on the cuffs and call it a day. No, apparently this woman was taking to the role of Domme—and relentless tease—like a duck to water.

Cuffs in hand, she climbed on top of him and straddled him. When she leaned forward to fasten one of the cuffs, she pressed against his cock, and her clothed breasts were just inches from his face.

The cold cuff closed around his hand. Another click-creak, and he was bound to the bed. Kent squeezed his eyes shut. He trusted her. He wanted her. He wanted this. If he wanted to move, well, he was fucked, because now he was completely at her mercy.

Sitting over him, she said, "Safe word?"

"Republican."

"Good. Now don't move." She picked up the pair of nipple clamps, and Kent briefly second-guessed the wisdom of bringing them out tonight—just how big of a sadistic streak did she have?

He was probably about to find out. He held his breath as she carefully closed a clamp on his left nipple. At first, it was dull pressure, but as the teeth really sank in, the burn started. Faint at first, intensifying as his nerves figured out that the clamp wasn't actually going anywhere and probably decided his brain needed a stronger signal to let him know about the danger. When she put the second one on, his body skipped right over the dull pressure and went straight to the eye-watering sting.

"How does that feel?" The playful note in her voice told him she knew damn well how it felt.

Kent swallowed. "Hurts."

"Can you handle it?"

He nodded. "Yeah."

"Good. Now you're going to hold this"—she lifted the cord between the clamps with her finger—"in your teeth."

"In my—"

Her eyebrows flicked up. "Is that a problem?"

Kent's lips parted. What the hell *did* she have up her sleeve? "No, ma'am." He took the cord and slipped the center of it into his mouth.

"Now that you're not going anywhere…" She held up—

Oh fuck.

The Wartenberg wheel.

Kent squeezed his eyes shut as goose bumps rose over every inch of his skin. His naked, vulnerable skin.

"Not yet, though," she said. When he opened his eyes, Carlene had his necktie dangling from her fingers.

Kent swore under his breath.

"You are okay with being blindfolded, yes?" she asked.

His heart sped up, but he said around the cord in his teeth, "Mmhmm."

"Good." She winked. "Because I want you to feel everything."

Shit…

"You're not going to make a sound. You're not going to move." She trailed a finger down the middle of his abs, and when his muscles contracted beneath her touch, Kent understood why the cord was between his teeth—one subtle movement of his head or his torso pulled it tighter and tugged the clamps. Twisted them even—she'd put them on so that an upward pull turned them slightly.

Oh. *God.*

She'd definitely been paying attention. Maybe even done a bit of reading on her own. She was clearly getting the hang of the art of enhancing senses by taking others away. Of using someone's powerlessness to fuck with him, of finding creative ways to…not force someone to bend to her will, but make it very much in his best interest to do so.

Carlene let him let go of the cord while she fastened the necktie around his head, but as soon as she was finished, the cord went back into his mouth. And he was at her mercy. Blind. Unable to move without his nipples burning.

Panic tried to flare up in his chest—he wasn't crazy about being blind or immobilized, never mind at the same time, but this was safe. He trusted the woman who now had control over him, and she would see to it that he made it through without harm. He'd be a sweating, shaking, fully aroused mess by the end of it, but he'd be all right.

Breathe in. Breathe out. She isn't going to hurt me any more than I want her to.

Carlene had a Wartenberg wheel at her disposal, and her featherlight fingertips, but for a long time—at least a minute, though it felt like hours—she did nothing. The longer she stayed like that, still and silent on the bed beside him, the more he had to struggle against the urge to squirm. Without his sight, his other senses searched frantically to fill in the gaps, his nerve endings grasping at even the faintest stimuli, be it the warmth of her body nearby to the subtlest shift in the mattress.

The bed creaked quietly, and the mattress dipped a little. Heat near his chest warned him she was close, but he jumped when her hair tumbled onto his skin. Again when her lips brushed just beneath his nipple. The clamp tugged slightly, sending a burning jolt through him, and he had to grip the cord even harder between his teeth just to keep himself silent.

And she didn't let up. Little kisses. Teasing his skin, his nerves, his—oh, fuck, his nipple. Her lips and tongue were exquisitely soft and gentle, the ticklish sensation extra intense when it was coupled with the sting of the clamp, and his senses went haywire. His body didn't know whether this was too much, not enough, good, bad, incredible—he couldn't make sense of anything, and he couldn't move.

She continued down, letting her hair drag along his skin as she dropped light kisses all the way over his chest and his abs. The Wartenberg wheel was there in the background, quite possibly in the hand that wasn't touching him. Where it would touch him first was anyone's guess, and every gentle kiss and ticklish touch startled nerve endings that were anticipating cold spikes. Christ, was he shaking already?

By now, James would've been a million miles away, lost in that space that came so easily to him. Kent, however, wasn't wired for that complete and total submission, and he stayed in the here and now—turned on, turned inside out, trying and failing to anticipate her every move. As coherent as a man could be when he was this fucking hard with a gorgeous woman screwing with his senses at every turn. He might not have had a submissive bone in his body, but this was *hot*.

Carlene's lips stopped just above his hipbone. When they pulled back slightly, he knew what was coming, and he braced, not daring to move, but when her teeth pressed into his skin, he squirmed anyway. His nipples burned. The place she'd bit stung. And his cock seemed to get even harder.

And that was the moment she picked to go down on him. One second she was teasing his skin with soft kisses, the next she'd sunk her teeth in, and now her hot mouth was around his dick, and Kent clenched his fists, straining against the handcuffs and the urge to curse aloud.

Her mouth was as talented as her husband's, and Kent…couldn't move. He held his breath and focused on staying perfectly still as she squeezed with her lips and fluttered with her tongue, because even the slightest movement tugged at his tender nipples.

The pain was intense, but he liked it, especially coupled with the sensual way she sucked his dick. The contrast was bizarre, and hot, and that whole "not coming until she gave the word" thing was getting more difficult by the second.

Kent opened and closed his hands, struggling to stay still, but also fighting the urge to hit the safety latches on the cuffs. Let himself go, pull off the blindfold, spit out the cord—reclaim control, goddammit.

No. No, he'd asked her to do this, and he would see it through. He focused on the sensations—the bite of the clamps, the tension of the orgasm he was barely holding on to, the softness of her touch—and tried not to think about the cuffs, the chains, the clamps, the commands that held him in place. He bit down hard on the cord because he would not let the safe word slip past his lips no matter how much his heart pounded and the confinement drove him insane. She was safe, and he trusted her, and nothing bad would happen this time.

Carlene moved slightly. The Wartenberg wheel rattled so quietly, he wouldn't have heard it at all if he hadn't been so tuned in to everything she did. He held his breath. His muscles were tense from his clenched jaw to his curled toes.

She ran her tongue around the head of his cock, and slowly took him deeper into her mouth, and then soft fingertips grazed his belly, and he jumped and yanked the cord and…pain. Pleasure. So many dizzying sensations collided, none of them made sense, and he didn't know if he was ready to cry out or come, but both were verboten, so he just held his breath again and tried to calm down.

Carlene wasn't having any of it. She taunted him with ticklish touches on sensitive skin while her lips and tongue relentlessly teased his cock. The wheel rattled once again, putting him on edge, but where he expected teeth, she gave him fingertips.

He lost track of time, and when he realized he'd forgotten where he was, he also realized he didn't care anymore. He just wanted his hands free, his vision back, and, for the love of God, let him come. Over and over, he reminded himself why he was doing this, that he'd asked her for this, and he knew damn well what he was getting into, and just as he started second-guessing if he could make it through this after all, Carlene stopped.

Her fingers broke contact. She let his cock slide free from her lips. She was still there but not touching him, and he squirmed as much as the nipple clamps would let him—she'd been oversaturating his senses, and now they were starved for contact, and…fuck, she was good.

"I'm getting off the bed," she said, her voice calm and even, "but I'm not leaving. I'll be right here."

Kent couldn't speak very well with the cord in his mouth, but he didn't dare nod either, so he just murmured, "Mmhmm."

The mattress dipped, then came up again, and her feet landed on the floor. She was moving. Clothing hissed and rustled, and a couple of times, a joint popped quietly. Her ankle, her knee, her back—hard to tell.

Then the mattress sank slightly beside him, and his skin tingled as his nerve endings searched for her body heat.

"I don't think you need this anymore," she said, and gently removed the necktie.

He blinked a few times to focus, and when he looked up, his pulse soared.

She was almost completely naked now. While he watched, dumbstruck and immobile, Carlene climbed on top of him. She sat perfectly so her pussy—

her hot, wet pussy—was right against his dick, and he groaned around the cord in his mouth.

"I think you've had these on long enough." She gently removed one nipple clamp, then the other.

Kent dropped the cord and exhaled hard, his nipples burning furiously even now that the clamps were off.

"You've done well," she said. "Not a sound. Good."

He licked his lips. "Th-thank you."

She leaned down, and her pussy pressed against his cock as she kissed him. Barely breaking the kiss, she murmured, "I think you should be rewarded."

He lifted his hips and pushed back against her pussy.

She grinned into another kiss. Then, "But you still can't make a sound. And don't you dare come until I say so."

Fuck...

"Understood?"

"Y-yeah. Understood."

"Good." She kissed him once more and sat up. Then she turned around— still straddling him, but now her back was to him.

Oh God. She wasn't...

Yeah, she was.

Carlene lifted herself up, and slowly, she lowered herself onto him, giving him the most amazing view of his cock disappearing inside her.

And of course, she didn't stop. She took every inch of him, lifted up again, came down again, and Kent could do nothing but watch her and enjoy this and try not to move or come or lose his mind. From this angle, every motion of her hips drove him insane. The way her pussy felt, the view of her hips and ass, her hair tumbling down her back over her bra strap...

Fuck. Oh fuck.

Her hand disappeared in front of her, and Kent mouthed a curse just before her pussy tightened around him. She moaned softly, fingertips brushing the shaft of his cock as she—he guessed—played with her clit. Shit, this was too much. Too hot from every angle—the view, the way she felt around him, the little moans she released as she no doubt drove herself closer to the edge.

Fuck it. Fuck it, he couldn't... This was too...

"Please," he whimpered. "Please, m-may I come?"

"Not yet." She was out of breath, which didn't help him stay in control at all. "Not until...after I do."

Oh God. Oh God. Oh fucking God.

Carlene threw her head back. Her pussy clenched around him, and her rhythm fell apart, and goddamn, Kent almost fell apart too. He strained against the cuffs, letting them bite into his wrists and center him, giving him something to focus on besides how badly he wanted to come in her tight pussy.

As she came down, she didn't stop. She still rode him slowly. Then she turned her head, bringing her flushed profile into his line of sight. "You've done everything perfectly, Kent. I want you to come."

He didn't need to be told twice. Her approval and her permission and her hot, perfect pussy all conspired to send him right over the edge. He thrust up, digging his heels into the bed and forcing himself into her as much as he could from this position, and strained against the handcuffs as his back arched and his toes curled and his whole body shook with the force of his release.

She rode him all the way through his orgasm until he begged her to stop, and then she lifted herself off him. Kent was out of breath, shaking, his mind a mess and his vision completely unfocused, but he was vaguely aware of her gently cleaning him off while he settled back down.

After she'd gotten rid of the towel, she undid the cuffs. He rubbed his tender wrists gingerly.

"How do you feel?" she asked, lying down beside him.

"Like I could sleep for a month."

"I believe it."

"You never used the wheel."

"Oh, I did." She grinned wickedly. "I used it to fuck with your head before I put the blindfold on."

"That's just evil."

"Mmhmm. That's the idea, isn't it?"

"*Oh* yeah."

She caressed his face. "I have to say, I didn't think you had it in you, but you are a great submissive."

He smiled and held her closer. "Just don't tell anyone. Our little secret."

She laughed and kissed his forehead. "Our little secret."

Chuckling, Kent lifted his chin, and Carlene pressed her lips to his. Then he rested his head on her chest. In her arms, he drifted in and out for a little while, riding the last stretch of that delicious high as he slowly came back down to earth.

Eventually, they agreed it was getting too hot, so they drew apart, but neither made any effort to leave the bed.

"I'm curious about something," she said.

"Okay." He smiled. "I think I kind of owe you one, right?"

She laughed. "Well, maybe. But you don't have to answer."

"Try me."

"When we first started this, you said no one dominates you." She gently ran her fingers through his hair. "What changed your mind?"

He hesitated, not quite sure how to word the answer. "I needed to."

"So you really are submissive sometimes?"

"No, I'm…I'm definitely a Dom. What we did tonight, there's a good possibility I'll never have any desire to do it again. But I…" His neck prickled as the memories clawed their way to the surface. "I did it a few times in the past. It wasn't my natural inclination, but I was experimenting. I was curious. And I also thought I should experience it for myself so I knew what I was doing to my subs."

"Don't tell someone to do something you wouldn't do yourself?"

"Pretty much. So one night, I was in a club. One of those leather dungeons that I don't dare take you and James to. I had some trusted friends there who I could play with, and I let one of them dominate me that night, and they…" He shuddered, phantom welts burning on his skin like a looming combat flashback, but tried to tamp it all down. "Long story short, they took advantage of my trust. Of me. While I was helpless."

Carlene pulled in a sharp breath and placed a warm hand on his arm. "Oh my God."

He willed the panic in his chest to ease. That incident was in the past where it belonged. There was no danger now. No reason to freak out. As his heart rate came down a little at a time, he said, "After that, there was no way in hell I was going to let someone top me." He met her eyes. "Not until tonight."

"But, why would you? I mean, if you're not a submissive, and—"

"Because I needed to put that experience to rest," he whispered. "It's been a long time, but it's been eating at me ever since. I needed to do it once, see it through, and be okay at the other end so I could walk away from it. The bad experience, it wasn't because I was submitting, it was because some asshole decided to take advantage. And I've never quite been able to leave that experience behind."

She nodded. "So you want to have a good experience with it so you can put the bad one to bed?"

"Yes. Exactly." He absently ran his fingers through her hair. "I'm not wired to be a submissive. I don't go into the same space James does. But the only way to let the past go was to do this someplace safe so I can be absolutely sure that the reason I don't want to be a submissive in the future is because I'm not a submissive, not because I had a bad experience. If that makes sense."

"It does. But…" She searched his eyes. "Why me?"

He smoothed her hair. "Because I needed to do it with someone I trust."

Carlene stared at him.

"You trust me with your husband." Kent held her gaze. "And I trust you with me."

Chapter Twenty-Six

The life of a First Lady was exhausting. Carlene had barely had time to dust off and grab a shower after that night with Kent before she was heading off in all directions for her various engagements. Sometimes she was with James—and Kent—but frequently, she was on her own. Or with the kids.

It was feast or famine too. She could have a reasonable schedule for a month—speaking here and there, accompanying James to visit heads of state, and spending some time with her children for once—and then the next month, she'd be darting all over the known universe for back-to-back-to-back

After nearly three weeks of running themselves into the ground, she and James were finally back in Washington. There was some precious downtime, too—barring any global crises or disasters in the next forty-eight hours, they didn't have to leave the White House for a couple of days.

She and James slept like the dead the first night. The second night, after she'd tucked in the kids, she stepped into the master bedroom, and—

They were both there.

James sat on the edge of the bed. Kent stood beside it.

And they were both looking at her.

Like *that*.

She closed the door and eyed them both. "You guys are plotting something."

The guys chuckled, exchanging knowing glances.

"Are we that obvious?" James asked.

"Uh-huh."

"We did some talking while you were traveling," Kent said, "and we decided that for everything you've done lately, and helping James figure out what he needed, we owed you one."

James stood. "So we decided we should give you the night of your life."

"The night—" Her eyes darted back and forth between them. "The night of my life?"

"*One of our favorite things to do together,*" she heard James saying, "*was take a woman to bed and show her the time of her life. Two men completely focused on her.*"

Oh God.

She moistened her lips. "You guys are serious."

"Both of us," James said. "Focused on you."

Kent nodded. "No dominance. No submission. It's all about you and you alone."

The shock was starting to wear off, and the truth was setting in—both of these men? Focused on her in bed?

Carlene shrugged off her jacket and draped it over the armrest of the antique chair. "Well, all right, then. Game on."

The guys looked at each other, and the grins they exchanged sent a jolt of electricity right through her. Oh Lord. This was going to be crazy, wasn't it?

James put an arm around her. Then Kent did. James pushed her hair back over her shoulders, exposing her neck, and they both descended on it at the same time, kissing her from either side.

Carlene closed her eyes. She thought she heard herself moan, but maybe not. Moaning required breathing. Breathing wasn't happening. Not with lips on her neck. A hand under her blouse. Another sliding over her ass.

In between touching her and kissing her, they made short work of her clothes. Theirs too, apparently, because as James laid her down on the bed, his bare skin was nearly feverish against hers. Kent joined them, warming her from the other side.

When they said they were going to focus on her and her alone, they weren't kidding. Lips drifted all over her neck, her chest, her stomach. Fingers trailed over curves and planes. Someone gently parted her thighs while the other teased her hard nipple. It was like they knew—intuitively, telepathically, *something*—how to intensify what the other was doing, like opposing tastes enhancing each other's flavor. When James teased her clit with a featherlight touch, Kent pressed his teeth into her nipple. When Kent's soft lips skated along her throat, James's coarse stubble grazed the other side. They never did one thing for very long, either, keeping her constantly guessing and constantly cursing. James went down on her. Then Kent did. Someone kissed her. Someone fucked her just enough to tease her, then pulled out. She was dizzy, overwhelmed, neither bound nor blindfolded but still barely able to keep track of who was doing what and where.

James stopped teasing her clit, and she had a few seconds to catch her breath before Kent took his place.

"Holy… shit…" She arched off the bed, and she cursed again when James closed his lips around her nipple. Lying back and simply taking pleasure from two men was easy—not going insane or bursting into flames was the hard part. If she didn't come soon, one of those things was inevitable.

And damn it, what Kent did with his mouth was amazing, but it wasn't going to get her off. Even when he added two fingers, he kept her orgasm well out of her reach.

Carlene whimpered in frustration, pressing against his face and trying to encourage his hand to fuck her faster.

James chuckled and lifted his head. "He's one hell of a tease, isn't he?"

Carlene swore. Shit. He was doing this on purpose?

"She's getting all fired up," James murmured between kisses as he inched his way up to her jaw. "Maybe you should let her come."

Kent didn't make a sound, but he definitely heard James loud and clear. His fingers crooked against her G-spot, and his tongue was suddenly firm and determined against her clit, and Carlene would have cried out if James hadn't picked just that moment to cover her lips and silence her with a deep kiss.

She gripped James's hair in one hand, Kent's in the other, as if that could somehow keep her in the here and now while one man kissed her and the other worked his magic on her pussy.

And everything went white.

Her whole body was electrified, shaking and hot-cool and tensing and relaxing all at the same time, and as she dropped back onto the mattress, James broke the kiss.

She gasped for hair. Panted. Had just enough coherent thought to nudge Kent away before her clit turned too sensitive, and he didn't resist.

"I'd say she's good and warmed up," Kent said.

Warmed up?

Oh fuck.

James laughed. "Yeah, I think so." He circled her nipple with a fingertip. "What do you think, baby? You ready for more?"

She shivered beneath his soft touch. "What do you have in mind?"

"Well, you always said you wanted to take two men at once."

Carlene's breath caught. Between her orgasm's aftershocks and her husband's words, her mind was rapidly short-circuiting. "Uh…"

"If you're game," he murmured, "so are we."

Kent lay down beside her, propped up on his elbow. "I'm definitely game."

"M-me…" Carlene licked her lips. "Me too."

"I thought so." James kissed her again. Then he rolled onto his back and gestured for her to come with him. Kent moved out of the way, Carlene got on top of James, and before she'd even found her balance, James pulled her hips down and buried himself inside her.

The mattress shifted slightly behind her, and James whispered in her ear, "Is this what you want? Kent and me at the same—"

"*Yes.* Um…just…" She swallowed. "Slowly."

Kent ran a hand up and down her back. "Of course. We have all night, and I promise we won't hurt you."

"Have you guys done this before?"

The guys tensed, probably exchanging a glance over her shoulder.

James drew his thumb around her nipple. "Yes, we have. We know what we're doing."

"Good." She sucked in a breath through her teeth as he teased her sensitive skin.

The bottle top clicked, and Carlene closed her eyes. She knew damn well they wouldn't deliberately hurt her, but she'd never done this before, and wasn't entirely certain how kind the laws of physics would be, especially with two men who were…blessed. Even if they had done it before, apparently without it ending in disaster.

The bottle clicked again, and Kent's cool, slick fingertip met her anus. She gasped. *Oh God…*

His finger pushed in. She leaned forward a little, which changed the angle of James's cock inside her, and she bit her lip. She slowly rode her husband, and as she did, Kent gently worked his finger into her ass. Then he pushed a second slick finger into her. From beneath, James moved his hips to keep her from catching her breath.

Carlene closed her eyes and exhaled. "Just *this* feels really good."

"As it should." Kent kissed the back of her shoulder. "We could keep doing this. Or…add more."

What they were doing was already intense as hell, but she was curious what it would be like to take both their cocks.

"More." She licked her lips. "Definitely more."

"Thought you'd see things our way." Kent kissed her neck, then withdrew his fingers. He shifted around behind her, his legs brushing hers as he positioned himself. Once he was situated…

Oh God. Here we go.

No one moved except for Kent. He eased himself in a fraction of an inch at a time. Carlene had had anal before, but never like this. Never while she already had another man's cock inside her. She held her breath even as she tried to relax, reminding herself they apparently knew what they were doing. Relaxing wasn't easy, of course, especially since she was pretty sure this could very quickly go from *oh* to *ow*.

True to Kent's word, though, they were careful. He took his time as if they really did have all night, and he intended to use every minute of it.

"Breathe." James lifted his head and kissed her. "Breathe, baby."

Carlene breathed. Her body yielded to Kent, and as she finally started to relax, he sped up *just* a little. Moving smoothly in and out, he found a careful, easy rhythm. Then James started moving too, rocking his hips ever so gently in time with Kent. They both moved slowly, one sliding in as the other slid out, and it felt…unbelievable. Like something that *should* have hurt—and easily could have—but didn't. With any other pair, she'd have been afraid one or both would get too rough, pinching that sensitive wall of flesh between them and turning this from pleasurable into excruciatingly painful. But she trusted them not to go too far. As much as both of them loved to fuck her until her bones ached, they were slow, careful and downright sensual, letting her feel every single inch of their steady, practiced strokes. Oh yes, these boys knew what they were doing.

And it was…

Amazing.

Absolutely amazing.

Hands all over her. Two gorgeous men against her. Two cocks moving inside her in perfect sync. Why in the world hadn't she begged them to do this sooner?

James looked past her, and she swore she could feel the two of them making eye contact. Something telepathic must've passed between them, because Kent slowed, pushing all the way inside her, and stopped. James nudged her hip. Carlene lifted up slightly and couldn't help a soft moan of disappointment as his cock slid out of her pussy, but that disappointment didn't last—James's hand materialized between them, and when his fingertips found her clit, Carlene closed her eyes and shivered.

Kent started moving again. He didn't have to go slow and easy now, and oh Lord, he didn't. He fucked her good and hard, and he was impossibly in synch with James—James's fingers teased Carlene at almost the exact same speed Kent fucked her ass, and it felt…it felt…

"Oh my God," she whimpered. She rubbed against James's hand, which only encouraged Kent to fuck her faster, and Carlene was in heaven.

"*Fuck,*" Kent groaned, and thrust even harder. He couldn't have fucked her like this while James was still in her pussy, but now he wasn't going to hurt her, and he must've known it—he pounded her for all he was worth. That alone was hot. Coupled with James's talented fingers? She couldn't have kept her orgasm from happening if she'd wanted to, especially not when Kent gasped and shuddered, when his fingers twitched on her hips and he released the most delicious, helpless cry.

Carlene slumped over James, her whole body shaking and tingling and coming apart at the seams, and both men drove her on, and right when it was about to become too intense, they both stopped. Kent withdrew. James took his fingers off her clit. Oh, but he wasn't finished yet—then guided his cock back to her pussy, and suddenly she was being fucked again. Her whole body was electrified from her orgasm, and James slid across nerve endings that were tingling and aching and totally overwhelmed. She didn't have another orgasm left in her, but Jesus, he felt perfect, and he fucked her from below until she couldn't even breathe because, holy hell, this was…

"Oh my *God*," she moaned.

James's breath caught. He pulled her hips down onto him, and he kept thrusting even as he held her there, and then he shuddered and groaned.

Carlene collapsed over him. Kent collapsed beside them.

And all three of them just breathed.

Chapter Twenty-Seven

Lying in bed with his wife between him and his best friend, all three of them satisfied, showered and exhausted, James tried and failed to ignore the ball of lead forming in his gut. They'd set out to give her the night of her life, and if the way she was barely staying awake between them was any indication, they'd succeeded. But…

James brushed a few strands of hair out of her face. She looked up at him and smiled sleepily, and he returned it, but when he met Kent's eyes, his own apprehension was looking right back at him.

James broke eye contact.

He and Kent had talked last night and decided Carlene would enjoy this. And she had. They all had. But there were things that hadn't crossed his mind until it was too late. Things like how much it had always turned him on to watch Kent drive a woman wild. How much of a thrill it had been to know that later on, he'd have Kent all to himself. After they'd seen the lady off for the evening, they'd wind up in bed together, reminiscing about the threesome until they were turned on again. Since they'd both be a little tired by then—as tired as early thirtysomethings ever were—they'd take it slow, and they'd have languid sex until they were too tired to go on. Orgasms were even optional by that point.

But tonight…

James trailed his fingers along Carlene's arm and struggled to look at her or Kent. Was it wrong that he wanted Kent like that again?

It wasn't any lack of desire for Carlene. God himself couldn't make James walk away from her, but every time he and Kent touched, those age-old feelings deepened, and by this point, his love for his longtime friend went all the way to the bone. He could tell himself all kinds of lies about how he loved him in a million different ways besides the way he loved Carlene, but lying here like this tonight, he had to accept that was exactly what they were—lies. He was in love with Kent. Deeply, irrevocably, way beyond blood brothers and bonded through combat and baptized by fire, he felt for Kent what he'd only felt for one other person in his entire life, and that person was lying here too.

He gazed at Kent. *How do I tell you that I love you the way I love the mother of my children?*

How do I tell her?

God, what do I do?

In between Kent and James, her body warm and aching, Carlene could barely stay awake, but she couldn't quite fall asleep either. Physically, she hadn't been this exhausted in ages. Mentally, she was on edge.

Why the hell had tonight felt so different from the other nights she'd played with both of them? They hadn't gotten into anything kinky—well, no dominance or submission, anyway—so it should have been simple. Just fun, playful sex. Nothing more.

But nothing felt simple now.

She loved seeing James as turned on as he'd been tonight, but was it too much to ask for him to be that turned on because of her? Because of—as Kent had said this night would be—her and her alone?

Oh, they'd both been focused on her, no doubt, but there was no pretending they didn't arouse each other. Or that tonight was any kind of isolated incident. Ever since Kent and James had gotten intimate again, James had come alive. His smile was brighter. His eyes were clearer. When he slept beside her most nights, he rarely made a sound. No panicking at some dream, no calling out Kent's name. Whatever she and Kent had done had worked.

And, at the same time, she was afraid it had backfired.

The guys hadn't gone into detail about the things they did alone, and she hadn't seen or heard a thing they'd done behind closed doors, but there was no denying that things had intensified between them. Whenever James stole a glance at Kent, his breath hitched a little. More than once, she'd caught Kent gazing at James with a palpable longing in his eyes. He'd done that forever, but recently, that longing smoldered more visibly than ever.

And there were those playful little smiles they'd exchange when they didn't think anyone was looking. When they didn't realize how much it broke her heart to see that glint in their eyes that was for them and them alone. It was all subtle enough that she doubted anyone else noticed, but she certainly did.

Though they'd brought her into it and shown her how to be what James needed, it had become abundantly clear that what James *wanted* was Kent. Tonight had only made it worse. They'd done this for other women before—women whose names they probably didn't recall—and they were good at it. Everything they did was practiced and perfected together. After experiencing them like that, it was impossible to believe that it was just sex between the two men, or that she could even try to compete with the connection they had—their history was too long, their intimacy too deep. That connection was enough to make her burn with envy. Well, when she wasn't ready to crumble into tears at the realization of just how easily James could slip between her fingers and happily settle right in the palm of Kent's hand.

At least he'd be with someone who loved him, but damn, it was killing her. What she wouldn't have given for James to look at her the way he looked at Kent. For their eyes to lock the way the two men's eyes locked, the whole world vanishing for a moment. They'd obviously enjoyed pleasing her together, but there was no way it would've been the same with another man in Kent's place. The telepathy, the simmering desire for each other, the way they so easily worked together to give her an amazing night. It would have been different if another man had been in Kent's place, but what about if another woman had been in *her* place?

Because she couldn't help thinking it was only a matter of time before there was no more room for her.

Kent lingered in his best friend's bed for a while, but he couldn't get comfortable. Eventually, he kissed them both and pretended things were fine, then dressed and bowed out for the night.

In his own bedroom down the hall, he stood at the window and gazed out at the sleeping city.

Well, this evening had certainly been interesting. The nights they'd shared women in the past were legendary. They'd fuck her within an inch of her life until she couldn't remember her own name, never mind either of theirs, and they'd make damn sure she was good and satisfied before sunrise. No woman had ever spent a night between them without walking away smiling in the morning. Most of them never even knew that James or Kent were bisexual or had even the slightest inclination toward men—when they took a woman to bed, those nights were about her pleasure.

That was what they'd set out to do tonight with Carlene. They'd given her the ride of her life, and she'd ended up boneless between them, exhausted and grinning, exactly as they'd planned.

And when it was over, she hadn't been the one walking away.

He was.

Kent exhaled, fogging up the glass in front of him. He pressed his arm against the window and rested his forehead on it, closing his eyes.

Carlene had brought him and James back into each other's beds, and she'd found a way to help her husband cope with a job so demanding it threatened to kill him, and they'd vowed to make sure she had several orgasms tonight for her trouble. And they'd succeeded.

But in the end, after the orgasms had faded and the sweat had dried, they'd succeeded most spectacularly in reminding him of where he stood in this arrangement. He was the third party. The only one in the room with no tan line on his left ring finger. The onlooker invited in, only to be dismissed before daybreak, and that was how it needed to be.

It just wasn't supposed to hurt like this.

Chapter Twenty-Eight

As soon as Kent reported for his shift the next morning, James's stomach wound itself into knots. He hadn't imagined the awkward "what the hell did we do?" feeling, had he? No, definitely not, if the discomfort in Kent's posture was any indication. He stood rigid and straight, his lips twisted and brow knitted like they'd often been when he'd been waiting for a commanding officer to rip him a new one over something. Nervous. Twitchy. Every inch a man with either a guilty conscience or something he needed to get off his chest. Maybe both.

James's job being what it was, getting a moment alone with his head of security was about as easy as getting a moment alone *without* his head of security. They were constantly within arm's reach of each other, but there were too many other people around. Advisers. Cabinet members. Interns. Secret Service.

Then a meeting concluded, and people dispersed, and just like that, they were alone. Kent. James. No one else. Standing in the Oval Office, they faced each other, and James's own panic was written all over Kent's rising eyebrows and creased forehead. James had been chomping at the bit all goddamned day for a moment alone to talk, and now that they'd found the opportunity, he wanted a phone to ring or a door to open or *something* to interrupt them.

Well, if they didn't do it now, God knew when they'd have another shot, so James dived right in. "Did last night feel weird to you?"

"Yeah. It, um… I can't even explain it." Kent paused, gnawing his lip. "I guess it felt a little too much like old times. More than it should have, if that makes sense."

The admission smacked James in the gut. "Yeah, it did. Now that you mention it, that's it. Exactly it."

Their eyes met, but only for a second before they both broke away, fidgeting uncomfortably. Last night had been like those times in their past life, hadn't it? They'd set out to do last night what they'd done back then—give a woman the night of her life—but things had changed in ten-plus years, hadn't they? The woman between them wasn't just someone they'd met in a bar. They were all sober, and the wild-eyed hotheads had faded into the past, leaving behind two more or less mature men who genuinely cared about not only Carlene, but each other. Nothing had driven that point home harder than putting themselves into those age-old roles and seeing how much they didn't fit anymore. How much things had really changed.

James took a breath. "We should talk about this somewhere else."

"Good idea. I can meet you in the master bedroom. Separately, so no one knows what's going on."

Always a strategy, always the need for discretion—fuck, this kind of thing was exhausting. But there were security cameras and people around everywhere else, so they didn't have many options.

James left first. Fifteen minutes later, Kent joined him, and they faced each other in the room where so many things had happened recently.

"So, about last night…"

"Yeah." Kent swallowed. "Look, I have to be honest. I'm… I'm not sure if I can keep doing this."

James's heart fell. "What do you want to do?"

"I want to—" Kent cut himself off. "What I want to do and what I need to do might not be the same thing."

Don't. Kent, don't…

James reached for Kent's waist, and when Kent didn't recoil from his touch, he couldn't help releasing a relieved sigh. They drew each other in, and their lips almost brushed, but they both held back.

"This got more complicated than it was supposed to, didn't it?" James whispered. As if there were ever any doubt that it *would* get complicated.

"Yeah, it did. And you know I…" Kent touched his forehead to James's. "For the record, you know I'd never do anything to break up your marriage, right?"

Not deliberately. But you exist.

James just sighed. "I know you wouldn't."

They were quiet for a long moment, just standing there in a loose embrace, forehead to forehead, a breath away from a kiss, but James was too afraid to take that breath.

Kent cupped James's cheek, his callused fingers light. "I love you, James. I have for a long time. And that's…lately…" He ran his thumb along James's cheekbone. "This hasn't helped. At all."

James drew back enough to meet Kent's eyes. He'd been about to say something, but God only knew what—now that he was gazing up at Kent, words weren't coming easily because Kent's had hit him squarely in the chest.

"We've tried before," James said. "To make something work, I mean, and I almost lost you in the process."

Kent flinched and broke eye contact. "Yeah, I know. I was there."

James watched him for a moment and finally inclined his head. "I feel like there's something you want me to say right now, but damn if I know what it is."

"Neither do I." Kent rubbed the back of his neck and exhaled sharply. "I don't know what to say or what any of us should be doing. I just know that ever since last night, I've been thinking a lot about what we did in the past and what we've been doing recently." He dropped his hand. "And the way I feel about you, it's not going to work. Not if I want to keep myself sane."

James swallowed. "What do you suggest, then? We've got a history, and there's feelings, but…" He gestured at his wedding ring. "I'm…"

"Believe me, I know."

The faint note of bitterness in his tone gave James pause. He narrowed his eyes. "Is that a problem? Because if it is, we can stop this conversation right there. I made a vow to my wife, and I meant it."

"Yes, I know." Kent's voice softened. "I don't want…" When he continued, his voice was a little unsteady. "I've told you a million times that I would never do anything to come between you and Carlene." He pushed his shoulders back and barely whispered, "But don't think for a second that it didn't hurt like hell when I stepped off that plane and saw you with her. Or that it doesn't hurt every fucking time I see you two together now."

The words and the pain in Kent's eyes nearly sent James back a step. "But why…why did you agree to head my security team? If it hurt that much…"

"Because it's even worse being away from you," Kent said softly. "Being around you, that was the lesser of two evils. People were already threatening your life before the election. At least this way, I could be there if someone tried to act on it. I could keep you safe, and I…" He winced and cleared his throat. "I could be close to you."

James's chest ached. "I didn't realize it was that hard on you."

"I know," Kent said. "I should've said something. I should've told you ages ago." He ran his hand through his hair and let it rest on the back of his neck. "I should've told you a lot of things ages ago."

The ache deepened. "I get the feeling we should've done a lot more talking back then."

"Yeah. You could say that." Kent sighed, letting his hand drop. "You know, that mission while you had to stay home and recover? When you—"

He stopped himself, but James heard the unspoken "*When you met her.*"

Kent cleared his throat again and continued. "All the way home from that mission, the only thing I could think about was you. I didn't want to be away from you anymore. I wanted…" Kent's eyes unfocused. Then he shook his head and cleared his throat. "It doesn't matter."

"It matters to me."

"What difference will it make?" Kent growled. "By that point, she had you. And she's had you ever since. And that's…" He shrugged. "That's the way it's been. Until recently."

"What do you want me to say, then?" James showed his palms. "You and I tried. Do you want me to apologize for moving on when it didn't work?"

Kent's jaw tightened.

James exhaled, dropping his hands to his sides. "What was I supposed to do? We agreed it was over. I don't know what I was supposed—"

"Of course you had to move on," Kent said softly. "I don't hold that against you. I really don't. The thing is, we can't change anything. I know you love Carlene, and I would never want you to leave her for me or anyone else." He paused, sweeping his tongue across his lips and avoiding James's eyes. "But that doesn't change how I feel about you."

"Kent, we—"

"I'm not finished."

James stopped. They locked eyes, and the silence lingered for a good minute.

Kent took a breath. "There is almost nothing I wouldn't do to keep you sane and keep you safe, even if it means driving myself crazy in the process." He swallowed hard. "But I have to draw the line this time."

Kent's tone more than his words sent James's heart into his feet.

"What do you mean?"

"I mean I can't keep doing what we've been doing." Kent took another step back, drawing himself just out of James's reach. "In bed. None of it."

"But we—"

"No." He looked James in the eye. "You and Carlene have what you need to get you through the rest of your term. But..." He took a deep breath. "But I can't be a part of that anymore. The way I feel about you isn't just sexual, and I..." His voice caught. He cleared his throat and shook his head. "I'm sorry, James. I'll stick by you as your head of security, at least for now, but everything else... I can't."

James wanted to step closer and reach for him, but his legs refused to work. "What do you want me to say?"

"There's nothing you can say," Kent said. "It's no one's fault, it's just...the way it is. I know you love her, and I'd never ask you to pretend you didn't. I don't want to break up your family. But I can't keep torturing myself either."

"But we—"

"Don't. Please." Kent widened the gap between them even farther, inching toward the door. "Just don't."

James opened his mouth to protest, but Kent had already turned to walk away, and the panic—*come back! Kent!*—choked him and lodged the words somewhere in his throat.

Kent walked out, and the door clicked shut behind him, and James sank onto the bed. In his mind's eye, he saw himself running after him, stopping him in the hallway, and bringing him back in here.

To...what?

This wasn't one of those arguments they could fuck away. If they talked, then what? Kent had stated his case. He wanted something James couldn't give him, not without choosing him over Carlene. No matter what James felt for Kent, he also loved his wife. He'd sooner chew off one of his own limbs than walk away from her. So why the hell did letting go of Kent hurt as badly as he imagined it would hurt to let go of his wife?

He pressed his elbows into his thighs and rubbed both hands over his face. When they'd started all this at Carlene's insistence, James had hesitated because he knew how much sex could complicate things. He'd anticipated jealousy between Carlene and Kent. A guilty conscience on his part. A tug-o-war between the three of them.

Sooner or later, one way or another, he'd known this would end. They'd all known that from the beginning. Either Carlene would get the hang of everything Kent taught her, and he'd be able to bow out, or there'd be some big fight and an ultimatum and they'd agree to go back to the way things were. It had always been a temporary situation. As far as James knew, the only variables were when it ended and with how much drama, and he'd hoped and prayed from the start that it would come to a gentle close without any hard feelings.

He just hadn't realized how much it would hurt to watch Kent walk away.

All through dinner, James picked at his food. Joey chattered to him about what they'd done at kindergarten that day, and damn, James tried to give the little boy the attention he needed, but his mind wasn't there. He could think of nothing except the conversation with Kent, and about his wife sitting across from him. Part of him wanted to pull her into his arms and promise that nothing would ever come between them. Part of him couldn't deny the simmering resentment that the distance between him and Kent precisely matched the width of her shoulders.

He sighed and rubbed his forehead.

"Daddy?"

"I'm sorry, kiddo." He looked at Joey and forced a smile. "Tell me that again?"

Joey giggled and went off again, chattering about a game they'd played at school, and James focused as hard as he could.

With a hell of a lot of effort, he made it to the end of Joey's story, and he made it to the end of dinner. Then it was Mario Kart, which was mercifully mindless. Anything to put his brain on lockdown for a little while and shut out everything except navigating an animated car around a crazy track littered with turtle shells and mushrooms.

After he'd played a few games and then tucked the kids in, James went into the master bedroom and sank onto the edge of the bed. All the thoughts he'd banished for the night had come crashing back in. There was no escaping it. Not until he'd settled all of it, and how the fuck was he supposed to settle something like *this*? And he wasn't sleeping tonight, was he? Fuck no. Not with all this weird tension hanging over him. Not with the afterimage of Kent's back burned into his retinas.

"James?"

Carlene's voice sent a jolt of dread through him. Shit. Because the conversation with Kent hadn't been bad enough.

He lifted his head and met her eyes. "Hey."

She came closer. She'd dressed down, trading in the professional look of the First Lady for a football jersey and a pair of shorts. "You've been quiet tonight."

She sat on the bed beside him and put her hand on his leg. "What's going on?"

He raked his fingers through his hair. "Does it have to be anything?"

She stiffened slightly, and he realized there'd been a touch of venom in his voice. She folded her hands in her lap. "Maybe there doesn't *have* to be, but I have a feeling there is."

He sighed. "It's Kent."

Carlene took in a sharp breath through her nose. "I see." The suspicion simultaneously made his skin crawl with guilt and his blood boil with anger. She sat a bit straighter. "What about him?"

"I think…" He swallowed. "I think things are more complicated now. We can't keep doing this. With him, I mean." *Because it hurts him. And it hurts me to see him like this. And I'm…and he's…and we're… Fuck, why can't this be simple?*

"Oh. Okay." She gnawed her lip. "If you or he don't want to, then we certainly don't have to."

James winced. *Don't want to? Oh, that doesn't begin to scratch the surface.*

"What about everything he taught me?" She lifted her eyebrows. "Do you still want to do any of that?"

How the hell was he supposed to answer that? He needed the domination as much as he needed Kent, and the former had the latter's indelible fingerprints all over it.

"James?"

He exhaled sharply. "I don't even know. I really don't."

Carlene eyed him. "Have I done something wrong? Because you sound like you're a step away from bitching me out for something."

James gritted his teeth. "When you approached Kent about me, did you ever stop to think at all about how this might end?"

"End?"

"Yes. You didn't think you and Kent would be happily taking turns on me forever, did you?"

Carlene narrowed her eyes. "Don't you dare put this on me, James. I was trying to help you. I didn't know what else to do, so I gave you what you apparently needed."

"So, what? You helped me by forcing my hand?"

"I helped you by giving you what you kept begging for in your sleep. And to answer your question, no, I didn't think about this in the long term. I was too busy being worried that your job was going to *kill you* in the short term to think that far ahead."

He pressed his tongue against the roof of his mouth. Fuck, what was he supposed to say to that?

Carlene wasn't done yet anyway—she pushed herself up off the bed and stood in front of him, glaring down at him. "I thought about all kinds of different scenarios and how things could happen, and yes, I knew this could end in disaster, but quite frankly, taking the risk made a hell of a lot more sense than just watching you wither away." She set her jaw. "I did what I had to, and don't you try to tell me it didn't help you. Because I will not apologize for trying to keep my husband out of a fucking psychiatric ward or a goddamned morgue."

James blinked. "Look, I get that." He patted the air between them with both hands. "I do. But I…" He exhaled, his shoulders sinking. "Fuck, I don't know. There had to be another way."

"Oh yeah?" She folded her arms tightly across her chest. "Such as?"

Yeah, James. Such as?

"I don't even know."

"Not that it really matters. What's done is done. So, the question is, what do you want to do now?" She lifted her chin. "I did the best I could because I didn't know what else to do. It doesn't mean I know what happens next."

"What *should* happen next?"

"You tell me, James. Because I don't fucking know."

"I don't either." He kept his gaze down for a long moment. Then he put up his hands and met her eyes. "Maybe we should sleep on it for now. We don't have to figure things out this instant, and tomorrow's…tomorrow's going to be a long day."

"Of course it will." She sighed. "I'm going to take my contacts out."

She didn't wait for a response and disappeared into the master bathroom.

James exhaled, his shoulders dropping. He pinched the bridge of his nose.

What the hell did they do now? Because, goddammit, he couldn't look at her without thinking about Kent now. He couldn't look at Kent without thinking about her. He desperately wanted both, and standing between them, knowing he had to move on with one and leave the other behind, was excruciating.

Whether Kent decided to stay or go, James was staying with Carlene, but he was scared to death of what this meant for his marriage. Would she be suspicious? Would she second-guess him until she got sick of it and left? Would he ever be able to exorcise this resentment that had taken up residence in his chest? Carlene hadn't done a damned thing wrong. She didn't deserve to be with a man who was pining after another man, and she didn't deserve an ounce of that resentment. But it was there.

How the hell do we get through this?

Carlene returned to the bedroom and didn't say a word. He went in, brushed his teeth and stripped down to boxers. By the time he came out, she'd climbed into bed but hadn't turned off the light yet. He joined her, stomach twisting—they hashed things out in bed all the time, but he wasn't even sure where to start this time. They could hardly fall back on their usual way of ignoring the problem and just making sure they were okay—sex was the root of all this, and having sex now wouldn't help at all.

James killed the light. As they lay there, side by side on their backs with the noise of DC buzzing in the background, their California-king-size bed suddenly seemed miles wider than it had ever been.

She didn't reach for him. He didn't reach for her.

She didn't speak. He didn't say a word.

And neither of them slept.

Chapter Twenty-Nine

The next morning, Kent could barely look at James.

Back in their SEAL days, when they'd mustered at shit o'clock in the morning after they'd had one of their famous blowups, it played out one of two ways. One, they worked it out through the haze of their hangovers, laughed about how stupid it was and moved on like it never happened. Two, they couldn't look at each other, didn't speak to each other, and could drag that shit out for days until the rest of the team finally shoved them each onto a barstool, set shots of tequila in front of them, and told them to either sort it out or drink it off. Most of the time, that second option led to an argument in the parking lot that neither would remember the next day when they woke up—hungover, naked, together.

Now, drunken fights and even drunker makeup sex weren't options.

Suited and booted, clean shaven and looking like professionals, poker faces on and no sign of anything amiss, they walked through the corridor from the White House to the West Wing. James had a meeting with a congressman about...hell, Kent couldn't even remember what this one was about. Always something. So with knots in his gut and a throbbing hangover that he didn't dare show, Kent followed him. Strictly business today. Duty and protection, nothing more—the ever watchful Praetorian guard escorting the Emperor of Rome.

Every step hurt like hell. They both had to pretend everything was fine so no one else would catch on, but that wasn't easy when it hurt just to be this close to James.

By James's third meeting of the day, Kent couldn't avoid the truth anymore—he couldn't keep doing this. He was only deluding himself if he thought he could be this close to James and not touch him. That had been hard as hell before, but now that they'd been together again, the platonic distance was excruciating.

The minute his shift was over, he went straight to his bedroom to grab his keys and a few other things. He hadn't been back to his apartment in a while, and there was no way in hell he was sleeping under this roof tonight. Traffic be damned, he had to get out of here.

As he was locking his bedroom door, Carlene's voice startled him: "Can we talk?"

Kent hesitated. That request was almost as unnerving as when she'd approached him at Camp David a lifetime ago to give him her blessing to take James to bed. "Sure. Yeah." He glanced at the door he'd just locked and then at her. "We could, um…"

"Here is fine. Or we can go somewhere else."

Somewhere else would've been a lot easier to cope with. Talking about all this right at the scene of so many crimes was a fuckload of salt in an open wound.

But walking in silence through the White House in search of a private place to talk without anyone noticing them wouldn't be any better, so to hell with it—Kent unlocked the door and gestured for her to go in ahead of him.

She glanced up and down the hallway, likely to make sure no one happened to be wandering through, and then stepped inside.

Behind closed doors, just steps away from the bed where they'd done so many amazing things, they faced each other. Carlene folded her arms loosely beneath her breasts and avoided his eyes, her lips tight and eyebrows pulled together. "We need to talk about James. About what we've all been doing."

Kent flinched.

She took a deep breath and looked him in the eye. "I came to you in the first place because I didn't want to lose him to his job."

"Yeah, I know. Turns out I didn't want to lose him either." *To his job or his wife, but what can I do either way?*

Carlene nodded. "That's…that's what I wanted to talk about."

Kent eyed her but didn't speak. In the beginning, Carlene had begged him not to rub it in that he'd won. That her husband still wanted him, that James wanted Kent even when he had her by his side.

Now he was the one with defeat pressing down on his shoulders, and he silently begged her just like she'd once openly asked him: *Don't rub it in. Please.*

Carlene blew out a breath. "What the three of us were doing, it wasn't just sex. It never was, and I think we all know it. It's nowhere near that simple."

His mouth was dry, and it was a struggle to force out the words: "Then what was it?"

"Kent, I know you two love each other. And there was a time when I resented that, but now I've seen what good it does for both of you to be able to have each other."

Kent's heart dropped. "But you and James are—"

"There's no reason we can't *all* make this work."

He blinked. "What?"

"He doesn't want to leave me, but he doesn't want to do without you either. I was afraid of that, but now…now it's…" She sighed and threw up her hands. "Look, this isn't a game, Kent. It's not a competition. It's not a war. One of us isn't going to walk away with the spoils and pretend that's the end of it." She swallowed hard and set her jaw. "James loves you, and he loves me. Asking him to choose one of us and live without the other is… It's just inhumane."

Kent raised his eyebrows. "So, that's it. The three of us just…what? Live as a triple instead of you two as a couple?"

"Any other ideas?"

"Not…not really."

"I don't have any either." She wrung her hands. "Look, we're all idiots if we believe you and James can be around each other without letting this thing do what it's going to do." She pursed her lips. "And we're all idiots if we think for a second you two can be apart."

Kent clenched his jaw. "We've tried to make it work before." He shook his head. "It blew up in our faces."

"Maybe you just weren't ready for it yet." A cautious laugh played at her lips, and her eyes sparkled as she added, "Maybe you needed a woman to knock your heads together once in a while."

At that, Kent couldn't help laughing. "Yeah, you might be right. But, I mean... There's compromise, and there's *compromise*."

"This isn't a compromise," she said. "I want my husband to be happy. If he's happier with the two of us than with only me, then that's how it needs to be. It doesn't do me any good to have him all to myself if part of him is hurting for you."

"And you're really willing to share your husband with me."

"Kent, I've been sharing him with you from day one. I think we'll all be happier if we stop pretending that isn't the case."

He chewed on the thought. "What about us?" He gestured at himself and her. "We've got chemistry and attraction and all that, but we know it's not that simple in the long run. Fact is, besides James and sex, we barely know each other."

"Maybe we should do something about that."

He raised his eyebrows.

"You said yourself that I trust you with my husband, and you trust me with you." Carlene swallowed. "That's a pretty good start, isn't it?"

"It's..." He paused. "Why *didn't* you like me before?"

She kept her gaze down for a moment. "I was afraid you were a threat. Yes, I was jealous." Carlene met his eyes. "But I've seen how torn James is about both of us. I pushed him, and I wanted him to make a choice, and now he's hurting." She pressed her lips together and shifted uncomfortably. "Maybe he shouldn't have to make that choice. If it hurts him this much to choose between us, then maybe he really does feel that strongly about both of us. Who's to say he *has* to choose?"

Besides every social more that had been drilled into them their whole lives? Sure, they'd violated those by the dozen recently, but turning their marriage into an emotional triad? Was that even... Could they...

"Think about it," Carlene said. "I don't want to lose my husband. You don't want to lose him, and I know he doesn't want to lose you. And I... To be honest, I don't want to lose you either." He tilted his head, and she sighed. "Look, We were both wrong about each other. The thing is, you don't take away from what I have with James. You bring something into the picture that I never could, and you make my husband happy in ways I can't. It isn't just the domination. It's... Kent, it's you. He loves you, and he always has. And when he doesn't have to pretend he doesn't feel anything for you, he comes alive, and so does my marriage." She pushed her hair behind her ear with a thin, unsteady hand. "When..." She shook her head. "I know, it doesn't make any sense, but you were a piece of this marriage that I didn't know was missing."

His lips parted.

"You're not coming between us, Kent," she whispered. "You're completing us."

All the breath rushed out of Kent's lungs. "Carlene..."

She stepped a little closer. "I mean it. I want you and James to be together. I want us all to be together." Her eyebrows rose slightly, as if to add, *Please tell me there's a place for me.*

Kent's emotions threatened to get the best of him, and he wrapped his arms around her, gathering her into a gentle embrace. There were so many things he probably could've said right then, but all he could do was hold her against him, close his eyes and try to breathe while he gathered his thoughts. Finally, he whispered, "I guess you were right—we don't have to be rivals."

"No." She returned his embrace and tucked her head beneath his chin. "I don't want to be your rival."

"I've never wanted to be yours." He kissed the top of her head. "James is happy when he's with you."

"He's happiest with both of us."

"Then that's what he'll have." Kent smoothed her hair. "This could royally fuck up his political career, though."

"Honestly?" Carlene drew back and shook her head. "I don't care. I don't.

His political career damn near killed him. Given the choice between watching that implode so we could be together, and my family being healthy and sane, I don't think I have to tell you my preference." She held his gaze. "And yes, when I say 'my family', I'm including you."

Kent's heart flipped. "You... Really?"

"Absolutely. I'm just sorry it took this long to realize how much you two need each other."

He exhaled, raking a hand through his hair, and met her eyes again. "James is one hell of a lucky man. You know that, right?"

"Of course he is." A tentative grin played at her lips. "He gets fucked by a SEAL."

Kent laughed. "So do you."

The grin came to life. "Well, if things work out, then I get fucked by two SEALs."

Kent's teeth snapped shut. "You really are serious about this."

"Yes." Her expression turned stone-cold serious. "And as far as his political career, and our extended families, and the public..." She half shrugged. "You two were Special Forces. I'm a SEAL's wife. We all know how to be discreet, so no one else has to know."

"But...the kids..."

She lifted her chin and pushed her shoulders back. "They're too young to understand right now anyway. When they're older, well, maybe we'll have enough of a grasp on what we're doing to explain it to them."

Kent chewed the inside of his cheek. He touched her face. "So what about right now? What should we do?"

"Now," Carlene said, standing up straighter, "we talk to James."

Chapter Thirty

When James stepped into the bedroom, he halted so sharply, Carlene thought he was about to go right back out into the hallway.

His eyes darted back and forth from Kent to Carlene, and his forehead creased. "Uh… This is unexpected."

"I know." Carlene inhaled slowly. "But we need to talk." She glanced at Kent for reassurance, and when he nodded, she faced her husband again. "All three of us."

James glanced over his shoulder, as if there might've been someone eavesdropping from the hallway. Then he stepped inside and shut the door, studying the two of them uncertainly as he did. "Okay. I think I can guess what it's about."

"I think so," Kent said. "Which means we might as well get straight to the point."

James hooked his thumbs in the pockets of his trousers. "All right."

"Carlene and I talked. We… Well, we realized…" Kent chewed his lip.

"We think we can make this work." Carlene reached for Kent's hand. "All of us."

James stared in disbelief at their joined hands. "What?" He shook his head. "Like, a three-way relationship?"

"Yes," Kent said. "Discreetly, of course, since this sort of thing doesn't mix with politics."

"With politics?" James blinked. "Does it even mix with"—he gestured at the three of them—"us?"

"We think so," Carlene said.

Eyes closed, James touched his fingers to his temples as if he could manually work all of this into his head. Then he dropped his hands and shook his head again as he looked at Kent and Carlene. "But you two... Up until recently, you could barely be in the same room."

Kent smiled playfully. "Being in the same bedroom helped, I guess."

"Okay, but..." James rubbed the bridge of his nose. "This is... This is insane."

"Do you have any other ideas?" Carlene asked. "Because, quite frankly, I don't."

"No, but this is way more of a compromise than I have any right to ask either of you for. Neither of you should have to have half of me while I get the two of you."

"We're not getting half of you," Kent said.

"Exactly." Carlene glanced at him and nodded. "You're happiest with both of us. You're more...*you* when you have both of us."

"We know this is unorthodox," Kent said. "And none of us have ever done anything like it before, but I can't think of any alternative that doesn't end with someone getting hurt."

"Neither can I," she said.

James held her gaze. "But how do we know this won't end with all of us getting hurt?"

"We don't," she said. "But I don't know what else we can do. Every other option means someone's getting hurt now. Going that direction, well, we've at least got a fighting chance of everyone being happy. Especially you." She paused. "If we went back to the way things were with just you and me, would you really be happy?"

"Of course I could," he said. "I love you, Carlene."

"And you love him too." Carlene released Kent's hand and came closer. "Honestly, I don't know how you've made it this far pretending you didn't."

James winced. She guessed that Kent probably did too.

She stopped in front of James and touched his face. "James, you're my husband, not my possession. I want you to do what makes you happy. If you've got room in your heart for two, and you love him as much as you obviously do, then love us both."

James held her gaze. Then he looked past her. Though she couldn't see Kent, and she couldn't hear either man's thoughts, there must have been something passing between them. Something telepathic as always.

After a moment, he shifted his attention back to her. He cradled her face in both hands. "You're an amazing woman, Carlene." He kissed her softly. "I was right when I said I'd be stupid to let you go."

She smiled up at him. "Good, because I don't want to let you go either." She glanced over her shoulder. "And neither does he."

James looked past her again. Carlene released him and stepped aside, and her heart pounded as the two men faced each other. After all these years, they could openly admit how they felt about each other. She held her breath, wondering how this would play out.

James stepped closer. So did Kent. For a long moment, they just gazed at each other from a little less than an arm's length apart.

It was James who moved first. He reached up tentatively, letting his hand hover for a moment, and then touched Kent's face. "All of this is all right with you too?"

Kent nodded and wrapped an arm around James's waist. "It's more than all right. All I've ever wanted is for you to be happy." He ran his fingers through James's hair. "And, admittedly, I've always wanted you too."

"I am so sorry," James whispered. "I didn't know you—"

Kent cut him off with a kiss, and everyone in the room exhaled. "I don't want you to apologize," he whispered against James's lips. "I just want us all to be together."

"Still…" James drew back and met his gaze. "I'm sorry." His eyes darted toward Carlene. "To both of you. For…putting you in this position in the first place. You're both more than I've ever deserved, and I…" His voice cracked. "I am so sorry."

Kent pulled him closer and kissed James's forehead. "Apology accepted."

"Same here," Carlene said. "We both love you, James. That's the important part. We'll figure out the logistics and everything as we go."

James's eyes lost focus for a moment. Then he glanced at her, and finally looked up at Kent again. "It's taken me way too long to say this, but…" He took a deep breath, and though it seemed to be a struggle, he held Kent's gaze. "I love you."

Kent's voice shook as he whispered, "I love you too." He wrapped his arms around James and kissed him again.

Carlene's heart went crazy. The first time she'd watched them together, she'd been blown away by how sexy it was to see two men kiss. This time, the sexiness didn't hold a candle to how beautiful and moving it was—two people who'd been in love for so long, finally letting their guard down and letting themselves be in love.

Her throat tightened with the threat of tears, and she muffled a cough as she tried to keep her composure.

Both men turned to her.

"You all right?" James asked.

"Yeah." She cleared her throat again. "You guys?"

He looked at Kent, and as they both smiled, he said, "Yeah. I think so."

Kent nodded. "I'd say I'm better than I've been in a long time." He embraced James again, but looked at her. "Thank you, Carlene. For letting me in."

"You're welcome." She stepped closer and put a hand on his lower back. "The only thing I'd change is how long it took for us all to figure it out."

"Better late than never," James said.

"Agreed." Kent put his arm around Carlene and pressed a soft kiss to her lips. As he drew back, he exhaled. "Well, I guess that's all settled, then."

Carlene also released a breath. "Finally, yeah."

"Yeah, I guess it is." James chuckled. "Now what?"

"Now?" Carlene folded her arms. "Now you're going to get down on your knees and suck his cock."

James blinked, and she swore she could feel his heart skip. "What?"

"Um…" Kent cleared his throat, and when he spoke again, his voice had hardened. "I don't think she's joking, James."

James looked at him, then at her, eyebrows up.

She lifted her chin and narrowed her eyes.

He gulped.

And then dropped to his knees in front of Kent.

As James fumbled with the zipper and belt, Kent turned to Carlene, his eyes heavy-lidded, and he beckoned for her to come closer. As soon as she was within reach, he grabbed the front of her blouse and pulled her all the way to him. Before she could even regain her balance, he kissed her hard. She hesitated, but then wrapped an arm around him, both to stay upright and to hold on to him.

She rested her hand on the back of James's head as he sucked Kent's cock, and Kent's kiss damn near drove her to her knees right beside her husband. Would the emotional logistics be complicated? Oh yes. But the sex? Good Lord, they were compatible there.

Kent broke the kiss with a soft grunt and looked down. "You're too damned good at that." He nudged James off him. "I don't want to come yet."

James sat back on his heels. "What do you want me to do?"

Kent beckoned again, and James scrambled to his feet. Kent took him by the front of his shirt, pulled him in for a brief kiss before he whispered something in his ear that Carlene couldn't hear.

Then Kent licked his lips. He hooked a finger under James's chin and tilted his head up so they were eye to eye. "Understood?"

James swallowed. "Y-yeah. Understood."

"Am I missing something?" Carlene asked.

Kent flashed a grin. "Not for long, no." He gestured at her clothes and then tugged his own shirt free from his waistband. "But the sooner you get undressed…"

Well. She was hardly going to stay dressed around these two any longer than she had to, so she quickly got out of her blouse and pants while the guys stripped too.

She was just dropping her panties to the floor beside James's boxers when Kent—fully naked and very hard—pulled her to him. He kissed her, and he slipped his hand between her thighs. Gentle fingers found her clit, and he drew lazy circles that made her knees shake. He teased her, and kissed her, and good God, he knew how to turn a woman's bones to liquid.

Oh, but as always, he wasn't done yet.

"Your husband likes watching us fuck," he said between kisses. "Think he should get a show?"

Carlene pressed her hip against his erection just enough to make him groan. "You tell me."

His lips curved against hers, and he kissed her again. "Over here." He led her toward the overstuffed antique chair where she'd sat and watched them the first time. He took a seat and gestured for Carlene to join him, but with her back to him. Oh, he liked that position, did he? Good.

As she sat down, he slowed her with a hand on her hip, and he guided her onto his cock.

James watched, mesmerized and hard, as Carlene took every inch of Kent. He licked his lips. Carlene did the same. This position was strange, but if it meant James had this kind of view, she was totally on board.

Then Kent parted his legs, which pushed her legs apart in the process.

"James," Kent breathed, "get down on your knees and make your wife come."

Carlene's whole body tingled. *Make me come? How is—oh.*

James knelt between her legs, and his mouth on her clit felt…fucking… amazing. She pressed against Kent, reaching back to grip his hips for balance. The position was a little awkward—she could barely move, and Kent could barely move—but James had total access to her clit. With his mouth working its magic and Kent's thick cock inside her, she was going insane.

"Holy shit," she murmured. "You guys…"

Kent gently tilted her head back onto his shoulder. His lips brushed her neck, as did his deliciously coarse stubble, and she gasped. His other hand snaked around her waist and up to her breast, and he pinched nipple, and her vision blurred. God, he knew every way to drive her insane.

Kent's cock seemed to get even thicker, and he managed to thrust up into her—or pull her down onto him—enough to hit her G-spot just right, and she damn near levitated right up off him. He didn't let that happen, though, and kept fucking her while James kept teasing her clit, and a split second before she would've cried out, Kent clapped a hand over her mouth, and somehow that made the whole thing even hotter, and she fucking lost it. Her body trembled and tensed, both men sending incredible waves of pleasure through her, and just before it would've been too much, James backed off. Kent eased her down onto him, letting her sag against him while the last few aftershocks rushed through her.

Kent brought his legs back together so she could do the same, and he gently lifted her enough to pull out before he let her sink back against his chest. "Had enough?"

"Enough?" she panted. "Not even close."

A hot huff of laughter rushed past her shoulder. "Good." He paused. "We're all getting on the bed. James, I want you to get on top of your wife and fuck her, and while you do that, I'm going to fuck *you*."

James's eyes widened.

"Get the lube," Kent ordered. He nudged Carlene's hip. "Can you stand?"

"Uh…maybe."

While James fished some lube out of the nightstand, Kent helped Carlene to her feet. Her body was limp, but with a little aid from Kent, she made it to the bed and onto her back. She parted her legs for James, her heart beating faster as he climbed on top. James slid all the way inside her, and took a few slow, deep strokes, but then stopped.

He bit his lip as Kent positioned himself behind him. James swore under his breath as Kent, she guessed, pushed into him, and just like that, they were both in motion, and Carlene's pulse was out of control. Watching Kent fuck James the first time had been hotter than she'd imagined. Being beneath them? With James's cock inside her so she felt every one of Kent's thrusts? Unbelievable.

Above her, James's eyes closed and his lips parted as he moved inside her and as Kent moved inside him. Behind him, Kent's brow was furrowed and his lips taut with exertion, and every time he brushed a kiss across the side of James's neck, Carlene's heart skipped. How she'd ever thought it was strange for two men to have sex, she would never understand, because watching them now—seeing, feeling, hearing—was breathtaking.

She still didn't quite know what she felt for Kent, and she was pretty sure they would never have connected—never mind thrived—on their own, but watching him make love to James was enough for her to want him to stay forever. Maybe the connection she had with him wasn't perfect on its own, but the love between him and her husband was palpable.

Kent met her eyes over her husband's shoulder, and they both grinned. She dug her nails into James's arms, driving a whimper out of him, and Kent fucked James harder, forcing James to fuck Carlene harder. James gasped. His arms trembled from holding himself up. Sweat gleamed on his forehead and his flushed neck and shoulders.

Kent put an arm across James's stomach. He nipped his ear, then closed his eyes and groaned, "You're so fucking good, James. You're gonna make me come."

James shivered. He tilted his head, baring his neck to Kent's mouth.

"And you're not gonna come till I do, are you?"

James whimpered softly. He started to speak, but Carlene dragged her nails down his chest, and he shuddered hard, driving himself deep inside her. "Fuck…"

"Answer me," Kent taunted. "Or I'll pull out, and we'll start over with—"

"I won't come," James blurted out. "N-not till…till…"

Carlene rolled her hips as much as this position allowed, and James's response melted into a string of slurred profanity.

Kent grinned against the side of James's neck. "Not till when?"

James swallowed hard. He took a few gulps of air and finally murmured, "Not till you do."

"Good," Kent growled, and slammed into James. Together, they fell into a whole new rhythm—not quite as fast as before but harder. Much harder. Kent drove into James, and James kept on driving just as hard into Carlene, and every thrust knocked the breath out of both her and James. They were in synch and yet seemed to be fighting each other—James trying to move faster than Kent would let him, Kent refusing to give up control or his orgasm, keeping James's orgasm out of reach in the process.

Carlene tried like hell to watch them because they were just so amazing to see like this, but was on the verge of giving up and enjoying the ride, knowing James was falling apart because of her just as much as he was because of Kent. Between the two of them—literally—James looked and sounded and felt like he was in heaven.

Kent was obviously holding back, struggling against his own climax. He was even more flushed than James, and he grimaced with what must've been both exertion and restraint, and he was—

There.

He threw his head back, and his eyes squeezed shut and his mouth fell open in a soundless cry, and the cords stuck out of his neck as he kept right on thrusting into James.

And then James was there too, seemingly collapsing and tensing at the same time, as if his body didn't know what to do with all the sensations coursing through him right then. His arms shook beneath him, and his voice shook as he murmured, "You two are fucking amazing."

"So are you." Kent kissed the back of his shoulder. "And your wife needs to come."

Carlene grinned. "You two already made me come."

"I didn't say you hadn't come." He kissed James's shoulder again, and his smoldering eyes met hers. "I said you needed to come."

She whimpered.

James pulled out, and he'd barely collapsed beside her before Kent went down on her.

"Holy shit," she moaned.

"That's fucking hot," James said, his voice slurred.

"Tell me about it." She grabbed him and pulled him into a kiss. His mouth tasted faintly of her pussy, which only made her that much more aware of what Kent was doing with his own mouth. Jesus Christ…

Though she'd already come once, Kent was gentle enough to keep her from getting too sensitive. Every soft swirl of his tongue, coupled with the feverish way her husband kissed her, sent her closer and closer, turning her knees to liquid and her spine to pure electricity. She kneaded each man's scalp, gripping their hair for dear life and holding them in place—Kent against her pussy, James against her mouth—while she fell to pieces between them.

As the dust settled, they separated. All three were shaky and lethargic, but managed to clean themselves up, toss the towels more or less in the direction of the hamper and then fall back into bed. Arms draped over bodies. Legs tangled beneath the covers. Everyone breathed, but nobody talked, and Carlene felt fucking great.

Nothing about this made sense in any traditional context. Part of her still tried to line up their relationship with every cultural imperative she'd been raised to accept, and none of it meshed, but she couldn't make herself believe it was wrong.

James loved her. He loved Kent. Kent loved him. With James between them, Carlene and Kent found some common ground, not to mention a deep trust she'd never imagined finding with him. More and more, she believed that trust and common ground would evolve into something stronger. Maybe not the same as the decades-old bond between him and her husband, but strong enough to keep this strange little triangle together.

Maybe this wasn't a traditional thing that the voting public would ever accept, but behind closed doors, the three of them could have their own little heaven. Their own flavor of happiness.

And tonight more than ever, Carlene thanked God she'd worked up the nerve to ask Kent to sleep with James.

Chapter Thirty-One

Somewhere in the middle of the night, James's eyes fluttered open.

He hadn't dreamed. No past missions. No reelection anxiety dreams. No sitting alone in a barracks room in Germany. Just dark, peaceful sleep. Though it was oh-dark-thirty in the morning—three forty-seven, according to Carlene's alarm clock—he actually felt rested.

To his left, Carlene had rolled onto her side, the sheet draped over her waist and the streetlights illuminating her bare shoulder. To his right, Kent was sprawled out on his stomach, face buried in the pillow and one arm hanging off the side of the bed.

James resisted the urge to run his fingers over Kent's tattoos or tame a few stray strands of Carlene's hair. No sense waking either of them up.

He closed his eyes and smiled to himself. This was the first time they'd all fallen asleep in the same bed. It should've been weird. In a way, he supposed it was. Mostly, though, it felt like it was a long time coming. Like they should've done this weeks ago. Maybe years ago.

No. Years ago, none of them had been ready. Even a few weeks ago, they hadn't been. But now they were, and lying here like this in the master bedroom of the White House, naked and exhausted and together, just made sense. As if everything that had ever happened had been leading them to this.

And finally, they were here. And he could breathe.

Everything was as it should be.

Deep down, he knew that going forward like this wouldn't be easy. A relationship with two people? In the very, very bright spotlight of his political office? That would definitely be challenging.

And yet, somehow, it was simple. He'd never loved another woman like he loved Carlene, and he'd never loved another man like he loved Kent. His wife was right—he did have room in his heart for both of them. He'd just never imagined that the two people he'd fallen this hard for would accept that he felt this way for both of them.

They had, though, and now everything was right.

Someday, they'd figure out how to explain this to the kids. Maybe by then, they'd have the words to describe it. If their families or, God forbid, the media ever caught wind, they'd cross that bridge when they got there.

But for now, James knew. Carlene knew. Kent knew. They trusted each other and needed each other. As far as James was concerned, that was all that mattered.

And as far as James was concerned, he'd make it through his time as president as long as Kent and Carlene were there to make him kneel.

About the Author

Lauren Gallagher is an abnormal romance writer who has recently been exiled from the glittering utopia of Omaha, Nebraska, to an undisclosed location in South America. Along with her husband, a harem of concubines, and a phosphorescent porcupine, she remains, as always, in hiding from the Polynesian Mafia. For the moment, she seems to have eluded her nemesis, M/M romance author L.A. Witt, but figures L.A. will eventually become bored with the wilds of Spain and come looking for her. And when that time comes, Lauren will be ready. Assuming L.A. doesn't have her hands full keeping track of Lori A. Witt and Ann Gallagher, which she probably will.

For info about Lauren and the rest of the Gallagher-Witt quad, check out www.gallagherwitt.com or @GallagherWitt on Twitter.

They could be each other's second chance…unless their mistakes are too big to overlook.

I'll Show You Mine
© *2014 Lauren Gallagher*

When Alyssa Warren meets Shane McNeill at a wedding, sparks fly. Despite a litany of mistakes no one will let her forget, she can't resist indulging in one hot night…one that leaves her hungry for more.

Alyssa's not ready to let her past scare Shane off, though, so she proposes a casual arrangement—live in the moment, no discussing ancient history.

Shane's on board with that. No-strings, kinky sex with a beautiful woman who has no interest in his past—and with a libido that matches his own? Hell yeah. If she knew about the monster mistakes he's made, she'd run for the hills, so he's all for enjoying this wild ride for as long as it lasts.

As they delve deeper into each other's kinks, though, it's only a matter of time before trust and intimacy start entangling their hearts. But before a future can take shape, they'll have to come clean…and hope their confessions don't drive them apart.

Warning: Contains a woman who knows what she wants in bed and isn't afraid to demand it, and a man who's more than happy to give—or take—anything her body desires. In between making deliciously dirty demands of his own, that is.

She's got the moves. He's got the heat. Will their hearts catch the rhythm?

The Princess and the Porn Star
© *2013 Lauren Gallagher*

Rachel Taylor's manager has to be kidding. A porn star dancing beside her in her next music video? She didn't claw her way back from near obscurity in the pop music world only to become a laughingstock all over again.

Yet the moment she meets Lee, a.k.a. the infamous Buck Harder, their chemistry sizzles. There's much more to the man behind the stage name than the obvious attributes that make him so successful, and soon she's fantasizing about sharing more than just a stage.

In only a few steps, they find a perfect, dance-floor groove hot enough to melt the camera lens. But when the video's release blows up in their faces, her record label exercises an obscure but ironclad clause—stay away from each other. Or else.

Meeting in secret seems the most delicious solution. But they can't hide this kind of heat for long…and when the paparazzi sniff them out, she realizes choosing to stay with the man she's fallen for could cause her to fall off the pop music map—permanently.

Warning: Let's just say there's a reason Buck Harder went into his line of work, and it ain't his pretty smile. Wink wink.

Everyone's bringing baggage to this baby shower.

Who's Your Daddy?
© 2012 Lauren Gallagher

After her divorce, Carmen James is still trying to get back on her feet when fate pulls the rug out from under her. She's pregnant—and she's not sure who's the father. Just one more thing for her impossible-to-please family to worry about. On the bright side, there are only two candidates: her best friend, Donovan, and Isaac. His boyfriend.

A little too much wine and the desire to comfort lead Donovan and Isaac to a night they both hope Carmen doesn't regret. When she drops the bomb, though, Donovan's plate, already crowded with a teenage son and a disapproving father, gets fuller.

And Isaac, who's still coming to terms with his bisexuality, wonders how he'll handle fatherhood at forty.

Above all, both men worry that whatever the answer to the ultimate question—which of them got her pregnant—it will forever alter their longstanding friendship with Carmen. While they're waiting for that answer, though, continuing their casual sexual relationship with her feels natural. But when emotions get involved, the cracks in their logic threaten to drive Isaac, Don and Carmen apart just when they need each other the most.

Warning: This book contains three people in one hell of a pickle (anyone have any ice cream?), parents who suck at parenthood, parents-to-be who think they'll suck at parenthood, a relationship-friendship-sexual-kind-of-thing that keeps getting more complicated, and a Chuck Norris joke.

It's all about the story...

Romance

HORROR

Retro ROMANCE

www.samhainpublishing.com

CPSIA information can be obtained at www.ICGtesting.com
Printed in the USA
BVOW08s1317260515

401616BV00003B/6/P